FROM DARKNESS

A NOVEL OF THE ANCIENT ROMAN WORLD

C.K. RUPPELT

Other books in the REPUBLIC'S END series

INTO DAWN (Coming soon)

2nd Edition 2019, Reedit 2020

ISBN: 978-1-7329076-2-1

All contents created by the author, including maps, artwork, diagrams and cover design.

For detailed color versions of the maps, more historical background and related original artwork visit the author's website at:

www.ruppelt-pdx.com

DEDICATIO

Thank you, soldiers and veterans, for fighting so others can live their lives in peace.

Thank you, brave individuals, for standing up to become fearless warriors at times of human tragedy.

Thank you, brave citizens, for seeking common ground with others to build bridges across what divides us.

For all humans are people, united in the need to belong, to love, and to be loved.

The Roman World in 59 BC

Tagus	River	AEDUI	Tribe/Kingdom
MARE	Ocean	**NUMIDIA**	Nation/Province
PYRENAE	Mountains	• *Oaxos*	Home Town or City
∘ *Scalabis*	Town/City	∘ *Aquileia*	Official Legion Base

Travel Routes

- Caesar 81 BC
- Caesar 75 BC
- Caesar 69 BC and 61 BC
- Oz and Adhe 66 BC - 65 BC
- Nico 62 BC
- Numerius 59 BC

© C.K. Ruppelt 2018

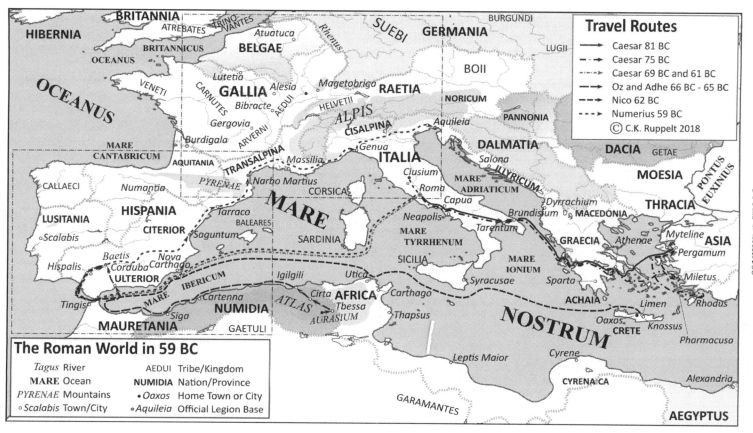

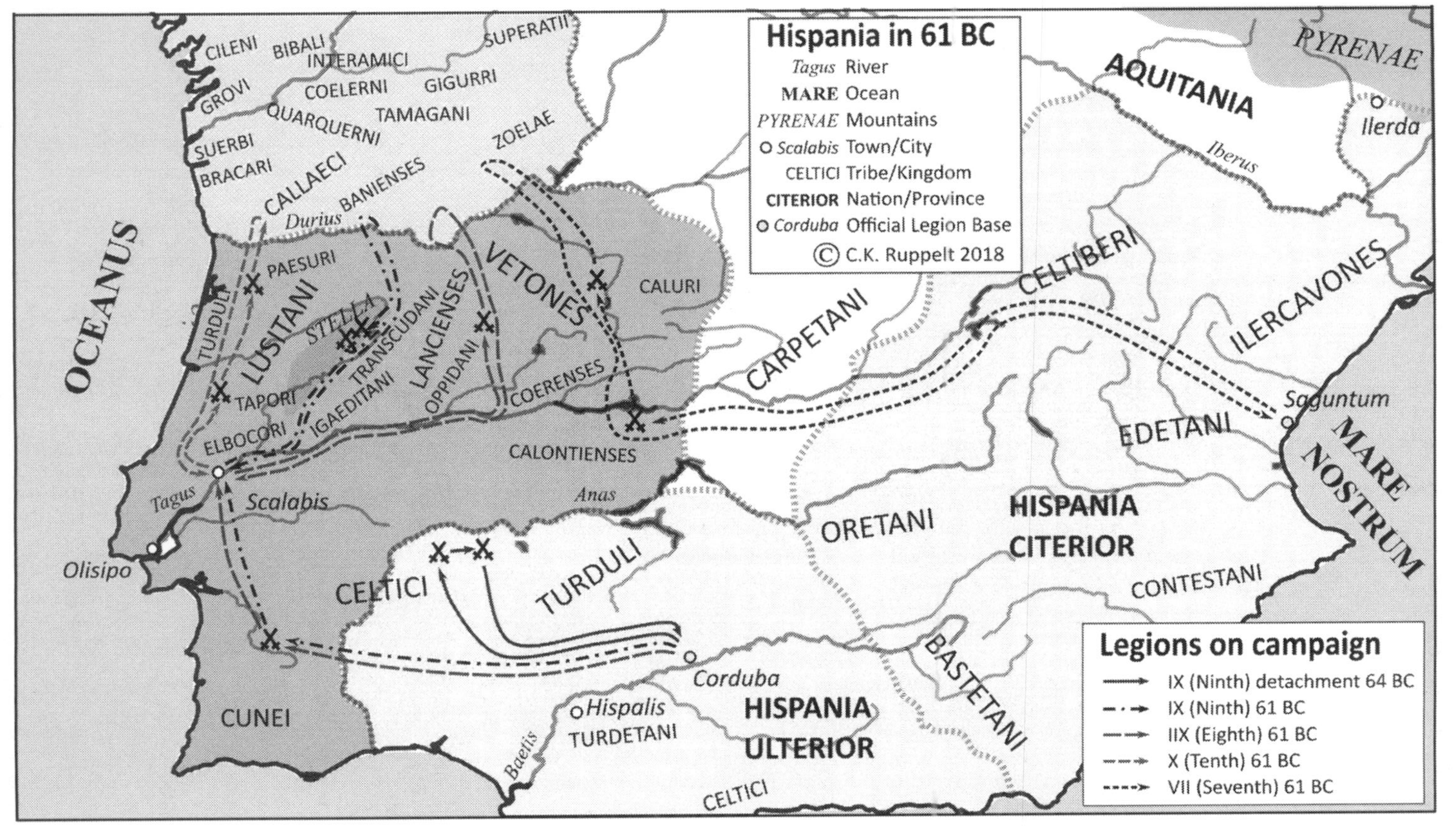
Hispania in 61 BC
Tagus River
MARE Ocean
PYRENAE Mountains
o Scalabis Town/City
CELTICI Tribe/Kingdom
CITERIOR Nation/Province
o Corduba Official Legion Base
© C.K. Ruppelt 2018
Legions on campaign
IX (Ninth) detachment 64 BC
IX (Ninth) 61 BC
IIX (Eighth) 61 BC
X (Tenth) 61 BC
VII (Seventh) 61 BC
OCEANUS
CILENI
BIBALI
INTERAMICI
SUPERATII
GROVI
COELERNI
GIGURRI
QUARQUERNI
TAMAGANI
ZOELAE
SUERBI
BRACARI
CALLAECI
BANIENSES
Durius
PAESURI
TURDULI
LUSITANI
STELLA
TRANSCUDANI
LANCIENSES
VETONES
CALURI
OPPIDANI
TAPORI
IGAEDITANI
COERENSES
ELBOCORI
CALONTIENSES
Tagus
Scalabis
Anas
Olisipo
CELTICI
TURDULI
CUNEI
Corduba
Hispalis
TURDETANI
Baetis
HISPANIA
ULTERIOR
CELTICI
AQUITANIA
PYRENAE
Ilerda
Iberus
CELTIBERI
ILERCAVONES
CARPETANI
Saguntum
EDETANI
MARE
NOSTRUM
ORETANI
HISPANIA
CITERIOR
CONTESTANI
BASTETANI

Campaign/Travel
Aedui Army
X (Tenth)
Caesar
Helvetii
VII, IIX, IX + XI, XII
VII, IIX, IX, X, XI, XII
Elsed's Aedui
Velia
© C.K. Ruppelt 2018
Gallia in 58 BC
Dubis River
MARE Ocean
ALPIS Mountains
Bibracte Town/City
AEDUI Tribe/Kingdom
BELGAE People/Province
Bailenua Home Town or City
Aquileia Official Legion Base
OCEANUS
BELLOVACI
BELGAE
REMI
Mosa
TREVERI
Rhenus
UBII
SUEBI
MARCOMANNI
VARISTI
TULUNGI
MEDNOMATRICI
CIVITATES
Durocortorum
Divodurum
GERMANIA
Lutetia
CATUVELLAUNI
Sequana
LEUCI
Mosella
TRIBOCI
VOSAGO
LATOBRIGI
SENONES
TRICASSES
LINGONES
RAURICI
Agendicum
Andematunnum
Magetobriga
RAETIA
CARNUTES
Alesia
MANDUBII
Bailenua
AEDUI
Dubis
Vesontio
Avaricum
HELVETII
BITURIGES
CUBI
SEQUANI
Bibracte
ALPIS
Lemonum
Arar
AMBARRI
GALLIA
ARVERNI
AEDUI
JURA
Rhodanus
PICTONES
ALPIS
Geneva
Aquileia
LEMOVICES
Gergovia
GRAIAE
SEGUSIAVI
Mediolanum
SANTONI
ARVERNI
ALLOBROGES
CADURCI
VELLAVI
COTTIAE
Uxellodurum
GABALI
GALLIA CISALPINA
Rhodanus
RUTENI
MARITIMAE
Padus
Genua
Ravenna
VOLCAE
GALLIA TRANSALPINA
ARECOMICI
Faesolae
NOSTRUM
VOLCAE
Tiber
ITALIA
Massilia
Narbo Martius
Aquae Sextiae
Clusium
Asculum
TECTOSAGES
MARE
Roma

DRAMATIS PERSONAE (Cast of Characters)

Roman/Italian

Sextus Albatius: Fictional figure, legionary in the Ninth

Titus Balventius: Historical figure, served as centurion in the Gallic War

Gaius Blandius: Fictional figure, legionary in the Ninth

Publius Ventidius Bassus: Historical figure, POW as child, later mule driver and highly successful Roman general

Gaius Julius Caesar: Historical figure, successful general, consul

Aurelia Cotta: Historical figure, mother to Caesar

Cornelia Cinna: Historical figure, Caesar's first wife

Lucius Cornelius Cinna: Historical figure, Caesar's brother-in-law and close friend after Caesar helps him back from exile

Calpurnia: Historical figure, Caesar's third wife and granddaughter to Lucius Piso

Julia Caesar: Historical figure, Caesar's daughter

Gaius Marius: Historical figure, uncle by marriage to Caesar, successful general, 7-time consul, enemy of Lucius Cornelius Sulla

Quintus Pedius: Historical figure, son of Julia Caesaris Major, serving under his uncle Caesar in Gallic War

Aulus Hirtius, Gaius Oppidus, Lucius Cornelius Balbus: Historical figures, close friends of Caesar

Velia Churinas: Fictional figure, freedwoman, sister to Numerius, friend to Lethie

Numerius Churinas: Fictional figure, freedman, legionary in the Ninth, brother to Velia, friend to Vibius Clarus

Marcus Tullius Cicero: Historical figure, close friend of Caesar, famous orator who speaks out against Caesar as member of the triumvirate, takes side against Caesar in the Roman Civil War

Quintus Tullius Cicero: Historical figure, younger brother to Marcus Cicero, close friend of Caesar

Vibius Clarus: Fictional figure, legionary in the Ninth, friend to Numerius Churinas

Marcus Licinius Crassus: Historical figure, general, consul, part of the first triumvirate with Gaius Julius Caesar and Gnaeus Pompeius Magnus

Marcus Licinius Crassus: Historical figure, older son to Crassus, tribune under Caesar in Hispania, later quaestor, proquaestor, before legate under Caesar in the late Gallic War

Publius Licinius Crassus: Historical figure, younger son of Crassus; while too young to receive a senate commission, he served as tribune under Caesar in the Gallic War

Fraucus, Luctatus and Postumus: Fictional figures, clients, confidants of Marcus Licinius Crassus

Pompeius Magnus, Gnaeus: Historical figure (Pompey the Great), highly successful general, consul, member of triumvirate

Celtic

Aina: Fictional figure, Aedui warrior, daughter of Drestan, married to Bradan

Brenna: Fictional figure, Aedui warrior, friend of Drestan's children, married to Elsed

Bradan: Fictional figure, Aedui warrior, friend of Elsed, married to Aina

Rionach and Orlagh: Fictional figures, Aedui warriors, friends of Drestan's children

Daleninar: Fictional figure, Celtici, becomes common-law wife of Gulussa

Divitiaco/Divitiacus: Historical figure, Aedui Vergobret, council member, master druid, friend of Liscan and Drestan

Divico: Historical figure, Helvetii chieftain, council member, and war-king

Drestan: Fictional figure, Aedui chieftain, husband to Ganna, father of Elsed, Aina and Morcant, brother of Liscan/Liscus

Elsed: Fictional figure, chieftain of the Aedui, eldest son to Drestan, husband to Brenna

Morcant: Fictional figure, son to Drestan, druid

Haerviu: Fictional figure, chieftain of the Aedui, father of Drestan

Liscan/Liscus: Historical figure, Aedui Vergobret, council member, brother to Drestan

Orgetorix: Historical figure, Helvetii chieftain, council member

Numidian

Ozalkis/Oz: Fictional figure, Numidian archer of auxilia of the Ninth, later decurion, uncle to Adherbal

Adherbal/Adhe: Fictional figure, Numidian archer of auxilia of the Ninth, nephew of Ozalkis

Massinussa/Massi and Gulussa: Fictional figures, brothers, Numidian archers in auxilia of the Ninth, friends with Oz and Adhe. Gulussa married to Daleninar (common law)

Greek

Alketas: Fictional figure, Cretan archer in auxilia of the Ninth

Andrippos: Fictional figure, first decurion in Cretan auxilia of the Ninth, friend of Capussia, Titus Balventius and Gaius Seppius

Nicolaos/Nico: Fictional figure, Cretan archer in auxilia of the Ninth

Timon: Fictional figure, young slave, love-interest of Nico

PROLOGUS

Omnia Mutantur (Everything Changes)

"Hope is the pillar that holds up the world.
Hope is the dream of a waking man."

Gaius Plinius Secundus

647 Ab Urbe Condita, After the Founding of Rome (107 BC), Southeast of Burdigala, lands of the Aquitani, free Gallia

Beloved husband, I am overjoyed to tell you we now have our long-awaited son. Our girls are excited about their little brother and are giving me a hard time when I want to keep little Lucius to myself. We receive many letters of congratulations every day, most addressed to you. People are glad that your and your forefather's name will carry on. The boy and I are in good health, and we all miss you terribly. I pray to the gods every day L. Cassius Longinus will finish this ugly business soon and bring you home to us.

With tears in his eyes, Lucius Piso, legate and former consul, rolled the letter back up to store it in the document bag hanging off his saddle. He straightened, seeing his friend and consul Cassius riding over. *I need to be careful to keep my disgust from showing.*

"Watch out, he is coming over for a visit," tribune Marcellus told Piso. "I knew the Senate had to act with the Germanic Cimbri and Teutones people crossing over the Alps, but why did they put Cassius Longinus in overall command?"

"They could not pass him over another time as this year's senior consul, could they?" Piso answered. "And you can't fault him for making haste with our three legions. Well, at least once the Helvetii tribes came out of their mountains to join in the ruin of southern Gallia and our Roman province here."

And to my surprise, so far, so good. We divided the Helvetii and chased after this Tigurini canton for weeks into this wild hinterland. Yet, they just kept running, and our discipline keeps declining. His legion was the only one still bothering to march in tight formation, and Cassius kept declining his continuous offers to send out scouts. Piso shook his head, realizing it was time to turn his horse to face the newcomer. "Salve, consul," he shouted as Cassius reined in.

"Greetings my friends. See, the fortifications they built overnight look ever more chaotic the closer we get. I declare them ripe for the taking," the consul stated, grinning ear to ear.

That's exactly the problem. This feels too easy by far. "Do you want me to continue as the left flank? Or would you allow me to march my men around the hill to hit them in the rear?" Piso asked.

After a short hesitation, Cassius shook his head in reply. "No need, dear friend. One on one, our men are the better fighters. Once our front ranks hit them, their warriors will break."

By Hades, why do you have to be so cocky? We're not invincible. "May we at least use some of the lighter artillery to soften them up first?" Piso asked.

"Good idea, I'll give word. With our heavy bolt-throwers pushing their missiles into their low palisade walls we'll see them scramble to safety, mark my words. I want your men to be ready to pursue once that happens. Show no mercy, we need to get as many of them as we can so we have less to fight later."

Piso held his tongue about his friend's carelessness. After all, their own forces seemed like a tidal wave eager for a chance to get at the enemy. He sighed. *Let him have his moment of glory, the situation seems obvious enough.*

Loud shouts rang out from the side. A good number of Tigurini warriors surfaced from what must be a low creek bed. Their war cries only the beginning, many more appeared from around the side of the hill, all adding to the din. Piso pointed forward. "And now they're attacking from the top of the hill as well," he said. Tens of thousands of Celtic warriors pushed through various openings in their palisade walls and careened toward them. "No longer cowering in fear. Damnation, this was well-planned." Now more enemy warriors made it to the third legion on their far side. *And there it is. Still feeling self-righteous and arrogant, dear Cassius, invincible like a Greek Titan of old?*

"Now they have us from three sides, and they have the numbers. We need to get back to camp, now," Cassius finally said.

"I agree, that is the only move we have left," Piso answered, guiding his horse toward his legion's signalers and cohort prefects. "Blow the command for retreat," he called. He looked back as his old friend rode away and put his fingers to the side of his helmet for a mock salute. *Maybe I will be able to forgive you at our next reunion, be that in camp or on the fields of Elysium.*

As far as Piso could see, the legionary lines were in disarray, entire cohorts turning to run for their lives, the enemy breaking through in masses. He looked back to the Roman fort they had left only an hour ago, so close across the valley, yet so far away. The rumble of many thousands of horses drowned out the noise of slaughter and the cries of people dying. The Tigurini cavalry had come from behind the hill to cut right between the legions and their camp. Piso focused for a moment on several overrun legionaries, all raising their empty hands in unison after hastily throwing away their swords and shields. Despite their gesture of surrender, they were slaughtered with little hesitation. His stomach turned. *They are too many, this is already over no matter what else we do.*

He put his hand on the small bag containing his wife's letter and hung his head. He closed his eyes, ignoring the stench of fresh blood wafting across the battlefield, the clanging of weapons on metal or wood, the screams of anger or pain. *I will watch over you all from Elysium, my beloved family, though you might curse my name with Cassius's over the dishonor I brought to you and to Rome.*

He pulled his long cavalry sword from its sheath and scanned the field. There. His legion's First Cohort stood solid as a rock amid a raging sea, their lines tightening into a small square. He nodded and waved to his officers and signalers. "Command a square formation, to be centered on the First Cohort." He kicked his mare's side to follow them to the space that would become the center of the square. *Maybe we can hold out a while longer, but I have little doubt this is our last stand. All we can do now is make them pay for it.*

***

"I can't believe it worked. Well done," Divico's father shouted at him from twenty feet away. Divico just smiled in response, for the first time in his young life truly content. *You screamed at me for my impertinence two weeks ago when I challenged you for leadership in front of the council. You called me a young welp barely weaned from my mother's teats, and yet here you are, congratulating me when you would have kept running forever.*

He swung himself out of his saddle and looked down at one of the Roman leaders sprawled out on the ground. The man was twice his age yet had fought well. He admired the Roman's sword skills and honorable death.

Out on the fields, warriors pushed each other in their excitement, cutting enemy heads as trophies and searching bodies for loot. Divico shrugged. *Let them do as they please. They followed me to victory today; they deserve so much more.*

Enjoying the sensation of sweet triumph and his new-found standing within the Tigurini, he didn't miss the glances of the men around him. Most smiled at him happily, some showed genuine awe, all shouted congratulations. He looked down at his sword, realizing it was still coated in blood. Bending down, he cleaned it on the tunic of the Roman officer before sheathing it. His eyes turned to the fortified camp across the valley. He raised his hand to garner attention from the many warriors and chieftains lingering close by. "We are not yet done. Some Roman dogs made it back to their fort. Let's go and knock on their doors." The declaration was greeted with a loud cheer.

"I feel like we should be generous, maybe we'll let them and their slaves live if they beg and hand us all they possess." He mounted, receiving giddy and roaring laughter in return. *That, and the loot of the dead will get us enough food for the winter. We can go back home to our mountains.*

PRIMUS

Ante Lucem Tenebras (The Darkness Before Dawn)

"…and the still more hostile Romans, whose arrogance we cannot hope to avoid, not even by submission and servitude. They have plundered the world, stripping naked the land in their hunger… they are driven by greed, if their enemy be rich; by ambition, if poor… They ravage, they slaughter, they seize by false pretenses, and all of this they hail as the construction of empire. And when in their wake nothing remains but a desert, they call that peace."

Cornelius Tacitus, The Agricola

668 AUC (86 BC), summer
Rome, Italia, Capital of the Roman Republic

Caesar sat on the bench of his old family house's atrium, reading the second book of "Alexander's campaigns" by Ptolemy Soter. Alexander the Great was his latest obsession, and this was the third series about his hero he had borrowed. Still alone, he was the first of his family in the atrium, enjoying his free time until their expected dinner guests' arrival. He used to love visits by his uncle, but now that Marius had changed and could exhibit unpredictable fits of rage at any time, he dreaded them. Still, he was excited to see his beloved aunt and his older cousin.

"How is that book?" his oldest sister asked from behind him. "Any better than the last ones?"

With a slight jump, Caesar looked up. "It's very different from Callisthenes's Deeds of Alexander. It doesn't merely describe military matters, it also talks about how the fame went to his head and how he started to act like a Persian king of old, persecuting anyone who spoke up against him or his plans."

"Does that remind you of someone we know all too well?" Julia major asked, her usually expressive face deadpan.

"Unfortunately, it does," Caesar answered, slumping his shoulders. When Sulla had been made dictator, his uncle had to flee for his life to Africa. Later, when his rival travelled to Greece to fight a war, Marius had come back with many loyal veteran soldiers. Ever since, the now seven times consul ruled the city through terror, putting all real or merely imagined Sulla supporters to death. The man they had all loved seemed gone.

They stayed in silence for a moment until they heard the house servants rushing to open the front door. The visitors had arrived.

***

After a lengthy and mostly quiet dinner affair came to a sweet end with honey drizzled desserts, Marius moved off his couch to approach Caesar. "Nephew, would you mind stepping out of the room for a moment?" Caesar nodded and stood up to follow his uncle who led him out of the dining room to one of the alcoves off the atrium.

"I'll keep this brief. You are fourteen years of age, and my co-consul Cinna and I have been wondering about your future. We noticed the looks between you and his daughter Cornelia last month. I mean during the second dinner with her at my house." He openly grinned. "We wondered if there was a possibility for her being with child from you already?" Caesar turned bright red. "I guess you don't have to say anything, I can see you'd rather not." Marius laughed open-mouthed, his lopsided face turning into a scary grimace. "You would probably prefer to be anywhere else but here with me right now, am I right?" Caesar shook his head, unable to say anything.

"Cinna gives you his blessing if you want to marry her, but only if you can provide for her. What would you say of becoming the next high priest of Jupiter? The old priest passed away recently, meaning there's a vacancy that needs filling. Holding the title would automatically emancipate you. You could leave your father's house to move into the official priest's residence with Cornelia. More importantly for me, you would have the right to attend the Senate where you can observe for us from the rear benches, which would be very useful."

"But…I'm not old enough for the priesthood, am I? Is it even possible?"

"Age is not a factor, believe me. If Cinna and I are supporting you, it's as good as done." Marius put his hand on Caesar's shoulders to push him back towards the dining room. His excited thoughts about Cornelia must have been well reflected in his face since his uncle started to laugh.

I've met the girl of my dreams, no other compares. And now she will be my wife! Joining his uncle in happy laughter, he walked back to their family in the dining room. Surprisingly, today had turned out to be very good indeed.

668 AUC (86 BC), summer
Farmstead outside of Bibracte, Free Gallia, Nation of the Aedui

The day was warm, allowing Drestan to take off his shirt. He proudly showed off his new tattoo, a blue bird on his upper left arm. He had plans for another bird and an oak tree on his right, and a yew tree on each wrist. A warrior now, born to one of the noblest families of his nation, he couldn't wait to show the whole world. Oh, how he had begged his father to let him get his first one! Every warrior could wear a torc around their neck, its decoration or choice of metal whatever he or she could afford, but only noble warriors, the nation's leaders or master druids, were deemed worthy of tattoos.

Weapons training on their estate was for all children, including those of his father's retainers. Several of the teenagers were good enough that Drestan still felt challenged. During their training, nobody made any distinctions about one's birth or family, just like later when fighting side-by-side in real battle. A good family connection, however, would get you noticed. His father Haerviu was chieftain of a prominent clan of the Aedui in their nation's heartland, a member of the council and recently elected as Vergobret to rule as king of the Aedui for one year in all but name, eligible for reelection after waiting another. Having a father at the top of Aeduan society did not mean that his sons, including seventeen-year-old Drestan, would automatically follow in his footsteps, but it did give the brothers a distinct advantage.

"Good, keep your footing," his stout, muscled father commented. The much slighter Drestan held on to his heavy oaken training sword and his even heavier shield while fighting against a similarly equipped young woman barely younger than himself.

"No! Don't overreach! Stop for a moment, both of you. Son, I know you're good with a sword, better than most of my warriors, but you're overconfident. If you face a respectable swordsman, he or she will take advantage of that." Drestan raised his eyebrows in disbelief.

"Alright, I need to show you." Drestan's father sighed while holding out his hand to the girl. She handed him her training sword and stepped away. Haerviu was rarely on their farm, spending most days and nights in the city. It was a treat to have him home; even more so to have him teach or train them.

"Here we go. Now try that again." Drestan performed the same feint, followed by a thrust meant to stab into his father's gut. Haerviu, slow and careful most times, broke into a burst of speed to sidestep the blade and move in closer. He pushed Drestan's arm with his left, keeping him from moving the blade back to intercept. They both stopped, the tip of his father's sword against his throat.

"Let's do this one more time. Your enemy has other options," Haerviu said, waiting again for Drestan to move first. This time, when he moved in, Haerviu moved right, dropping his sword arm and rotating his body into Drestan on the inside of his outstretched blade. His right arm caught his son's sword arm while the left moved in from below to form a complete trap. The force of the continuing rotation pulled Drestan forward, making him lose his footing and fall forward onto his own shield.

"I think I made my point. When you lean that far out with your feet still behind, you cannot move back fast enough to react to my moves. If I had a shield, I would have broken your arm between my right hand and the shield edge." He handed the sword back to Drestan's sparring partner.

"You'll be fighting with me next time we ride out to raid. Meaning, you have a few short weeks to forget about how good you are."

He looked around the courtyard and raised his hands.

"Gather round, gather round!" he called the youngsters, waiving for them to stop their mock battles and come closer.

"Drestan, it's time we repeat the twelve doors to the soul for everybody. Why don't you demonstrate with the sword while I recite them?"

Haerviu looked at the others as they approached.

"Ganna, you do the same with your spear." They moved over to a thick pole of green fir, sunk into the ground for use as a training dummy. A smaller pole pushed through a hole at shoulder height represented arms, and a rusty old helmet completed the setup.

"You have all heard this before. We Aedui believe everybody has twelve doors to the soul. You need to know these doors until they are the first thing that comes to mind when you see your enemy. You need to start by finding whichever one is the least guarded and the easiest to reach. You older ones already know this by heart." Drestan's father pointed at the youngest. "Why don't we have the younger children answer. Who can tell me where our souls sit?"

"In the head. That's why warriors always wear helmets," a small boy answered.

Drestan and Ganna both stood ready. Haerviu continued. "Right! The first door, as you said, is the head, or to be specific, the very top of it." Drestan moved his wooden sword onto the helmet, with the cutting edge facing down. Ganna placed the wooden ball on the tip of her training spear right next to it.

"You can see the issue reaching it when your enemy wears some protection. You need to push off the helmet first or hit hard enough to split it. That only works with a sword or an axe, if at all, and you won't get a second try. Think about how you open your guard when you do a mighty overhead swing. Let's move to the second door. Who can tell me where that is?"

"It's the hollow in the back of the head," a small girl piped up. She seemed a feisty one, standing with both her hands on her hips, swinging her long red braided hair as she looked around the group. Drestan had to grin at the sight. His father nodded, pointing at him and Ganna to step around the dummy for the lower back of the helmet.

"Feel the back of your skulls, where the bone ends, and the soft tissue starts. Yes, that's the point. Same issue as the top of the head, many helmets cover the back, but some don't cover low enough, so it's still a valid move. But who knows the issue with using the second door?"

He pointed at a small boy, barely big enough to hold his training sword. "How about you?"

"Is it because the back of the head is used for punishing murderers?" came the reluctant answer.

"Very good! Killing somebody from behind in battle is done as a last resort or if you need to save someone. It's not an honorable thing to do, and the warriors don't take the enemy's head after killing that way. Now, let's move on. What's the third door?"

"I know that one. It's the temples!" the same young boy answered again. Nodding, Haerviu pointed to his own temples to illustrate the point. "Some helmets cover them, but some don't." He motioned for Drestan and Ganna to point to the dummy's head before moving on.

"What's next?" They moved in rapid succession through the doors, from the apple of the throat to the spoon of the breast and the sixth door, the armpit. Drestan had his sword pointed at the joints of the wooden dummy. When Haerviu continued, Ganna shoved Drestan's sword tip aside with her spear tip. Drestan looked at her in surprise. She showed him her teeth in a wide grin. His hands turned sweaty, and he felt his heart racing. *How am I supposed to react to this?*

"Don't forget—instead of stabbing to kill, you can also slice, which will make the arm useless," Haerviu said. Drestan walked to the front of the dummy to hold his sword to the joint, then made a pulling motion. He glanced at Ganna to see if she was still smiling at him. She was.

They moved on to the breastbone, then to the naval or womb, the area's names depending on the enemy's sex. Drestan found it increasingly hard to focus as Ganna toyed with him. His father droned on about the remaining doors, from elbow to the ham at the back of the leg, to the groin area, to the foot. Giving himself a jolt, Drestan decided to look back at the girl, keeping eye contact. She was fifteen, and only half a head shorter than him. He had known her all his life as the daughter of one of his father's most trusted retainers. She lived with her parents in a house right across the courtyard from his house, yet he had somehow missed her turning into this intriguing young woman.

She seems perfect.

He knew what she could dish out with her spear. Her smile added to the sunlight. Her watery blue eyes drew him into her depths until, amazingly, he found brown flecks the same color as her hair.

The remainder of the training session finished much too quickly for his taste since he knew he would be bound to his father's side as long as he was on the farmstead. Though that wouldn't keep him from dreaming about spending time with her.

669 AUC (85 BC), summer
Rome, Italia, Capital of the Roman Republic

Gaius Julius Caesar, now fifteen, was beyond himself. *Why did this have to happen to my own father?* At age fifty-five, Gaius Julius senior had sat down on a bench in the vestibule to put on his street shoes and passed out. His father's death had been similar to the story he remembered about his grandfather, who had fallen dead one morning during a visit to Pisa forty years ago, also without apparent cause.

"Ready?" Caesar whispered to his mother Aurelia, finally letting her out of his embrace. He hugged both of his sisters before getting in place behind his mother. Tears flowing, he searched for his young wife Cornelia's hand to hold. Instead, her arm reached around him for a tight squeeze. His mother now started the long walk away from their domus, and the family followed with a longer and longer procession forming behind them. Right behind the main family, his father's most treasured clients carried his body in a wooden sarcophagus to the eastern Necropolis, one of several big cemeteries outside the city limits. Aurelia had hired over two hundred professional mourners, who now walked all around the wooden box in darkened togas, loudly wailing. Many wore the ancient wax masks of the Julii family ancestors over their faces. He was grateful. A procession this size left little chance of his father's spirit escaping along the way to become a shade to haunt the living.

They arrived at the cemetery and promptly walked up to the hole dug in preparation. The sarcophagus was lowered, and while it was covered, everyone loudly lamented the early demise of Caesar senior. With the burial complete, Aurelia sent the professional mourners away while the inner family lined up next to the burial site.

Caesar spotted his aunt Julia and cousin Gaius Marius next to uncle Sextus's widow Horatia and his young cousin Sextus Julius

Caesar. They were close to the end of the many people moving through to give their condolences.

He received a hug from six-year-old Sextus, and another one from his aunt before they moved on to his wife and his mother. Cousin Gaius Marius stepped in to give him a solid arm grip before making way for Gaius Marius senior.

"I am so very sorry about your father. He was a great man," his uncle said. "You are now the head of the family. Let me know if there's anything I can do to help you. Anything."

His aunt Julia was next, enfolding him in a big hug. On a sad day like this, he appreciated the family's affection. He wiped his eyes with the back of his hand as he heard Aurelia excuse herself from the line to come over. "My son, it's time to prepare for the eulogy. Are you ready?"

He nodded and made his way to the small podium. He stood there waiting until all mourners had taken their seats. His mother had rented many stools, anticipating a big showing, but obviously not enough. As it turned out, there were at least as many guests standing as sitting, maybe more. Since he was now the official high priest of Jupiter, almost all of Rome's priests and many Vestal Virgins had come to honor his father.

The first two rows were filled by family, the next several by long-standing friends and family clients, and all now looked at him in anticipation. He nodded to many familiar faces in acknowledgement before looking down to face his script and gather his thoughts. It was time.

"Family, friends, clients. Thank you all for coming to honor the life of my father. As is custom, I will start this eulogy with our family's ancestors."

He pointed at the incredibly lifelike death masks of his ancestors, now on little stands on small tables to either side of the one taken from his father's face.

"Our family was founded by Aeneas, prince of legendary Troy, son of prince Anchises and the goddess Venus, cousin to king Priam's sons Hector and Paris. After Troy fell to Agamemnon's host, Aeneas led a group of survivors to Latium, where he founded the kingdom of Alba Longa. His son Ascanius Julius is the first to bear our family name. His line also led to Romulus and Remus, the founders of our beloved Rome."

He went on to name every single one of their ancestors, an endless litany stretching from the early days of Alba Longa through the forced joining of that kingdom with the kingdom of Rome, listing the varied history of the following rule by the Senate and People of Rome, finally arriving at his own father's time. Only now was he allowed to talk directly about Julius Caesar senior and his achievements.

"My father was that rare politician, both skilled and beloved by all, chosen to become proconsul without ever holding the post of consul." His voice breaking, he paused, closing his eyes and holding his breath for a moment before being able to continue.

"My father was that exception among his peers, caring only for the common good. A man who loved his family, his city, and his countrymen in equal measure." He looked down, carefully wiping his eyes with the back of his left hand.

He knew this would be a long day. A lengthy feast back at his parents' house was waiting after he wrapped up here. He would need to attend until every single guest had left, and his sadness already made him feel weary to the bone.

Both of his sisters came up from behind to join his wife Cornelia and his mother Aurelia, already standing in close support. They would all get through this day together, a simple family grieving for a father and husband.

672 AUC (82 BC), late fall
Praeneste and Rome, Italia, Roman Republic

Marcus Licinius Crassus sat on his horse atop a hill overlooking the small city of Praeneste. Exhausted, he slumped his shoulders. The fields of a heavily farmed countryside framed a city gleaming in the setting sun. The view presented his tired eyes with a peacefulness so very unlike the brutal reality surrounding it.

"You don't look too well, Marcus!" Sulla called from his side. Crassus turned to the general who had ridden up on his famous white horse. The man who had brought a huge force of five veteran legions from Greece two years ago to take back from Marius what he considered his own looked no less tired, blue eyes warily peeking out from under unkempt flaming red hair. They had both seen constant campaigning in Italy while fighting the Senate and its troops, all still loyal to old Marius. The old thorn in Sulla's side had died close to three years earlier after catching a cold, soon after the start of the man's seventh consulship. Sulla had also been through many years of continuous fighting in Asia, while Crassus had hidden in Hispania ever since their enemy had his family killed and their property confiscated. The moment word had reached him of Sulla's arrival in Italia, Crassus had raised his own force to join the fight.

"Too bad that Pompeius is not here to share in our glory when we sack the city," he said in reply. Gnaeus Pompeius was their third commander, currently holding Italia's north for Sulla's forces. "The young pup down there doesn't have the balls or the skills of his old man, so it shouldn't take us too long." Crassus referred to Marius's son, who had made a desperate retreat into Praeneste after losing an open battle, only to be besieged there by Sulla's men.

"Don't underestimate him, Marcus. His name alone will keep his men fighting to the bitter end. I can fault my dead archenemy all I want, but he inspired a devotion in his sycophants and their soldiers that still holds." Sulla turned in his saddle to face Marcus. "Change of plans. We will not be able to attack Praeneste soon. Our scouts reported that the senatorial relief force we've blocked from relieving the city has instead marched out this afternoon. They turned north, towards Rome."

"No rest for us then, they are the bigger threat," Crassus responded wistfully. "I better let my men know we need to break camp in the early morning. I assume you want us to follow them posthaste?"

"Yes. I already sent all the cavalry ahead to hold the field in front of the Colline gate, so we won't lose access to the city. We'll only leave enough men here to keep the siege going."

Deep in thought about what needed to be done, he turned his horse and rode back to camp.

***

Early morning the following day, Crassus rode at the head of a single column of his own men, paralleling a bigger force on their way to Rome. Once the city was in sight, Sulla's men spread wide to cover the left and middle, and he gave the command for his soldiers to become the right flank of the attack line. Their forces reached the nearest wall and gate before the enemy showed itself. Hidden in nearby woods, the Marian forces rushed to trap all attackers against the wall. Sulla's left wing became overwhelmed, and the Colline gate, standing wide open in apparent invitation, became a rallying cry for the troops. Many of the soldiers and the loyal senators traveling with them ran for presumed safety.

"Hold men, hold!" Crassus screamed when he realized that some of his own men started to make for the gate as well. In horror, he watched the gate's garrison suddenly dropping the iron grate portcullis right into the fleeing masses. Some were killed outright; the following screams clarified that whoever had made it through had run into a slaughter set up by the guards. The troops still outside had no choice but to face the enemy once more.

He turned his horse to glance over to the west. Sulla's ranks were even thinner than his own. Despite their impending doom, Crassus could spare some admiration for Telesinus, the enemy's commander. They had fallen for his trap without a second thought.

The opposing troops reformed for a phalanx maneuver, succeeding in pushing a wedge into the small space between his own and Sulla's soldiers. The now divided parts of the army drifted apart, with Crassus soon losing interest in anything besides keeping his men alive.

***

With a gleam in his eye, Crassus looked over his thinned ranks, grinning despite the long and bloody struggle. He loved these boys. The late morning had turned to noon, noon to afternoon, and now dusk was close. Yet they were still holding their position against overwhelming numbers. His grin faded. How much longer could they do this? It was time for a desperate gamble.

"Luctatus, rally all remaining cavalrymen. I want you to try to get at Telesinus from behind. If we can take him out, we'll break their army." He watched his friend and client make the rounds until a small group of about fifty riders had formed. Crassus rode over so he could keep his voice low. "We'll make it look like you are fleeing…" After he had layed out his thoughts, he waited for the signal from Luctatus before waving the centurions on.

"Push! Push! Cuneum formate, form a wedge!" he heard the shouts at the northern side of their square. The legionaries did their best to push forward, the center of their line shoving the enemy line out further and further. The men rotated sideways at the last moment to let the galloping riders through from behind. The opposing forces had thinned enough that forty of the riders made it, with the remainder either killed or having lost their horses. Crassus's eyes lit up in satisfaction as he saw his cavalry ride hard as if fleeing for their lives, going east to leave the enemy forces behind with none of the Marians bothering to pursue. *Good.*

In the far distance he observed Luctatus and his men reining in to turn south. A few minutes later, he knew the mission had succeeded when the enemy line's center started to waver. For a brief time, his own riders became visible behind the enemy foot soldiers, many of which turned in response to the shouting behind them. Crassus's men pushed hard and thinned the center's confused enemy ranks with ease.

"Their whole line is caving! Keep pushing!" he shouted in elation. Another few minutes of heavy fighting saw the enemy lose more ground. "Single line! Flank them! It's now or never!" Crassus screamed at his centurions. The rear ranks moved out to stretch the frontline, with both ends enveloping the senatorial army's flanks. The enemy center panicked; many of the rear ranks turned to flee. It took the opposing front's soldiers a moment to realize what went on behind before an avalanche of them turned and ran from the center outwards, hoping for safety in the woods half a mile away.

"After them, boys! Take down as many as you can!" he yelled, urging his tired horse to follow. The animal wearily stepped over countless bodies. The metallic smell of blood mixed with bodily fluids wafted up to him, but he barely flinched. All that mattered now was winning.

His legionaries ran after the enemy, cutting down any stragglers from behind. Riding in from the north, Luctatus with his few survivors had backtracked just in time to join the rout.

He signaled them until a couple men split from the group to come over. "Tell all the remaining prefects and centurions that I want the men to form up outside of the forest. We need to comb through it as a group, the enemy might still rally." He looked up at the sky. The sun was about to set, yet they could not let up.

***

The next morning, Crassus called out to Sulla. "There you are!" After his own men had followed the fleeing enemy throughout the night to the small town of Antemnae, where the last pocket of enemy survivors had fortified themselves for a final stand, he had sent out scouts to find Sulla and to let him know where to meet.

"I had thought all was lost," Sulla responded. "Until your scout found us holed up in our old fort, I assumed you and your forces were dead."

"I am very happy to say you were wrong, Lucius. My men won the day and broke the Marian's back. I don't think they'll recover from this."

"I'll pray the gods agree," Sulla answered, his face suddenly darkening. "I came by the Colline gate on the way here. One of my centurions gave me the numbers for the dead on the ground. He estimated nearly fifty thousand, counting both sides. The blame solely rests on the traitorous senators' shoulders." Sulla's eyes narrowed. "I gave specific orders to burn all enemy bodies. I won't have any burials for them."

Crassus raised his eyebrows. Sulla's eyes seemed crazed as the man looked out over Antemnae. Or, possibly, mad with barely contained rage.

"I will make them pay for this; I swear by all the gods. For the wrongs done to me, and for all loyal friends and soldiers they murdered," the general fumed.

Anybody siding with Marius would be fair game now. Crassus had no doubt Sulla would show them all what it meant to invoke his righteous wrath. Though Crassus looked forward to his own revenge, adding some financial opportunities in the process, he involuntarily stepped back from his commander. He hoped the man's fury was not contagious.

"I will demand the Senate appoint me dictator again. Once I have my special powers, I will fall on the traitorous and corrupt senator swine like a bird of prey. I will shred them to pieces with my talons. None will stay alive who supported Marius." Sulla's forehead glistened with sweat, his eyes narrowed to small slits. "The gate garrison that turned on us? Kill them all. Telesinus' surviving legionaries? Kill them all. Do the same with these here at Antemnae. My mercy has run out."

672 AUC (82 BC), fall
Rome, Italia, Capital of the Roman Republic

How come I am a child again? Caesar wondered.

He found himself walking with his father through the Forum Romanum on their way to his aunt Julia and his uncle Marius's new domus, located in an upscale neighborhood of the Viminal hill in Rome. He closed his eyes for a moment. When he looked again, they were already rushing through the main entry door to get out of the blistering morning sun. "Hand your toga to the servant. That will keep it clean and your mother from chiding you later," his father told him.

He walked into the atrium, where he spotted his aunt close to the pool. After they hugged, he searched the room for his older cousin, to no avail. The memory of the impressive atrium decorations was crystal clear. The floor with its beautiful mosaics, with geometric patterns flowing from the entryway to the pool area, where the blue tiles depicted all manner of interesting ocean creatures. The walls painted with realistic nature scenes of bare, gentle hills around the vestibule, changing to herds of deer on luscious grasslands around the pool area and into forests before changing again to snowcapped peaks at the back of the room.

"Come here, young man, let me have a look at you!" Marius called from across the atrium. There he was, his beloved uncle.

He turned towards the voice with a big smile, only to instantly freeze. His uncle's familiar face, framed by the same balding head, looked much different than he remembered, with his left cheek and eyelid hanging low. Odd. At least his remaining hair was trimmed nicely, and he looked as fit as ever. His father had told him about something called apoplexia, but he had not imagined that his uncle would have changed. The boy made a slow procession across the room. Marius looked him up and down. "You need to start your martial training soon. You don't have any muscle, and with your pale skin you look like you stay indoors all day. Well, at least that skin tone compliments your eyes." His uncle chuckled. Caesar's family trait was dark rings around the iris, and he had been the target of many derogatory comments about his piercing gray eyes. At his uncle's jest, he stopped walking and stiffened.

Marius pulled up his shoulders in apology. "I see you don't like anybody teasing you. You need to toughen up, you hear me?" Caesar closed his eyes again, this time in emotional pain. When he reopened them, he walked behind his uncle down the hallway. "I thought that I could show you my collection of Cimbri and Teuton weapons. What do you say? We'll leave your aunt Julia and your father to catch up."

He hurried on. "Yes, uncle, I would love to see those! Do you also have Numidian weapons from when you fought Jugurtha in Africa?"

Marius laughed aloud. "I should have figured you'd ask that! Yes, I brought some of their spears and bows with me. Come on." He took Caesar's hand to lead him away.

"Wait!" The boy turned and waved at his father and aunt, receiving a couple of warm smiles in return. "Now we can go. I can't wait to see the spears!"

"But to be clear, my boy, I don't have the king's weapons, they went to Lucius Cornelius Sulla. Do you know who he is?"

"He was your second in command in Africa, right?"

"Yes, that's right. I sent Sulla to get the king to surrender and to ship him to Rome, and he delivered." He closed his eyes again.

When the eighteen-year old Caesar reopened them this time, he was in his bed. *Not my bed,* he reminded himself. His wife Cornelia was next to him, and it was late afternoon. *I wonder why I dreamed about that day again. Was it the last time I wasn't scared of my uncle's fits and wrath?*

He sighed and turned his head to look at his wife. Her head rested on his arm, which was asleep and in pain. *Time for us to get up and ready.*

Later that night, Caesar and Cornelia moved through the darkened city, the same as every other day, to stay with yet another set of friends or relatives before moving on once more. Roaming the city streets well after midnight, when decent citizens were at home, meant their only encounters were with the unwanted, the indecent, or the many delivery workers whose carts and wagons were banned from the streets during daylight.

"I am so tired of doing this," Cornelia said, raising her voice. "Putting on disguises, having friends and loyal clients walk us from hiding place to hiding place is wearing on me. If we could at least start out earlier!"

"We would run into everybody coming home from dinner parties. We wouldn't be safe even in these disguises," he answered. From under his thick hood, he watched a young delivery cart runner pass them by, the cone of his torchlight playing on the facades of the houses as he gained distance. Once at the next intersection, the boy would block the entry to the narrow street for his cart team, allowing them to pass without running into head-on traffic. Caesar's gaze moved back to his own small group of ten people.

His wife Cornelia wore a black wig over her luscious curly, red tinged brunette hair, with a cheap, dirtied stola hanging around her thin frame. This completed the change in her appearance, successful despite her unmasked face and distinct dark blue eyes, which now looked his way with a hint of challenge. His heart melted. She was the only reason he hadn't succumbed to despair.

"I am sorry. You know we can't stay longer anywhere. We've been caught five times already. I am racking up huge debts with my mother's family from the payoffs to the crews to let us go." With an incredible two talents reward on Caesar's head, they were not about to stop looking. "Our only chance lies with my uncles getting Sulla to issue a pardon."

His client and friend Gaius Oppius walked up from behind. "You should stay quiet," he told them in a subdued voice. "We're nearly there, you can talk more later." Oppius wrinkled his nose. "We should walk on quickly, though, away from this vomit." The façade of the closest house reeked of the results of excessive love for wine.

At the next major intersection Caesar stopped to check the proscription posting on the wall, and Cornelia came up to hug him from behind. Yes, his name was still there. The shock was still fresh from the first time it had been included in this list of people Sulla wanted dead. The high reward, equaling one hundred forty pounds of silver, was enough to tempt anyone from lower and middle classes to try their luck as an executioner. The only escape was to pay even more when caught.

Dear Jupiter, help my uncles come through for us soon. "Even with a pardon, my estate is gone, and my priesthood too," he said, with a breaking voice, "but the worst thing is this feeling of helplessness and being at the mercy of others." He paused before continuing, louder. "I swear to you, from here on out I will do anything, whatever it takes, to never again be this helpless." He nearly shouted the last sentence, and now fearfully looked around before starting down the road again.

As they hurried to their destination, Cornelia never let go of his hand. *As long as you're with me, I can weather even this.*

672 AUC (82 BC), early winter
Rome, Italia, Capital of the Roman Republic

Caesar walked into his uncle Gaius Aurelius Cotta's atrium looking for his mother, and found her sitting on a stone bench close to the pool in the midst of several small potted maple trees, engrossed in a conversation with his wife Cornelia. Good, they both needed to hear what he had to say. Though grateful for their support beyond words, he recognized their suffering throughout the ordeal, born with few complaints.

Ignoring the two for a moment, he looked around the well-lit room to prepare himself. It had been dark, with only a single oil lamp burning when they had arrived in the early morning hours. His uncle's domus, newly renovated since his last visit, had the previous scenes depicting the Roman pantheon of gods replaced by exciting scenes of Homer's Iliad, his uncle's favorite Greek classic. One side of the room was taken over by a huge mural showing the siege of Troy, while the other had several smaller scenes depicting the various heroes involved, including Achilles and Hector during their final showdown. He finally walked over to the bench, silently squeezing between the two most important women of his life. Their conversation stopped.

Caesar turned to his right. "Mother, I am grateful that your brothers and great uncle Aemilius Scaurus managed to get me pardoned"—he took a deep breath—"but I can't divorce Cornelia, no matter that Sulla demands it. I just cannot do that."

He turned to his beloved wife, who had lowered her head, likely to hide the tears Caesar knew to be there. His heart skipped a beat, while his left hand reached out to find her right, squeezing it tightly. "I want you to know that I sent Sulla a letter, begging him to forgive me for not going through with his request. Nothing can change my mind." His wife looked up, a deep joy shining out her wet eyes that tugged at his soul. She was breathtakingly beautiful in her new stola, tightly wrapped around her body. He appreciated how the blue offset the red sheen of her hair.

Now that he was eighteen, his marriage to Cornelia had already lasted through three tumultuous years. Her current status of disfavor stemmed from her father, who as co-consul to his uncle Marius had bitterly opposed Sulla until being killed by the hands of mutinying legionaries.

"My name was struck so recently from the proscription list that I don't want to take any chances. Sulla must be angry at my defiance and could change his mind any day." Caesar looked back at his mother. "I would like Cornelia to stay with you, while I will leave Rome. If I'm out of sight, I'll be out of Sulla's mind, which will be easier on all of you, including aunt Julia. I'm grateful that her good reputation has kept her out of harm's way. May the gods praise the Vestal Virgins for their help." The Vestal Virgins, women priests for Vesta, the goddess of home and hearth, had publicly spoken out for his aunt.

"Where will you go?" his mother Aurelia asked. All his money and property had been confiscated, including Cornelia's dowry and the old family home, forcing Aurelia to stay as a guest in her brother's house.

Caesar's lips parted until he showed his mother the boyish grin of old. "When Sulla stripped me of my priesthood, he unwittingly allowed me to join the Cursus Honorum. Maybe he didn't realize that I was barred from a political career as a priest. Not anymore! Of course, the Senate won't issue me a legal commission as a tribune, but I can go as an unpaid military aide. If things here change, the service time might yet be credited towards time served. I am hoping that uncle Gaius Aurelius will write a letter of recommendation to Marcus Minucius Thermus, who has now been confirmed as propraetor governor of Asia province for next year. I know they are friends from the time of Sulla's eastern campaigns."

"As much as I hate the thought of not seeing you for a long time, I admit this makes good sense. Also, my brother will surely give you some money to get you started." Her lips moved into a slow, small smile; transforming her worried face. "What are the expenses? There is the travel itself, plus provisions. What about armor?" His mother's thoughts lingered, as ever, on the practical.

"For the last, I was able to save father's, which fits well enough, and the swords he bought for me for my military training at the Campus Martius are still the best money can buy." He had started his sword training at eleven years of age. What a happy time that had been—now it felt like many lifetimes ago.

His mother nodded, looking around him to her daughter-in-law. "Cornelia, what do you think of all of this?"

Caesar's wife straightened when facing her mother-in-law, her adoration for the older woman apparent. "I don't like the idea of my husband leaving, but I don't see a lot of choice. And, I would be eternally grateful if you and your brother would let me stay here. I would appreciate not having to fear for my life anymore."

Aurelia nodded. "Consider it settled." She stood up to lead them out. "Let's go to the study to talk to my brother about the details."

673 AUC (81 BC), summer
Pergamum, Roman Province of Asia

Tribune Caesar had been called to the office of Propraetor Marcus Minucius Thermus, current governor of the Greek Province of Asia. The man administered his realm from an impressive old palace that had served as the province's headquarters for half a century. As the seat of the former rulers of Pergamum for centuries, it looked beyond ancient to him.

He waited in the entryway until he saw a young Roman scribe return.

"Follow me," the young man told him.

Caesar walked down several long and dark hallways, only lighted enough by occasional oil lamps. He scrunched his nose when the building's wet and moldy odors assaulted him. The impressive façade was no indicator of the state of the roof, which was in severe need of repair. They stopped outside Thermus's office, the governor visible through the open door. The provincial ruler sat behind a large and impressive Corinthian-style desk made of a thick polished maple slab resting on six ornately carved legs.

The aide knocked on the open door to get the governor's attention. "Sir, Gaius Julius Caesar is here to see you."

"Have him come in." Thermus waved the aide away and pointed at one of the several chairs in the room.

"Salve, sit down. I'll be done in a moment."

Caesar studied the man he felt enormous gratitude towards. The governor, trim, in his mid-forties with short-cropped gray hair, was currently engrossed in a scroll. Thermus finished reading, removed the weights needed to keep the scroll from rolling back up, and then added the roll to a growing pile on the right side of the desk before looking at the smaller pile on the left, where most scrolls were still sealed. He sighed. "The bane of any magistrate, I'm afraid. Nobody ever told me how much tedious paperwork there is for the likes of us." He barked a deep and infectious laugh, now turning to give Caesar his full attention.

He leaned forward. "Let me be very honest with you. I wasn't sure about you at first. I knew of your connection to Marius. Understand, most of my family has been supportive of Sulla. Well, except for my younger brother, of course, who served for the other side. Without your uncle Gaius Aurelius Cotta vouching for you, I would've never taken you on. Anything with the potential of earning Sulla's wrath should not be taken lightly."

Thermus looked to the side, out the window, at the swelteringly hot countryside visible behind Pergamum's city walls and collected his thoughts.

"That said, I'm glad I took you in. You've done a spectacular job for me reorganizing the administrative office. When I asked you to go to Bithynia to talk old king Nicomedes into giving us his fleet in support against Pontus, I didn't think you could succeed."

That mission was a sore spot for Caesar. It had taken him a full three months to change the king's mind, and with the monarch known in the Roman world as a connoisseur of young men, the provincial rumor mill had produced the overwhelming conclusion that he must have sold his body to earn the fleet.

"You came back later than expected, though with a better agreement than anybody could have possibly hoped for." Thermus paused to stand up and pour water for both of them from a big earthen pitcher. He handed Caesar one of the cups.

"Next, you excelled when asked to advise at local legal proceedings."

He'd had all the complaints about previous governors collected throughout the province, filed, and copied. The activity had been enlightening, to say the least.

"Finally, when I asked you to consider current issues with our military supply logistics, you came up with a great number of suggestions for improvement. As a result of all your hard work, I applaud you for your vigor and attitude." Thermus leaned back in his chair, giving Caesar a wide smile. "I'm going to give your career the push it needs. You might think it a punishment, but please be assured that's not my intention. You don't have any true military experience as you've never been in battle, which is why I'm sending you to serve under Lucius Licinius Lucullus."

In response, Caesar hissed through his teeth in disapproval. Thermus held up his hand to stop him from protesting. "Lucullus just started a campaign against Mytilene, which was accused and found guilty of harboring pirates. I know that as a stout supporter of Sulla he sees you as a nuisance at best. Overlook that. Instead, when you deal with him, think about Lucullus as the gifted military man he is, the famous general with his legendary victories against Mithridates. Sulla wouldn't have been able to overcome Pontus without that man by his side."

Caesar was devastated at the turn of events. He'd encountered Lucullus a few times. A fanatical follower of Sulla, the man had previously made a point of showing him what little he thought of his family connections. "I don't like it, but if you think it best, of course I'll go. As to the mission, by the gods, pirates are the scourge of the Mediterranean. I am eager for a chance to get involved." He averted his eyes, focusing on the desk's surface. *But did it have to be Lucullus?*

"I just hope that he will let me get close to the fighting."

673 AUC (81 BC), late summer
Mytilene, Island of Lesbos, Greece

Caesar rushed down a major road to reach one of the supply warehouses on the other side of camp, where he hoped to get new leather straps for his father's worn armor. Before crossing the next major intersection, he paused to see if the coast was clear. Lucullus was to be avoided if possible. The legate had continued to treat him with disdain at every opportunity, making several comments within Caesar's hearing about having to babysit against his better judgment. Thermus's orders must have been quite clear in their intent, or Lucullus would have sent him back immediately.

"I was just thinking of you!" Lucullus called from behind. A groan escaped Caesar's lips before he could stop himself. He turned around to face his tormentor.

The general moved up close. "The sappers just reported that they are nearly done. If their calculations are correct, we will see action tomorrow." Lucullus cleared his throat and barely turned sideways before spitting on the hardened dirt ground, no more than a foot away from Caesar's feet.

"Which brings me to you. I have just the right command to keep you away from trouble. I promise you will have hell to pay if you mess this up somehow and get in the way of your betters."

Speechless, he stood frozen as Lucullus turned and walked away.

***

Years ago, Demotimos worked as an honest trader following in the footsteps of many family generations. Lately, few goods still flowed through normal channels, and he had barely scraped out a living until the city had decided to ally with a group of pirates, providing them safe harbor, a chance to buy supplies, and a market to sell their spoils.

Many of the citizens hated that decision, although for his family it had seemed a blessing. The city had a new lease on life, and his wife and five children could eat their fill again. Now, the Romans had come to punish them, making him wish the city elders had never made the fateful decision.

He drank the last of his water skin and put his helmet back over his dark hair, stepping back out onto the main plaza to continue his training with other city defenders.

"I'm ready, let's resume where we left off," he told his sparring partner. They were both part of the city's small elite that owned full hoplite suits of armor, handed down through generations. The polished bronze and steel sparkled in the sun, both spear tips and swords well sharpened in expectation of what was to come. As Demotimos moved into a defensive stance to ward off future attacks, he briefly glanced at the sea, visible from this side of the plaza. How he wished he could board a ship with his family and leave all this behind. "Begin!" he said with a heavy heart.

***

With the men around him preparing to leave, Caesar put his helmet on and tied the straps. They stood in the small space between two tent rows in the northern army camp, and he had ample time to mull over Lucullus's lack of fairness. Of all the possible choices six cohorts conducting the siege would give, he was now to lead eighty of the oldest veterans. He was nineteen, and some of these men sneering openly at him were at least twice his age. He assumed they thought of him as a spoiled youngster they had to endure for the day. Officially, they were the reserve, and he was acting as their centurion. Unofficially, his job was to keep them out of the fight. The siege seemed well in hand; the plan of action laid out by Lucullus long ago. Once the army breached the walls, it would be up to the regular soldiers to storm in and win the day.

Though it was still early in the morning, the men seemed ready. He raised his hand. "Let's march." As they proceeded towards the camp's eastern gate, they encountered a growing number of legionaries and their officers.

"Have a good rest," a centurion hollered at his troop. The men standing in an inspection line behind the centurion broke out into hoots and laughter.

A tribune stood waiting for them to pass before crossing the camp road behind them. "I hope you have wine and dice with you," he shouted after them.

By any legion standards, these veterans had served long enough to deserve a break and were more than happy to just observe. The motto was always that the greener the soldier, the more fighting he had left to do. The longer the legionary's service, the better his excuse, except for situations that required all hands on deck. He just wished he wasn't the one who had to lead them.

"Let's move up to the top of this hill!" Caesar shouted so they would all hear him. He had scouted the place last evening. Half a mile away from the city wall and the siege works, it gave good vantage. As they arrived, a few of the men sat down to look at the city in expectation. Others, though, chatted away from the view; a few even pulled out dice. He walked up to a big boulder, climbing for the best outlook over the city, only pausing to take off his hot helmet.

Mytilene was built on a small spit reaching out into the ocean. Located about halfway up the eastern coast of the island of Lesbos, it had a natural harbor on its south side and a twenty-foot-tall stonewall that had kept its twenty thousand inhabitants safe for centuries. The vista was beautiful in the morning sun, showing whitewashed houses with red clay roofs. He knew this had once been a bustling community with a busy harbor, which had changed because of too many greedy governors over the last two decades. He had heard of overzealous Roman publicani, contractors acting as government taxmen, shutting down many honest business ventures in the provinces, and he wondered if this city's trouble was related. The Roman Republic sent quaestors to assess a territory's tax value but left the tax collection to the contractors. Apparently, the system was rife with bribes and corruption, with local populations suffering.

One of the younger veterans climbed up to join him, and they shared the view in silence for a few minutes. "A shame, what is about to happen down there," the man finally commented.

Caesar nodded in agreement, though the idea of financial compensation for a successful capture of the city was also exciting for him. Just being part of the sack, even if he only stood here throughout, meant he would receive a part of the spoils. No small thing, considering how badly in debt he was and how many more loans he would need to finance elections once he became eligible for a seat in the senate.

"Our troops are ready." He pointed at the lines of men in the nearby northern camp. The two forts were about a quarter mile from the siege works, and about half a mile from each other. Caesar's hill was west of the northern part of the city wall. He scanned the Roman siege works, which formed a one-mile-long second wall made from timber, encircling the city's defenses at a distance of a hundred feet. The Roman wall was built to the same height as the city walls, with towers to match and access stairs every few hundred feet on the inland side to allow fast troop deployment.

A section of Caesar's view was obscured by smoke blowing out from a mine shaft entrance behind the northern end of the Roman siege wall. The smoke was billowing over to the city wall, dispersing out to sea with every gust of wind.

A deep rumble shook the hillside, accompanying the rise of a huge cloud of dust and debris. A couple of minutes later, he heard cornua and tubae, the ancient trumpets used to relay commands to Roman legionaries, calling for attack. The sappers had been successful, part of the wall had collapsed.

The dust in the air spread, removing all visibility. Caesar looked at the veterans, feeling strongly that they needed to get ready, just in case. He straightened and smoothed his face before addressing them. His voice started out as a whisper and he caught himself, repeating as loudly as he could. "Veterans, I know I'm little more than a fresh recruit to you. I cannot change that"—he briefly paused before continuing—"but it is our job to be reinforcements, so I expect you to stand ready nonetheless. If there is a clear need to move, I will not wait for anybody. Stragglers will have to deal with disciplinary action afterwards."

He scanned the men's faces. Some looked away, though he was sure they had heard him. Others seemed to grumble under their breath, too low for him to make out. He looked at every veteran in turn until the grumbling died down. *I might be young and green, but they know I am aide to the governor. I outrank them, even without a senate commission.*

He adjusted the sheath of the gladius on his belt to have it ready for easy drawing.

"Rare, that. Don't see many officers with a gladius," the legionary on the boulder with him commented.

"I don't think we'll see a lot of cavalry action today. Do you?"

The soldier showed him a wide grin, clearly appreciating his response. "I'd wager you're right on that account, sir."

Caesar loved to wield the longer spatha so many officers preferred. He had a fine Gaulic example waiting in his tent, though he was practical enough to understand that a spatha's extra length was handy on a horse, yet unwieldy in close quarters.

The man stowed his food bag. Caesar felt a pang of regret about the troops having to grab rations of old bread, cheese, and stalks of celery thanks to his decision to leave before sunrise, removing the joy of hot porridge or fresh bread made over the morning tent fires.

The smoke blew out to sea, making the Roman cohorts visible again as they streamed down the siege wall over a temporary ramp, allowing for quick descent towards the breach in the city wall.

Off the ramp, the legionaries formed groups on both sides of the breach. As they advanced and changed into battle lines after climbing over the wall remnants, the noise grew dramatically. Caesar saw volley after volley of arrows hitting the oncoming Romans, with many men dropping. From the slow going, he assumed the city defenders had also built barricades to deter the attackers. The legionaries formed into testudo, a formation named after the tortoise, compact and minimizing exposure to arrows. Only the first rank kept their shields forward while the ranks behind held theirs upward to cover the men from fire from above. As the troops advanced into the city, only the rearmost of the men stayed visible. Caesar decided to check both sides of the wall instead and spotted a group of men moving at the farthest edge of the siege works. Only lightly armored, they must have climbed up the cliff wall from the rocks below.

"Look!" He shouted at the soldiers around him, pointing. "There, local Greeks climbing up the cliffs to the north. Seems around five hundred already, with more coming." He could see a steady stream of heads popping up over the edge. "They're heading for the breach to trap our troops."

He closed his eyes and pushed his rising fear into a dark corner. He knew the enemy force climbing the Roman wall could turn the tide, so he could not idly stand by. He untied his plumed helmet from his belt to put it on his head again. Next, he pulled his gladius. Taking a deep breath, he shouted, "Follow me!" before running down the hill toward the siege wall closest to the breach. *Please, Jupiter, let the men be behind me.*

He did not have the heart to turn around. He only relaxed his tight face when the unmistakable clanging of sword sheaths on chainmail and pila on shield rim reached his ears. It was impossible for legionaries to run quietly, especially when carrying two six-foot pila inside their big oval shields.

As they descended the hill, he realized the defenders' timing had been impeccable. All the Roman troops had left the siege works, with only a small token force sprinkled along the towers to watch the city's walls. The dust of the breach had perfectly hidden their ascent up the cliff.

The Greeks entered the siege wall at the first set of steps and spread out to quietly take care of the distracted sentries one by one, the battle noise from inside the city masking everything. Caesar veered away from his original target for a still empty section of the siege wall. He made it to the wooden staircase and hurried up, finding himself on the other side of the long ramp from the Greeks. Catching his breath, he scanned his men as they came up behind him. The wall was wide enough to allow a six-legionary-wide front rank when deploying their shields. With the first thirty or so ready, there was no more time to waste.

"Attack! Throw your pilum as soon as you can!" he shouted, letting them go ahead to the thirty-foot-wide ramp. As his first veterans came close to the enemy, they slowed to throw their spears before forming a shield wall. As enough men for the next rank pulled up, they threw their pila above the heads of the first line. Many of the lightly armored enemy force went down in screams.

Caesar ended up pushing himself into the sixth line from the front. Here, he figured he was close enough to the front for a good view of the engagement without being in the thick of it. "Push! Push them back from the ramp!" he shouted. As veterans, the men didn't need any more direction. The first line pushed a step forward, holding their shields edge to edge, making some of the closest enemies fall. Next, they rotated their bodies and shields slightly left, creating an opening wide enough to allow for each gladius to stab out for soft bellies before pulling their hands back in. Now, they rotated the shields back, again edge to edge with their neighbors', and took another step forward in unison.

"Inpello! Push through," the first two lines called out together to keep each step synchronized. The second and third lines were busy dispatching trampled enemies underfoot who still showed signs of life. Caesar felt light-headed from the sight. The downed men begged for their lives, quieted only by ruthless stabs into their throats. The metallic stench of blood and the stink of emptying bowels made him retch. His stomach convulsed and he breathed only from his mouth to steady himself.

His men moved past the width of the ramp. A few hundred Greeks were running through the breach, having made it down before his century closed the gap.

"Advance halt!" he shouted. "Hold your ground!" He turned around. "Last seven ranks, follow me."

As they moved down the ramp, he addressed them again. "Stretch out into two long ranks. Close your shields, let's chase them into the city!" He marched with his soldiers into the breach. Most of the Greeks ahead didn't notice his small group of Romans advancing on their backs until his men stabbed many from behind.

Caesar saw the third rank of Lucullus's original cohorts detaching to face the Greeks in their rear, now trapping them in turn. His own two lines of twenty men each filled the width of the breach perfectly, removing any chance of escape.

He laid down his small round officer's shield and picked up a discarded infantry one instead before stepping into the second rank of his veterans. He wondered why he had bothered with his own shield at all. Commonly known as a buckler, the officer's small variant was out of place in a legionary line.

The man in front of him received a cut in his leg from beneath the shield and toppled to the ground. Caesar lunged at the enemy who had stepped in for the kill and pushed his gladius up for a stab into the man's throat, pulling his sword back out as the Greek collapsed. Blood sprayed everywhere, including over his face, his helmet and his breastplate. Half blind, he rapidly blinked to clear his vision. Another warrior tried to take advantage of the opening. Without conscious thought, he stepped forward to push his shield into the man. The hard impact shoved the attacker backward into his own people. Caesar moved up and closed the shield line, relieved at his success. Suddenly, he gagged as some of the blood entered his open mouth. He shivered in revulsion.

A few more steps forward, a few more thrusts with their swords, and the threat was over. Most of the trapped Greeks had been slain, and a few threw their weapons to the ground, wailing, their desperate gamble lost.

Lucullus stood between the Roman lines, about forty feet into the space behind the breach. Caesar started moving towards him, but Lucullus waved him off angrily, shouting for the original third attack rank to change their focus back to the city defenders, which had come out from their barricades in support of their fellow townsmen.

He stopped, baffled by Lucullus's detestable manners. Turning back to his veterans, he contemplated what to do next. A glimpse at the siege works stopped him in his tracks. The job wasn't finished, there was still more to do.

"Reserve, follow me!" he called on the soldiers one more time. They hurried back to the ramp and to their fellow veterans still fighting on the siege wall. The six ranks he had left behind were reduced to little more than four, but the men had successfully held back the much larger Greek relief force.

"We are back!" Caesar shouted and the relieved men whooped in response. The Greeks lost heart once the Romans made a hard push and cut down the entire enemy front line. The remainder turned to flee down the length of the wall.

"Let them go, we can't catch them anyway," Caesar shouted at the legionaries, who were too heavy in their armor for effective pursuit.

As he walked back down to the breach, he heard cheers. A runner passed by on his way to camp, shouting at him about the main force having pushed through the barricades into the open streets behind to search for remaining pockets of resistance.

The older of the veterans talked to each other until they turned and crowded him. The excitement of the fight still raging, he suddenly turned wary. *What is this about?*

His eyes started scanning for a way out when a deep chant started. "Caesar, Caesar, Caesar," louder and louder. Two of the men dropped their shields to lift him up onto their shoulders. The chant continued until the men were shouting at the top of their lungs. One of the legionaries carrying him looked up and saw his bewilderment, thankfully screaming an explanation up at him over the roar. "You saved most of the troops, maybe all of us, when you led us to the wall. We are all Roman citizens, now we bear witness for a Civic Crown."

Caesar's hand tightened in shock. The Civic Crown was rarely awarded, and only for saving Roman citizens' lives. A wreath of oak leaves to be worn at any Roman public gathering, it also gave him automatic access to all senate meetings. Not to mention the senators would be law-bound to applaud him on entry. His lips relaxed into a satisfied smile. The soldiers' euphoric mood was infectious. Everywhere he looked, he saw joking, smiling, and laughing. Now that the fighting was over, every veteran made guesses about their portion of the pillage. As was tradition, all belongings found in the city went to a common stockpile. After the sale of the goods, everybody would get a fair share, thanks to the cohort prefects, centurions, and optios. When it came to spoils, hundreds of years of experience had taught the army to be fair to its legionaries. The alternative was certain mutiny.

***

The Roman front line separated and their soldiers scrambled up the Greek barricades to fight his fellow defenders man to man. Demotimos fought off one opponent when he saw another coming at him from the corner of his eyes. He had no time to react as the legionary's sword hit the side of his head. Hard. Falling backward, he slid down to street level before pushing himself off the ground. Many dead or wounded defenders lay around him. "Run! It's all over!" a man screamed at him while hurrying past.

Demotimos began to walk, frequently glancing behind him. In a wave, the whole defensive line broke and the few surviving townsmen rushed away from pursuing legionaries. He shook his head to clear it, spraying blood in all directions, and ran down the street. As he unstrapped his helmet and pulled it off his head, the ensuing pain nearly made him faint. The dented and bloody piece of bronze in his hands had a big open cut, and parts of his scalp and pieces of his skull were stuck to the inside. He dropped it, working on discarding his shield next before moving on to his armor. After turning left, off the main thoroughfare, he stopped to take a breath. His hand came away drenched from the side of his head, indicating a steady trickle of blood. Feverishly opening the last leather straps, he finally dropped the heavy plate and started to move again. Now lightheaded, he settled for a slow jog over a full sprint, willing himself to last.

All I want is to see my family one last time. He and his wife had discussed what to do if the Romans captured the city. The plan had been to accept slavery and make the best of what lot the gods would give them. She had given him her blessing to remarry if circumstances allowed, and he had given his to her. Though all that was meaningless now.

I will be dead soon, at most I have a few more minutes. He wiped the tears from his face. He was so close, just two more streets. He kept moving, one foot in front of the other.

***

Caesar walked the streets with a group of his veterans, noticing many buildings with belongings collected in the street in front of them and a large letter V painted above the front door. The V was indication the house was *vacuus*, meaning emptied. Some of the former inhabitants had died in the fighting, but many others were being led away. Caesar arrived at a large, official looking building, and found it yet untouched. They all drew their swords before going inside.

Workers hid in the upper levels, and some of the soldiers volunteered to walk them out to the other captives already outside the city. He figured the slave traders, never far from Roman legions, would take over transporting them as soon as the tallies were completed, and their contracts signed. As he moved with the men through the bigger offices on the ground level, they collected many valuables found and came across several dead magistrates, often in the midst of their deceased families. Many well-dressed figures, some older, some younger, lay scattered on the floor. The bodies had settled in random positions and at first seemed to be sleeping, though their vacant eyes stared into nothingness. They were well on their way to the underworld and Charon, the ferryman who would cross them over to Hades. Thinking of his own family, his dear Cornelia, or his many cousins and their children, he wondered how easily the roles could have been reversed. *Would I have reacted the same way?*

Finally, when he came across the body of a small girl, three or four years old, he couldn't look any longer. A pang of guilt managed to get through his elation for their victory, and bile rose in his throat. He shook his head to recover from his sudden unease, but it did not go away. Waving at the soldiers in silent good-bye, he quickly headed for the door. *I can't wait to get out of this godsforsaken place.*

676 AUC (78 BC), late fall
Rome, Italia, Capital of the Roman Republic

More than three years after his experience at Mytilene, Caesar walked up the street to the front door of his uncle Gaius Aurelius Cotta's townhouse and knocked. A familiar old face opened the door for him.

The servant greeted him with a warm smile. "Young master, it is good to see you again."

"It is good to be back," he replied with a nod and a smile of his own. He stepped to the side to allow the hired helper carrying his travel trunk to enter. "On the vestibule floor is fine." Caesar had to shift various bags and scrolls in his arms to reach his purse. "Thanks for your help, here is your money."

He stepped from the vestibule into the open atrium and heard a loud scream from above. He looked up to see Cornelia running to the stairs from a small guest room off the atrium's upper balcony. She must have heard him arrive. *My sweet Cornelia!*

His heart skipped a beat. He had dreamed about this reunion for nearly four years. He melted in joy as his wife jumped the last few stair steps and threw herself into his arms. He had to drop everything in order to catch her.

"I missed you so much," she whispered. Caesar could not respond, his throat too dry. He held tightly as if to never let go again.

"I missed you more," he finally replied, unable to look away. Somehow, she was even more beautiful than he remembered.

"I was so afraid you would die in Lucullus's campaign or some of the unrests after. I'm so happy to have you back!" She turned her head to the house slave that had opened the door earlier. "Please, fetch Aurelia, quickly!"

Two more servants arrived to collect his belongings off the floor as he led his wife to the benches around the atrium's pool. "The maple trees have grown tall," he commented before he saw Aurelia running at him.

"My son, my son!" Still breathless from her rush, she gave him a tight squeeze. "How often I prayed to have you home again, safe and sound." She noticed the servants behind the two, holding his belongings. "Let's get your things put away in your room, we can talk there."

He held hands with Cornelia while his mother led the way to the guest room, now to be both of theirs. He had his few loose things dropped on the bed and directed the other servant to put the trunk down in a corner. Once the three were alone, he sat down next to his wife and put his arm around her. His mother took the only chair in the room and sat down in front of the couple. "You must have so much to tell us. You never went into much detail in your letters. I am just glad that you came home so soon after Sulla's death."

"The only time I was close to real fighting was in Mytilene, and that campaign turned out to be quite memorable for me." Caesar walked over to the trunk and opened it. "I had to change out the leaves a few times since I received this, they dry up rather quickly." He pulled out his Civic Crown and put it on his head. Both women gasped.

"Are those oak leaves?" his wife asked.

"A Civic Crown? And, it is truly yours?" his mother added with wide eyes.

"Yes, yes, and yes," Caesar answered, presenting his boyish grin of old. "Mytilene was nothing at all like I imagined. Every boy dreams of big battles, thinking it's all glorious, that our soldiers always prevail like some mythical Greek heroes. But when you are there in person it feels different, and not for the better. All the dying, friend and foe alike—the messiness of it, the screams, the blood, and oh, the smells. Nothing prepares you for the smells." He frowned as unbidden visions filled his memory. After a moment, his eyes cleared, and his smile was back. "The good part is that I learned how to lead men into battle while keeping my wits about me." His mother's scrunched face showed him her worry. "I mean to keep going with the Cursus Honorum, but don't worry, I'll stay home for a while. For now, I want to work as a lawyer in Rome. You wouldn't believe the kind of atrocities I uncovered while working for Thermus. Some of the previous Roman governors in Greece and Asia need to be held accountable, and I hope to make a name for myself by prosecuting the worst of them."

His eyes narrowed. "And I have a mind to go after some of the worst of Sulla's henchmen while I'm at it"—Cornelia hugged him tight, face frowning in worry—"but for now, I'd like a bath, a dinner, and this bed. In that order." They all laughed in relief.

***

The next morning, he found Aurelia sitting on a small bench in the kitchen amidst the servants of the house. "Good morning, mother. Where is uncle Gaius Aurelius? I can't seem to find him. Did he leave for the Senate already?"

"He did. My brothers are meeting early these days to strategize about next year and brother Marcus's praetor post. You don't know yet that he was elected. The three have made interesting alliances lately."

"Really? What kind of allies are we talking about?"

"The most important one is Crassus. He offered to finance all their election campaigns for years to come."

"Crassus? As in Marcus Licinius Crassus?" His mother nodded. *Unbelievable. How could they? The man is a monster.*

He shook his head. "You can't mean the man who swooped in to help Sulla come back to Rome and then made incredible riches by working the proscription list? The same Crassus that bought half of Rome for cheap at the auctions?"

The success story of Crassus was well-known all over Rome, and even Caesar had heard many anecdotes in Greece. When the proscriptions had been in full swing, the despicable man had bought slaves skilled in construction. With his first team of five hundred established, he bought burned-out buildings across the city and later adjacent properties as well, rebuilding or renovating to resell for huge gains. Lately, Crassus concentrated on growing his business of slave trading. The use of Sulla's contacts in the east had made him a favored source of slaves for many senatorial enterprises.

"I know you don't think highly of him, but please hold your judgment until you meet him. He was here for dinner a couple of months back, when we had a long conversation about his upbringing and his role with Sulla. I didn't know that his parents had been rather poor or that they had shared a small house with both his older brothers and their families. I knew he was related to many former praetors and consuls, so the apparent lack of money surprised me.

"Marius proscribed and killed his brother, his father, and many of his close friends. He was forced to flee for his life, and hid in a cave in Hispania, close to the sea. Can you imagine living in a cave?" His mother shook her head to emphasize the point. "He raised his own army after he heard of poor Cinna's death at the hands of his own troops." She paused to thank a servant for bringing her a loaf of fresh bread. "You know most of what happened after. Crassus is not quite what you think, he is an interesting oxymoron. Charming, well educated, he holds no grudges and is a great public speaker. Always willing to help others, yet he's also quite boastful and easily flattered. Then, there is his boundless ambition and greed, which I think overrides all other considerations." She took a breath. "I believe that if you can deal with that greed as a constant, he could make a useful and predictable ally."

"I will think about it, mother," was all Caesar could reply before walking off deep in thought.

***

A few weeks later, Caesar, Cornelia, and Aurelia walked down a bustling city street in the Subura, buffered by a group of servants. Cornelia walked between mother and son, arms linked all around.

"It's in the neighborhood of our old family home, Gaius," Aurelia told him while watching one of their servants shooing away a beggar by waving his cudgel.

"But the Subura, Aurelia?" Cornelia asked. "I heard of a few surviving old pockets of nicer houses, but it's certainly not a high-class location these days."

"I know, Cornelia, but remember our lack of coinage. Please look at the house first before you make up your mind. It's supposed to be in good shape, with no repairs needed." Aurelia sighed. "My savings are meager, and you two have little to contribute. I assume that the lawyering will pay off in the long run, but it's not helping much now, and I didn't want to ask my brothers for more charity. Not after all they've already done for us." She looked back at her son. "Speaking of money, have you met with Crassus yet?"

"No, but your brothers arranged a meeting a couple of days from now. It seems they have a good relationship with the man; Crassus confided that he plans on switching to the Populares after some of the mighty nobles of the Optimates faction stated their goal of curtailing his business expansions. He started to hide some of his more lucrative activities from them and is biding his time until he has an issue for the Senate that makes the move a truly worthwhile surprise."

"That means my brothers will do the same when the time comes. Feels like Marius's Populares faction is rising from the dead," Aurelia mused.

They turned off the main street to reach a neighborhood of older but nicely kept townhouses. Gone was the bustle of the Subura's famous insulae, cheaply built apartment complexes housing most of Rome's population. After the tremendous noise, the peace and quiet they walked through now felt like heaven to him.

After several peaceful blocks, Aurelia waved the servants to a stop. She pointed to a freshly whitewashed façade with no windows. The stately, well-built door of solid oak had a small opening at eye height, covered from the outside with iron bars.

"Here it is. What do you think of the location?" Aurelia asked.

Caesar looked at Cornelia, who nodded to his mother. "You are right, Aurelia, it's not too bad. There are several blocks between this and the next insulae, and most importantly, no brothels in the neighborhood. Let's go and look inside."

He knocked on the door and waited until an older slave looked out through the iron bars in greeting.

Aurelia stepped up. "We are here to look at the house, as was arranged with your master." The man moved back from the door, opened it, and let them enter.

"Ah, the atrium dates the house a bit. The old-fashioned style with columns all around the pool," Cornelia said.

Caesar gave her a hug. "I rather like the columns. Even the walls look great." He pointed out the paintings, consisting of geometric patterns on white walls, with a few small sections depicting harvest scenes, musicians, and festivities. They might be original or newly done in a remodel. Either way, they were pristine. He pulled her along, eager to see more of the dwelling.

"I agree, they are bright and friendly, not like most new houses where everything is painted in dark reds or blues. Look, the dining room is similar. I am surprised that I like this domus. Let's take it," Cornelia said with a smile.

My career is looking up, I have the woman of my dreams, and now we have the perfect home to start our family. Warmth spread upwards from his belly, flushing his cheeks. The bright colors and friendly scenes in the well-lighted rooms became a reflection of increasing delight. *Finally, everything is going my way.*

678 AUC (76 BC), summer
Forty miles southwest of Tbessa, Kingdom of Numidia

Oppressive heat added swirls into the air. Seventeen-year-old Ozalkis and his seven-year-old nephew Adherbal stalked a group of red deer in the afternoon sun. Oz raised his hand, indicating the need to stop. For once he wished they had brought long spears instead of their bows and knifes. Ranging farther every day into the mix of sparse evergreen woods, bush, and dry grasslands at this southern edge of the Aures Mountains in the eastern Atlas range, the two were happy to encounter any game, be it barbary sheep, boar, gazelle, screwhorn antelope, oryx, or hartebeest. Though now he had spotted another kind of hunter and knew they were in trouble. A Barbary leopard had joined them, one of three dangerous local predators. The others were the Barbary lion and the Atlas bear. Though perhaps less powerful than a pride of lions or a mother bear, a leopard's inquisitive nature meant it wasn't shy when encountering humans.

Oz pulled on the cloth of his tunic where it hugged his chest. It stuck to his sweaty skin, which was annoying now that he had become tense with worry. He studied the boy next to him. They shared a distinct brown complexion, curly dark brown hair, and brown eyes. All traits that were different from those of the common lighter-skinned Numidian people. Adhe's nose, though, was slightly smaller and less sharp-edged than his own, which had a hook reminiscent of an eagle's beak. He sighed in resignation. *I won't let anything happen to you.*

"We need to hide in the bushes. Stay silent," Oz whispered. They both pushed into the acacia growth to kneel, snapping dry branches in the process. Though their simple cotton tunics, left unbleached in their light brown color, helped them blend in, the key was distance. Oz and Adhe always stalked their prey from downwind and, of course, the huge leopard had the same idea. Creeping, the cat made its way closer to the deer until it was only a couple hundred feet away from him and his nephew. It sniffed the air, turning sideways until it stopped in the direction of their hiding spot. Ozalkis's shoulders slumped and he closed his eyes. *Oh no. Now a showdown is unavoidable.*

He turned to see a frightened Adhe looking back with big, round eyes. "Promise me you will wait until I shoot before you let your own arrow go. I want the cat to go after me in case I only wound it," Oz said. He waited for a clear nod from Adhe before pulling his string close to his cheek, keeping the nocked arrow pointed at the big cat as it stalked towards them. He let fly at twenty feet. The cat increased its pace at the last moment, resulting in the arrow only grazing its right shoulder and causing a roar of anger. The leopard sprinted the last ten feet before leaping. Oz had just enough time to drop his bow and draw his long thin knife, holding it outstretched in his right hand in anticipation. Quick movement from the right let him know that Adhe had launched his arrow, clearly missing his target. The huge cat hit Ozalkis like a battering ram and launched him backward. The back of his head exploded with fiery pain before everything went black.

***

"Salpo, come quick, your brother needs our help!" Oz heard Mipsa shout from afar. He glanced up. Though late in the day, the two had been out weeding. Before he had to close his eyes again, he saw them drop their tools and run over. He stumbled; his legs didn't have much strength left.

"What happened, Adhe?" his sister Salpo asked her son. Oz felt her moving in on his left side. When she took some of his weight he sighed in relief. Now his brother-in-law Mipsa took over from Adhe to support his right side, and they sped up.

The boy still breathed hard and could not muster enough air to answer. He had half-carried Oz for several miles.

"Is that leopard skin?" Mipsa suddenly asked, staring at Adhe's bundle. His tone was incredulous.

Salpo hissed through her teeth. "I am just glad you both got back. Let's move Oz into the house, I need to look his wounds over."

On their walk to the family home they drew attention from Adhe's three older siblings as well as the children of their closest neighbors. Soon, they all pelted them with questions.

"They ran into a leopard. That's all we know!" he heard Salpo answer. The shadow from their porch roof felt good on his heated, torn skin. "Turn, go sideways," his sister commanded Mipsa. "The kitchen table will work best."

They both grunted as they helped him up onto the table. Flat on his back, he opened his eyes again. His skin was on fire and the cool table felt good. "Help me get his tunic off," Salpo asked her husband. "Here we go. These claw slashes on his left, by the gods, they are very deep. I need to clean those first and sew the skin back together."

"Mother, also look at the back of his head please. He's bleeding there," he heard Adhe, who was finally able to speak again.

He turned his head to his left. Salpo walked to the food counter on the side of the room to fetch their red wine vinegar. She poured enough to fill a wooden bowl half-way, then added water before sponging it into Oz's wounds.

"We will work on his head after I've done his chest and he can sit up." He saw Salpo look over at the children. He felt dizzy and closed his eyes again. "It's important not to use too much vinegar, always remember that. If it's too much, it attacks the skin itself and the wound won't heal as well, but if you don't use enough, the wound can get red and inflamed." Oz had kept quiet so far, but now he couldn't hold back any longer, and moaned from the pain. *Is this it? Will I die from this?*

Someone grabbed his left hand. Oz squinted to the side. *Adhe, dear, incredible boy. You got me home, impossible as it seems.* He looked on as Salpo worked his wounds, moving to the deep cuts on his left side. Before he passed out, he saw a whole sheet of his skin move sideways.

"Mother, I think he's losing consciousness," was the last thing he heard.

As he slowly became aware of his surroundings again, the first thing he noticed was a strange pulling sensation on his skin.

Without the pain, the rhythm of the pulls might have been lulling. His whole body was on fire, the pain worse than before he had passed out. With a groan, he opened his eyes.

"Are you back with us already? I hoped you would stay out a little longer, at least until I'm done," Salpo said. She smiled at him as she moved needle and thread deftly with expert hands. "At least, now I know you have a good chance to get out of this with a few beauty marks. It doesn't look like the leopard got to anything vital." She cut the excess thread of the suture and threaded the needle again with a new length.

"So, what about you, Adhe? You are all bloody yourself. Is any of that yours?" he heard Mipsa ask across the room.

"No, none of it. Some of it is uncle Oz's, but most of it is from skinning the leopard." After a brief pause, his nephew continued. "I thought uncle Oz was dead after his arrow just seemed to make it mad. My own arrow missed, that cat just ran so fast. Then it jumped him and threw him down. My second arrow went into its side, but I think it was uncle Oz's long knife that killed it. They were both lying still afterward, the cat right on top. It took me a while to pull it off, and I was surprised to see he was still alive."

"I am proud of you, my son. Sounds like he might not have made it without you," Mipsa replied.

"Now, why don't you all go outside?" Salpo asked the children. "Adhe, you need some cleaning up yourself, and later you can tell your siblings and the neighbor children all about what happened. Mipsa, help me get Oz off the table. He should sit up, so we can look at his head next."

Two pairs of hands reached for him. "Ouch." *How is it possible this can hurt even worse?*

"Sorry, dear brother. I'll try not to touch your wounds again."

He slid off the table and made for the chair. His sister started to explore the back of his head with her fingers, pulling on his hair.

"Certainly not worse than the rest of you."

He put on a shaky smile for his sister. *Oh, how I wish I could pass out again.*

679 AUC (75 BC), early spring
Bibracte, Free Gallia, Nation of the Aedui

Drestan and Ganna emerged onto the main plaza from the ornately decorated Great Hall, which served both as palace and meeting place for the council of chieftains of the Aedui. The plaza seemed eerie with the late morning fog still hanging on. The sky above was heavily overcast; the day felt like it was on the cusp of bringing late spring snow.

Little Aina came running up to them. Drestan smiled at Ganna before dropping to his knees to open his arms wide. Since their days of budding warriors training together, they had shared a fairytale romance culminating in a big wedding. He was still as happy as when they snuck away from their chores to spend time together. The feeling of fresh new love had changed over time to something deeper, involving trust and deep understanding of each other.

The only thing dampening their joy had been the losses through the years of some of their beloved children to sickness or accidents. Drestan knew that no parents were immune to this, yet he wished the pain would ease quicker. Their focus had narrowed sharply to their three surviving children, two glorious boys plus little Aina, whose happy disposition was an endless well of joy. At eight years she had decided to skip marriage and motherhood to focus on becoming a famous warrior. She loved playing with her brothers, especially when that play involved learning how to fight.

"Aina, sweet girl, look at how dirty you are! Well, certainly my mistake for letting you dress yourself in your best clothes," his wife chided the girl in a stern voice. Aina wore a long overshirt against the cold, in a beautiful orange, purple, and blue plaid pattern, with big patches now covered in brown dirt. He glanced at Ganna and realized from the quiver in her cheeks that his wife had to work hard to suppress a smile. The dirt would wash out, and Ganna doted on Aina as much as he did.

"I was fighting a battle while you were inside!" their daughter shouted in excitement. "And I won!"

"Who did you fight as? If it was Andarta, I hope you didn't say that out loud again," Ganna asked Aina quietly, followed by their daughter's quick smile and a shake of her head.

Aina had recently gotten into trouble when pretending to be the goddess of war during one of her games, shouting that she had changed out of her she-bear form to fight alongside mortal humans just as an old druid walked by. Daring to impersonate a god had resulted in a caning on the spot. Drestan knew that only druids were supposed to have a direct connection to the divine, except when some of the gods decided to walk among the common humans to mingle, yet he had told the man in no uncertain terms what would happen if he were to ever a lay a hand on one of his children again. The druid had never returned to his farmstead.

"Drestan, we should pack right away." Ganna turned to face him. "We need to get east soon if we're to have a successful harvest and enough food for next winter. If it's as bad as what we just heard from your father and brothers, there won't be many hands left to help farming."

"First, I need to ask all our local people to see who will come with us. The more we can talk into joining us, the better our future there."

His oldest brother Liscan, the current Vergobret, had just offered him a heavy responsibility. He would now be chieftain over a vast stretch of fertile land in the eastern border region, tucked between the tribes of the Lingones to the north and the people of the Sequani to the south. The area had seen many raids from both, and a desperate call for help had reached Bibracte after the old chieftain and most of his warriors had been killed.

Ganna hugged little Aina, while Drestan embraced them both in a bear hug. "I can't help but be worried if this is the right thing to do for us."

Ganna kissed his cheek before whispering into his ear. "You complained about not feeling challenged just a few months ago, don't you remember? It will be good for us, you'll see."

Oh, my love, I hope you're right.

679 AUC (75 BC), early summer
Island of Pharmacusa, Roman Province of Asia

It was another day of perfect blue sky above the azure waters of the eastern Aegean Sea, though that was where the similarities to a boring and uneventful yesterday ended. Caesar turned to his friend Quintus, who looked miserable standing on the deck of the small bireme galley, hands tied just like Caesar's.

Looks like Quintus needs some cheering up. "You know, it's all your brother Marcus's fault," he said, forcing a grin. If his friend Marcus Tullius Cicero had not boasted about how much could be learned about the finer points of rhetoric at Apollonius Molon's school on Rhodus, neither of them would be in this predicament.

"I'll give him an earful when we get back." He was rewarded with a smile from Quintus. Marcus was only a few years older than Quintus or Caesar but already a former praetor and aedile of Rome. Also, since Cicero was a highly successful lawyer, they frequently crossed paths at the courts.

"You certainly wouldn't have joined me"—he looked beyond Quintus, now wistful—"and I wouldn't have brought all of them along." His group contained several friends, clients, and servants. The distinction between the three categories had blurred for him since Sulla's time. Every major family in Rome had clients rendering help in exchange for patronage, legal representation, loans, employment, or even elections for public office. Out of fear, few of Caesar's original clients had stayed loyal to his family throughout the years of persecution. His thankfulness to the remaining few made him consider them close friends. He felt responsible and would do whatever he could to help them rise during his own career.

He noticed that the little flotilla of two pirate galleys and Caesar's leased trading vessel had turned into one of many coves of the island of Pharmacusa.

"Look at how ecstatic these sorry excuses for Greeks are at catching so many Romans," Quintus said, nodding to a group of pirates standing guard, joking to each other amid frequent laughter.

"Yes, they blame us evil Romans for all their plights; personal ones and the rot afflicting the Hellenistic world in general," Caesar replied. "Sadly, they are likely right. Until we became masters of the eastern Mediterranean, Greece and Asia province were wealthy and mostly peaceful. There is a good reason why everybody in the known world calls pirates Cilician, no matter their true origin. Cilicia is just southeast from here." They both looked at the pirates. Caesar smiled as he continued to talk in hushed tones. "I read that a hundred thousand slaves are changing owners every single day at the auctions on Delos. Even though that number seems unbelievable, if only a fraction is true, it tells you how bad things are here in the east. The common people have three choices. They either work for us, turn to banditry or piracy, or are threatened with slavery by the bandits and pirates—or by our Roman publicani if they can't pay their taxes."

What he didn't say out loud was that most of the slaves not sold to the Parthian empire ended up being shipped west to Sicilia, Sardinia, or Calabria, where they worked on one of the many wheat, olive, or wine plantations owned by Caesar's peers, the noble and rich rulers of Rome. The richer these men became, the more slaves were needed to cover their ever-rising demand for labor.

The galley's pirate captain walked up to the group, inspecting him, his friends, and the trader's original crew. "These are all yours?" The man asked him and Quintus, opening his arms to encompass all of their entourage.

"Yes, as I told your men earlier, they are with me and we are not to be separated. Consider us a package." Caesar answered with a steady voice while holding his head high. The pirate's nose started crinkling before his face changed to an open sneer. He held his gaze while noticing from the corner of his eye that Quintus had turned away from the man, no longer able to hide his disgust.

"We shall see," the pirate said before moving on to inspect the trading ship's captive crew. He stopped in front of a sailor wearing a clean tunic. "You must be the captain. Are you Greek?" The pirate received a nod. "Where are your men from?"

"From Apollonia, like me, except for these two over there. They are from Brundisium in Italia." The captain pointed to two men fearfully standing off to the si.de. The Italian crew members now drew the pirates' attention.

"Put the Greeks into the pens," the pirate captain ordered, pointing at the captain and his crew. "We will sell them tomorrow at the slave market in Rhodus." He turned to wave at the two Italians. "As for these two exalted guests, bring them our finest shoes and togas."

Amidst much laughter, a pirate rushed to a big travel trunk at the back for two pair of each. He held them out with a wicked grin on his face. "Put them on. Now."

The men stripped and did as they were ordered. The pirates started to cheer and mock them with rude gestures and profanities amid constant cat calls, whistles, and laughter. Caesar felt sorry for the two sailors, he could not imagine any scenario that included mercy for them.

The galley had made it to the beach. The men at the oars upped their speed for the last few feet to get the ship as far onto the sand as possible. The pirates standing at the bow jumped down to help drag it up further before the momentum was gone. A wide plank was thrown over the side.

"Take them to the camp!" the captain commanded.

Caesar raised his hand, again acting the belligerent nobleman in the hope of saving the lives of his servants and less wealthy friends. "Wait for me, I need to be first," he shouted. His entourage moved only after he stepped onto the plank. "Ah, here is our honor guard. Lead the way," he told the pirates, who stood with swords and pikes in hand, ready for any attempt at escape.

They walked off the beach toward the camp that was hidden in a slight depression half-way up the hill, invisible from the sea. The guards guided Caesar and his friends through the campsite. The stench of unwashed men combined with the rot of old food or worse to make him nauseous. Gagging, he walked past a pirate defecating at the edge of the perimeter, thanking the gods for the steady breeze blowing over the island. Still, this was preferable to the slave pens on the galley with the possibly short and brutal lives that went along with them. He wondered where the former crew members would end up. With few other skills beside sailing, they would be working silver, copper, or gold mines, stone quarries, or worse, lime production, with its caustic burning of limestone or seashells.

His group settled down as best they could. A couple of hours later, a pirate brought a sack with stale bread and a small earthen jar filled with olives. Before Caesar could eat more than a handful, two grizzled men came for him. "You, come now," one of them commanded.

He slowly stood up and followed them across camp. The two men halted in front of the pirate captain who had commanded the small galley, who waved for Caesar to move on. "Keep going, he is expecting you," he said pointing at another man a few feet away, who was lounging close to a fire on a fine and expensive looking couch. He walked up and the pirate leader slowly turned to show him a crooked smile. He was small, heavy-set, with a big hooked nose over a full black beard giving him a hawkish countenance.

"I will ask for a ransom of twenty talents for you, young Roman. That's the amount I get for Roman senators, not the likes of you, but I am making an exception. I've heard from my captain that you are acting like a haughty swine. I doubt you'll be worth much to anybody, but I want to make a good show of effort for my men. If we end up with little or no ransom money paid, I'll have the pleasure of killing you and perhaps some of your friends and selling the rest with your servants."

It was abundantly clear the man hated everything Caesar stood for and that greed was the only thing keeping him alive. As Caesar scrutinized him, he suddenly had to laugh out loud. The heavy-set pirate had donned Caesars' own lorica musculata, ransacked from his travel chest. His father's old-fashioned Roman armor was of the kind only worn these days by higher ranking officers to distinguish them from the rank and file that wore scale armor or chainmail. As its center piece, it had a polished bronze breastplate surrounded by wide leather strips meant to extend the armor's coverage to shoulders and thighs. The pirate had tied the breastplate tight at the top, but then by necessity had to keep the sides loose to allow for his ample stomach. Comically, this resulted in the plate sticking out at forty-five degrees. Caesar was sure the man had meant to impress him, showing that Caesar was at the mercy of the pirates. Instead, he felt amused by the theater.

"I tell you what, oh mighty pirate leader. Why don't you ask for fifty talents instead of twenty? I'm worth that much at least. I believe you have no idea who you are dealing with. My name is Gaius Julius Caesar, I am the scion of the ancient family of the Julii."

The man's grin was even wider now. He gave a loud chuckle before shouting at his men to gather as many crew as were close.

"Tell them again what you just told me!" he commanded his Roman captive.

"Very well." Caesar turned to look at as many of the filthy former sailors and fishermen as he could before continuing. "I told your mighty leader here to ask for fifty gold talents as my ransom. I'm a Caesar of the Julii family, which means I'm worth that much and more. If you want that ransom paid soon, I suggest you let some of my servants and friends go. They need to arrange the money in the bigger cities of Asia province and Graecia. I also feel compelled to warn you right now—once the ransom has been paid and you set me free, I will come back to crucify you all," Caesar said, lips parted for a wide grin. The whole group of pirates let out loud hoots and laughter. Some, already drunk from celebrating their catch of the day, fell to the ground to hit the dirt with their open palms.

They must think me extremely funny, maybe even insane. They will see. He resolved to stay aloof throughout captivity, reinforcing their thought of him as a half-wit.

"Get him back to the others!" the pirate leader shouted to be heard over the commotion. The same two men from earlier took him by his arms and led him away. "Let's celebrate a good day. Wine. Bring wine!" the leader demand from the midst of his troupe of ruffians as he was led back through camp.

679 AUC (75 BC), summer
Miletus, Roman Province of Asia

He paused to smile at his close friend Quintus Tullius Cicero and the two servants who had suffered through captivity with him, before they were escorted the last stretch from the camp to the galley waiting at the beach.

The pirate leader's voice shouted at him from the direction of the camp. "I still can't believe your friends came through for you, and after only thirty-eight days. I never thought we'd get a full fifty talents!"

Caesar's smile dropped, his eyes filling with loathing for the man. He did not want to acknowledge him. As they approached the galley, he heard loud applause from behind, and only then did he look back. The few pirates guarding the camp had all gathered to send them off. Whenever he had deigned to talk, it had always been in a joking manner, and he had frequently joined the pirates' exercises or games to pass the time. One night he had ordered some of them to shut up and stop drinking so he could sleep in peace, which had ended in the opposite, with the pirates laughing the night away. He smiled when he thought of what Quintus had told him several times. "Your behavior will stick. You'll always be a pompous ass from now on."

They boarded the galley, which was pushed off and rowed out to open sea. Once out of the bay, he saw the second pirate vessel tied to a small ship that must be his friend's.

The moment the galley docked with the smaller vessel, Quintus, Caesar, and his servants climbed down over the side. "Friends!" Caesar shouted amid relieved laughter. He clasped arms all around. "Thank you all for my freedom." He moved back a step to enjoy their friendly faces. Then he became pensive before he asked, "you have to tell me right now—which cities did you solicit for help with the ransom, and which of them contributed?"

"We asked at many, including Athenae, Pergamum, and even Miletus, which is just ten miles from here. Those three were the ones willing to help," his long-time friend Gaius Oppius answered.

"Good." Caesar turned to the sailing ship's stern to shout at the sailor manning the tiller. "We go straight to Miletus!" The crew got busy with turning the ship and hoisting the sails.

***

The ship headed into a gigantic bay, the sailors tacking at a slow pace around a hill at the end of a land spit. As they turned south, the city of Miletus became visible. It looked to be a couple of miles wide, its harbor facing away from the open ocean.

"The birthplace of the great Greek philosophical and scientific traditions," Caesar said to fifteen-year-old Aulus Hirtius. They stood at the ship's starboard side, enjoying the view together.

"I know, Gaius Oppius told me all about that already this morning," Hirtius replied.

Caesar smiled at the boy. *How eager he is to prove his worth.*

They watched as their ship made it into harbor to dock at one of the many piers, then Caesar jumped off-board before anybody had time to lay a gangplank and rushed up to the unmistakable harbor master. The man wore a big golden chain around his neck as a symbol of his ultimate power over the harbor fees and tariffs to be paid for goods.

"My name is Gaius Julius Caesar and I represent one of the oldest families of Rome. Please, tell me if there are any Roman officials currently in Miletus."

"Yes, sir, a Roman procurator arrived yesterday from Pergamum. You should ask at the town magistrate's office where he's to be found. Congratulations on your freedom, I saw your group leave this morning to ransom you."

"Thank you." He shook the man's hand in gratitude for his friendliness, then turned to his group. "Who knows where the city magistrate's office is? We need to hurry."

"I know the office location; we were there just yesterday," Hirtius answered. "Though maybe Gaius Oppius should lead?" he added after a quick glance at Oppius, who simply nodded and started walking. Hirtius was the bright son of a long-time family friend, which was the main reason Caesar had brought him along for the trip to the school. To learn rhetoric and eloquent oratory was a mandatory requisite if one wanted to become a successful politician. It seemed the teenager also had initiative, which made him a young man after his own heart.

Caesar followed them up the inclining main street, leading to the top of the city's main hill. After pushing through throngs of traders and shoppers, they arrived at a very old and official looking building sporting a massive colonnade of Doric pillars. In the middle of the row of columns, a wide and open doorway became visible, guarded by two Greek Hoplites whose bronze armor glinted in the sun.

Gaius Oppius rushed ahead to inquire about the Roman procurator, though the rest caught up to him quickly. "He's in the building, meeting with the magistrate of Miletus. His office is at the end of this hallway," Oppius said. Caesar pushed inside to take the lead, rushing down the hall and through the office door without so much as a knock. As he saw the men look up in shock at his rude entry, his lips parted into a wide grin. Here was none other than Publius Servilius Vatia, a good friend and fellow staff member from his time serving under Propraetor Thermus. "You came back to Asia as procurator for governor Junius Silvanus? How wonderful to see you! Your timing is impeccable." Caesar beamed and moved in to clasp arms with his old friend.

"Gaius, I'm so glad you are free. I came to Miletus to help with the ransom, though from what I just heard, your friends had things well in hand."

"Thank you for that, I'm grateful." Caesar turned to the other man in the room. "You must be the magistrate. I apologize for barging in like this," he said.

"Anaxidamus, at your service. I'm the representative of the city council of Miletus. Congratulations on your freedom, I am glad our city could be of help."

Young Hirtius spoke up. "Miletus indeed gave graciously towards the ransom. The council here knew of your fair service under Thermus, and it seems that news of your court cases against former governors have reached the wider world, garnering good-will among the city's council members. The fact that consul Marcus Aurelius Cotta is your uncle might have clinched the deal," he explained, grinning ear to ear. Caesar clapped the boy on his back, grinning right back. He leaned against the wall while observing the assembled men before raising his hand to get their full attention.

"I need your help, urgently. The pirates are very close by, their camp is at the end of a small bay on Pharmacusa, invisible from the sea. I believe they will celebrate their payment today rather than move on as they should."

He looked at the city magistrate. "I'll forever be in your debt for your help, but I hope I can pay back your gracious loan by the end of today. How many armed men and galleys can you raise on short notice? I'll pay whatever the men ask, as long as they can be ready soon after noon."

***

It was only early afternoon when the small fleet of galleys set out from Miletus. In satisfaction, Caesar watched four smaller biremes and one massive trireme follow his flagship. A small army of several hundred fighting men was spread across all vessels.

As his company neared Pharmacusa, the pirate galleys remained conspicuously absent. *They think they are safe in their hiding spot.*

He had memorized the landmarks well. "This is the opening, right here!" he told the navigator, pointing at a small, unremarkable channel.

The pirates' two galleys had been drawn up on land, and once the attacking ships beached on either side, the city's soldiers eagerly jumped off. By the time Caesar walked down his trireme's plank, the first pirates had already effortlessly been rounded up. With the many soldiers coming for them, they had realized a fight was pointless.

He hurried down the beach and on to the camp, searching the faces of the captured pirates he encountered. *There he is!*

The old pirate leader was quite drunk. "You son of a Roman whore!" he swore in defiance while Caesar shook his head.

"You should have left right after you had the money. I told you again and again that I would come for you. All of this"—he gestured at the pirates being led to the ships—"is on you for not believing me."

He walked away to talk to the captains of his assorted fleet about getting the pirates to Pergamum. *I need to ask the governor for permission for what comes next.*

683 AUC (71 BC), late summer
Via Appia, 60 miles south of Rome, Italia

Marcus Licinius Crassus stood below a tree in the growing dark as he watched one of the wagon drivers handing out food to the slaves in his charge. This driver's wagon was close to the front line of their long trek now, the man would likely be free of his charges within a couple of days. Another one of his many hundreds of clients, all working for him in exchange for his patronage and support. He knew he was a demanding employer, changing their work focus quickly to whatever he thought most useful. In return, his workers made good money as long as they helped him make profit. He turned to look down upon the many other wagons parked to the side of the road, all with fires close by for food and warmth. Their long line had started with six thousand slaves back in Capua, moving excruciatingly slow towards Rome ever since. They were only two-thirds there, so it would be a few more weeks before the last cross was built and the last slave crucified.

Crassus wandered back towards the front of the convoy until he came to a fire with two of his better-known helpers. Fraucus was the brother of Luctatus, his closest confidant, and Postumus was the brothers' close friend. These two had worked for him for some time; the rise of his own fortunes had meant the rise of both of theirs. Crassus decided to stay hidden in the shadows to listen in on their lively conversation.

"I am still not sure I believe you, Fraucus. I get that Crassus is crucifying these poor souls along the Via Appia to appease the Senate. It makes a public statement for all slaves not to run away or incite rebellion again. Also, it shows foreigners that Rome is back in control. But is this"—he moved his hand wide to indicate everything around them—"enough of a distraction to keep the Senate from figuring out what we did in Calabria?" Postumus asked.

"Just think how well everything worked out for him since Sulla. He's going to get away with this too, you'll see."

Spartacus had wiped out two Roman legions last year on his way north to flee across the Alps. *I sent Luctucus to meet with him. He miraculously talked him into turning south, feeding him lies about passage on pirate ships for all his revolting slaves. Spartacus was convinced the ships would take him from Calabria all the way back to his homeland in Thracia, or wherever else the man wanted to go. I need to give Luctatus another reward for that. Once I sell my new tens of thousands of slaves to Parthia in the east.* With the wide-spread fear of Spartacus, it had been so easy to make the Senate agree to give him overall command. All he had to do was spend his own funds to raise six legions.

"I wonder how much money all those slaves we caught last fall are worth," Postumus said.

Fraucus laughed out loud, while Crassus smiled to himself.

A lot. Enough that it's time for me to stop simply meddling in politics. I need to raise the stakes and play for keeps. He had in mind several candidates he could support for elections in return for later help to further his own agenda. Young Caesar sprang to mind. The boy might be a long shot, impoverished and full of mistrust towards Crassus as he was. *Doesn't help that we were on opposing sides under Sulla, but he might be worth it, seeing how obsessed he is with keeping his word. What a rare and refreshing thing these days, and how predictable.* He switched his focus back to the conversation.

"I've always said Crassus is a genius, ever since he signed on with Sulla. No wonder he's now the richest man in Rome." Fraucus stoked the fire before continuing. "What do you think about that pompous ass Pompeius? He came back from Hispania just in time to catch five thousand slaves himself."

"Well, I would say that must have made the boss unhappy," Postumus replied.

Crassus smiled. He liked men who were smart enough to see things clearly, but he had heard enough. Clearing his throat, he walked up and stepped into the light. He just stood there for a moment, enjoying the saucer-like eyes on both men's faces after they realized who had walked into their conversation. Sitting down on the ground next to Faustus, he spoke in a casual tone. "You two have to learn to keep things behind closed doors. Out here, you never know who might be listening." He noticed with satisfaction their faces draining of all blood. Good, fear was the reaction he wanted to see most. Time to bring these two into his inner circle. "You both have done good work, and I want to move you up. Once your load is done, you will serve as my personal servants until we get back to Rome." He grinned. "Of course, that includes a raise."

Both men exhaled in relief. "Thank you, sir. We will not disappoint you," Fraucus said, his voice breaking.

Crassus looked at the other man, who seemed unable to speak. Postumus' nodded instead; his body trembling and tears running freely. Crassus stood up. "Welcome to the inner circle. I will expect more of you, but the rewards are much higher." He nodded and walked away, satisfied with himself. *Having you close also means that I can keep an eye on you.*

***

Crassus sat at a small folding table at the side of the road. He was done with his correspondence for the day, and his boredom returned with a vengeance. At least they were finally close to Rome and his triumphant return to the Senate. He decided to write one more personal letter but cut it short when a light rain started. He mounted his horse, letting the two new servants Fraucus and Postumus pack his belongings. He rode up to the next chosen spot, where he observed the few remaining wagons. Good, Litaviccus was next, a Numidian and one of Spartacus's closest followers. The slave army's leadership had been saved for this last stretch of road leading up to Rome itself. He scrutinized the man as he was walked over where several legion specialists had the lumber ready to proceed, one stepping up to untie Litaviccus's hands while another held a pilum ready just in case.

"Take your tunic off," the first soldier commanded. The resigned Numidian did as he was bid before getting pushed on top of two rough logs, both notched in the middle and tied securely together to form the letter X. Crassus had to admire the efficiency of his engineers in streamlining the process. He was especially grateful they had avoided the use of expensive iron nails. The wrists and ankles of the man were now painfully tied to more notches hewn into the logs to secure the ropes in place, keeping their victim from sliding the cord to relieve the pull on his arms.

The next step was breaking the man's legs, and Crassus didn't look away. It was done to shorten the man's suffering after all. The Numidian endured in silence until the men raised the cross up and he couldn't hold back his screams any longer. When the contraption was just shy of standing fully upright, a third man secured it by attaching a simple third log to the back, which rested in another notch at the center of the X.

Crassus looked up. The man stared towards the Roman capital in the distance, its walls shining brightly in the late morning sun despite the cold rain. Suddenly, he spat as hard and as far as he could. Crassus had to chuckle. *A nice, albeit final display of defiance.*

Spartacus and his people had earned his respect for not making his job easy. He watched the soldiers clean up their tools before storing them for the next crucifixion. His men walked on to the next spot without so much as a glance back.

685 AUC (69 BC), spring
Clusium, Etruria, Italia

Little Velia chased her brother Numerius through their father's small bakery, running between shelves of cooling fresh bread and the hot oven. She heard her father let out a long line of swear words in frustration. Next, she felt his hands as he grabbed his six-year-old daughter by her arm.

"Children, I know you are bored. Having to be with me this early is no fun, I understand that, but I can't have you run into things here. Every one of these loaves sells for half a sesterce, that's two asses. Any we lose means less money for me to buy grain next week and feed you. Or, worse, I might not be able to pay the rent," he chided her and her brother.

Velia looked at her brother Numerius, one year older than her, to avoid her father's gaze. She was ashamed for having been careless. She knew their father struggled to provide for them and there was nothing extra to go around.

She started to cry. "I am sorry!" She moved in to hug him hard and relaxed only when he hugged her right back.

"Hush, little one, hush. It's alright. I did not mean to scold you two. Numerius, come here," her father whispered, now opening his right arm to let her brother close as well. "I shouldn't worry about a loaf or two. You children are the most important thing in my life."

Her father had been a kitchen slave in the household of a wealthy and childless widower. She knew all the stories about them being freed by the man on his deathbed, in appreciation of their father's long service and loyalty. She had been too young to remember their mother, sold long before they were all freed.

Upon becoming independent, father and children had taken the old master's name Churinas as their own. Unfortunately, the master had been a foreigner without Roman citizenship, which would have transferred to his former slaves.

She was old enough to understand her father needed to pay every week for the loan he had taken out to start the bakery, that the little money they had went to pay rent for the small store with its single backroom used as the family's shared bedroom. The business had started out well but turned into a struggle soon after. Grain prices had fallen for several years, taking baked bread prices down with them. Her father told her and Numerius that the grain came from big plantations on Sicilia and Sardinia. They continued to produce more each year, but she did not understand why that also meant they had less money to spend.

Velia relaxed, feeling safe in her father's strong arms. With a loving papa like hers, the world around her held no real dangers.

685 AUC (69 BC), fall
Small village thirty miles west of Tbessa, Kingdom of Numidia

"Oz, Anno is gone!" Adhe ran up a dusty street through their village, tears streaming down his face. "I just went to see her, but her house was empty. The neighbor told me the whole family packed up and left for one of the big cities. They just walked out without knowing where they would end up."

"I am so sorry, I know how much you liked that girl," Oz replied, giving the boy a tight hug. *Another family gone; on top of the horrible news I have to bring home.*

Anno's family was one more in a steady stream of locals heading out east to Tbessa or north to any number of Numidian cities in the hope of finding work and food, or at least enough charity to take the edge off their loved ones' hunger. "You can't blame her parents. The soldiers are eating the little food still left in our village, while the drought is worse than ever. Even our new well is running low, and we are part of the lucky few with any water left at all." He slowly started walking.

"I had even heard some families talking about going south to join the nomads, but now the king's soldiers showed up and took everybody's horses. Our village is going through hard times as it is, and having the soldiers here, eating what little food people have, is not helping."

Oz knew all the stories about how Numidia had been full of horse-riding nomads until a few generations ago, when the new nation's first kings dreamed of following the Carthaginian and Roman examples. They had forcefully bought up horses everywhere to compel the tribes to settle. The families opposed to the new lifestyle had moved south to continue in the old ways on the plains along the southern edges of the Atlas Mountains, outside the sphere of influence of the kings. Which was why the Numidian soldiers where here now. They had stopped at their village on the way back from capturing slaves among the free nomadic tribes.

Adhe was first through their front door, followed by Oz, who was glad to see all their family assembled, including his beloved new wife Niptaso. He held out his arms for her, and she walked up for a tight squeeze. She let go and they both turned towards the lively discussion at the table.

"We still don't know how much longer the soldiers are going to stay. In the meantime, they are tyrannizing everyone. Worse, they take any remaining food and animals without even asking. All for provisioning themselves and their new slaves for the trip back to Cirta," his sister Salpo said.

"I know, and they justify it by calling us kin of the free folk of the plains, seeing as we're far south from the capital," Mipsa added from across the table. "The captain told the village elders that the king can no longer pay the high tribute to Rome with wheat or marble alone, which is why they look for slaves instead."

Oz's father Isalkis cleared his throat. "He only told us that so the village would understand his threat that he might just take our people next year if we don't freely hand over our animals."

The family seemed to hold its breath in reaction before everyone started talking at the same time. Isalkis held up his hand, effectively cutting off all voices. "Let's eat first. With the little we have left, it would be a shame to let this meal get cold."

With all conversation postponed for the moment, the family settled around the dinner table. Oz appreciated how lucky they were to have enough food for one decent meal a day. They also still had water for their field and the meat he added from his hunts. So many of their friends were going hungry.

The food on the table quickly disappeared before the spoons were laid down and their bowls shoved to the center of the table. Mipsa spoke up first, looking at his father-in-law for approval. "Our family needs to stay quiet. I do not want any of us to meet the soldiers again. They already took half of our herd, don't give them reason to come back for the rest."

Isalkis nodded. "My thoughts exactly. I already told the other elders we shouldn't meet anymore until after the soldiers ride back for Cirta."

Oz cleared his throat and received his father's nod to talk next. The usually so energetic family sat quietly and expectantly at the table. *Now I will give them even more bad news. The worst kind.* He took a deep breath.

"I've been over to Hiempsa and his family with a little food. You all know that he complained directly to the captain yesterday about the soldiers taking all his animals." He saw the nods and held his breath for a moment, Hiempsa's wife and their children's pain too fresh in his mind. "This morning, he got so angry that he hit one of the captain's lieutenants. The man had his soldiers kill him for it."

"Oh no, not Hiempsa!" Isalkis blurted out. The man had been a long-time family friend.

On the other side of the table from Oz, Salpo started crying. Hiempsa's wife was a close friend of hers.

"That's not all. As if killing him was not enough, the lieutenant took his men back to their farm and cleaned it out. They even burned the furniture, leaving nothing for the family."

They all absorbed the news until Salpo stopped her sobbing and stood up. "She has family in Tbessa. With Hiempsa dead, I'm sure she will go there as soon as she is able. I'll visit them now, feel free to join me."

Isalkis muttered to himself while they gathered a few essential items they could share with Hiempsa's family. There was little left.

***

A couple of days later, what remained of the village rejoiced when the soldiers and their slaves left for the king in Cirta.

Oz and Adhe immediately went out on another hunting expedition to help top up meager supplies, hiking across the top ridges of the hills a few miles south of their home. It was fall, but the day's heat still felt like full summer. Oz scanned the brown-green hilltop, which was spotted with lots of shrubs, always keeping a wary lookout for hidden vipers. When he glanced up to peek past the razorback ridge into the valleys, he saw dust rise in the distance.

"Adhe, look," he said, pointing to the southeast from their position.

"What's that, uncle?"

Oh no, that can't mean anything good. Oz felt sick to his stomach as he looked back at his nephew. "That means riders, Adhe, lots of riders. They are coming from the south, likely headed for our village. We better get back home. And I mean now." He started running, trusting the young boy to follow.

As they came closer to the village, he saw thick smoke. Some of the mud-covered houses and grass patched roofs were burning bright.

Who is this? On the last hill before entering the village, they saw a body with several arrows sticking out. The man's dark tunic seemed very familiar. *Oh gods, let it not be true.* Oz repeated the phrase in his mind over and over as they approached. As he stood next to it, there was no more doubt. *Oh, father.*

Momentarily overwhelmed, he slid to the ground. Ever so slowly, he reached out with trembling fingers. Holding on to his father's right shoulder, he hesitantly turned the body on its side. Isalkis's face, always showing a quick smile for his children and grandchildren, was frozen in an expression of alarm. His fearless father had been murdered from behind while running back to warn the family. He gently closed lifeless lids before pressing his forehead to his father's.

May we see each other again in the next life. I am so sorry; I don't even remember how long it has been since I told you that I love you.

His tears flowed freely, covering his face and blurring his vision. Adhe dropped down beside him. "Grandfather? Grandfather?" the boy wailed. Oz grabbed Adhe and held tight, rocking him for several minutes until the fear for their other loved ones pushed through his immediate grief.

He scanned northeast towards their side of the village and their own home at the outskirts and took a deep breath. "We have to go, Adhe, we need to look for the others. Are you ready? We need to stay low and quiet. Do you understand?"

Adhe nodded. They were both in a bad state, shaken to their core, but he needed them to keep going. Oz strung his bow and nocked an arrow while cautiously moving. They saw nobody else, though a big plume of dust showed that the raiders headed back south from the burning buildings at the other end of the village. After that, he ran the remaining distance to their house with Adhe close behind. As they approached, the blood on the ground turned his stomach. *Please, please, no.* He stopped, frozen to the porch in front of the door, staring at the big dark-red stains on the stone steps leading through the entrance. Continuous wailing from the inside finally broke through his apathy.

"It's Adhe and Oz," he called before bursting through the heavy curtain in the doorway. He stopped, the stench overwhelming his senses. He tried to make sense of what he saw, but his mind couldn't handle the impressions right away. Finally, reality snapped into focus. The blood on the floor in front of him trailed into different directions. His brother-in-law's powerful body lay on the floor close to the big table, a hole in his chest. His eyes moved on to Salpo. His lively, always strong sister kneeled helplessly next to her husband, wailing. His eyes moved to yet another body. He pushed himself to take a step forward before he saw it was Malamsa, his oldest nephew. His head had been cut open, his usually quick and intelligent eyes now staring, lifeless. Another, second noise was audible beside his sister's cries. He slowly turned until he saw young Adhe. The boy had come in behind him, and had slid down the wall, holding his head and repeating guttural sounds deep in his throat. Oz snapped out of his pain to grab the boy, pulling him outside to the bench on their front porch. "Please, stay here, don't move." He gave Adhe a quick hug before going back inside. "I'll be back with your mother." As he walked up to Salpo he noticed Sophona, Adhe's middle brother. The boy sat silently in the far corner with his head in his hands. Upon closer inspection, Oz found a grisly cut in the side of the boy's upper stomach, freely bleeding. He tenderly lifted Sophona before he felt the boy go slack as he carried him outside. He gently lowered him to the ground and leaned his back against the wall. It took all he had to keep going. He went back to pull Salpo away from Mipsa and Malamsa.

His sister started fighting him, hitting and screaming, until he pulled her close for a tight hug. "Shh, shh. It's Oz." Her eyes focused enough to recognize him. "Come outside with me." He guided her through the front door and sat her down next to Sophona. When he took his hands away from her back, they were red from more fresh blood. He tried to lift her tunic, but she held his hands tight, shaking her head. She continued to softly cry until she caught herself enough to speak.

"They came over the hill with no warning, killing all the men outside. Mipsa, Malamsa, and the girls had already gone back to the house for lunch. Sophona and I were following when the screams started. We walked on until we saw hundreds of riders, free Numidians from the south, looking just like our own men. They were so very angry about the raid by the king's soldiers last week. I tried to stay hidden with Sophona at the edge of the field, but when I saw Mipsa coming outside to see what was going on… He walked right up to a couple of them, asking them what they were doing. And one of them just shoved his spear into him." She had to stop talking for a moment, holding on to Oz tightly. After a deep breath, she continued. "I screamed when they did that to my love, I just couldn't help it. If I hadn't, they might not have found us. I guess I passed out when one of them circled around and stabbed us from behind." She closed her eyes, reliving the horror of the last hour.

"Salpo. What about Niptaso? And Juvo? Where are they?"

She opened her eyes and focused on him. "When I came to, I saw them drag the girls out of the house. Niptaso bled from her side when they led her away, she must have fought. Then the last of them moved on to the other side of the village, and Sophona and I made it back to the house." Salpo stared into nothing, unable to focus through her tears. "There may be little hope, but you must follow them." She pulled Sophona close. When Adhe dropped off the bench to join, she included him in the circle of her arms.

Oz took a long look at his sister and the boys before leaving the house at a run. He started towards the burning houses at the far side of the village. As he got closer, he saw more and more bodies of villagers through his blurry eyes, plus several dead horses. He understood now. The farther away from the initial attack, the more warning their friends and neighbors had to gather for a semblance of defense. He hoped that meant that at least some of their women and children had gotten away. He kept wiping fresh tears as he moved to cut across the raiders' path leading south. After following for a couple of hours, he started to feel odd. His tears stopped flowing and a cold filled him, suppressing all feeling. It did give him back some ability to think. *I won't reach them in time when they are on horseback, but I need to try.*

He knew if he didn't catch up with the raiders before they reached the foothills of the Aures mountains, he would lose them for good.

***

It was the end of the second night. Though he could not sleep more than an hour or two at a time, Oz rose long before daybreak despite his exhaustion and started to hike. He knew time was running out, and growing thirst and hunger added to his urgency—the few pieces of dried meat and the half-empty water skin left from their hunting excursion had not lasted long. Still half a day behind the raiders, he was sure they would reach the open grasslands later today.

The sun came out to light up the ridges all around him. Though usually a beautiful sight, today it seemed an omen of impending doom. He kept methodically walking, following the path of the raiders through foothills that had changed from the usual rock and stone to overgrown sand dunes. The raiders' hundreds of horses had left a wide swath impossible to miss.

As he rounded another bend, he saw abandoned fire pits. Approaching, he made out a figure lying face down on the far side and hurried on. The work tunic was a common sight and could have been anybody's, but the curly dark brown hair looked like his wife's. His stomach dropped. *No, by the gods, not you.* He reached the woman and fell to his knees. The whole side of her body was a mix of dried and wet blood. He turned her around, the sense of dread overwhelming him. *My beautiful Niptaso.*

The moment he saw her beloved face, now void of all expression, he screamed uncontrollably. He held her body tight, rocking back and forth, unable to control the torrent of anguish rushing through him. After what seemed forever, a stray thought pushed him back up. *My niece is still out there. I need to try to find her.*

He moved in a pain-induced trance; no hope left that he could reach the raiders before they were lost in the vastness of the open lands. Yet, he couldn't stop.

He walked all day through until he reached the open sands. There were no landmarks visible across the vastness of the desolate landscape, and the heat had become unbearable. His mouth was too dry to swallow, every breath painful. *I'll die if I don't turn around. I need to get back to Salpo and the boys.*

He sunk to his knees in defeat. *I'm so sorry. Forgive me, Juvo.*

***

Three days later, Oz tumbled through the doorway and fell to the floor. After what seemed like ages, he pulled himself up with the help of the kitchen table. The bodies had been dragged into a corner, blankets loosely draped over them. A sweet smell of decay filled the room and he retched, but his stomach was empty. He pushed on for a few more steps to the room at the back of the house.

Sophona and Salpo were both lying on sleeping cots, with a defeated-looking Adhe sitting between them on a small stool. Sophona had a makeshift wrap around his stomach. The boy's lifeless eyes stared at the ceiling. Adhe kept mechanically dabbing Salpo's forehead with a damp towel. Oz moved closer to his sister, who was on her side, until he could see her once so beautiful face had turned ashen. He put a comforting hand on his nephew's shoulder. "Come with me to the porch. Your mother"—Oz' hoarse voice broke. It took a moment before he could pull Adhe off his stool to hug him tightly. "Your mother is gone. They all are," he whispered, and the boy finally responded with a crying fit.

On the way outside, Oz grabbed the water urn from their little kitchen area. They sat on the bench, and he drained the thing in one long drink. He felt a little steadier, but knew he needed a few hours of sleep before he could tackle digging graves, even if he kept them shallow. The boy needed him now more than ever. He could not let himself stay in his grieving stupor of the last few days.

As he looked out at the setting sun, a new feeling set in. Anger. First just a hint, it steadily grew stronger until he was consumed by rage against the world.

My sister, my nephews, Mipsa. Niptaso, my precious, beautiful wife. I will see you all again soon, whenever the fickle gods decide it to be my time to follow you. Curse the king. Curse the gods that allowed this to happen.

685 AUC (69 BC), summer
Corduba, Capital of Roman Province Hispania Ulterior

Caesar sat in his small office in the Roman headquarter of the province of Hispania Ulterior, holding a letter from his mother Aurelia. He looked out the window, but his eyes couldn't focus on the clouds floating by. Unwillingly, his mind drifted back to a conversation he had with his wife late last winter. It had been an especially cold day, colder than any other winter he remembered.

"So, that means you will be gone for a whole year?" Cornelia asked Caesar.

The couple sat around a small portable coal brazier burning on the desk of Caesar's study. Their six-year-old daughter Julia was with her tutor in one of the open alcoves off the atrium, where a huge Caminus burned big pieces of split wood, staving off the chill of the day.

"Yes, definitely a whole year," he replied. "As soon as the spring weather permits, I'll sail to Hispania. Gaius Antistius Vetus is governor this year, and I've been allotted to serve him as quaestor."

Cornelia sternly looked at her husband, folding her arms over her slightly swollen stomach.

"That means you will miss the birth of our second child. I have a feeling you only did this because you don't want to be here when there's no sleep to be found at night, with a new baby crying." When Caesar cringed, his lovely Cornelia grinned from ear to ear before squeezing his shoulder.

"I am teasing, Gaius. I know how much the post means to you and to our future. If I would have thought the timing through beforehand, I would have kept you out of our bedroom for a few months." Caesar laughed, leaning over for a kiss. Cornelia moved in to hug him tightly.

"Do you think there will be war in Hispania? Is it peaceful there right now? It's only been two years since the traitor Sertorius was killed." Cornelia's tone had turned serious again.

"As far as I know, the province is quiet, and as quaestor, my focus is on finances and the assessment of local taxes. Meaning my travel around the province will be limited to inspections. Otherwise, I'll be at the office at headquarters, tallying numbers. I doubt Vetus will let me do anything else; he wants to know the numbers as soon as possible to see how much he can squeeze out of the locals for himself."

Cornelia relaxed. "No war, that helps. I don't want to have to deal with a new baby and worry about you fighting or being in danger."

His mind drifted back to the present. He looked at the scroll on his desk, which contained the message. It was the second letter his mother had sent him to Hispania, the first telling him of the passing of his beloved aunt Julia, widow of Gaius Marius. But now this. He had a hard time seeing the writing clearly, his eyes betraying him.

Childbirth had not gone well for his wife. His mother had explained the details, but he had stopped reading beyond the fact that both his beloved Cornelia and their second child had died.

My whole world ended while I sat here every day, far away from you, drafting ledgers, sorting accounts and auditing these damn taxation lists.

He sat for a while in silence, not able to process the variety of emotions flowing through him. Finally overcome by his inner turmoil, he wiped everything off the table. He stood up, voicing his rage in a deafening, visceral scream. He grabbed his chair and threw it against the wall, picking up and throwing the bigger pieces again. Next, he flipped over his big desk, which landed with a deep thump. He kicked one of the table legs until it broke, screaming throughout.

The door flew open and several guards rushed in, looking for the expected attackers killing their quaestor. With nobody else in the room, they looked at Caesar for guidance. He held his breath. Unable to utter a word, he successfully waved them back out the door with balled fists. Alone again, he slid down the wall, the rage leaving as quickly as it had come, and he started to sob, laying his face into his hands and surrendering to his grief.

688 AUC (66 BC), summer
Bailenua, Free Gallia, Eastern part of the Aedui Nation

Drestan stood on the roof of the town wall's gatehouse, taking in the sight of the many houses illuminated in the morning's tender light. Overcast, the sun had still enough power to turn the dampness of the thatched roofs to steam curling up into the sky. He was so very proud of everything they had achieved here, despite the initial, daunting challenge. He thought back to the endless wagon trail of five hundred families and their belongings that had made the trek east ten years ago. His first decision upon arrival had been to abandon the remains of the burned old farming town, built for convenience close to the fertile fields. A new, much more defensible location was soon found atop a gentle rise close by. The new fortified town had risen quickly that first year, with sixteen-foot-tall walls of timber set on earthen ramparts adding another few feet. The tall gate house provided a clear view of many miles in all directions. Vesontio, a northern bastion of the Sequani nation located only twenty miles south, was still the biggest threat for raiding parties coming their way.

Ganna climbed up the ladder to the top platform and walked over.

"Ah, my love," Drestan greeted her. "Glad you could join me. How do you feel this morning?"

She gave him a quick kiss, stopping right next to him to look across their town. "Better, but I still feel a tingling in my side." She put her hand over her heart to illustrate. "I am lightheaded just from climbing up."

He gazed longingly at his wife, still as beautiful as ever, and put his left arm around her lower back to feel closer to her. He couldn't help but worry after she had complained about chest pains for the best part of a week. He decided to change the subject. "I was just reminiscing about the first years here. Remember how we were lauded as saviors when we came? And how that changed when the first summer ended abruptly in a cold spell, leaving people hungry and on short rations through the winter?"

"I thought the demands and grievances would never end," Ganna answered with a knowing smile. "But we made it through." Purchasing extra food from traders with their own money had helped everybody. The people still loved them for it, and the community and surrounding lands were now thriving. The population had skyrocketed to several thousand, with many new families joining their clan from neighboring lands to share in the town's good fortune.

"They want me to lead more raids, now north to the Lingones. As if repercussions from raiding wasn't what started the problems of this area in the first place." He sighed. "I guess the new generation of warriors does not remember the bad things the same way our older folks do."

"Don't forget, the younger ones grew up seeing the many enemy heads you and your men brought back over the years. Or the many enslaved Aedui you freed," Ganna added.

"I understand that," Drestan said, "but I have a feeling we need to keep our strength for what's to come. I am uneasy about the reports the traders bring us from the Sequani." Several of them had now seen Germanic people there from across the Rhenus.

"I think those must be just rumors. I can't believe they would do such a thing," Ganna replied.

"I don't know. They've been jealous of our nation for a long time. I wouldn't put it past them." The Aedui held the status of Gallia's most populous and powerful nation, with exclusive control of all trade flowing through and around their lands.

"I feel weak," Ganna said unexpectedly. "Help me sit down, please."

All other thoughts vanished as he gently let her down to the rough floor of the timbered platform. He sat down with her. "Can I do something to help you?" he asked her.

But instead of answering, Ganna closed her eyes and leaned into him. "Just hold me," she whispered.

He sat holding her, and felt her life leaving her little by little. She was about to leave him behind. Though grateful to be close to her during her last few breaths, a deep sorrow washed over him. He kissed the side of his love's head, over and over, until she made her last, rasping breath. In the ensuing silence, a bottomless emptiness spread through him. *Love of my life, my best friend. It wasn't time for you to go, not yet.*

He gazed up at the sky through blinding tears. *Gods, why are you so cruel to us?*

Continuing to rock her body back and forth, he looked out over the land without seeing anything. He vaguely noticed a voice behind him. "Go get their sons and daughter," it said.

688 AUC (66 BC), late summer
Small village thirty miles west of Tbessa, Kingdom of Numidia

There were few neighbors now. Most of the mud houses in the village were empty and had fallen into disrepair. Everybody still living here struggled for survival, their despair palpable.

Oz sat down on the old porch bench and stared in a wave of melancholy at the graves twenty feet away. The simple mounds of dirt had no means of identifying who was buried in which. But Adhe and Oz would never forget.

His mind drifted back to some of their happy days. A few years earlier, the family had built their new well a few hundred feet to the east of their house. It seemed like a lifetime ago, yet he could still feel his sweet Niptaso running up from behind to squeeze him, like she so often had. The whole family had worked together for several days to dig that well, desperately needed when their old one had dried up. Niptaso and himself, his sister Salpo, her husband Mipsa, their daughter Juvo, and their sons Malamsa, Sophona, and little Adhe dropped everything else to get it done, while his old father Isalkis stayed with their goat herd. Shortly after they struck water, the dirt they all carried away in their baskets had turned into heavy mud. On one of his many trips from the well hole, Malamsa had made it halfway to the top of the slope when Oz saw him slip and fall. He had to laugh as the fond memories flooded his mind, clear and brighter than today.

Keeling over, the boy threw his basket forward while freeing his hands to catch his fall. The basket's contents sprayed all over Juvo's back. "Eew! Malamsa!" his dear niece screamed. Oz hooted so hard he dropped his own basket, splashed mud over Niptaso in the process. At that point, little Adhe bent down with a wide grin, taking some of the mud with his hands to fling it at Oz. He tried to avoid that volley, accidently pushing Mipsa sideways and making him step out and slip on the fresh mud from Oz' own basket. The whole family ended up on the ground, laughing and flinging mud at each other, with no thought of tomorrow.

Oz smiled and cried at the same time at the flood of bittersweet memories. *Will we ever find true happiness again? This empty place has lost its meaning. Gone are all the love and laughter.*

He wiped his eyes when Adhe came back to the house. Now sixteen, the boy was coming of age. Once the energetic and lively youngest sibling, these days he was quiet and subdued. Except, now he seemed excited as he ran toward Oz. *Like much better times. How I wish it were so.*

"Uncle, the trader just told me the Romans are recruiting Numidians as auxilia archers. I guess our bows are better than what they can build themselves," the boy said, breathing hard from his run.

"I saw a Roman bow up close many years ago, when I went to Tbessa as a little boy. It was made from a simple, thin piece of wood, rather weak compared to ours."

Adhe sat down close to him and Oz continued. "Grandfather once told me that our bow-making comes from the Carthaginians, who had learned it from Phoenicia in the east. Now, about that trader." He expectantly looked at the boy. "Did you get any details about what the Romans offer? I am ready to leave, there is nothing left for us here."

"The trader said recruits get signed for service with a standing legion. He also thought there may be a form of citizenship offered as part of the deal for the service." Adhe looked down. "I don't see how we could stay here much longer. Without our hunts we would have starved long ago."

The boy looked back at him, and he nodded in agreement. "Where is the trader now?"

"Traveling to the next village, where he will spend the next day before heading back to Tbessa. We can catch up and ask him more details," Adhe answered.

"Or we could go directly to Tbessa instead, to find a Roman who can point us in the right direction," Oz countered.

Time to leave the ghosts of their past behind.

688 AUC (66 BC), late summer
Bailenua, Free Gallia, Eastern part of the Aedui Nation

Aina was giddy with excitement as she looked at her skewed reflection in her father's polished helmet. She could make out her red tinged brown hair and her light green eyes. She was seventeen and supposed to stay at home so close to her wedding. With time on her hands, she had invited her best friends over and hoped they would arrive soon.

"Aina!" One of her father's servants called. "Your friends are here!" She rushed out of her father's bedroom to the common space. "Brenna! Rionach!" she shouted in greeting, before flinging herself at them for hugs.

"Did you already start drinking without us?" Brenna asked in mock incredulousness.

"What else am I supposed to do?" Aina asked back. Her two friends laughed in reply.

Aina fetched three drinking horns and went to the sunken cellar at the back of the house to bring several amphorae of imported wine. The three started to drink in earnest, and before long, Brenna and Rionach had caught up to Aina's level of intoxication.

"What color is your wedding dress?" Brenna asked Aina to interrupt Rionach's monologue about her preference of sword over spear in battle.

"It's bright blue. You know, to symbolize my virginity." They all giggled.

"I know you are a virgin, but I think that's more to do with circumstances." Brenna winked at her friend. "I am thinking about that boy in the woods a few years back. What was his name?"

"Brenna, don't say that!" Aina burst out laughing and shook her head. "But, you're right."

"Where is your father? Or all your visiting family?" Rionach asked unexpectedly after looking around the big family room.

"Our family arrived yesterday. Father and Morcant are showing them the town and the surrounding lands," Aina answered. "So, only Elsed and I are home today. Though I wish Bradan could be here as well," she said with a dreamy look in her eyes.

"I am *so* jealous, Aina! Your groom is such a famous warrior, and so… well built... Seeing him all the time on the sparring field makes one wonder, you know." Brenna smacked her lips loudly before laughing out loud. "Can I make you a deal? If you ever feel like sharing, I'll pay you off with some sheep, or maybe a nice dress or a sword?"

She batted her eyelids in playfulness. Rionach snorted loudly, blowing some of the wine in her mouth out through her nose, and then breaking out in a loud coughing fit.

Aina laughed hard as well, punching Brenna on the arm before patting her other friend's back.

"If I do ever feel like sharing, you can have him for free. But I'm warning you, that might be a long wait. Better bat your eyes at Elsed instead."

Brenna's eyes regained some focus. "You know I'm interested in Elsed, but I don't think he even notices me." She let her shoulders sag before turning back to Aina. "Do you think I could get any help from you with that?"

"Yes! And I sure hope it works out, because I'd love to have you as a sister!" Brenna smiled and gave her a brief hug before looking at Rionach. "I know you are not interested in men, but you should still marry one, at least to get the children part over with. Once you have a couple little ones, nobody will give you grief anymore, or care about what else you do," Aina told her, grinning widely. "Or with whom you do it."

"Do you know any boys that you would find tolerable?" Brenna added.

"You know I can't think of men like you two. And it's not like I don't get plenty of invitations to get to know some better," Rionach said, dramatically rolling her eyes upwards. Breanna and Aina both broke out into laughter again. Though their friend was considered short, she was quite pretty, with her dark-brown hair and green-flecked brown eyes, and had no shortage of hopeful suitors.

The door opened and Aina's brother Elsed entered. Brenna squealed at his sight. A head taller than his sister, he was broad and well-muscled. His light brown eyes seemed magnetic, framed by his wavy dark-brown hair.

"Speaking of your brother…." The alcohol had taken away all her natural inhibitions, and she shamelessly let her glance wander up and down his body. After working outside splitting wood with an axe, he needed clean clothes and a wash. "Elsed, do you need any help...?"

Aina punched her friend so hard that she fell off the bench. "That's disgusting!"

Brenna started giggling, followed first by Rionach and then Aina. Elsed walked off, but Aina caught him giving Brenna a long and thoughtful glance over his shoulder before he walked through the inner doorway. Aina had always thought of Brenna as very attractive with her bright orange-red hair, dark green eyes and a face full of freckles. Just maybe her brother thought so as well. She grinned at her friend.

"Goodbye, Elsed!" Brenna shouted after him. "See you tomorrow at the wedding!"

Aina's thoughts drifted to her own big day. The day after tomorrow, she would no longer live in her father's house, but move in with Bradan instead since his family had no other surviving siblings left in a big house with room to share. She hoped that her marriage would turn out to be a lasting one, not like the current fashion of year-long bindings without signed contracts, or the quick divorces happening for all kinds of silly-seeming reasons. Fortunately, her own parents had been a good example to follow. A hint of sadness about her mother overcame her before her friends' antics made her laugh out loud again. *How I wish you could be here, Mam, to share this happy time with me.*

***

The sky was overcast and gloomy. Of course, it would have to be, but she decided to ignore the weather on what she hoped would be the happiest day of her life. As she walked to the sacred grove, she saw the druid and several of his helpers waiting near the sacrificial altar. Aina and her family approached the sacred place from the north, while Bradan's family came from the south. She walked ahead, with her older brother Elsed to her right, her father Drestan to her left, and her younger brother Morcant just behind.

There he is, and he can see me now. She stared across the grove at her husband-to-be. Bradan was an enigma. He was so strong, yet so lithe. He could be silly, a daredevil, yet also smart and understanding. Most of all, he was just as compassionate to those around him as she was. That more than anything else had drawn her to him. Well, his good looks hadn't hurt. Nearly as tall as her brother Elsed, he had short dark-blond hair and bright blue eyes she wanted to drown in.

They came close to the grove's center before she glanced at the despised old altar and its dark bloodstains reminiscent of countless human sacrifices. She vividly remembered the last one, a melancholy and willing highborn son of a friend of her father. The summer's drought had threatened a winter without food, resulting in the druids calling for a sacrifice to Toutates, the chief protector of most Celtic clans and tribes. His wrists bound, he had been laid on the altar and cut into, the blood flowing freely down the stone into a bucket. As the boy had become lightheaded from the blood loss, the druid had pushed his head into a bucket of water, at the same time strangling his throat until the sacrifice was complete in its whole trinity. Two days later, the drought had vanished, and the harvest had recovered fully.

Aina figured that sometimes human sacrifices might be needed for the greater good, but she hated the idea of the gods demanding them in the first place. She shook her head to dispel the darkness in her thoughts. Today would be a day of joy, and they would stay away from the dreaded altar.

As the families gathered, Aina stepped ahead to a stone stele sunk into the ground. The eight-foot-tall megalith had a hole carved through its middle at stomach height. The druid stood to the side, shifting his attention between her and the other side of the stone slab. "Are you prepared for this contractual union?"

"I am prepared," she answered, hoping Bradan had done the same since she could not hear him on the other side. The druid looked around at all the other party members. "Are all of you prepared for this contractual union of families?"

"We are prepared!" she heard them answer loudly and in near unison.

"I see our great god Sucellos standing ready, with his big mallet lifted to strike asunder any attempt at a union not pleasing to the gods," the druid continued. "Nantosuelta, his wife and companion, lifts her hand to the crow on her shoulder in warning. If you are both sure, step forward." He now started a singsong in the ancient and secret druidic language. As he sang, he walked behind the stele to Bradan, and soon she saw her groom's hands emerge in the hole. The druid came back to Aina's side, and now it was her turn to move in, holding Bradan's hands in the middle of the megalith's hole. The druid ended his song on a nice high note, showing off an exceptional singing voice.

He gestured for them to let go before ushering them to the side of the rock. Aina knew the common ceremony to bind any union, contractual or one-year casual, was next on the agenda. "Hold all four of your hands together." They did. "Sucellos and Nantosuelta were pleased." He pulled out two lengths of cord, wrapping each around their wrists and then tying them both together, securing all four hands. "Let nothing break this union except for the gods' will. I declare you joined and wish you many children. Now, celebrate your new life together!"

Aina hugged her new husband, and they kissed to loud whooping and laughter. The next hours seemed like a dream to her. As she expected, the celebration became loud and rowdy, with the guests enjoying themselves in the mead hall. Many flagons of imported wine, local mead, and beer were emptied, with the servants refilling the drinking horns again and again. The least hardy of the guests started slipping off their benches shortly after dinner. Aina and Bradan kept holding hands throughout, both increasingly drunk themselves. Every time somebody congratulated them or held a speech, they had to join the toast. Finally, it was time. She had dreamed of this night with Bradan for ages, but the moment they got up and started walking, her head spun. She felt sick to her stomach. "How do you feel?" she whispered into his ear as they walked to their designated bedroom for the night. "Any better than I do?"

"I feel like I had an ungodly amount of that wine. I better stick with mead in the future," Bradan answered with a wobble in his voice. He followed her into the room, tripped over a stool and fell flat on his back. They both laughed.

"How about we wait with that," she looked down at his midriff, "until we can both enjoy this more?"

"I think that's a good idea. For now, I'm just happy to have you alone with me," Bradan answered. He seemed to have a hard time untying his laces, so she helped him take his shoes off. Next, she laid down beside him on the bed and reached out for his hand before instantly falling asleep.

688 AUC (66 BC), fall
Cirta, Kingdom of Numidia

It took them three weeks to arrive at the Roman recruitment center in Cirta, a sprawling compound on the outskirts of the large Numidian capital. Oz and Adhe walked through the entryway to the open courtyard, happy to use the shade of the compound's walls to avoid the strong morning sun. A grizzled man with short cut gray hair and a face full of scars walked up to them.

"Good morning, my name is Barbus," he greeted them in Latin. "I'm the head-recruiter here."

"Salve, I Ozalkis, this boy nephew, Adherbal," Oz answered in a heavy accent.

Barbus raised his hand and shook his head. "Wait." He turned and walked away.

Oz and Adhe looked at each other. Oz shrugged. Two minutes later, the man walked back with a young Numidian in tow. "I'm to be your translator," the man said in Numidian.

Barbus apologized with his hands held up. "I don't speak or understand any of the Numidian dialects, and I simply cannot understand your horrible Latin! If you end up signing, I suggest you learn it properly." He lowered his hands. "You know how to handle these bows of yours?" After Oz nodded, the man continued. "Good, the generals are hiring archers for all our legions. We used to sign whole mercenary groups, sometimes whole tribes under chieftains or nobles, but had a lot of problems with that over the years. Some chiefs thought to renegotiate their terms right in the middle of a shitstorm."

"So, Pompeius changed the rules and we opened this." He pointed at the compound behind him. "we're signing you on as individuals now for specific legions." Barbus paused to inspect their clothes and their gear. "Before we get into more details, I want to see your bows."

Oz took his weapon from his shoulder to hold it out. Adhe followed suit.

"Nice. Strong wood, glued with horn for strength, plus joints wrapped in leather for protection. Straight rather than pre-curved when unstrung, and quite long. Hm." He nodded. "Unusual length, but fine bows. May I see your arrows as well?"

They both pulled a couple of their small selection of arrows from their quivers.

"Just what I thought," Barbus replied. "Your bows are taller than we usually see from the locals around here. I bet you won't get a full draw with our shorter arrows." He turned to shout to another Roman currently bent over a ledger inside an open doorway across the training ground.

"Heius, forget about your paperwork for a moment! Bring me some of the big arrows from that last shipment from Utica." He turned back to the two Numidians. "You must understand, Rome wants you and your bows if you know how to handle them properly, but we cannot rely on your own arrows. Those are fine for hunting, when you can stroll up and collect them again afterwards. But for a soldier…" He shook his head. "Surest way for any archer to die is going into battle with only a handful of arrows."

The other Roman returned with a couple of sealed packages. Barbus opened one and pulled out the arrows from inside. "Ah!" he exclaimed. "I thought so. We received some of the longer arrows the army buys for Cretan archers. Their bows are much shorter than yours, but with a hefty recurve that gives them a longer draw. Note that these arrows aren't just long, they are also quite heavy. Feel the weight of the heads."

Oz inspected the big steel head on the arrow and discovered that it was countered by much bigger fletching on the other end.

"Let's see what you can do, and if it's not too bad we'll talk details. See these targets?" Barbus pointed to three straw bales at different distances from them. They had black dots painted roughly in their middle. "Start with your own arrows and try to hit each of the three distances with your first one, then try again with our arrows. I'll watch from over here."

Both Oz and Adhe strung their bows and took out three arrows from their quivers. They nocked the first one while holding the other two squeezed between the fingers of their left hand and the right side of the bow. Oz glanced at Adhe, who nodded for him to go first. To the side, he noticed Barbus raising an eyebrow, likely because of their hunting habits. Oz sighted to shoot and emptied his mind before letting go of the string. The middle of the first target. Good. Close to the middle on the second. One more. Just above the middle on the third. He had taken only a few seconds between each shot and now took a deep breath as he stepped to the side.

Adhe set up next. He hit the bullseye of the first but missed the second target completely.

"Relax!" Oz said. "No need to be nervous. Empty your mind like I taught you. Just imagine yourself hunting. You are hiding in a thicket, waiting for your one chance at a good shot."

The boy drew the string on his third arrow, took a few deep breaths, and released. He barely scratched the corner of the third target, the arrow going down to the ground twenty feet beyond. Oz glanced at Barbus. The man scowled.

"Kid, the third target is only fifty yards out. You will need to shoot a hundred yards in battle, with angry enemies running at you. I don't think you are up for this."

Oz looked from Barbus to Adhe, who looked down in apparent shame. *He can shoot much better when he's not this anxious.*

He walked to the side table and picked three of the Roman made arrows. They were indeed much heavier than his own with their thick shaft and much bigger arrowhead. He weighed one in his left hand and put the other two on the ground. He drew it fully and released at a much steeper angle than before. It hit the first target, though barely at its lower edge. The stiffer shaft gave it less wobble in mid-air. *Nice.* He grabbed the second arrow and sighted at an even steeper angle. *Hm, close to the upper edge. These will take some getting used to.* He took his time aiming for the third target. *Release. Bullseye!*

Barbus applauded but held up his hand when it was Adhe's turn to walk over to the Roman arrows. He turned to Oz. "I want to sign you but send the boy home. He should come back in another year or two, after his skills have improved."

Oz shook his head in response. "Adhe usually shoots as well as I do. And since there is no more home for him to go back to… I'm sorry, it's both of us or neither."

Barbus scratched his chin in thought, then he nodded to Oz before walking off.

A minute later, he was back with a scroll in his hand. "I'll sign you both. I'd be stupid not to." He opened the scroll. "There are currently two options for deployment, either Greece or Hispania. The second is much closer and would be with one of Pompeius's three new legions raised there. He is asking for a large contingent of Numidian and Cretan archers for each. The duty, at least for now, would be keeping the peace and enforcing Roman law. Hispania hasn't had real fighting for a few years, and the previous legions stationed there are shipping East. If you sign up to go to Greece with those, you'll be right in the middle of the third war against Pontus. That would likely mean good money from the spoils, but I would choose Hispania for the sake of the boy. There, he might have a chance of growing into it." He closed the scroll.

"Now to the details. There is no predetermined service duration, but it's usually around twenty years. The legions get directly sworn to any new legate, or a provincial governor if he's in overall command. A governor would also have the right to dissolve legions after successful campaigns. If that happens, you will get a discharge bonus, but don't expect that for at least ten years. I've been discharged twice, took close to fifteen years both times. So, after a discharge you can always sign up again if you want to keep going." Barbus held up his hand and coughed.

"Now to your pay. You will start at a third of standard legionary pay, four hundred sesterces a year. That's equal to one hundred denarii. If you get promoted to decurion, which is a squad leader, it's going to be half again as much at six hundred, and so on." He looked up from his scroll.

Oz had raised both eyebrows. "I don't know what the numbers mean, exactly."

"Oh. I guess you don't know Roman sesterces and denarii? It's a lot of money for a year, more than most people here make in a lifetime. Once the legion does go to war, which it will sooner or later, you will get a portion of any spoils. That can amount to much more than the salary, but hey, there's no guarantee. If you survive until your discharge, there is also a good chance for a full Roman citizenship to look forward to. At the very least, every auxiliary will get Latin rights plus a small parcel of land, wherever your commander can manage." He paused, looking to see if they had any questions for the translator, and looked at them both.

"Your choice, sign up now and get a signing bonus, come back later, or don't come back at all." He spread his hands, palms facing upwards. "I've said my piece."

"Let me discuss this with my nephew," Oz replied and took Adhe by the arm. They walked over to the wall of the courtyard.

"Are you truly ready to do this? You just heard we could be stuck with a legion for twenty years. The citizen status and money sound enticing, but we won't be able to just leave if we don't like it anymore…"

Adhe rolled his eyes at Oz in response.

"Uncle, come on. We'll always have something to eat, and we'll see Hispania. I've heard it's much greener there."

Oz had to smile at the last comment. He turned to Barbus to give him a nod.

"Tell us where to sign."

689 AUC (65 BC), spring
Port southeast of Corduba, Roman Province of Hispania Ulterior

"How long since we walked into Cirta? Three months?" Adhe asked, standing with Oz at the railing of the main deck of the big trading vessel.

A quick glance up let Oz know the westerly breeze was still strong and steady, filling the sail as the ship tacked back and forth to make headway. "Four. Finally, we're close to our new home," he replied. "Barbus said we'll be either Eighth or Ninth legion. Don't know that I care which one."

"Ho, Oz," he heard from behind. He turned to see Massinussa walk up, followed by his brother Gulussa. The two were from Southwestern Numidia and as dark-skinned as Oz and Adhe, which had instantly endeared them to each other in the midst of name-calling by lighter-skinned recruits. Oz was especially glad for Adhe. The boy had trouble investing emotionally and still had few words for anybody, but had opened up enough with these two to hold normal conversations.

"Ho, Massi!" he said in answer. "We're nearly there. I thought we'd never leave Cirta. Adhe and I celebrated when we reached two-hundred recruits and they finally shipped us out."

"And that long march to Igilgili through the mountains was something else," Gulussa added, now standing next to Adhe.

Two groups of fifty had traveled on foot to Igilgili, followed by two more on horseback. Barbus had explained there was no difference in pay between foot or mounted archers, except that the men bringing their own horses would sell them to the legion's camp prefect on arrival, earning them a bonus and relieving them of the need to buy tack or fodder.

Igilgili was the next closest port from Cirta, where passage had been arranged on three big merchant vessels.

Two of the nearly five weeks of travel had been spent lying at anchor in some bay or other, waiting out raging spring storms, with Adhe seasick for the first week before finding his sea legs. "This must be our port!" he shouted now, pointing at some barely visible buildings along the coastline.

"Finally! I can't wait to get off this tub," Oz grunted. "The legions are stationed straight to the north. The sailors told me there's also a river that could be sailed later in the year, but for now they won't chance it. The mouth of that river is on the other side of the Pillars of Hercules, where the spring storms are much worse and the waves taller than any ship."

"Not sure I would want to be riding them in a ship, but I would love to see waves like that," Massi answered. They held their spot at the railing as more of their fellow archers came out to join. The sailors trimmed the square sails, cussing at their passengers for not moving out of the way quickly enough, and rowed the last half mile into the harbor against the wind.

The ship docked at one of several wooden piers, and a simple gangplank was pushed out from the side. Several men in legion armor had gathered during their slow approach and now guided the newcomers into a single line toward a massive desk set up in the open space between the piers and several warehouses. As they crept up the line, Oz saw it was occupied by a single man in Roman officer's armor, checking over several rolled-out scrolls. The line was moving slowly enough that they were anxious long before getting close.

"Next!" Finally, his turn had come. "Your name!" the officer bellowed.

"I'm Ozalkis, and behind me is my nephew Adherbal."

The man looked down the names in the first scroll, then halfway down the second. He started making marks and spoke without looking up.

"Welcome to Hispania. You're now both part of the auxilia of the Ninth legion. Go stand with your legion's standard in the plaza behind me. Next!"

They walked on and quickly found their place under a standard with the number IX embroidered in two big black letters below a brown bull over a red background. Their group was steadily growing. "Look, Adhe, Massi and Gulussa are coming over, they also made the Ninth."

He hadn't realized how tense he had been until that moment. *Nothing like keeping friends by your side.*

690 AUC (64 BC), summer
Thirty miles north of Anas delta, Border area, Roman Province of Hispania Ulterior and Lusitania

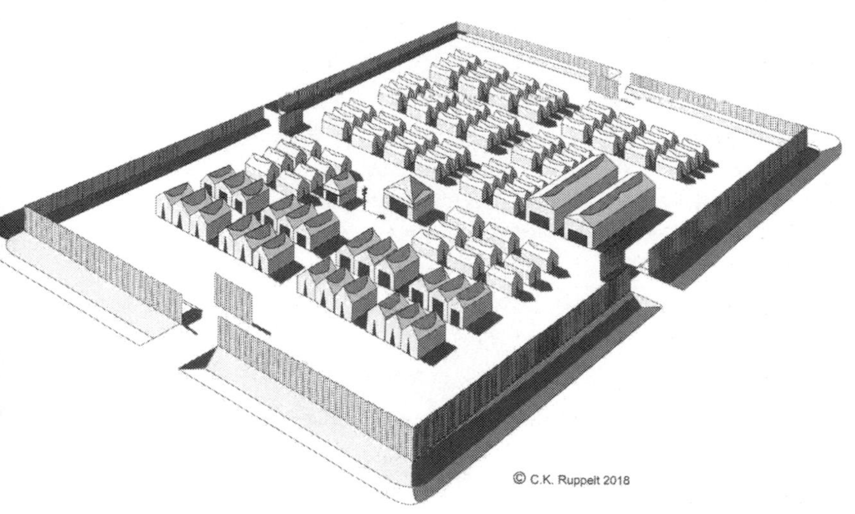

Illustration: Typical Roman Cohort field camp

"We hardly had time to figure out how things work around here," Oz complained to Adhe as they marched out of their camp close to Corduba, the capital of the Roman province. It had only been a month since their arrival, and they were already on their first campaign of sorts.

"It was long enough to figure out that the Cretans think we are barbarians," Gulussa interjected. The Numidian archer's barracks were located on the other side from the group of Cretan archers, with Celtic cavalry between, and they had quickly figured out the reason.

"Doesn't matter to the Romans though, to them we're all stupid and unworthy foreigners," Massi added. His whole tent group started laughing.

They marched with half of the Ninth's Numidian and Cretan forces behind three of the legion's regular cohorts.

"So, does anybody know where we're going?" Massi asked.

"Our decurion said this is a punitive expedition against a clan of the Celtici people that fled into the hills to the northwest of here," Oz answered in Latin. "But he didn't know why they deserve punishment."

Since enlisting in Cirta, they each took every opportunity to practice their Latin. Though Oz's speech was still badly accented, he had improved his fluency. Adhe had made more progress, though he still preferred listening to speaking.

But Oz's nephew now surprised everybody by asking in nearly flawless Latin: "Anybody know why the Gallic cavalry is not coming with us?"

"Maybe because we're going into the hills," said Massi. "Or maybe because some of our cavalry are local Turdetani. Would they try to help the Celtici?"

"I don't think that's the reason," replied Oz. "Since coming here, we've heard that the Celts fight amongst themselves all the time. At least if they're still independent, like the ones in the west or in Gallia to the north."

The Celts attached to their legion had been recruited from all over Roman Hispania and southern Gallia, yet seemed to share the same culture, language, and similar dress, with at least one piece of their clothing made from colorfully plaid cloth. They usually had blue, green, or gray eyes, while the brown eyes he had seen around Corduba and their camp belonged to Iberian, Greek, Carthaginian, or Phoenician people, with the latter three descendants of centuries-old colony cities.

"Well, I'm sure the Celtici will wear open torcs around their necks to show their prowess for battle," Gulussa said. "All Celts do that. But what I really want to know is what kind of stuff they put into their hair. Is it going to be whitened with limewater like what the northern Celts seem to prefer? Or, are they using the sap-based stuff like the locals here close to our camp, to turn their long hair into impressively tall spikes?"

"I'll bet anyone that it's going to be the wood resin," Massi said.

"You are on!" Adhe spoke up. "I bet you five sesterces that it's neither and that the Celtici do something else with their hair."

Massi smiled and nodded to Adhe. "We'll see. I hope myself that it's not the tall spikes, we'd be safer in battle." The whole group laughed.

"Talking about Celts. Have you two gone to one of the local smithies yet?" Oz asked.

Massi and Gulussa shook their heads. "No, did you?"

"Yeah, I took Adhe to a big one. I've never seen swords and spears like those. No simple weapons to be had there; some are quite beautiful with lots of decorations."

"I'd like to see those!"

"The best thing though is their chainmail. That looks so strong, I bet nothing gets through.We need to save, so we can buy some. Even if it's heavy, hey, if it keeps arrows out, that'd be enough for me."

Making Adhe and my friends safer would be priceless. The thought of possibly losing somebody else close to him put him into a melancholy mood and he kept silent for a long while as they marched down the Roman road paved with large slabs of white local stone.

***

A week later, the legionaries all took turns using their field shovels and their wicker baskets to collect dirt from a ditch for a berm meant as base for a simple ten-foot tall log palisade. Oz looked away from the men to gaze at the approach up the hill, where several more mules brought the men's tents and additional palisade logs.

"I'm glad we're standing watch instead of digging like our heavy infantry," Capussia said from his side with a chuckle. The man was first decurion of all the legion's Numidian turmae and seemed to be a natural and smart leader. Oz liked him immensely. "But never forget that we're in enemy country. Don't take your eyes off the horizon for long," he continued. Oz nodded and waited a few minutes before giving the current construction site another quick glance. Their camp was to house a single legionary cohort, two turmae of Numidian, plus one turma of Cretan archers; a turma consisting of thirty soldiers divided into three squads of ten, each led by a decurion.

Similarly to their permanent Roman fort, the four gates of this smaller one were carefully laid out from east to west and north to south, with the roads connecting at the center of the camp. The only concession he'd seen for the size was the lack of hinged gate doors; instead, permanently open gaps were used in the wall. A recessed palisade blocked the direct view to the inside for anyone approaching, and the openings could be blocked by additional sections kept ready nearby.

He looked the other way again. The beautiful view seemed peaceful, though the late afternoon sun parched his throat. "Do you think the enemy will come looking for us here?" Adhe asked from his side.

"Maybe, if we don't find them first. I'm sure our cohort prefect will send search parties out the moment our camp is secure," Oz answered.

They all kept staring at the edge of the woods. Oz hoped they would get through the rest of the day without any excitement.

***

For two weeks the troops had gone out every day. The Celts had ambushed several of their skirmish units, and Oz figured that proved their cohorts were closing in on their target. This morning, while on sentry duty, he stood on the slightly raised dirt berm of the western wall used as a catwalk, watching their cohort prefect lead a tight formation of five centuries of legionaries out.

All archers plus a single century of legionaries stayed behind to secure the camp. Once the troops were out of sight, he returned to scanning the tree line. Some of the louder birds chirped a few hundred feet away in what was left of nearby woods. The cohort had cut firewood and replacement stakes for the fort's palisade, and the colorful animals had complained loudly before taking flight. *I'm so glad they are back. We never had that many in our village, or ones that sing this beautifully.*

Many hours seemed to have passed since he started his shift, and he checked the length of the shadows to gauge the time. Though his stomach growled, it wasn't lunch time yet.

"I can't wait to eat!" he said to Massi, who stood a few feet away.

"I'm happy we always have enough rations, but I'm more than bored with our food," Massi replied. "We have all the wheat we'll ever need for bread and porridge, but otherwise we only get salt, chickpeas and lentils. The worst thing is that I am all out of spices. If you can spare something, anything, I would much appreciate it."

"Don't forget the free garlic and olive oil." They both laughed. As far as Oz could tell, garlic and olive oil were used as meal ingredients by every soldier for every single meal, including fresh bread and porridge at breakfast. "I will gladly share my spices with you, I stocked up before we left camp. Don't know what half of the local stuff is, but that just makes it interesting," Oz said, still laughing. "I also want to ask Capussia if Adhe and I can go out to hunt. We could use some variety."

Ozalkis checked the shadows again. It was close to noon now. Good, their shift change would happen in another hour or two. He paused. Some feeling in the pit of his stomach made him turn back to look at the forest.

Why? What's wrong? He stood there for a moment in silence. *The birds! They sound agitated.*

He scanned from the hill ascent to the trees covering the ridge of the hill. *There is movement. Several people.*

He looked left to Massi and saw his friend walking away to the stairs. He turned right to wave to the next sentry in line. "Can you confirm that?" he said, pointing at the tree line.

The Cretan archer nodded. "Yes, there's movement."

Oz turned toward the inside of the fort to see a single legionary strolling down the main east-west road.

"Hey, you there, legionary! Alarm the centurion that we have movement in the woods to the west." The soldier nodded and took off at a run.

Three minutes later, he saw Titus Balventius rushing toward their part of the wall with his optio at his side. The boyish-looking junior centurion had overall command of the camp in the prefect's absence. Oz heard the cornicen and tubicen, the century's two trumpeters, blowing a call to arms.

"Who called this?" the centurion shouted from the few boards acting as stairs to the catwalk.

"I did, sir. Ozalkis." He pointed at the tree line. "I saw movement over there, and this man here confirmed it."

The Greek archer drew himself up in front of Balventius. "Klearistos, at your service. Don't know exactly how many I saw, but it was several."

Titus Balventius looked at the forest. "Seppius, assemble our century here at the western gate."

He turned to look down into the fort. The two highest ranking auxilia officers had arrived with several of their squad commanders. Capussia, tall and broad, represented the Numidian contingent. His stature made him overshadow the thin and hook-nosed Cretan leader named Andrippos.

"Both of you, get the rest of your men onto the wall to give us cover. Except for a couple of squads that go out with us. Andrippos, please, personally lead those."

The Cretan nodded and spoke to his two decurions, while Capussia ran to the tents of his Numidians, soon reemerging with the remaining squads.

"We are to mount the western wall, follow me!" Oz heard him call as his fellow archers ran up the stairs.

Ozalkis was once again impressed by the level of organization within the legion. Within a few short minutes, the century of legionaries was perfectly arranged in front of the gate and ready to march out.

***

He might have many years of service experience thanks to lying about his age when signing up as a fifteen-year-old, but Balventius still thought of himself as too young to lead a whole century.

Perhaps feeling unworthy is why I'm not cursed with the same prejudice against non-Romans my colleagues seem to have. It's supposed to be about how people behave, not where they're from. He really liked the Numidians and their leader Capussia. They seemed refreshingly honest and straight-forward people, not trying to play games and politics for advancement like the Roman officers were wont to do.

He walked away from the men who'd raised the alarm, pushing through the archers streaming onto the western catwalk. When he made it down, he walked through Andrippos's group of twenty Cretans to the infantry behind. Seppius stood with the century's standard bearer and their two trumpeters. The squad leaders all called in the troop's readiness before he raised his hand. "Let's march!"

"Blow the signal!" Seppius relayed to the cornicen. The man deftly used his instrument.

The century moved through the gate in rows of four, immediately spreading out into their long traditional formation of three ranks deep. As always, the freshest recruits walked in the front row.

Balventius glanced over his shoulder at the Cretan archers spreading out into their own loose line right behind the Romans. The formation marched the few hundred feet to the tree line without any issues.

As they approached the woods, the officers and the men in the formation's center faced a grisly display. Severed heads of Roman soldiers sat on spikes rammed into the ground, located only a few feet behind the undergrowth of the tree line. *Why would the enemy do this here? Did they mean to draw us out of the camp?*

Balventius's eyes grew big as he recognized the horse's head in the middle of the spikes. This could only be their prefect's chestnut, identifiable by the big white blaze running down its face. Now he also recognized the head next to it as the prefect himself.

The other centuries must be dead. And he had played into the Celts' hands by bringing his men out to investigate. Hopefully it was not too late.

"Halt, now!" he screamed. Most of the first line had already reached the edge of the forest. "Orbem formate!" he called, commanding to form a loose circle. The sides of the battle line started moving back and inwards. The men had drilled this maneuver often enough that they smoothly created a near perfect circle when both ends of the line joined. "Retreat to the fort!" he shouted, wanting all his men to hear him directly. The formation moved as one. He warily scanned between the underbrush and the trees. *Good, the last men of the front rank are out of the forest.*

A big roar sounded through the woods as several hundred Celtici jumped out of hiding. The warriors ran by the severed heads as Balventius swore. Thank the gods he hadn't waited any longer before calling the retreat, or it would have been much worse. "Steady, men, steady!" he shouted. The first warriors of the Celtic charge hit the legionary shields with tremendous force. Some of the green recruits had left their rank's shields misaligned, causing several of them to be killed or wounded. The men of the second line stopped their backwards march to fill in where needed.

Now that the shock of first blood was behind them, the legion fell into well-practiced motions imprinted by continuous drilling. The rear arc of the circle formation directly involved in the fighting started a running change-out for an orderly retreat. The more seasoned second and third ranks of the rear section rotated their bodies ninety degrees to stand sideways, allowing the first rank to squeeze through to reform behind, again keeping the same gaps open. The soldiers of the second rank had become the front, rotating their bodies to again present a continuous shield wall to the pursuing enemy. Twice, they opened their shield briefly to stab at the enemy, then squeezed backwards to let the next rank behind them become the front line. His century managed a slow, yet orderly retreat.

Halfway back to the wall, Balventius heard the thundering of hooves long before he saw a line of horsemen riding up to cut them off from the fort's gate.

Merda. They're not letting us get away that easily.

The archers manning the wall collected a heavy toll from the Celtici riding up. Balventius grinned when he realized that the cavalry's shields were all pointed towards the legionaries on the ground, exposing their right sides fully to the volleys from the fort. Many of the warriors twisted in their saddles to avoid incoming arrows. Good, time to change orders. "Second rank!

Put your swords away and hold your first pilum ready!" he ordered, not waiting for his trumpeters to pick up on the command. "Second rank, move forward!" The men moved to become the new first rank, while the horses filled the space in front of the gates. "Throw, throw! Second and third ranks, grab your pilum!" He repeated the same process, switching the ranks until they had all thrown both sets of pila. The use of the small iron-shafted spears proved deadly for the cavalry, their small shields leaving both men and horses unprotected. A quick glance back to the forest showed that his men's pila there had entangled many shields of the pursuing foot warriors who tossed the now unwieldy contraptions to the ground, allowing the legionaries to fell them by the dozens as they freely stabbed out from behind their shields into suddenly vulnerable bellies, groins and legs.

The Cretan archers in the midst of their small group kept a steady stream of arrows flying over the legionaries' heads. They would run back a few feet, stop and shoot another volley, always careful to keep ahead of the retreating legionaries.

The circle now pushed through the horsemen, the men climbing over dead horses and dispatching wounded enemies along the way. Balventius, focused to the side, stepped on the innards of a horse and slipped.

Seppius was there instantly to pull him back up. "Thank you, my friend." He looked down at his gore-drenched armor in surprise. *Incredible, I can't believe how focused I am. Even the stink doesn't touch me as it used to.*

The circle broke against the gate opening and split into two open ends moving along the fort's wall. As soon as his soldiers reached the palisade, they turned back toward the middle and hurried through the gate.

"Decanus, stop!" Balventius shouted at one of the men running inside. "I need you to organize three parties for the other gates. We need to close them all before the enemy goes for them, do you understand?" The man nodded. "Hurry!"

A few minutes later, Balventius rushed towards the gate himself. "Turn, form testudo!" he roared at the last two squads, joining their front rank. "Keep them out!" Stabbing a lone warrior, he saw the remainder of the Celts rush away to get out of range of the fort's archers. Standing several feet higher on their catwalk, the Numidians and Cretans on the wall finally commanded the enemy's respect.

"Switch!" Balventius pushed through the rank behind him to see another squad stand ready with the loose wall section. "Retreat. Close it up, quickly!" He watched the last lashing being tied into place from within the wall before glancing up at the sun. It had barely moved. *Really? I thought we were out there for hours.*

He walked away to check with the squad's decani about how many men they had lost. Every answer added another twist to the knife in his back. The total came to fifteen dead and five wounded badly enough to be out of the fight. Down to sixty able legionaries and surrounded by the enemy, yet they were still alive. *Thank the gods for our auxilia.*

***

Three days had passed since the sortie. The Celtici warriors camped in big groups within sight of the four gates and had hundreds of their horses grazing in full view of the camp, illustrating to the defenders that escaping was not a viable plan.

Oz sat on his cot in his squad's tent, polishing the exposed wood sections and leather-wrapped joints of his bow with a patch of raw sheep's wool. He smiled when he saw Adhe finally corner Massi.

"You owe me five sesterces!" his nephew demanded.

"I guess I can't argue with that. Most of these Celtici seem to color their hair red with Henna like they do in Mauretania and western Numidia." Massi smiled as he got his coin purse out, counting the money loudly as he handed it over.

Capussia peeked in through the tent flap. "Oz, I need to talk to you."

"Come on in," he told the first decurion, who took one step before scrunching up his nose.

"Quite rank in here. I guess that's what happens when we're short on water," Capussia said. He looked around at the other four men present. "Sorry, but we better talk alone."

Oz followed out of their tent and over into one of the camp's many newly empty sections. He touched Capussia's arm. "This should be fine." They stopped and faced each other.

"First things first. Since your tent's squad leader died, and since the other men respect you, I hereby declare you their replacement decurion. Do you accept?" Oz hesitated. He didn't know if he was the most qualified, though he supposed there were worse choices. He liked the idea of double pay, which might let him help his friends to buy chainmail sooner. Oz nodded and stood straighter. "Thank you for your trust, I'll do my best."

"Good. Now to the other part of my business. I just spent a few hours in the command tent with Balventius, Seppius, and Andrippos. The situation is of course bad, though we have many weeks of food stores. The water supply is our main issue. It's much worse than we let the men know so far. At the current rate we'll be out in a week."

"Meaning we can't wait this out," Oz answered, swallowing hard after the severity of the situation sank in and fear for Adhe and his friends rose inside him.

"Correct. We need a couple of squads to sneak through the enemy lines and go for help. Most of the Celtici clan is here, penning us in. We're hopeful that the other cohorts can make it here before we die of thirst."

He looked out over the tents, then turned to Oz again. "Sorry to lay this at your feet. Are you up for this?"

"I don't think we have a choice. If nobody goes, we all die. If whoever goes doesn't make it, we all die. At least, Adhe and I know how to stay quiet, so we might have a chance."

Capussia reached out his hand. Oz shook it.

"You know how much rides on this. Leave tonight. Early morning might be the best chance to slip through unnoticed. Now let me explain what we know of the other two camps' locations."

***

Akuia found her husband Mezugenos at a small campfire, warming his chilled hands. Like her, he was full of anger at the aggressive Romans. In early spring, the hated people had sent a tax collector and several soldiers to the clan's two small towns, stating that the clan's territory officially belonged to the Roman Province of Hispania Ulterior, meaning it owed taxes.

She smiled. It had not ended well for the arrogant publicani and his men. *Would the man still insist on them paying their taxes from the afterlife?* True, there were Celtici clans east of here paying tribute to the loathed Romans. *But not us, never us.*

Her leather boot came down on a small twig and snapped it. Mezugenos jerked around with his hand on his sword handle, smiling at her a moment later. She knew he was proud of her part in their successful ambush where they wiped out most of the camp's troops. *If we kill enough of them, I hope they'll never come back.*

He touched her arm. "I am the envy of all men. I still don't know why a beautiful woman like you married this ugly scoundrel." He pulled her close for a quick kiss. "But I'm not complaining." She smirked back at him, fire building up inside her. "Do you think we could ask somebody else to take over our watch…?" he continued.

"You would like that, wouldn't you?" she answered him with a wide grin. "As would I," she added, pulling her husband close for another kiss. "Let's find somebody to help us out." She put her arm around his back, gently guiding him towards one of the bigger campfires where they saw a young woman standing in front of the fire's flames, her silhouette outlined by the flickering light. "Hello there, Keka, we have a favor to ask. Do you have sentry duty tonight?" The woman shook her head. "No? Could you cover for Mezugenos?"

"That depends. What's in it for me?" The young woman replied with a hint of a smile.

"How about I'll take your next two sentry duties? Plus, some of our ham to sweeten the deal."

Akuia knew the woman couldn't resist their smoked ham and chuckled at Keka's sudden enthusiasm. She nodded in thanks before pulling her husband along to find a quiet corner.

***

Ozalkis slowly closed in on the Sentry, hiding in the darkness. He had shot at many riders during the battle, and he was sure he had killed several of them. But this, this was something else entirely, close and personal. He observed the woman standing at the fire and realized how young she was.

She looks no different from the local women around our big camp back in Corduba. In fact, she looks a lot like the girl Gulussa likes so much. But he knew he had no choice. He needed to do this for them to get away and survive. He finally stepped in to put his hand over the Celtici's mouth from behind. How he had hoped that they could slip through undetected! But the enemy had established a decent gridwork of guards and sentries.

Merda! He loathed himself as he slid his knife over her throat. He suppressed the sickness in his stomach, and the urge to cry. *I need to think of Adhe.* When he returned to where he'd left his squad, he couldn't find his voice. Instead, he gestured for them to follow, motioning for Adhe to take the rear. They were inching forward, changing directions several times when hearing voices or seeing lights in the distance, until he finally found neither. The next challenge was to cover their tracks since the enemy would hunt his men soon enough.

He took a branch from the ground. "Adhe, you lead for a while," he whispered. "Go off at an angle from here and change directions for a bit, but always get back to following the moon. Let's go, we need to be as far away from here as we can when the sun comes up." He turned around and walked backwards after the men while swiping their footprints. The path behind him looked clean in the moonlight, but he doubted it would hold up in daylight.

They made it down a ravine and into a small creek. Adhe led them downstream through the water for a while. *Good boy.*

Oz dropped the branch. He wondered and worried about his nephew. They had trained for many months now, but actual fighting and killing was a whole different thing. Men you've talked to and joked with had been cut to pieces, their bodies and body parts left rotting in front of the fort, affecting them all. He had thought himself numb since the loss of his wife and family. He knew now there had still been something intact deep inside of him, because it had shattered to pieces tonight.

***

He counted the nights in his head. *After this one it will have been seven days since we left the fort.*

The distance could have been traveled directly in two days or less, but with the Celtici patrols out and about they had to change directions frequently. Oz led his squad through another rocky ravine to hide their path, which had worked so far, but they'd had two random close encounters with Celtic search parties. Was this to be the third time? He heard the noise of a large group close by.

"Hide!" he hissed at his men. They all scrambled into bushes and thickets, trying to blend in as much as possible; except for one of his friends who was still clearly visible. "Massi! Move farther back!" he hissed. *Better, nothing left now but to wait.*

The noise grew and he wondered. Could it be? Was that the familiar clanking of pila on shields and sword sheaths on chainmail? A single legionary hesitantly moved out of the trees fifty feet away from them. The man looked around as if scouting ahead for a bigger group. A second legionary left the woods a few feet from the first.

"We made it!" Oz stood up and raised his right hand in greeting. The men around him came forward as well.

"Greetings, friends!" he shouted. "You can't imagine how glad we are to see you. We are auxiliaries with what's left of the second cohort. We need to talk to whoever's in charge."

I hope it's not too late yet.

***

Akuia led her horse as fast as she could. Most of the small group of disheartened survivors around her were too exhausted for anything but stumbling forward. The sun would set soon, and they could get some rest, though she knew she would not easily go to sleep. Not after today.

The noise of fighting had woken her in her husband's arms at first daylight. The Romans had come up from behind, running in force through the forest to catch her people unprepared. The lookouts able to warn them of approaching forces had covered the access road—nobody had thought to see long battle lines of Roman legionaries hurrying through the woods. The slaughter she had witnessed had been horrible. *My Mezugenos, stabbed and trampled...*

At that point, she had decided to run, grabbing the first horse she found and not looking back. She joined several other survivors on her way north, and the small band headed back to their people's main camp to find it under siege by yet another group of Romans. They turned to ride west, away from the hated aggressors and their own homeland.

"Let's stop here!" she called out at a small copse of woods with a stream. Getting off her horse, she was exhausted enough not to care if the others would follow her example. After loosely tying her reins to a bush, she walked to a tall chestnut tree, turned, and slid down the trunk. Mezugenos's last moment flashed through her mind again, but she resolutely pushed the thoughts aside. *I cannot get bogged down now. I need to keep my wits about me.*

She folded her hands over her stomach and watched the few other wretched clan members settle around her. Her husband was gone, but she had some small hope and a need to survive, thanks to the child growing inside her belly. *My love, may you live on in our son or daughter.*

691 AUC (63 BC), summer
Limen, Knossos, Crete, Roman Province of Crete et Cyrene

Nicolaos looked up from his ledger to see his favorite older brother standing in the doorway of the slave trading office. He jumped up from his stool. "What are you doing here? Come on in! What brings you to Knossos? Can I get you something? A cup of water, perhaps?" he babbled in excitement. He had not seen any of his family for many months, and here was Penthylos in his office.

"Hello, little brother! I decided to kill two birds with one stone, checking the local markets and comparing them to ours in Oaxos. It's clear we could get a lot more money for our wool and cheese if I could talk father into bringing them here. Plus, I couldn't wait to see how you are doing. It's been a whole year since you started as Zenodoros's apprentice."

Nico had left his home at the age of fifteen to come to Limen, the massive urban harbor settlement serving the ancient city of Knossos just up the hill, to learn the slave trade from a distant relation on his mother's side.

"So far, father was right. It's never boring and it pays well, or it will soon enough, once I'm no longer a mere apprentice. I'm happy with my new life. Knossos und Limen together are several times bigger than Oaxos, and there is so much to do and explore here. How long will you stay? Can I take you to one of the many eateries here? They have all kinds of foods." Nico was too excited to wait for answers.

Penthylos held up his hand and laughed. "I'm glad to see you haven't changed. I can stay the night before traveling back. So, I am yours if you want to give me a tour of the town."

"Great! It's nearly lunch time. Let me go find Zenodoros to tell him that I need the afternoon off." Nico ran out through the doorway and out of the main slave market building. He was back within two minutes. "Let's go! There is so much to show, I don't even know where to start. There's this huge library that's open to all citizens and freemen, and it's next to the one of the three theaters for comedies. The play tonight is supposed to be very funny. If there's still time after that, we could browse some of the stores with exotic goods."

They walked out the main colonnade into the slave market itself. "I have to admit I didn't think the slave trade was this big here," Penthylos said, indicating the size of the huge open market square. Many platforms showing off shackled people for sale were strewn about the large plaza.

"Zenodoros said that our market's trade volume is only behind that of Delos and Rhodos. All three are in competition for the slavers to bring their wares. That means we have a lot of pirates come through," Nico replied.

Penthylos made a face as if he had bit into a sour lemon. "I guess I knew that, on some level, but it's wrong to buy and sell people that were free like us not long ago." He took a deep breath. "I am sorry, I don't want to start an argument. Let's enjoy our afternoon. So, where to next?"

"Would you like to try Egyptian food? Yes? I can't wait till you see the dishes they serve, come on!" Nico took his brother by the hand to pull him along right through the open plaza dividing the slave market from an area with decent shops and cheap eateries. He was ecstatic. *I did not realize how much I missed him.*

***

Two months had passed since his brother's visit, and Nico often thought back to that day. He still missed his family, though Zenodoros had given him many important tasks to occupy his mind, like writing contracts and drawing signs for the slaves to wear around their necks in the market square to advertise their skills and attributes.

He walked up to the slave pens to interview the latest batch of newcomers for resale. Close behind, Zenodoros followed him into the holding. "Ah, Nico! Are you ready to process this lot?"

"Yes, great uncle. I'll ask them about their specialties."

"Good, good. Always remember they are property, nothing more, nothing less. An investment that needs to be cared for until we can sell them." The old man patted Nico's shoulder. "I guess I better go and talk to our auctioneer. He has a good voice, but now wants more money for it. We'll see about that," Zenodoros added with a cackle.

Nico watched him shuffle out before turning back to the slave pen. He walked over to the small bench and table in the corner of the room and nodded to the guard.

"They all have separate irons?" He asked. The guard nodded. "then please bring them out one at a time." Nico sat down with his wax tablet, ready to take notes.

"Go over to the table and talk to the young master!" he heard the guard command. He looked up to see the first slave arrive, a man perhaps only a couple of years older than himself. His heart fluttered as he studied him. The man was attractive, with his chiseled chin, unruly black hair, and dark brown eyes scanning him with warmth despite the situation. He looked down at his tablet and took a deep breath.

"What's your name?" he asked.

"Timon. I am Timon, son of…" The young man stopped when Nico raised his hand.

"Just your name." He cleared his throat. "Where' are you from?"

"I grew up in a small town outside of Smyrna."

Nico jotted down Smyrna. "What are your skills? What services are you qualified for?"

"I had good teachers and tutors," Timon answered in an educated voice. "I know numbers and all the classics. Most recently, I served as a household tutor for a rich family, educating their two young sons."

Nico scratched on the tablet. He was intrigued and would have liked to ask more. Still, he knew better than to get involved.

"Have you been sick recently?"

"Not for a while."

"That should be enough." He turned to the guard. "I'm done with this one. Bring me the next!"

***

Nico marched the last batch of eight new slaves around the market square as a chained group, gathering potential customers for Zenodoros's auction platform. A local man he'd seen about the market before waved at him.

"Hello, I'm Parmenides. This one's sign says that he has experience as a tutor and knows all the classics." He pointed at Timon. "I am in dire need of a teacher for my children. Is there any chance I could buy him directly? I am not after a discount, I am willing to pay a fair price. I just don't want to leave without him. I've been looking every day for weeks, and he's the first one that seems like a decent specimen."

Nico's initial reaction was to say no since he knew that Zenodoros frowned upon direct sales and preferred competing bids at auction. Yet, when Nico followed the man's gaze to Timon, he suddenly decided otherwise.

"I am not supposed to sell directly, so please don't make me regret this. Why don't you meet me at the auction building in a few minutes? When I'm done with this walk, we can go to one of the backrooms to discuss what you have in mind."

He finished his round and brought all the slaves back to the pens in their building, except for Timon. "Remove his chain but keep his shackles on," he commanded the guard. He grabbed the little box with his scribe set and bid the young man to follow. When they were out of hearing range of the slave pens and the guards, Nico slowed to look back at Timon. *I can't believe I'm doing this. Something in this man makes me like him more than I should, makes me want to help him.*

"I really like you," he blurted out. "I agreed to talk to the man about selling you to keep you here, in Knossos. I don't know how you feel about that." Nico avoided Timon's eyes.

"I can see that you're not like the other slave traders. Your heart is not hardened yet and you still care, though you are trying to hide it."

Nico took a deep breath before he looked back, right into dark brown eyes full of warmth and tenderness. Timon's smile melted his heart.

"Do you know much about the buyer? If you don't, there are no guarantees he will treat me well or ever let me leave his house." Timon sighed, and his smile slipped. "Hestia knows, I have experience with bad treatment.

"I don't know him, not really," Nico answered. "I only know that he's a local and I've not heard anything about how he treats his slaves. Of course, I'd only hear about bad treatment happening in public."

Timon nodded. "Alright. It might still be a better shot than waiting for the auction. Thank you for trying to help me."

They walked down the long hallway to the reception area in the front of the building. Parmenides waited anxiously, stepping back and forth until Nico waved him in. "Follow me."

They walked down a long hallway, and he opened the door to a small room stuffed with a table and two benches.

"Please, sit down. Water?" He poured a couple of cups from the fresh pitcher on the table.

"Now, to business. What can you offer me to keep this slave from the auction block?" Nico asked.

"How about six hundred silver drachmae?" Parmenides suggested.

Nico figured that this was simply the opening move for the age-old ritual of haggling. He stood up to head for the door. "Come, Timon, let's go. That man has no shame."

"Wait! I may have underestimated the worth of a good tutor. How about eight hundred?"

Nico turned back. "I've been at every one of our auctions for the last year. I know he would sell for a minimum of fifteen hundred there. You said yourself that good tutors are hard to find." He shrugged dramatically. "Since you are a good local citizen, I'll let you have him for thirteen hundred."

With another two counteroffers back and forth, they shook hands at eleven hundred and fifty. Parmenides brought out a small sack containing golden drachmae and counted out the equivalent of the negotiated sum. Nico sat down to log the sale on a papyrus containing Zenodoros's running tally. When he had counted the coins himself, he handed over an official seal of ownership.

Parmenides shook his hand. "Thank you for your help."

Nico walked them into the hallway and watched them leave through the main entry. *Sorry, Timon, I wish I had the money to buy you myself. I hope to see you again.*

He pulled himself together. He still had to get seven slaves ready for the upcoming auction, and there would be a reckoning to look forward to. Zenodoros would be livid about his direct sale, though the fair price Parmenides had paid would help to smooth things over.

***

"You've proven yourself with the children exactly as advertised. I'll take a chance and have your shackles removed, but I will not allow you to leave the house until you have convinced me you will not try to run away," Parmenides told Timon. Next, the new master turned to the aging majordomo. "See to it. I'll be leaving for the afternoon."

At least it's a decent-sized house, and I like the children. Timon followed the old slave to the back of the house, where another household servant took off his shackles. This had been the first time outside of his small bedroom or the dining room he used for tutoring lessons in several weeks. He wondered about the old slave running Parmenides's household. With a face of stone, never smiling or angry-looking, it was easy to see how uncaring he was. *Well, all the other servants' warmth makes up for the lack of his.*

"How does it feel?" the majordomo asked him.

Timon rubbed his sore ankles. "Much better," he replied. The man waved at him to get up, and he followed. They came to another section of the house, and they stopped in front of a doorway.

"The master is gone, and he will not be back for many hours." The old man suddenly showed a bright smile. "Which means we can all let our guard down for a little while. You only know me as the majordomo. My name is Leonas," he said as he ushered Timon through the door. "We got you a new set of clothes. Here's a clean chiton, and on the chair over there is a clean peplos to wear over that."

Timon only had eyes for the small bathtub built into the back wall of the room. He washed every morning with a bowl of water, but he hadn't been allowed to properly bathe since his first capture by pirates several years ago.

"I can't thank you enough, Leonas," Timon said, removing the knot holding his peplos over his left shoulder.

"Well, it was as much Cyanea's idea as mine. Why don't you thank our old kitchen mistress instead of old me?" He turned to leave. "I'll be back when it's time. We need to make sure all evidence is gone before the master is back," Leonas said, winking and showing surprisingly white teeth in a grin full of boyish charm and affection.

***

Four months later, Nico had long given up hope of seeing Timon again. He walked down the office hallway after paying some rather unsavory characters for a load of fresh slaves when a boy working for their auctioneer found him.

"Nico, there is a guy here asking for you. He says his name is Timon."

He stopped walking to keep from tripping. "Please, show him in!" he replied. He rushed into the office to put the purse and his papers away. "If Zenodoros asks, I am out on an errand!" he told the two colleagues sharing space with him. Back in the hallway, he saw Timon walking up, and his heart hammered away in excitement.

"Timon, I am so glad to see you. Tell me, how did things work out for you?"

"So far, so good. I came to see you, but don't have much time. I'm supposed to fetch papyrus for Parmenides. Would you mind walking to the store with me?"

Nico nodded and led them out of the building into the market area, and from there through a colonnade onto one of the main thoroughfares of the city.

"So, is your new owner a decent man?" Nico finally asked to break the uncomfortable silence.

"The treatment has been good, everything considered. Not as good as with my last owner, a rich Athenian, but that did not end well for me. I was on a ship with him, on the way to move his whole family back from Naxos to Athenae, when the pirates who sold me to your employer attacked. Of course, he spent the ransom money for his family, but he didn't want to pay for anybody else and left all his servants behind."

Nico was shocked into silence for a moment before he had the nerve for the next question. "You are from outside Smyrna, right? I would like to know more about how you became a slave in the first place. Having had good teachers and tutors usually means a wealthy family..."

Timon nodded. "My father was a successful trader who owned several warehouses filled with wines from the Greek mainland and the islands of the Aegean Sea. He also had vendors selling his goods at the Smyrna market, plus contracts to ship back out to other ports. He always lost the occasional load to pirates, but about five years ago everything changed when all his shipments were stolen. He made a big gamble and bought directly at the vineyard outside of Mende in Chalcidice. It took everything he could scrape together, and I came along for the trip. He said it was likely the last time we could afford to travel anywhere. We nearly made it back home before the pirates caught us. With no money left to pay for ransom, they sold us in Delos." His eyes teared up. "I have no idea where my father went, or if he's even still alive."

If this can happen to someone like Timon, it could happen to anybody. Nico stared at the young man walking beside him. "I can't promise anything, but I have been saving for several months. Maybe I could get enough together within a year or two to get you away from Parmenides. I would like to see you set free," he told Timon in a low voice.

Timon grabbed Nico's arm and studied his face. "I can see you truly mean this. Thank you, I would forever be in your debt." As Timon's hand dropped, Nico felt a jolt when their fingers touched. After that, it seemed only natural to hold hands on the way to the store.

***

Nico met Timon ten more times over the next two months, always during errand runs, and was content to simply enjoy his company. Today, though, Timon was clearly distraught. He barely said two words, while his eyes looked red from crying. Finally, Nico had enough. By now he cared deeply for Timon and had to know what was going on.

"It is clear that something is wrong. Can you please tell me?"

Timon shook his head, looking down at the cobbles of the street.

"If I don't know what it is, I can't help you. And all I want is to help you!" Nico blurted out.

"But you can't. No one can." When he touched Timon's shoulder, his friend looked up into Nico's eyes. "I don't know anymore. Parmenides often comes home late and drunk. The last few night's he came into my room. His wife knows about it, but she doesn't care. He used to have a steady male lover, but they had a falling out, so now he wants me to console him. I can't really say no. Not anymore." He pulled up his tunic and turned to the side, showing Nico massive welts on his back from beatings. "There is nothing to be done."

Nico broke out in tears and gently hugged Timon. "I will ask my great uncle for a personal loan, that's the one thing I can do. As soon as I have the money, I will tell Parmenides to set you free." He let go of Timon. "In fact, I will go find Zenodoros right now." He took off running but stopped for a quick glance back. *I can't wait to set you free.*

He sped into the office and from there to the holding pens where he found Zenodoros. "Great-uncle, I need your help."

***

The very next morning, Nico stood in front of Parmenides's door with a coin purse full of golden drachmae. He knocked, and an old servant opened. "I need to talk to the master of the house."

"As you wish. Who may I say is calling?" The man asked.

"Nicolaos. I work for the slave trader Zenodoros."

The man closed the door. A brief time later it reopened to show Parmenides starring at him. The man seemed angry and irritated. Nico's heart dropped.

"What do you want?"

Nico didn't hesitate. "I am from the slave market and work for Zenodoros. I sold you your tutor Timon half a year ago."

"Yes, I remember you. Again, what do you want?" His voice took on an even sharper tone.

"I want you to set Timon free. I will gift him the money or buy him from you first, whichever you prefer. I am prepared to pay higher than market price, just tell me how much you want." Nico saw the man's eyes turn to slits and hurriedly continued. "As per age-old tradition, you have to grant him his freedom once he is able to pay for it."

Parmenides's anger seemed to have reached a boiling point. "What makes you think I would set him free or sell him to you of all people? You must be the boy walking with him everywhere. Don't think I haven't heard about that. I won't allow his liberation, especially not when it's paid by you, you insignificant little worm, tradition be damned!" Parmenides screamed before slamming the door shut in his face.

***

Nico came by again that evening, hoping to find Parmenides gone from the house. *Maybe I can talk the old doorman into letting me speak to Timon.*

He knocked to see the older servant opening the door. When the man saw Nico, his stony face burst into tears.

"I am so sorry. The master sold Timon this morning, right after you left. Not through the market; he brought a buyer to our house." The man paused, composing himself. "We are all heartbroken, including the master's children. Nobody understands why he was sold to the copper mines."

Nico was utterly shocked and had to quickly sit down on the ground to keep from fainting. *My gentle Timon, to the copper mines? That is a death sentence, nobody lasts more than a few months there.*

He had seen many unfortunate souls sold to mine buyers and knew there was a reason these people continued to buy huge quantities of new slaves.

Nico clenched his teeth and swallowed. *I cannot give up yet. Not while there's still a chance I can find out more.*

"Can you tell me where Parmenides goes to drink every night?"

"He goes to a taverna not far from the crossroads of the Tripods' street and the Middle Road. It's two streets east from that intersection." The old man wiped his eyes. "I am very sorry. We all loved Timon and will miss him deeply."

Nico shook hands with the servant before walking home in a trance. He ate some bread and olives to steady his stomach, then gathered tools he figured he might need. He laid out a midsize cudgel on his cot, and one of his bigger knives, just shy of a short sword. He experimented with how to secure the weapons to his chiton and put on a light linen cloak over that to keep them from sight. He sat down to drink a few cups of unwatered wine to steady his nerves, until the sun had set. *All I want is to crawl under the covers and cry. Tears be damned, it's time to head out.*

***

Parmenides walked out of the taverna's door, clutching a small oil lamp in his hands. He turned around in the doorway to shout back obscenities.

Very, very drunk. Nico watched him turn the first street corner and started to follow. He knew where the man was headed; he could stay far away and out of sight.

At about half the distance home, Parmenides was about to walk past a small alleyway that Nico had scouted earlier.

Here we go. He started to run and shout with a changed voice to make his target stop. "Parmenides, my friend, wait up, wait up!" *Good, he stopped just in time.* Nico fingered the cudgel, removing it from the backside of his chiton and holding it ready behind his back.

"Who… is that you, Akadios? Or Tecton?" Parmenides slurred, trying to lift his lamp higher to make out his supposed friend.

Nico kept his head low and made it within a few feet before being found out.

"It's you! You filthy…" the man shouted before trailing off and falling down from being hit on his head. Parmenides's lamp had fallen, some of the burning oil puddling on the cobblestones. Nico looked up and down the street. *Good, nobody around to see anything.* He grabbed Parmenides arms to drag him into the dark alleyway and came back to use the still burning oil in the street to light his own lamp.

As Parmenides came to, the man's eyes widened. *Good, he has noticed my knife at his throat.* The man looked around in panic. The alley was filthy, and their spot was hidden from the main street by a pile of garbage. The stones beneath them had been recent targets of people relieving themselves, which added to the stink of many rotting kitchen scraps and worse.

"I already know that you sold Timon. Tell me who the buyer is, and I'll let you go. But you better tell me now," Nico said, full of loathing for this despicable man, pushing his big knife slightly forward.

Parmenides roared with laughter. "I knew you would try to find out, but I made sure you couldn't. You made it clear that Timon didn't want to stay with me. So, nobody else will have him now, certainly not you."

In his agitation, Parmenides had moved forward enough to nick his own throat on Nico's blade. He kept talking, seemingly unperturbed. "I had some luck with that buyer. I went down to the docks. The ships were already loaded, ready to leave. I made him an offer he couldn't resist, so he came back to my house to get one more slave for his mine." He laughed again. "The only one who can tell you where Timon went is me." The hated man seemed to enjoy himself. Now his eyes shrunk to slits in determination. "And I will *never* tell you!"

Suddenly, Parmenides grabbed Nico's right hand in a shaky attempt to move the knife to the side while jumping up to tackle Nico to the ground. They both fell, and the lamp went out. Nico sat up, his hand still on the knife's handle.

What is that? This smell... fresh blood? Yes, and lots of it. He slowly let go to feel around in the dark for his lamp. After a brief search he found it and moved around the garbage pile back to the street, where a small amount of oil was still burning. His lamp re-lighted, he moved back into the alley. The knife was stuck in Parmenides' sternum; the dead man's eyes stared at him in silent complaint. He shook his head as if to throw off the overwhelming despair he felt and pulled out the knife. After cleaning it on Parmenides clothes, he turned around to walk home to his room. Halfway there, it dawned on him the stink of blood still in his nose came from himself, and he looked down at his drenched chlamys. Suddenly lightheaded, he stopped to take it off. Walking on in his undergarment, he was surprised he didn't encounter any other early morning walkers. Finally, he burst in through his door and ran straight for his water bowl to clean himself up. Next, he dropped on his bed. As if in a stupor, he leaned back to close his eyes. Within moments, a wave of emotion hit him, tumbling his mind uncontrollably. *Timon will die, and I will never see him again. No, no, no!*

Reliving the day's unfortunate events and feeling the heavy loss that lay on his soul, he burst into fits of weeping until his physical and mental exhaustion finally caught up with him and brought him fitful slumber.

692 AUC (62 BC), summer
Magetobriga, Free Gallia, Sequani Nation

"Until now, I did not want to believe the Sequani would stoop so low," Drestan told his daughter Aina. They rode at the head of the Bailenau contingent of warriors on their way to join the great Aedui host led by his father Haerviu.

The Sequani and Arverni had always been jealous of the Aedui's hold on trade between the Rhodanus in the south and the mighty Rhenus to the east. For two years, rumors had made it to the clans about those nations bringing in warriors from Germania. Rumors no more, as they knew for certain now.

"Was it desperation that made them contemplate such a thing?" Elsed threw in loudly from Aina's other side.

"That, we will likely never know. It seems they feel invincible with the new Suebi king by their side. In his letter, your grandfather said that when the Sequani captured Magetobriga, they slaughtered everyone except for five old people which they gave horses and sent back to Bibracte to report," Drestan said. "They knew where to hurt us most." A remote outpost in the Vosago mountains, Magetobriga had been the linchpin for Aedui trade to the east.

Drestan had only visited the town once, but he knew the whole area was a melting pot, with the Sequani to the south, the Raurici people to the east, the Triboci to the northeast, the Lingones to the northwest, and the bulk of the Aedui nation far off to the west. Magetobriga's importance laid in its location close to several rivers—with the origin of the Mosella on the backside of the nearest mountain and the Mosa, the Dubs, and the Arar also nearby, it was a natural connection between Gallia, Germania, the lands of the Belgae, and the Mediterranean.

"And here we are, taking the town back for our people," Aina said.

"Right. I expect my father collected the biggest Aedui host in a generation. I hope to see some of my brothers." Several of Drestan's siblings were now active council members and constant contenders for the rotating Vergobret position.

"Look!" Aina called out, pointing forward to where the ancient Celtic road bent slightly as it exited the low hills. The road emerged onto a long plain, and the entire Aedui army became visible in the distance. The sight was breathtaking.

"Amazing, I have never seen so many people together. How many are there?" Elsed asked.

"Maybe fifty thousand?" Morcant, his youngest, answered. He had ridden up to Drestan's other side.

Drestan looked at his three children, seeing the awe in their eyes. "You need to look at the colors of the single clans," he explained. "When you start counting these, you'll see this looks like much more than fifty thousand. Your grandfather must have rallied every able body around Bibracte."

They urged their horses down the road to catch up to the host.

***

"Father!" Drestan called out a short time later, steering his horse close to Haerviu to reach out for a brief touching of hands. They both smiled, not having seen each other for many months.

"I am glad you made it in time. I'm sorry for the late message," his father said. "What do you say? We haven't had a gathering this big in fifty years or more. With the Sequani and Arverni emboldened by their new allies, the council unanimously agreed to a show of force. Look around, most everybody you know from back home is here."

Drestan scanned the group around his father until he saw grinning faces belonging to two of his older brothers. "Haedan!

Suibhan! It's been too long," he called as he rode over to them. "Are Nectan and Liscan here as well?"

"No, Nectan is Vergobret this year and felt he needed to stay in the capital. Liscan is traveling south to the Roman province for a trade deal," Suibhan replied. "You know, that makes you and me the only brothers that haven't been Vergobret. Yet." They grinned at each other, and Drestan realized how much he had missed this. It was good to see his brothers, and the easy banter made him feel as if no time had passed since their childhood at their father's homestead.

Drestan saw somebody else moving up from the corner of his eyes. "Divitiaco!" He moved in to clap his shoulder. "I haven't seen you since Aina's wedding." He grinned at his old friend, who was part of a rare breed of both warrior and journeyman druid. He wore different shades of white from head to toe and was cleanshaven as always, in contrast to the older warriors around him sporting heavy mustaches, or his own father with his full beard. "Is that a new golden pin holding your cloak?" Drestan sharply breathed in. "It's a yew?" Divitiaco nodded in response.

"Congratulations. You've always been a master with your weapons, and now you are also master druid. That must be some kind of record and worthy of a lot of ale or mead when we have time," he told his grinning friend.

"I frankly thought the studying would never end. It surprised me when my master said I was ready for the test." They both turned their heads to watch Haerviu and his grandchildren greet each other. *Oh, how good this feels. I need to visit Bibracte more often, and I should find excuses to take the children with me. Well, not children any longer, but they need the family connection as much as I do.*

Somebody shouted out, and everybody looked ahead at the vista in front. The host had come far enough to see the town of Magetobriga, located halfway up the slope to a mountain pass barely visible in the distance. The town effectively straddled and controlled access up the main road to where the rafts laden with goods landed after navigating up the Mosella river. The settlement itself, as well as half a mile of the open approach, was bordered by old-growth forest. The cleared corridor to both sides of the road was only a couple hundred feet wide.

"There it is," Haerviu stated the obvious as all of them took in the sight.

Though Drestan expected a long and prolonged fight, he had no doubt about the outcome. Even with the Suebi king Ariovist and his warriors in the mix, the Sequani and the Arverni could never equal the great Aedui host his father had gathered. He looked behind to find battle-ready warriors as far as the eye could see. "How many did you bring, father?"

"We should be about eighty thousand, more or less."

They rode on in silence for a few minutes, content with studying the land. Several riders moved out of the southern and northern forests, quickly approaching the head of the host. "Let's hear what our scouts found out."

The group from the north were first to make it to Haerviu. The scout leader nodded and spoke after receiving a nod in return. "We went up several miles into the northern foothills. The Sequani hold a fortified lookout there on this ridge"—he pointed up to the tall hill on their left—"with a few hundred men. We did not find anybody else."

In the meantime, the scouts from the southern forest had arrived, their leader coming over to report. "We rode in a wide circle around the forest and came back through the middle of it. No evidence of anybody having been through or hiding in there. We found some empty and abandoned old buildings, nothing else."

Drestan studied his father during the report. After a few questions for more details with no satisfying answers, he could tell by the look of determination on his father's face that he had made up his mind.

"We need to send warriors up to take the lookout from the Sequani there. Once that is captured, that party needs to watch for enemy movements in or around the town and report back. They are likely holed up in Magetobriga itself, but let's be sure." Haerviu turned to two of his older friends. "Once we reach the forest corridor, I want you to stay and hold the approach against anybody trying to get behind us." The men looked disappointed but did not complain. His father turned his horse back forward. "The main host will approach the town and check the wall for weaknesses, plus scout the immediate surroundings. I have my doubt that we can get them out for a pitched battle, though stay ready for the gate to open for a massive sally at any time."

He looked at Haedan and Suibhan. "We need a few hundred riders to comb the woods ahead of us to spring any traps they may have set." They nodded back at their father with an eager look in their eyes.

Then Haerviu's eyes settled on him. "Drestan, how would you like to lead the party to take the lookout? Yes? Good. Divitiaco, Feidelan, Nochtan, would you support him with your people?" Seeing the men nod, he continued. "That should be enough to make quick work of a few hundred Sequani." Drestan waited for his father to speak the customary blessing.

"The rest of you will follow me to the town." His father raised both his hands before he continued. "May Andarta, honored goddess of war, ride with us and guide us." Now, they all moved apart to gather their warriors, and Drestan pushed his horse to get his own clan's people.

***

An hour later, Aina, her husband Bradan, and their fellow scouts fell back to where her father and the other chieftains rode up the mountainside ahead of their warriors. Aina arrived first, pulled up her reins, and shouted so everybody present could hear. "They are settled in and it's a solid wooden fort, well built, with only one gate. The walls are ten feet, and that lookout tower itself is the only thing on this hill tall enough for vantage above the surrounding trees."

"That just reinforces the need to take the fort. We better do it fast," her father responded. "Let's get closer before we decide on how. Will they see us coming?"

"Yes, if we were to stay on this trail. We can turn left, and come from above and behind," Aina answered. Divitiaco and Drestan both nodded at her. "Follow me," she called, urging her horse off the trail to go around the next stand of trees instead of through. A few minutes later, she figured they were close. She raised her hand to stop everybody. "Time to get off." She fastened her reins to a small sapling and joined her father to walk to the tree line on the camp's backside. None of the enemy showed on the wall close to them. It seemed the whole force was at the front side, watching the trail to the west or the town to the south. She looked to her father, who had raised his head upwards.

"I think I have a suggestion on what we should do," he said in a low voice, with a glance at Divitiaco, Feidelan, and Nochtan. Drestan pointed at the two tallest trees facing the hillfort. Their eyes grew big as they nodded in understanding.

"Let's get back and see who brought axes," Nochtan replied.

A few minutes later, rhythmic noises echoed through the woods from axes slowly cutting down the two biggest trees beyond the camp's northern wall. Aina stood in one of the shield walls, ready and waiting. Not surprisingly, the enemy spotted them quickly, and soon after their archers started launching arrows at the axe men. The shields kept the fellers safe, though Aina jumped when an arrow went right into her shield with a loud thunk. The two burly men behind her hit the tree from each side, working in perfect synchronicity.

The other team was first to shout. "It's falling!" She could hear the tearing sounds of the tree's trunk parting, followed by the rumbling impact when it hit the wall. Divitiaco shouted. "Hold steady, people! Wait for it!" Within a couple minutes the second fir came crashing down. *Here we go.*

She moved aside with the other warriors to get out of the way of the massive trunk, which took down a huge portion of the wall. The very tip clipped the side of the tower, making her hold her breath. *We need that watch tower!*

The whole structure swayed back and forth a couple of times, before finally settling. "That was close," her father sighed in relief. "Let's get them!"

The Aedui around her surged forward. Her friend Rionach was the first through the breach in the wall, screaming swear words at the Sequani as loudly as she could while running straight at the first man standing in her way. She held her sword at half height, feinting a defensive position while the warrior prepared a downward strike. She broke her run on the dirt, sliding to the left at the last moment to stay out of the man's reach, but using her own sword to open his leg in the process. The Sequani screamed and went down. Now Aina was through the breach herself and needed to deal with a warrior running straight at her. The young man seemed distracted by all the Aedui around him, which allowed her to quickly take him out with a stab to the side. She looked up to see a female Sequani standing halfway up the tower, readying her spear for a throw. She followed the woman's aim and realized the target was her friend. "Rionach, watch out!" she screamed, but it was too late. The woman released her spear in one smooth motion. At the last possible moment, a tall blond warrior stepped in from behind Rionach's side to use her shield to catch the missile. It penetrated halfway through, stopping just short of her friend. Aina saw the tall woman smiling and winking at Rionach and had to grin. It looked like her childhood companion had found somebody to watch her back.

After the brief initial resistance, the much bigger numbers of the Aedui quickly overwhelmed the small garrison. She scanned the fort and saw no enemies left standing.

"There is a full battle going on!" came a shout from the top of the tower. Her father ran up the steep stairs, and she went to join him, with Divitiaco, Elsed, and several others close behind.

Her hands made involuntary fists when she saw the embattled Aedui host below. They must have made it close to the town before becoming encircled by a growing number of Sequani and Arverni, steadily emerging from both sides of the tree corridor and the open area around the town. A big number of the enemy had moved between the main host and the Aedui warriors stationed at the end of the tree corridor. That latter force now joined the fray. Somehow, the Sequani and Arverni had collected a much bigger host than any of her clansmen had thought possible, evading the Aedui scouts and patiently waiting to close their trap.

Her father turned to all of them. "We need to get back to our horses and join our people down there," he stated loudly.

"Wait!" Aina shouted and raised her hand. She had spotted a sizeable number of riders emerging from beyond the southern woods, galloping straight north until reaching the road and turning into the tree corridor. Aina's eyes narrowed, and she held her breath, shivering involuntarily. These must be the Suebi; they were unmistakable. The tribes across the Rhenus were legendary for their savage fighting abilities, and many Aedui parents used them as boogeymen for unruly youngsters. The Suebi's clothes were similar to the Celts', as were their helmets and shields. But these warriors down there all held spears, only a few had any kind of body armor, and their much smaller horses were shared by two warriors. One rode while another hung off the side, hanging on to the horse's four-horn saddles.

"How can there be so many of them?" her father said from her side. "We need to get to your grandfather and uncles, Aina. We need to move, now!"

She rushed after Drestan, down the tower's ladder and to their horses.

***

The small force galloped down the hill in a mad dash to get to the rear of the Suebi. How many warriors they were approaching was hard to tell, but they were enough for Drestan's force to be hopelessly outmatched. He looked at both of his sons next to him. Elsed had his sword drawn, eager to get at the enemy. Morcant, dressed in his white druid tunic, clutched a long spear he usually only used in self-defense.

"Time for you to fall back!" he told his younger son, who had come for his ability to save lives as a field medic, not to fight.

Their three thousand strong force crashed into the rear of the unsuspecting enemy and created havoc. He briefly saw Aina fighting close by and his son-in-law Bradan on the far side of Elsed before a Suebi fighter left him no time to worry. He cut through as many enemies as he could before the cluster of riders and horses blocked his way. He had hoped to see the main Aedui army beyond them by now but realized it had been false hope. *There must be twenty thousand or more German warriors between us.*

The Suebi quickly rallied against the attack hitting their rear, and Drestan saw more and more Aedui warriors taken down. With a heavy heart he made the decision to disengage. They would either fight another day or all perish. "Sound the retreat!" he shouted at the next man he saw with a carnyx tied to his saddle. With the call sounding, his warriors tried to get away, though many were cut down while turning their horses.

Drestan managed to break loose and looked to the side. He spotted Aina's husband in trouble and guided his horse in Bradan's direction. The young man's steed had been killed, and though he was still in the fight, his side was bleeding heavily. Drestan rode right into the Suebi combatant Bradan had struggled with and slashed downward with his sword. He pulled his son-in-law up until Drestan could hold on to one of the saddle horns and they rode west, away from the Suebi.

Some of the enemy pursued them, breaking off to turn back only after a couple of hours had passed. As soon as the Germans were out of sight, Drestan raised his hand to signal for the group to stop. His son-in-law let go of the saddle and massaged his cramping hands and arms. Aina jumped off her horse to check on him. "How does he look?" Drestan asked.

"It's a long cut, but not overly deep," his daughter replied, trying to make light of the circumstances. "I'll tease him soon enough about the scar he'll have from today."

Drestan scanned the familiar faces. He felt helpless. Waves of sadness and frustration rolled through him. Most of his people's expressions were solemn. *My family is dying out there.*

They walked towards a small wood, where the wounded could rest to catch their breath. Morcant was in his element now, administering first aid, cleaning and stitching wounds. "Whoever is able and willing, come back with me towards Magetobriga. We will see if there is anything left to do."

Drestan collected about fifteen hundred warriors and rode back to within sight of the captured town. From there, he watched the still raging battle from afar and sent scouting parties to take a closer look.

The gravity of it all started to sink in. The battle was lost, and with it the forces that had been trapped. *I know my father and my brothers will soon be dead if they are not already, fighting to the death rather than surrender like some of the younger warriors will. They won't become slaves of the Germans or the Sequani.*

Drestan kept his force in place until late into the night when they collected wounded survivors from the forest's edge, who'd hidden during the day and waited till after sundown to escape. Those warriors confirmed his worst fears. *The great and proud host of the Aedui is no more.*

SECUNDUS

Temet Nosce (Know Thyself)

"A bad peace is worse than war."

Cornelius Tacitus, Annales, book III

692 AUC (62 BC), fall
Rome, Italia, Capital of the Roman Republic

The ancient empires of the Mediterranean have vanished, or are shadows of their former selves," the tutor lectured. "Some have been conquered by the Senate and People of Rome, others are dependent on Roman help. In this year six hundred sixty-four after the founding of this glorious city, few regions are independent. Can you name the most important former powers I've told you about?"

"There is Macedonia, the heart of Alexander the Great's empire," ten-year-old Caesar answered.

"Good. What happened to it?"

He turned his head to follow the old Greek man's glance. His father stood at the back of the atrium. Gaius Julius senior's presence was the reason for an impromptu quiz.

"We conquered it sixty years ago. Macedonia is now a Roman province, and Graecia, the Hellenistic mainland, is a protectorate," young Caesar answered.

The tutor's glance moved on to his two sisters, keeping one eyebrow up in expectation. Julia major, Caesar's two years older sister, started to speak. "Egypt is another ancient power. The ruling family there are descendants of Ptolemy, who was a general for Alexander the Great. They have been killing each other over the throne for generations. We have arbitrators at their court to help them stay nice to each other. As a thank you they gifted Cyprus and Cyrenaica to Rome."

The old tutor cackled in response. "I am sure they only feel gratitude to the Roman Senate." The man pursed his lips to look serious again. Caesar knew he did that because of his father. Though a household slave, their tutor was usually strongly opinionated. "Julia minor, can you tell me about another big power? How about one that used to rival the might of Rome itself?"

Caesar's one year older sister Julia minor's face lit up when she realized she knew the answer. "You mean mighty Carthago! They felt threatened by us and started the first war by attacking without warning. They hurt us then, but we beat them in the second war, and all their territories in Hispania became Roman, as did Sardinia and Sicilia. Much later, our Senate declared the third war after the Carthaginians collected a Numidian army, and because Cato pleaded to the senators. We won, and our army razed the city, sold the people as slaves, and salted the fields so there would never be another Carthago to threaten us."

"Very good!" The old tutor beamed, patting his bald pate with his left hand in excitement. "One more. Tell me about another ancient power, one that is still powerful today, though farther away from Rome than the others. Anybody?"

Young Caesar broke the silence. "The kingdom of Parthia?"

"That's the one. It was called Persia when the three hundred Spartans made their stand. What are the three ancient heartlands of Parthia?"

"I think you mean Sumer, Akkad, and Babylonia," Caesar said with raised eyebrows, proud to be able to show off his knowledge.

"That's right, son," Caesar senior cut in from the back. "The Parthians have ignored us Romans for a long time. I know from Senate business about their problems in the east where nomadic tribes often invade."

Young Caesar watched his tutor closely and noticed a slight hardening of the man's face at the mention of the Senate. He knew his tutor's views and was impressed with the displayed self-control. He had overheard an impassioned conversation in the street close to their home, during which his teacher had freely discussed his opinions about Roman rule outside of Italia, talking of Roman governors as corrupt rulers with absolute powers, and of the Roman Republic as a once honorable institution long rotten from the inside. The conquering or governing of new provinces was the ultimate opportunity for personal enrichment, with the senate members masking it all by invoking the glory of Rome.

His father continued from the back of the room. "We've had many military successes that grew our small republic in the last two hundred years. I have a trick question for you, though. What do we call what used to be the Mare Internum?"

"Mare Nostrum!" all three children shouted at the same time. Caesar knew that name to be true. With most of its coastal regions Roman or at least dependent, the inner sea had aptly been renamed to Our Sea. Deep in thought, Caesar watched his father walk out. He knew the lesson was supposed to show the glory and power of Rome, but he had seen a different moral, one from the opposing point of view, and it had seemed crystal clear.

He woke up with a start, realizing immediately that he had overslept. He swung his feet over the edge of his bed to get ready for his meeting with Crassus. How fitting that he would dream of that childhood day from so long ago. The epiphany still seemed as appropriate now as ever and had guided him out from dark times. *Stay independent and powerful by any means necessary, or others will walk all over you.*

***

Caesar looked from Marcus Licinius Crassus to the new arrival who had just been brought to his study. He dismissed his majordomo and the six Senate bodyguards given to him for his position as praetor. The target of his gaze, young Publius Claudius Pulcher, was a very recent political ally and the newly appointed leader of the Populares faction's gang of brawlers. The man's style was flawless; his dark-blonde hair coiffed in fine waves, perfectly plucked eyebrows, and blackened eyelashes. The toga he wore somehow shined, the folds immaculate down to every crease. Caesar cared about his own looks, but he knew he and Crassus were amateurs in comparison to this man.

"Publius, sit down. Let's discuss what needs to be done next."

Claudius Pulcher took the chair opposite Caesar, nodding to Crassus. "Gaius, Marcus, thanks to both of you I'm still a free man. Without your help at my trial last week, Cicero would have eaten me alive. I just wanted you to know I am aware of how deeply in your debt I am. I will stick with you and the Populares as far as we can go. Especially you, Caesar, I cannot thank enough, considering..."

"That it was in my house and that you were after Pompeia, my own wife? With both my mother and sister present?" he cut in. "I do hope you will never forget my leniency in the matter and that your support will pay me back tenfold in years to come." He made a show of moving his face close to a small vase of white roses on the desk, smelling their sweet scent in silence.

Pulcher was a man of huge appetites and well known for his public sexual escapades with both men and women, trumped only by an unquenchable thirst for violence. His latest vice was unbounded hatred toward his former ally Marcus Tullius Cicero. Claudius Pulcher had loyally supported the man and the Boni of the Optimates faction for years, until Cicero backstabbed him over this Bona Dea scandal when named official prosecutor for the case. Pulcher had stood accused of entering the most important religious women-only rites for reasons of sexual conquest. As was customary, the Bona Dea festivities were held in the residence of the current Pontifex Maximus, namely Julius Caesar, and led by his own mother and wife.

"Cicero didn't dare mention Pompeia as your target," Caesar finally said. "We should be glad for that." That intention might have been deemed plausible, though the tight focus on intended incest with Pulcher's sister had been too much for the court to believe.

"I am very sad I caused you to divorce last week. I want to repeat that she knew nothing of my intentions, and that she would have likely denied my advances."

"Don't worry too much about that. You might have done me a favor there." His marriage to Pompeia had been one of convenience. Attractive, of ancient lineage and a granddaughter of Sulla, she had seemed like the perfect match after Cornelia's passing. The union had also worked well to stop many of Sulla's old allies from shaking their fists at him.

Love, however, had never entered their relationship. "I told the Senate that Pompeia never had nor ever would commit infidelity. When some of the senators asked me why I had divorced her, I told them that a wife of Caesar always needs to be above suspicion." His comment had resulted in many chuckles and some outright laughter since he had gained a reputation as womanizer. "Anyway, it was Marcus's money that saved you. My words might have helped, but ultimately it came down to him buying the jury."

Now Caesar looked at Crassus. "And speaking of thanks, you will always have my eternal gratitude for helping me finance my elections as Pontifex Maximus and praetor this year. Without your deep coffers, neither of us would be sitting here with you." Caesar grinned. "Especially considering the issue with Silanus."

Decimus Junius Silanus had not forgiven him for going against his brother Marcus when the man had been governor of Asia province, publicly condemning Caesar for his capture of the pirates and the resulting aftermath. Silanus ended up throwing a lot of money at the opposition.

He looked back at Pulcher. "But you have to promise to say nothing about Crassus's involvement. Not to anybody, you hear me? The longer it will take the Optimates to figure out that he's no longer in their camp, the better."

"Of course, I understand. That goes without saying."

"Good. Now it's time to work towards our bigger goals. Marcus and I want you to use the Populares legionary veterans as nucleus for a much bigger fighting force. Most of Sulla's old veterans have left the Optimates brawlers. Our enemies brought in hordes of slaves as replacement, armed them with bludgeons and promised freedom and money. They've been no threat so far, but they're also trying to recruit gladiators. That means it might get hard to keep the upper hand. Are you up for that, Publius?"

He received a decisive nod. "Absolutely, we'll show them who rules the streets," Pulcher responded with a predatorial grin. After all, street brawling was the man's favorite pastime.

"Good. My goal is to ask the Senate to give me one of the Hispania provinces for next year when I am propraetor. I may need help from you and the men to cower the opposition." He did not expect smooth sailing and was glad that Pulcher nodded eagerly in response.

Caesar handed him a long papyrus roll. "Alright, you know what's needed. Here are all the names of the veterans that have shown special loyalty and might like to join you. Please, check in in a few days and let me know if you need anything else." Caesar stood to grasp Pulcher's arm in goodbye and watched him leave.

"What's in it for him? I mean, what does Claudius Pulcher want next?" Crassus asked after the man was gone.

"He wants revenge on Cicero, pure and simple. It's all he can think about right now, and that's why he threw in with us and the Populares."

Crassus laughed. "Revenge? Well, we can certainly work with that. That means Claudius will give it his all when it comes to blocking Cicero and friends in the Senate." He looked back at Caesar, and they shared vicious grins.

"Our glorious plans are unfolding nicely." Caesar stood up and walked to the doorway. "Bring us some wine!" He turned back to Crassus. "Let's toast to our success, current and future."

692 AUC (62 BC), spring
Outside of Oaxos, Crete, Roman Province of Crete et Cyrene

Nico rotated his sling at high speed above his head. He took his time, aiming carefully. The stone hit the whicker target with a loud whack.

"Put that away, brother, and use your bow instead," Penthylos chided him. "If you want to sign on with the Romans you better concentrate on your archery."

Cretan younger male siblings trained from childhood with a traditional double-convex bow, the island's claim to fame in the known world and beyond. Made from a combination of wood, animal horn, tendons, sinew, and glue, they were similar to the eastern bows except for the specific wood used. Native Cretan Beech was very hard yet remained very flexible. This exceptional quality gave good range at a length easily manageable for deployment from horseback.

Archers from Crete had gone out into the world as mercenaries since time immemorial. Even the Macedonian legend, Alexander the Great, had Cretan archers to help him fight his way to India. And now, for the last hundred years or more, the Romans routinely hired from the island. If the archers came back home, they were rich enough to buy big farms or even estates. Of course, many never came back, either dying or settling in foreign lands.

"I guess you are right, brother. I left it in my room." They walked back to their parent's farmhouse, past sheep being herded to the foothills for grazing, a big new shed for cheese making, groves of olives in the middle of harvest, and a sheep shearing station that also housed spinning wheels to turn threads into wool.

After losing Timon, he had made up his mind to come home to Oaxos, at least for a while. He knew he could never go back to slave trading; his experience had opened his eyes. Slaves often were normal people down on their luck. *And no person should be treated without respect. This, I know now, deep in my soul.*

Since there was barely enough work here to support his older brothers and their big families, he had restarted his weapons training with the goal of signing up with the Romans. Penthylos had agreed to help him procure the best horse his savings would allow.

He glanced at his brother with a wistful smile on his lips and patted the weapon at his hip. A sheath was hanging from a long leather strap worn over the opposite shoulder. "I still can't believe you sold me your beautiful sword for half the price you paid yourself."

"Don't worry, Nico. You know I would never use it now that I have Eupraxia and the children. My dreams of foreign battles are long over."

Nico put his hand on his brother's shoulder in gratitude. As they approached the house, seven of his young nieces and nephews came running at them, chasing each other, laughing and screaming. Nico smiled and relaxed. For now, he would simply enjoy being at home and surrounded by friendly faces, until it was time to ship out to wherever the fates had decided for him.

693 AUC (61 BC), early spring
Corduba, Capital of Roman Province Hispania Ulterior

"I'm glad you could join me so quickly," Caesar told his young friend Aulus Hirtius. As usual during the last year, they walked in the midst of his six lictors. Most of his assigned bodyguards had become trusted friends.

It was a cool spring morning, and Caesar tightened his comfortable purple-striped senatorial toga against the chill as they walked down narrow streets in the provincial capital to reach the governor's mansion. He did not look forward to frequently wearing armor again. No need to cut out the small niceties just yet.

"Especially considering my rather hasty departure," he continued. He had needed to leave Rome before his official service time as praetor was over. One of his less savory creditors had lost patience with him, threatening to sue for payment the moment the immunity he enjoyed as a public official staying inside of Rome's city limits was over. Caesar excused his illegal flight with false news of calls for help from Roman allies in Hispania. Crassus stepping in at the last minute as guarantor for a portion of the debt had helped, but his financial situation was still disastrous.

"I'm well and truly beyond bankrupt. My debt was still manageable to a degree when I became Aedile of Rome.

Four years ago, the position of Aedile had helped him build a broad platform of public support. The two aedile city magistrates were responsible for upkeep of roads, temples, public buildings, and grain and food for the masses. Most important, though, was the organization of gladiatorial games. "But when I financed the games without my co-Aedile Marcus Bibulus, it got out of control."

Hirtius laughed. Caesar had certainly gained the adoration of the masses for breaking the record for the number of gladiators in a single season. "Well, did you really have to bring in a full three hundred and twenty pairs?"

With only a small budget allotted from the Senate, Caesar's resulting personal debt load would have crushed any less well-connected man. "You should know by now that I don't do things halfway. That includes my campaign for praetor for last year." That election had added significantly to his already lofty tally.

"Now that we are here, I hope you'll get the chance to make some money. You can count on my help, you know you are family to me." Hirtius paused as they walked by a throng of traders moving goods to the market. "At least get Papirius off your back. That man is insufferable, you should never have asked him for money."

They walked up to their offices, and Caesar paused in front of the doorway. "I was desperate, as you well know. Can you please bring Gaius Antistius Vetus into my office?"

Vetus was his officially assigned quaestor for the year and had just arrived in Corduba. Caesar wanted him to help review all financial documentation and all official missives for local and Hispania-wide issues, as well as anything pertaining to current legal matters. Hopefully, the young man would find something, anything, he could use as excuse for military action in or around his province. With a pang of guilt for overriding his moral values, Caesar motioned the approaching Vetus into his office. "Come in, come in! I hope you had breakfast and a good night's sleep. We have a long day ahead of us."

***

The morning of the next day, Caesar felt tired and sullen on his way to his office. He had wrestled with his conscience for most of the night. *In the end, my need for money overrides any other concerns. This is a matter of survival.*

"Ah, good morning," he greeted Hirtius upon arrival. "Let's go through what's needed today. First, we'll write official dispatches to the Senate to tell them that there's public unrest in both Lusitani and Callaeci lands, and that the nations there are moving towards open rebellion. Second, we'll ask around for names of local magistrates and businessmen we can strong-arm into corroborating our story. We need them to send their own messages to various Roman senators."

"Rome fought the Lusitani a few times before, right? Are they still a worthwhile target for us?" Hirtius asked.

"We fought them in the decades leading up to the second Punic war, which is close to a hundred years ago. Then, a second time after Proconsul Sertorius rallied them after he fled from Sulla."

Winning against Sertorius and his successor was what had cemented the rising star of Gnaeus Pompeius and made him into a much-lamented thorn in Crassus's side.

"If you consider that the Lusitani and their northern neighbors, the Callaeci, were left in charge and always paid their tribute to Rome on time, then yes, I believe there is still much to gain there." Caesar stood up and closed the door to his office.

"I should have done that earlier. So, here are my plans. I will take the Eighth and Ninth legions westward past the borders of Hispania Ulterior, towards the free tribes of the Celtici and Cunei. Before we leave, I will send word to the new governor of Hispania Citerior, asking for the Seventh to march towards Lusitania. I made an arrangement with him to borrow the legion, let's hope that he honors it. The trickiest part of all these plans is the time constraint. To wrap up any action against the Lusitani and the Callaeci in my single year of service will be very tight, even after adding the Seventh to our Eighth and Ninth legions." His face relaxed and he grinned at his old friend. Hirtius was hanging on his every word. "As propraetor, I am entitled to recruit new legions when the need arises. That need has now arisen. I want you to organize the recruitment for a tenth legion."

"A tenth legion? Has Rome ever had a Tenth?"

"No, it's the first time we're past nine. We're making history." Hirtius grinned right back at him, and they savored the moment. "For recruiting, I want you to focus on local Roman and Italian colony towns first, to speed up the process. I will also send word back to Rome to raise a few Italian cohorts, but they won't be able to join the new Tenth for a few months."

They both stood up and headed towards the door when Hirtius briefly paused. "I can't wait to get started. Many Roman towns I should visit are popping into my head. I have to get back to my desk to write it all down." He grasped hands with his mentor.

"Also, make a list of the staff you want for the recruitment process, and we'll meet again tomorrow to talk about the budget." Caesar's eyes stayed on his excited friend as he walked out the office and down the hallway. *No way out. I need to do this.*

693 AUC (61 BC), spring
Scalabis, Roman Headquarter for Lusitania, Hispania

"Aulus Hirtius, the man of the hour. It is good to have you back," Caesar called out to his friend entering his tent. Two months had passed since their last face to face meeting. They moved close and clasped arms in greeting.

"I just collected the last of the local new recruits," Hirtius said. "I brought a total of six plus a half-strength first cohort. That's all we'll have until the men from Italia show up." His friend's expression changed from his usual self-assuredness to something resembling uncertainty. "I had hoped to be here at least three days earlier, but one of our new centurions was overeager with the last squads and their final test. He had them start the obligatory march, you know, twenty-four miles and loaded with forty-five pounds of extra gear, in full sunshine on a scorching hot day. That by itself was fine, but he decided to forgo any of the usual water breaks. By the end of the day, close to half of the boys had dropped along the way. To add insult to injury, he wanted to wash them all out. After we rushed them all through basic training. That idiot!"

"So, what did you do?" Caesar asked with a flat face.

"I told him he was demoted back to decanus. He started to protest, and I shut him up by stating that if he's not happy about it, I'd gladly recommend a dishonorable discharge for him."

Caesar saw his friend's questioning glance. He held back his approval as long as he could, keeping his face stony before bursting out in laughter. "Thank you. Once again you show me what a good and capable friend you are." Affectionally, he put his hand on Hirtius's shoulder. "Let's go to the table, I need to bring you up to speed about our campaign."

After sitting down, Caesar continued. "As you know, I marched the Eighth and Ninth out to the territories of the Celtici and Cunei. They have no love for the Lusitani. We were welcomed with open arms, at least until I met with their leaders and told them of the new and favorable terms they could expect as direct subjects of the Senate and People of Rome." Caesar paused dramatically.

"I take it they did not like the terms?"

"The terms were not the problem. Some of the older chieftains were afraid what the Lusitani would do to them. They didn't believe me when I told them there was nothing to be worried about on that account. They refused to budge, so I decided to approach some of the more eager, younger chiefs in private. They listened and we have treaties with both tribes now. They made a show of good faith, bringing me many personal gifts, both valuable goods and gold. Oh, and some of the older chieftains aren't in power anymore." He grinned. "It's a good start toward my debt. I sent it all back under guard to the Governor's palace in Corduba. I'll take it with me when I come through there on my way back to Rome."

"That's all welcome news. We have the Eighth and Ninth, most of the new Tenth, and the Seventh is on its way, right?" Hirtius said.

"Yes, the Seventh should be close, following the Tagus river across Hispania." Caesar paused, adding a dramatic sigh. "I had reports yesterday that all Roman traders have been banned from

Lusitanian towns. That means the Lusitani won't be push-overs, and the easy part is done with." *I can't help but feel bad over what we're about to do.*

"We'll hit them as hard as necessary. It shouldn't escalate too badly if we move before they can combine forces against us."

"I hope so. I already sent out cavalry and scouts towards the Seventh. Once word travels back they met, we will start to roll up the clans and their hill towns one by one."

693 AUC (61 BC), early summer
Along the banks of the Tagus river in Lusitania, Hispania

The Ninth had received a sizable contingent of fresh horses, and the Cretan auxiliary unit had changed from a mix of foot and horse to exclusively mounted. Nico, now nineteen, was part of a combined group under the leadership of Quintus Titurius Sabinus, the cavalry prefect of the Ninth. The force consisted of some of the legions' Celtic cavalry, Roman equites scouts, and all the Ninth's Cretan archers.

He rode up to Andrippos, first decurion of the Cretans, as they came over the ridge of a hill just north of the Tagus river. "What exactly is our mission, oh fearless leader?" He felt at ease asking since the man had always been friendly to him. They hadn't been given any details since their morning call to ride out.

"Ah, young Nico. Sorry about keeping you in the dark, but I had orders to keep quiet. Caesar didn't want the legions to talk about stuff where it could be overheard by the wrong ears." He cleared his throat. "Our mission is to watch for any movement of the Lusitani along the Tagus river, while we travel to meet the Seventh legion. They are marching to Lusitania along the embankments from the other side of Hispania. We will always leave a few men as scouts when we pass the major tribes." They had already done so a few hours ago in the lands of the Elbocori. "They'll report back to Scalabis if there is any change, otherwise they'll wait until the legions march out."

"Do you know what the next people are called?" Nico asked.

"They are the Tapori," Andrippos answered. "Next, we'll be in the lands of the Igaeditani, and then the Celtic federations of the Calontienses and Caluri. Those are unrelated to the Lusitani and could be friendlier; I don't think so, but we'll see." He raised his right hand to ward off more questions. "Beside hearing their names in a briefing this morning, I know nothing about them," he continued while chuckling.

Though the Lusitani were people proud of an ancient heritage supposedly unrelated to the Celts, from what Nico could tell the differences seemed superficial. As they rode by several villages, he saw slightly darker hair and complexion, and many of the men favored a longer hair style, though he also saw fewer women warriors, which possibly indicated less cultural equality compared to the Celts. Though back in Crete, women fighters where indeed the rarest of marvels. The Greek world as a whole had few ancient heroines, usually from Sparta and Athens, and some female mythical demigods. Children grew up with tales of the all-female Amazons, though they were from outside the Hellenistic world as well as ancient enemies.

"After we meet the Seventh legion and hand over Caesar's orders to its legate, I will lead our Ninth's turmae back to the Igaeditani to wait there for the Ninth to catch up. As I understand it, all four legions are supposed to head north in parallel, with the Tenth closest to the coast, followed by our Ninth, and the Eighth and Seventh farther inland. I guess going separate might speed things up, but I hope the legions can move quickly to help each other if things get dicey."

Nico looked at his pondering superior and saw real worry. All he had known so far was the seemingly unbeatable discipline and strategy of the Roman legions and the legionaries' boasting of a long list of glorious Roman victories, though he knew there must have been disasters as well. He hoped their Ninth would only ever add to the list of victories.

He could see their prefect Sabinus raising his hand up ahead, calling for a short break. Some of the scouts moved out to keep watch, while everybody else dismounted, tying the horses to hedges at the edge of a small stand of trees. Most of the Cretans sat down together on a few big rocks in the middle of a field of wildflowers, and Nico and Andrippos walked over to join them.

"As far as I can tell, everything hinges on our new governor. We all swore loyalty to him, but what kind of man is he? Have you met Julius Caesar?" Nico asked once seated.

"Yes, in meetings, though only twice, and I didn't get to talk to him directly. Everything I know is second-hand." Andrippos glanced back at him and shrugged. "That said, I might have heard enough. The man is extreme in many ways, but also cultured and highly intelligent. I could tell he was well educated just from how he talks. When he made comments in Greek, he sounded as if he'd been raised in a wealthy household in Athens." Nico looked around to find that Andrippos had gathered quite an audience. Other Cretans were observing, and many had stood up to get closer.

Andrippos smiled at the gathered men and continued. "The man is considered a war hero. He was awarded a Civic Crown after he fought at the siege of Mytilene on Lesbos twenty years ago. I heard that's a rare honor to receive, so it's likely that he is a good leader that holds up under pressure. Let's see, there's one other truly notable thing I've heard—Caesar is fanatical about his word. I mean, he keeps it whenever he gives it or promises something, no matter the cost. That must be a huge exception for politicians, and especially a high-ranking Roman like he is." Andrippos chuckled, while many of them men burst into roaring laughter.

Klearistos, Nico's squad leader, cut through the laughter. "But what does that mean for us? That he is a truly good man?"

"Maybe he is a believer in stoicism," Nico threw in.

"I don't know about that, or if he is a good person," Andrippos answered. "All I know is that he goes to extreme lengths to hold his word, that he considers it the only currency that matters. Let me give you an example. Many of you know the story of how he was captured by pirates a few years back." Nico saw several people nod. "Nothing special, considering how many people get taken and ransomed all the time. However, you all know about Caesar's encounter with the pirates because he told them he was worth a lot more than they were asking for, am I right?" Again, more nods, and murmurs of agreement. "That is the story that spread fast and wide. There is a lesser known part to this, and much more extreme. I doubt many know about it." Andrippos added a dramatic pause before making his point.

"I heard this from one of Aulus Hirtius's men, and Hirtius was with Caesar when this all happened. Our governor told the pirates throughout his captivity that he would come back for them once he was free, and that he would crucify them all. They always laughed, thinking he was joking, but the same day he was freed he raised a small army in Miletus and captured them." Andrippos looked back at his fellow archers, all hanging on his every word. "He brought them to Pergamum, the capital of Asia province, where they went straight to jail. Next, he sent word to governor Silanus, who was away on campaign, asking for permission to crucify the pirates as he had promised. The governor wrote back, outright forbidding any action in his absence. Now comes the extreme part." He paused again, taking a sip from his water skin.

"Despite a clear order to the contrary, Caesar did what he had brought the pirates to Pergamum for. He lied to the jailors, saying he had clearance from the governor to do as he pleased, and had all the pirates crucified that same day. He stayed true to his word, but at what cost? He incurred the wrath of the governor, who had many strong and powerful allies in Rome.

"The Senate officially rebuked him for his apparent disregard of authority."

After a moment of silence, several people started talking to each other at the same time. "So, he always does what he promises," Nico, closest to Andrippos, said.

The first decurion raised his hand for quiet. "I believe that Caesar meant every word he said at the swearing-in ceremony. That we'll face hardships serving with him, but that he would also always look out for us. And that he's someone I would not want angry at me. Ever."

"I'd still prefer a liar and cheat ruling over a peaceful province letting us enforce the law or repair streets over an honest governor leading us into war," Nico said, earning everybody's laughter.

"I think most of us much prefer that, my boy." Andrippos said.

Nico stood up to stretch and glanced around. Elatos sat off to the side by himself, and Nico decided to walk over. The shy young man had given him a wide smile from afar late yesterday. He briefly hesitated, the loss of Timon still weighing on him from time to time. *It's been two years. Time for me to move on, and Elatos seems nice.*

As Nico walked up, he saw the same wide smile appear again. He grinned back, enjoying the moment.

693 AUC (61 BC), summer
Clusium, Etruria, Italia

Her older brother carefully noted the amount of money he had just dropped into a small lockbox in their bakery ledger. Velia Churinas was glad she had talked her father into buying the papyrus needed. Having a running tally had already proven helpful well beyond recouping expenses. She picked up a loaf of bread from the cooling rack and put it into the bag she carried.

"Is it alright if Velia and I go see our friends now?" Numerius asked.

Spurius looked at his fifteen-year-old son from behind his cooling racks. "Did you finish all your deliveries?"

"Yes father, except for the one to Lethie's family. I'll give that to her mother when we get there," Velia said. Her idea for a morning bread delivery service had helped the bakery survive these last few years. "Numerius finished updating the ledger, and the money from this morning is in your box."

Their father walked over to hug them both and watched them leave. They would pick up Lethie, Velia's best friend, and go meet Vibius, Numerius's best friend, at the courtyard of their tutor's insula. Some years earlier, their father had managed to find a friendly teacher willing to add a couple of older children to his small school in exchange for free daily bread. Velia and her brother had eagerly taken to it, becoming fluent readers and writers while making new friends.

She followed her brother across the street over the pedestrian crossing, happily skipping on the stone blocks that were raised above the street surface to keep pedestrian shoes away from the muck and left-over dung of the previous night's delivery cart animals.

"Vibius told me that signing up as a legionary would give me full Roman citizenship. Which extends to all my close family," Numerius said. "I think I should join with him when he enlists."

"He's been talking about signing up since he was eleven. I thought he would have grown out of it by now. What's the normal recruiting age?" Velia asked.

"You could join really young as a camp laborer, but the normal age for soldiers is eighteen. But Vibius doesn't want to wait that long, he wants to enlist two years from now, when we're seventeen. He figures that's old enough for them to take us."

Velia hated the idea of her brother becoming a soldier, leaving her and father alone, to fight and probably die in some foreign country. *I have two years left to talk him out of it. I better figure out how.*

693 AUC (61 BC), summer
Northern lands of the Igaeditani, Hispania

The Ninth moved away from the Tagus river, northwards through wooded hills, until it reached a long stretch of medium-sized mountains running north and slightly east. The legion's long marching line stretched out at the bottom of the foothills. Occasionally, small cavalry units were sent to scout the passes. Some of the legion's scouts had the unenviable job of finding ways across the mountains to keep communications open with the Tenth to the west, while the scouts heading east for the Eighth rode across easily passable flat plains. As the Ninth continued to head for the lands of people known to the Romans as the Lancienses Transcudani, a much taller group of mountains became visible on the horizon. Every day, they reached ever higher into the sky, white-capped peaks reaching above the clouds.

Balventius shared the slightly raised catwalk of the west facing wall with several other noncommissioned officers. The beautiful landscape was painted in shades of orange and pink by a stunning sunset. The few clouds and snowy peaks were lighted by a sun sinking early behind the mountains. After camp building and the evening's roll calls, the officers all had a little time on their hands.

"Seppius, what do you think? Will we have to climb some of these?" Balventius asked his friend while pointing north.

"I hope not, but if I know our lady Fortuna, it's likely we will have to. Tribune Marcus Crassus said that his scouts found fertile valleys with towns in these mountains, and fortifications that let the Transcudani cover passes and approaches. If I were them, and if I were to make a stand against us, I would have all the clans of the area collect their food reserves and hurry in. They could create good choke points to pick us off when we attack."

"Well, I hope they are not you, Seppius," Balventius replied with a chuckle. "But I agree, the easy part is behind us. The Igaeditani weren't ready for us, that surrender was entirely too easy. Though I won't complain about our growing stash of plunder."

Balventius glanced down along the wall. About fifty feet away, Capussia and Andrippos slowly made their way over, stopping for a short time here and there to greet Numidian and Cretan sentries on wall duty, and a few other centurions and optios out and about to enjoy the view. The bond built with the two foreigners during the siege of their camp by the Celtici three years earlier had held and evolved into a strong friendship.

"Ah, Titus Balventius. And Gaius Seppius, was it?" The young legate of the Ninth spoke up from behind, surprising them both. They turned, nodding respectfully to Publius Vatinius, who continued. "Nice balmy evening, right? Before long, I'm afraid the evenings will get rather chilly." Their commander looked them over with a critical eye. "You've seen real action before this year's campaigning, correct?"

"That's right, sir," Balventius answered. "We've done some fighting against the Celtici."

"Then what do you think of our deployment so far? You must agree that it has been quite successful. I can't believe we Romans left these people to themselves for several years," he added, smiling.

"I would not know about that last part, sir. I'm afraid it's been easy because we haven't run into any real resistance yet. I fear that we'll find that soon. The northern tribes have had plenty of warning by now," Balventius said with a serious look on his face. He couldn't make himself like their commander. Vatinius was too smooth and slick, and his easy smile felt too false, never reaching the man's eyes.

"That may be, centurion, that may be. We will overcome that as well, though, won't we?" the legate responded lightly. Balventius nodded, still unflinchingly showing his serious face. The legate frowned and stepped back. *I hope he finally realizes we don't care for his small talk.* Vatinius looked past them and frowned in sudden recognition, his nostrils distending. "I bid you good night," he said, turned around and walked away.

Balventius turned around to find Capussia and Andrippos close by. "I think he saw you approaching, that's why he left so quickly. The man despises Barbarians, even the ones that work for him."

"Was that our esteemed legate? He's too full of himself by far." Andrippos chuckled. "I'm quite happy he left before we arrived."

"You don't know the half of it. Tribune Marcus Crassus told me last week that Vatinius was accused by Consul Cicero of extortion and bribery, after serving as quaestor under him three years ago. Just last year, he was accused again for a second time when he served as legate under Praetor Cosconius. Listening to his smooth talk makes me believe that he's as guilty and corrupt as they come. I don't know why Caesar took him on," Seppius said.

Capussia narrowed his eyes in contemplation. "Maybe Caesar knows something important about the man that we don't?"

Considering that possibility, they all mused about what that might be. Their eyes followed the legate as he slowly talked his way through the other centurions before taking the short steps down from the wall.

693 AUC (61 BC), summer
Southeast of Stella Mountain range, lands of the Lancienses Transcudani, Hispania

A couple of weeks later, the legion had reached the foot of the tall and looming mountains. On the way, they had passed many abandoned settlements, including some big Oppida, local fortified hill towns. Seppius's prediction about the local clans gathering had proven true. The legion's string of good luck would have to run out at some point.

"Have you heard the troops are calling these impressive peaks the Stella mountains?" Seppius asked while the two walked to an early morning meeting in front of the legate's tent, at the camp's center crossroads.

"I heard that name comes from the locals. You are supposed to be able to touch the lights in the night sky from the two tallest peaks," Balventius answered. They both laughed at the ridiculous thought.

They arrived at the tent to find most of the Ninth's staff already assembled. All cohort prefects, centurions, and optios, tribunes, camp prefect, their cavalry prefect, as well as the auxilia's first and second decurions were now present. Close to a hundred men stood around and waited for their commander. The hungry officer's mouths were watering as the smell of fresh-baked bread reached them from countless portable clay ovens around them. They had all left their tents too early for breakfast.

When Legatus Vatinius deigned to show, he walked right into their midst and cleared his throat loudly, silencing several personal conversations.

"The scouts are very clear on the enemy's situation. The Lancienses people as a whole have chosen to resist us, and their Transcudani clans are all rallying inside these mountains." He pointed north. "It's a perfectly defendable setup for them. There is only one decent pass in from the South, cutting through two massive high tableaus that have their toughest fortifications. There is also at least one more pass into the valleys from the north, possibly two, towards the northern end of the mountain range. We have identified a possible approach through a ravine in the east, but the scouts say the locals have started to build a wall to close it off. That's it, no other obvious weaknesses. If we approach from the north, they can fight a retreat from their valley towns all the way up to the high flats." He looked around the group. "Any recommendations?"

Interesting, without the fake smile on his lips, he looks like he's constantly scowling. Balventius looked into the round, wondering who would speak up first. It was young Tribune Marcus Licinius Crassus. "Do we know if there are any goat paths going up? Something we could use to flank them with a cohort or two?"

The Ninth cavalry commander, a young man in his late twenties named Quintus Titurius Sabinius, raised his hand. "If I may answer that? My scouts saw several paths up the sides to the high flats, but all of them are exposed. The southern part of these mountains is too high for much vegetation, except for around two big lakes on top of the plateaus. But, the peaks of the northern part of the mountains are much lower and stretched out and there're long patches of woods. We should look there for a possible way in."

"I second that. I think these people still put too much emphasis on guarding against cavalry forces. They will likely patrol the ridges to catch any scouts we might put up there, but they won't expect a big force in that direction," Tribune Crassus said. "Anyway, sounds like we should only keep a few cohorts south, to secure the lower part of the pass and keep any reinforcements and food supplies from going in. Could the Eighth legion give us support? Do we know their current situation?" Everybody looked at their legate for the answer.

"The Eighth is bogged down besieging a town housing the entire Lancienses Oppidani federation's council, close relations of the clans here," Vatinius replied. "Their legate believes he will get a full surrender from all other towns once he takes this one. He is planning an all-out assault, and if successful, he agreed to send us several cohorts. Until then, we will move north and leave a small force at the southern pass as suggested. Three cohorts should be enough to keep them from going in and out. The rest of us will keep moving north along the mountains' eastern side. We'll decide how to best take on the Transcudani once we know how many forces the Eighth can send us, and when." He stepped back and looked at his officers. "Any other questions? No? Dismissed!"

The meeting dispersed and Balventius and Seppius walked back in silence, both men deep in thought, until Balventius suddenly pointed at the tall peaks. "Your prediction about the locals moving into these mountains? I hate it when you're right." They both chuckled all the way back to their men.

693 AUC (61 BC), summer
Stella Mountains, southern pass, lands of the Lancienses
Transcudani, Hispania

Gaius Blandius was a simple legionary and part of a detachment of three cohorts sent to guard the southern pass leading into the high plateaus of what the Romans now called the Stella mountains.

"Isn't there a better place for this damn fort? Preferably somewhere that's already halfway level?" one of Blandius tent mates complained.

The legionaries of the Ninth's third and fourth cohorts were building a fortified encampment on the east side of the long incline leading to the enemy. They were well over a mile up the path from the main tree line, which gave them a good view of any reinforcements or food transports coming for the Transcudani, yet also a mile away from the closest defenders.

"Sure, there are lots of flat places farther below. Do you want to camp close to the woods? Where we don't see anybody coming?" Blandius answered, while dumping his basket of dirt onto the slowly rising rampart, soon to form the base of the western camp wall.

Everybody was aware of the enemy watching, and the men's armor and weapons were never far away. Blandius glanced up at the three turmae of mounted Cretan archers standing by on foot, ready to shower approaching enemies with arrows. He for one was grateful the Cretan archers were here. Their ability for close hand-to-hand combat might be needed before too long. In addition to bow and arrow, every one of the archers was equipped with a small bronze buckler and a long, single edged steel sword. Blandius admired the weapon for its forward curve, appropriately called a kopis in Greek, meaning chopper. He bent down with his spade, hitting the rocky ground hard with the tool's edge to loosen the dirt.

"At least you know we'll be here for a while," Blandius said. "No more camp building for a week or two, maybe more, and no marching! It'll be nice to have a break from that, and from lugging dirt every evening. I heard there's going to be a wait for reinforcements from the Eighth before the other cohorts will attack from the north." *That would make for a nice break from the routine.*

Blandius was one of the original recruits of the Ninth legion's first levy. His little hometown outside of Fidanae had nothing left for him after his mother's death, and the few friends he had grown up with had all long since fled the impoverished area. He sold all belongings and marched the twenty miles distance to the city of Rome to sign up with the legionary recruiters on Campus Martius. He had made the right choice: the Ninth legion had become his home, and he knew others respected him for his skills with the sword despite his blind right eye.

He had long since made his peace with his handicap, earned as a fresh recruit just after his arrival in Hispania. His centuria's training had included a mock battle with wooden training swords. Green as he had been, he had given his opponent a wide opening, promptly receiving a hit in the face as a reward. The other man's blade hat impacted his right eye with its blunt side, and the eye had swollen enough that the medicus insisted on draining and removing it. He had resisted, and the eye had reduced back to its normal size just in time, turning milky white in the middle of his brown iris and leaving him with blurry vision ever since.

Blandius and his squad worked in silence for a bit, until his spade broke. *The ground is just too damn hard.*

"Merda," he loudly swore, knowing that he wouldn't be able to have it replaced until after the camp was built. "Anybody know where our muleteers are with the baggage train?" he asked without hope for a reply. They were likely still hours away, guarded by the seventh cohort and a few artillery men from the First.

Blandius wiped his dark-blond hair from his forehead, unhappily resigning himself to carrying the wicker baskets of dirt for his comrades for the remainder of their building activities, until one of the two architecti on loan from the first cohort walked up to him.

"What have we here, a broken spade? You are in luck, soldier!" he said to Blandius, who still held the broken handle in his hand. "I'll loan you my very own tool." Blandius took the offered utensil.

"We should be done with this section in another hour or two, then your group can shift to terracing the inside of the fort. We'll need to level for the tents, or all you sorry lot will roll out of your tents at night to make a big heap at the southwestern corner." The soldiers in earshot laughed at the witty comment. The hillside was indeed steep, so a heap of sleepy legionaries rolling off was easy to imagine. The walls would mostly follow the natural incline, with all excavated dirt from the ditches in front of the walls being used, as always, to even out and elevate the wooden palisades themselves, and to level the uneven walkways behind. That would still leave the camp's inside surface with a strong decline that needed to be dealt with.

Blandius looked up when two of the buccinators blew their buccinae, the legion's long curved trumpets, signifying a short break. The buccinators, the other horn blowers, and the cohort standard bearers were all exempt from digging, and were currently standing around in the middle of the camp laughing, joking, and earning the legionaries' jealousy.

Loud sighs of relief were audible all around him. The sweaty and smelly soldiers gratefully dropped their dirt or shovels and hurried to their bags for water and food.

The men around Blandius chatted and ate, the mood light despite the hard work. He finished his water skin and put it back in his bag, wondering about getting a refill, when both the cornua and tubae blew. At first, he thought they were called back to work, then he realized it was a call to arms. The centurions and optios started to shout. Blandius glanced at the mountain side above their camp and held his breath in shock. The Transcudani at the top of the pass had suddenly moved into action. *They must have realized how vulnerable we are with the fort incomplete and waited for a break when even our Cretans were distracted.*

It looked like close to two thousand riders were already halfway down the distance to the Romans, with another roughly three thousand warriors chasing behind on foot. "Hurry!" he urged his squad on, swearing to himself while clumsily stuffing his remaining food back into his bag. More successful with his armor, he donned it in record time and moved to help others to get theirs secured faster.

All the readied soldiers ran as directed by the centurions who shouted "Ad Signa," gathering into battle lines in front of the respective century standards. The nearly one thousand legionaries formed into three ranks that covered the open stretch between the two main sections of finished ramparts, a distance of about eight hundred feet, and a few men on each end covered the sides to discourage enemies from trying to climb over the ramparts to outflank the rest. The archers spread out evenly behind the legionaries for support, with a few of their number walking the Cretans' horses over from the middle of the campsite to hold them at the ready.

***

Nico stood holding his bow when he heard shouting behind him. He turned to see their detachment's two engineers and their helpers run towards the forming line, each lugging a heavy leather sack. One of them shouted at Andrippos. "First decurion, have your men move these sacks up to the front! They need to get to the first row of legionaries as soon as possible. We will bring up more."

"You heard the man! Move the sacks forward!" Andrippos shouted. Nico rushed to put away his bow and carried a sack forward, careful not to get hurt by the many sharp metal tips poking through the heavy leather. He handed it to the third row of legionaries, which handed it to the second, until it arrived at the first line. There, the men shouted excitedly after emptying the contents on the ground. Each heavy sack contained twenty-some iron caltrops, devices made of two slightly bent and sharpened iron rods joined to create a structure that would always sit solidly on three of its tips, with the fourth pointed straight up. He'd seen these things in the armory but didn't know how they were supposed to work. He saw the legionaries pick up individual caltrops to throw them forward, creating a danger zone of twenty feet for the oncoming riders, who were now only a few hundred feet away.

He moved back in position next to his decurion Klearistos and waited for the next load of caltrops.

Andrippos shouted loudly, his voice carrying through the din. "Klearistos, once the front line is fully engaged, move your own turma back and mount up. Ride to the opening at the western side of the rampart and wait. Just stay there to block any of their cavalry deciding to flank us. Send word right away if you need help, understood?"

"Yes, Andrippos. We'll block the gap, and I'll send word if we need help," Klearistos shouted back.

The second set of bags of caltrops arrived, and Nico helped move them forward. He walked back a few feet behind the soldiers and readied his bow. Now, there was nothing else to do but wait. Another couple of minutes and the cavalry came into bow range.

"Archers, release!" he heard Andrippos command. His call was picked up as a short note by their single Cretan liticines, their lituus blower, relaying the command to the men too far away to hear the first decurion's shout.

Nico had a hard time keeping his bow steady, and he feared he would lose his grip because of his sweaty palms. This was his first full-scale battle, after all, and they were fighting against overwhelming odds. After he released his first arrow into the sky, he stood still for a moment, his eyes following its flight towards the oncoming riders. He realized that everybody around him kept shooting at a rapid pace, and with a jolt he moved to pull out the next arrow, aimed, and let go. The last hundred feet of the enemy's distance shrunk so fast his third arrow's trajectory was nearly flat, flying right above the legionaries' heads.

Several of the enemy went down, either hit directly and sliding off their horse, or both horse and rider going down if the horse was hit, taking out other riders around them in spectacular fashion. *Let's hope this proves too much for them and they turn around. Oh, Tyche, who am I kidding?*

***

The cornua and tubae blew the command to brace, and Blandius gripped his pilum so hard his knuckles turned white. The entire first line of soldiers had dropped one of their pila and taken the other on from behind their shields in anticipation of the command to kneel. They would use their standard throwing weapon as a lance, digging the handle's back end into the dirt, and bracing the shaft with both hands. The row behind him held their shields high, ready to cover his line after the first impact. He smelled his neighbor's urine, the green recruit no longer able to control his bladder. This wasn't Blandius's first fight, and he knew waiting was the hardest part. Once the wait was over, so was the time of conscious thought and worry. His gaze followed the riders' approach, and he saw many go down from arrows that created chaos in tightly packed Transcudani ranks. The first riders, now in a much looser formation, came up on the caltrops.

The enemy warriors made it several feet into the caltrop zone before chaos ensued. The magnificent horses started to scream, their legs buckling from hitting caltrops in full gallop. They went down hard, dislodging their riders explosively. Still, a reduced number of riders made it through and came up on the first line. Blandius shivered from anticipation as he looked into the face of a proud brown stallion aiming straight at him. He got lucky: the horse slowed at the last moment, rearing instead of ramming the Roman line. Blandius knew to lift his pilum off the ground to push it at the horse's exposed neck, though the horse saw the weapon coming and turned away in panic, jumping right and colliding with another cavalry man. Blandius threw his weapon but missed as the horse jumped back and out of reach.

He had a short moment to look to the side. Many horses impaled themselves on the men's pila, falling forward and crushing legionaries in the process. Several of the second rank had pushed forward, attempting to fill the gaps and free trapped fellows. He turned forward and picked up his second pilum in anticipation of more cavalry. The initial hard charge had been stopped by the caltrops and spears, and the riders now tried to approach the Roman line slowly to make use of their long swords. The legionaries simply closed the line, joined shields, and stood their ground.

Blandius finally heard the call for the entire first line to stand up, long after the fact. "Pila iacite! Throw your Pila!" the centurions now shouted up and down the line. More horses and riders went down. "Two steps back!" This moved everyone clear of the horse bodies. Blandius drew his gladius.

With the entire first line standing at attention and holding their shields high against the cavalry, the riders had a hard time getting close enough to hurt the legionaries. The first rank started to go through the standard rotation, opening up a small space between the shields, stabbing out with their gladii into horse's sides or riders' legs. In a very short time, enough had come down that another "Two steps back!" was needed to clear the line and get the shields closed again. Soon the scene repeated itself, followed by another call: "Two steps back!" Blandius moved backwards. They had started their line anchored to the ditches on each end but now stood in line with the middle of the ramparts. *Maybe there is some hope.*

The encounter had gone much better than he had expected. He knew that Roman legions could face overwhelming odds and win, though, of course, he also knew that some legions had been annihilated even when winning seemed all but assured. Recent public losses included armies facing Germanic barbarians or, more recently, a rabble of slaves under the gladiator Spartacus.

His spirits lifted when the riders retreated and a flood of fresh warriors on foot pushed in. It was a hot day and many of the enemy hadn't bothered to don armor of any kind. Blandius grinned, hoping it would give his blood-spattered face a demonic expression. No armor against a line of legionaries was a serious mistake. They would know that once they went down dying.

He kept working in sync with his fellow legionaries. Lock shields, push shield forward, rotate the shield on his left arm to get enough opening to stab the tip of his gladius at any exposed skin. Over and over again. From the corner of his left eye he saw some of his colleagues go down only to be replaced by men from behind. The third rank pushed forward to fill the new holes in the second. The cornua and all the tubae blew for rank change, and it took Blandius a split second longer than the smelly recruit to his right to react and move. A wounded Transcudani lying on his side a couple of feet in front of him reached out swinging his long sword. As Blandius rotated, the heavy sword tip cut through his right caliga, splitting his open military boot and coming to a halt deep inside his foot. The man managed to pull his weapon back, cutting deeper still. Shouting and swearing, Blandius continued his turn to let his replacement deal with the wounded enemy. He rushed backwards through the third rank and looked down at his foot, seeing freely pooling blood. The medicus assigned to their detachment ran over to have a quick look. He had heard the man was not a studied doctor but raised from the ranks of the medical helpers based on his excellent triage capabilities. *I hope he knows what to do.*

"Sorry, no time to deal with you right now. Your caliga is doing a fine job of holding things together. Just lay down and elevate your foot, that will keep you from dying before things calm down again and I can help you." The man moved on to look at the next legionary in need.

Blandius hobbled back to the legionaries' packs and lowered himself to the ground. He got as comfortable as he could, always keeping a wary eye on the line in case the enemy broke through.

***

As the first of the enemy horses were impaled on the legionaries' pila, Nico heard their lituus blowing the call to mount. The line of archers turned their heads momentarily towards the middle, until they saw the raised standard of the second turma. The first and third went back to shooting while Nico released the arrow he held before dashing with his squad towards the horses. The thirty men mounted and rode a couple of hundred feet to the middle of the camp. Here, they reigned in and studied the enemy's movements. When he realized how hard the Transcudani cavalry had gotten decimated, Nico allowed himself a glimmer of hope, but then the first men on foot reached the battlefield and ran unscathed through the killing zone of caltrops. They jumped over bodies of horses and men alike, and for the most part had no problem avoiding the iron spikes. The cavalry men, now relieved from having to bear pressure on the Romans, gathered on the far side of the caltrops. His mood went sour when this group of about five hundred riders, the sole remnants of the original force of two thousand, moved into a trot downhill, intent on going around the camp's western rampart. The faces of the men around him turned grim as well.

Klearistos called. "Alketas, take word back to Andrippos that we're in need of all the help we can get," his decurion shouted. "For the rest of you, we can't keep them at bay with our bows, so one arrow only. After that it's down to how well we can chop with our kopis. We need to keep them away from our legionaries' backs as long as possible." Nico's eyes followed the flanking force which was now increasing speed.

"Follow me!" Klearistos shouted. He kicked his horse, and they rode to the opening between the mostly dug southern and western ramparts, spreading out with four or five feet of space between the horses. When they stopped, everybody nocked their arrows and held ready to release. Nico steadied his mount with his legs.

"Wait until they get close!" The first of the Transcudani now made it to the end of the rampart and turned inward and back upward toward the Cretans, now only twenty feet away. The enemy warriors spurred their horses on, racing with each other in their eagerness to be first to the archers.

"Release!" All arrows flew, several hitting the same few cavalry men that were closest. The first ten riders toppled, reining some of their horses to a stop in the process. The following riders had to swerve wide around now riderless animals. The Cretans dropped their bows and moved their small shields to their wrists before drawing their recurved swords. With a throaty shout, Nico moved forward to meet the Transcudani. He'd made it close to the riderless horses when the first enemy came at him from his right side. For a moment that seemed to stretch out forever, all he could do was parry the man's frantic slashes. But then his adrenaline overcame his fear and nervousness. *By Ares, I will not sell my life cheaply.*

He twisted to his right in his saddle, now finally able to catch the incoming blade on his buckler. His right arm was now free to slash downwards, and his blade bit deep into the enemy's upper leg, close to the groin. When he pulled his kopis back, the leg's artery started pulsing, blood spraying over both him and the enemy rider. Nico kicked his own mount left, trying to get some distance from the fatally wounded man who was now drooping in his saddle and pulling on his reins. The enemy's horse reared before it turned right, away from Nico, whose focus snapped to the next rider pushing into the opening. The woman wielded a solid iron spear, pointed right at his face. Nico had trained countless hours for situations like this and finally stopped thinking. He let the spear come very close until the Transcudani tried pushing it forward by stretching out her arms, expecting to end him. Instead of waiting for the point to hit him, Nico twisted forward and to the left, letting the weapon's tip glance off the right side of his chainmail. He caught the spear shaft with his left shield arm and pushed it down and away from his leg and his horse's side. Twisting back, he stretched out his right arm for a back swing. His kopis connected with the woman's face, cutting clear across the nose and eliciting a loud scream. Stunned by her injury, she hesitated enough to let Nico add a slash to her right thigh, cutting deeply. The woman warrior let go of her bridle and dropped to the ground, to be trampled by the horses of her eager fellow warriors. A different rider moved in, ignoring Nico to attack another archer. A glance at the other Cretans made him realize their line had changed. The other two turmae had come to their support, and Elatos had pushed in without Nico realizing. His friend was already engaged with a Transcudani to his left side and wide open to the enemy newcomer. With a start, Nico pushed forward, trying to shove himself between them. Just when Elatos looked to his right, the Transcudani warrior stabbed him hard with her spear, the tip going through the chainmail into the sternum. Elatos was thrown backwards out of his saddle, ripping the spear out of the warrior's hands in the process. *No, not you!*

While the woman fumbled to draw her knife, Nico slashed hard into her exposed shoulder, cutting deeper on the back draw. She screamed and dropped her knife in her attempt to stem the flood of blood rushing out of the severed artery. With her out of the picture, and now several riderless or downed horses between himself and the closest Transcudani, Nico had a moment to look around. He spotted Elatos, crawling away from the fight. He tried to wipe some of the blood from his face and realized how vast the sea of enemy riders in front of him was, all eager to get at him and his fellow Cretans. It seemed impossible to withstand this flood. The thought paralyzed him for a moment. *I will die here in these mountains, far away from the civilized world. At least I will see Timon soon, when we meet in the underworld.*

Just maybe he could give the two cohorts and Elatos a few extra moments to live. He spurred his mount forward, rushing towards the next warrior.

***

"Are we going to get there soon?" the man in front of Publius Ventidius Bassus asked in a whiny tone. They walked up a narrow path through slowly thinning woods, on their way to deliver supplies needed for the new fort at the southern pass of these mountains. Bassus figured the legionaries already there and digging would be ready for them when they finally arrived. He didn't mind their slow pace. He was content walking his mule while musing about the past and the future. How lucky he had been to meet old Albanius, who let him, a homeless and hungry orphan boy, walk the roads with him! The deep friendship with the old muleteer had saved him and set his current path. Albanius, old enough to be the boy's great-grandfather, had procured a second mule within a couple of months to let Bassus help with bigger deliveries. *I've been happy with my lot in life ever since.*

When Albanius died many years later from old age, his sons had inherited both mules and kicked him out. With little savings to his own name, Bassus had signed up as a muleteer for the legions. He'd never rued the decision. He loved working with the animals; it was as simple as that.

His mule's current load was for a tent group of the fourth cohort of the Ninth legion and consisted of poles and leather hides for an eight-men tent, as well as sleeping cots and a bread oven, several packs of spare clothes and tools, plus six of the heavy palisade stakes needed for the fort walls. He had long since stopped being amazed at what mules could carry for long distances. Forty of their almost three hundred animals behind him were weighed down even more, carrying the centuries' scorpios and half of the First cohort's artillery plus various ammunition options for each. Forty of the animals in front of him carried huge stacks of palisade logs, fortunately frequently waxed or oiled in the Ninth. With dry weather, they were relatively light, but he had seen other outfit's mules break down in heavy rains, unable to continue under water-logged loads. At the rear of the single file, yet more mules drove twenty of the camp prefect's wagons, heavily burdened with the staples of legionary food, mainly the obligatory wheat and chickpeas, and several weeks' mule fodder.

He shook his head at the legionaries of the seventh cohort marching to their side, feeling superior to him and his comrades and making fun of his fellow muleteers. The four hundred and eighty legionaries stretched out in single file, with five squads marching wide at the front, leading the entire baggage train, and another five doing the same as rearguard. The one hundred sixty artillery men travelling with the cohort marched between the single file and the rearguard, keeping an eye on the mules carrying the parts for their war machines.

Bassus looked up when he heard a commotion up front and saw men and mules ahead breaking into a fast trot. He followed, and as he neared the end of the tree cover, he could make out the muted but unmistakable sounds of battle. He urged his mule out of the trees and pulled to the side. His breath caught when he saw the desperate action of the third and fourth cohorts in the distance. *These men need help, and it can't come soon enough. Help us, Jupiter!*

Without thinking, he started stripping his mule's load and shouted at the other muleteers to do the same. He received a few blank looks, but most seemed to understand, feverishly emulating him. Muleteers usually played catch-up with marching legionaries in enemy territory, and they were encouraged to carry long knives, spears, or even cavalry swords for self-defense. They also had plenty of opportunities to train with the legionaries, and every mule driver worth his salt knew how to ride. There was no doubt in his mind what he needed to do. Bridle in hand, he jumped onto his animal. Once seated on the strapping used to secure the load, he pulled his long sword out of its sheath and looked around. About a hundred and fifty of the muleteers were in various stages of unloading or mounting their animals. The last of the artillery men and legionaries passed by in a fast jog, starting a long run uphill. Blandius counted the number of mule drivers already mounted and figured they were up to nearly a hundred. He was surprised when he realized the muleteers looked at him for guidance. *You want me to lead you? Really? So be it, if that's what it takes.*

He wasted no time. "You all see that desperate struggle up there, right? The closer ones have got to be the Cretans, trying to cover the cohorts' rear," he shouted as loud as he could to be heard over the noise of the unloading. "They can't hold out long enough, certainly not until our legionaries can get to them." Nobody else spoke, but many kept looking between him and the raging battle up the mountainside. "So, let's give them a hand, shall we?" he shouted, and with a roar, he kicked his mule into its ribs, launching it forward. He moved uphill at a sharp trot, the others following.

After a few hundred feet he passed the first of the jogging legionaries. The men had stripped off their extra gear and bundles, steadily advancing uphill. Bassus admired the men's stamina: they still carried over twenty pounds of armor and weapons up a steep incline. Few people outside the legions could match feats like this.

He looked at their target. The uneven struggle between the Cretans and the Transcudani had become desperate. From below, he could barely make out more than a handful of light beige and red tunics peeking out from underneath armor, stranded in a sea of local earthy browns and greens. "Sweet Perseus, you need to fly like the wind! Faster, faster!" he urged his animal. *Will we get to them quickly enough? Gods, help us all.*

***

Blandius saw the enemy climb over the finished ramparts to move around the ends of the Roman defensive line. *Took them long enough, they should have done that right away.*

He knew the prefects and tribunes had seen the flanking maneuvers, calling for the horn blowers and signalers to relay "agmen formate," meaning the formation of an open square. The men at both ends of the line stepped back behind the man next to them. They kept perfect form, exactly as drilled every week. The front line slowly shrunk, extending the sides farther and farther back. Even wounded and in pain, he was amazed to see how well the ceaseless and tireless drilling translated to battlefield action. This was the advantage against high numbers that kept the two cohorts alive, at least staving off certain disaster for now. Blandius pushed himself upwards, feeling faint. *If I can't reach the men around the cohort's standards, I'll be left outside the square, as good as dead.*

He shuffled over, sparing a glance at his feet. He could see Fresh blood ran down with each step. Weak and barely coherent, he tripped. Falling to the ground, he had no energy left to get back up. He closed his eyes. *This is it, then.*

Soon after, he felt his torso being lifted off the ground, though he was unable to move until he dropped back to the ground. The hand grabbed him again under his shoulder in an effort to lift him. This time, he came alive enough to try to get up.

"Quickly, man, on the double. We need to hurry!" somebody shouted in his ear. Moving as fast as he could, he turned to look at who helped him and was surprised to see young tribune Marcus Licinius Crassus.

They made it to the line just ahead of the first Transcudani warriors and Crassus ducked under the first swing, which nicked Blandius's cheek instead. The closest legionary moved out of his side-stepping line to stab the attacking warrior's side, allowing Crassus and the wounded Blandius to hurry past.

"We made it. Let's go to the medicus and his helpers." Crassus told him, keeping up his support until they were within a few feet of their target. Blandius stared at Crassus, attempting to commit the face with its big forehead and dark blue eyes to memory. *Why is he helping me? I am just a legionary, a nothing to the likes of him.*

"Ah, good, the fellow with the cut foot," the medicus said. "You, there, let's get his leg up, he clearly can't afford to lose any more blood," the man called to one of his helpers. Blandius's eyes scanned past him to follow a few enemy warriors now behind the Roman line and harassing the legionaries' rear. He couldn't believe what he saw next: the cohort prefects, both tribunes, all their aids and servants—even the horn blowers—drew their gladii and ran to engage the enemy, making short work of them. The legionaries could move quicker without the added pressure and closed the square. For now, that would be enough. His focus changed to the valiant Cretans a few hundred feet away. *Merda, they are done for.*

He heard a few prayers to Mars, god of war, for victory, but many more prayed to the spirits of their ancestors in preparation for the upcoming reunion. Finally, his lids turned too heavy to keep open and the battle noise and prayers seemed to fade into the distance.

***

Nico felt the impact of a sword on his right shoulder and the sharp pain made him drop his kopis. He had no time to check his wound and kept moving his shield into the way of wild slashes attempting to cut him down. Another Transcudani horseman shoved his attacker's horse to the side, and Nico took the short opportunity to slide off his own horse's far side. He remained upright thanks to his left hand's tight grip on the bridle, though hitting the ground shot pain like a lightning bolt into his shoulder, making him waver on his feet and howl. His blade glinted a few feet away, and he moved to pick it up. Jostled by the horses around him, he settled on a closer spear instead. Gritting his teeth, he pushed to get to the enemy he had fought against a few moments earlier. Holding the far end of the lance, he stabbed at the man's chest from several feet distance. The warrior turned, and the weapon's tip glanced off hardened leather armor and penetrated the man's left arm instead. Nico pulled the spear out and rapidly hit a second time into the man's side, pushing him off his horse. He glanced behind to see his fellow Cretans surrounded on three sides, with the fourth side covered by the end of the finished section of rampart. Riderless horses crowded them, thankfully making it hard for multiple enemies to engage simultaneously. *Otherwise this would have been long over.*

Just as he wondered how to get back on his horse, he saw an opening appear to the south side of the melee, where some of the Transcudani turned away from the remaining Cretans. *What is going on?*

He ran towards the opening but decided on engaging the next enemy warrior, allowing a fellow Cretan on the other side of the man to dish out a lethal hit. They both had a moment of breathing room before moving to support the rest of their swiftly shrinking unit.

***

Bassus saw some of the enemy peel off from the struggle ahead to face him and his fellow muleteers. A brief glance over his shoulder showed him a long line of mounted mules reaching back all the way to the woods. He figured there were now at least two hundred galloping behind him up the incline. He kept riding towards about sixty Transcudani bearing down on him before swerving sideways for the last fifty feet. This made the entire line of enemy riders spread out. *Good. This might actually work.*

Some warriors tried to cut him off, some were slowing, and the remainder kept on downhill towards the other muleteers. To his relief, the line of colleagues behind had followed his swerve. With his sword out, he targeted the closest Transcudani, hitting the man's shield with a glancing blow while riding by at an angle to avoid engaging more enemies. The man reined in and turned to follow him uphill.

He kept riding for another fifty feet while glancing over his shoulder. As he had hoped, close to forty of his muleteers had been able to avoid getting engaged and were close behind him. In comparison, only fifteen of the Transcudani had turned to follow them uphill, now close behind his small team. Bassus reigned in, and quickly turned his mule. With satisfaction, he saw the surprised face of the lead warrior. *Divide the enemy so you can deal with smaller numbers. I don't even remember where I heard this, but I am grateful I did. Here we go!*

Smiling grimly, he kicked Perseus forward.

***

Nico couldn't believe his eyes. The legions' muleteers crashed into the Transcudani riders right in front of him. He let out a wild laugh which eerily matched his exhaustion and pain. He didn't remember when he'd lost his helmet, but now he felt a gashing wound on top of his scalp. No matter. Reinvigorated by the sight of the mule drivers, the few remaining Cretans around him went mad with anger and grief, hacking into the enemy in a raging frenzy, finally taking down enough of them to clear the ground between them and the muleteers. Nico ran out from the mass of horses and sighted twenty Transcudani riding back up the mountain, chased uphill by more of the new arrivals of make-shift cavalry. He cheered and pumped his shield into the air despite his pain. Then he spotted the long line of the running legionaries of the Seventh cohort less than half mile away.

He looked at the two other cohorts. They had formed an open square, keeping at bay what seemed to be at least two thirds of the original foot warriors and a few hundred cavalry men who'd made it around the Cretans. The enemy there had paid no attention to the cavalry battle. Maybe this might give his Cretans and the muleteers a chance to clear things up here first.

Some of the twenty fleeing enemy barely hung on, clearly heavily wounded, and rode on along the camp's western rampart instead of joining the group clustered around the Cretans.

Nico couldn't believe what happened next. *These few fleeing enemy men are turning the tide in our favor.*

Some of the Transcudani in the mass around the Cretans noticed their fleeing fellows and spotted the pursuing muleteers and the seventh cohort.

With some of the stragglers of the mule drivers still barely out of the woods, there was no way the enemy could know how few Roman reinforcements were en route. More and more of the locals disengaged to ride back around the earthen ramparts to join the group at the upper part of the camp. While their foot soldiers stayed focused on breaking the Roman square, what was meant to be a regrouping of horsemen started an unintentional flood, many Transcudani misunderstanding it for general flight. Despite their still tremendous numerical advantage, the warriors suddenly all turned to flee up the mountain. Nico cheered, soon joined by all the survivors.

After a few minutes of simply breathing, his mind suddenly cleared. *Elatos.*

He started to walk around, pushing horses aside while looking for fellow Cretans on the ground. He found many dead bodies, including his turma's decurion, Klearistos. Andrippos, their first decurion, was still alive, though barely, with deep lacerations and a spear stuck in his stomach. Nico knew that the man's chances depended on what had been hit internally. *Not much hope there.*

Nico continued his search in an ever-widening circle until he ended up close to the rampart. Looking up at the berm he found Elatos. His friend had crawled up and away for a hundred feet before succumbing to his pierced lungs. Nico closed the unseeing eyes and stared at the bloody foam at the corners of Elatos's mouth. In an act of tenderness, he gently wiped his friend's lips.

With a sudden surge of emotion, reality hit, and he began to sob. *Why did I survive, why? Why could you feckless gods not take me instead, and leave poor Elatos alive?*

***

Bassus led Perseus back towards the woods in the midst of his fellow muleteers. Tribune Crassus commanded a century of legionaries as escort and as help for reloading the animals. The remainder of their battle-weary legionaries were finishing the remaining ramparts to get ready for the incoming palisade logs.

He knew the surviving soldiers would be rewarded with lots more digging and likely logging in the woods below. Maybe that was for the best. It would keep their minds off what just happened. From what he knew, the troops would build a raised wall section across the whole mile of the ravine to connect the fort with the ridge on the other side of the pass, likely adding several watch towers to receive some of the war machines like scorpios and ballistae.

Out of the corner of his eye, he saw Crassus move up to him, so Bassus turned to face the man. Of medium height, the young tribune had short and curly brown hair. He seemed rather average except for highly intelligent green eyes, which always perceptively scanned the men and their surroundings.

"You are Publius Ventidius Bassus?" Crassus asked. Bassus nodded before the man went on. "I heard from other muleteers that it was your idea to ride into battle. There's little doubt it was your valiant charge that saved the few survivors of our Cretans and likely all of us." The tribune paused briefly before continuing. "I have to ask, most mule drivers come from humble backgrounds and have one or two names at most, yet you have three like a nobleman. Ventidius sounds familiar somehow. Your speech doesn't sound like it, but is your family originally from Picenum?"

"Yes, it is, tribune," he replied. "Though I was brought to Rome at a young age and never found my way home." Crassus raised eyebrows at him in the hope of more information, but

Bassus stayed silent. The past was the past, all done with and behind him. Then he saw Crassus's eyes widen in recognition. He sighed. Now the man wouldn't leave him alone.

"Would your father's name also have been Publius Ventidius? With a different third name?"

Bassus sighed again. "Yes. Bassus is indeed my own nickname. I was a very fat baby, or so my mother told me. Though I'm not so fat or stumpy these days."

"I can't believe this. I actually saw you walk as a prisoner in Pompeius Strabo's triumph. You were just a little boy, and I was barely older. My father explained your situation to me, that your father was a nobleman he admired, from one of the best houses of Asculum that happened to end up on the wrong side of the Social War."

The man put his hand on Bassus's shoulder. "And here you are, a true eques if ever there was one, working as a simple muleteer in the Ninth legion. But not for much longer if I can help it. What would you say to becoming decurion of one of our Ninth's Roman scout turmae? Though we can't make that official until we're back with the rest of the legion."

Bassus looked intensely at the young man and tried to figure out why he was jesting with him. *He is not smiling… maybe… is he serious?*

"I could be open to that, but only if my one demand can be met. It's not negotiable," he answered flat-faced, not expecting the conversation to continue.

"Oh, and what demand would that be? You are in everybody's good graces, so I guess it's the right time to ask for favors," Crassus said, his formerly friendly face now looking disappointed.

"Well, scouts all get magnificent horses, but that's the problem. I don't want a horse. I don't want to be a scout leader if it would be without Perseus, my mule. We've grown quite attached to each other." Bassus patted his animal's shoulder. *The young tribune will drop the matter now and that would suit me fine.*

But, incredibly, Crassus started to laugh. "That, my friend, may be irregular, but it's no problem, truly! And I understand, believe me. I have just seen what your mules can do in battle."

Back in good spirits, Bassus continued his walk down the mountain; the first trip of countless he and the other muleteers would surely have to get through over the next days.

***

Blandius opened his eyes to find himself on a cot in his own tent. A cup of fresh water, some bread, and a bowl with ground chickpeas, garlic, and olive oil had been laid on a small three-legged folding stool next to him. He remembered waking a few times before, but his memories were blurry. He tried to sit up to drink, but the pain shooting up from his foot gave him pause. *Oh no, Merda. This really happened.*

Slowly pulling his blanket down, he saw his right foot's heavy bandage, but even so, it was much shorter than his left. His shoulders slumped. *Damn the gods, my time in the legion is over. What am I supposed to do now?*

He would likely be discharged once they got to their winter camp. *Will the legion pay for me to travel back to Italia? Do I even want to go back? I don't know where any of my childhood friends are. My life is here now, with the legion.*

He mused what he could and would do. First, he needed to become healthy again, and mobile. Hopefully he could still walk, that would be the most important part. If he couldn't, would he be able to at least ride? No, he was a horrible rider anyway, that didn't make sense. He could drive a wagon, though, something he had done frequently as a child. *But I don't want to drive somebody else's wagon. I want to stay with the legion! Is there any way?*

He swayed between the onset of major depression and his practical outlook, which always helped him through any decision he made in his life. *At least I'm alive. A lot of my fellow legionaries are not.*

The tent flap opened, and his surviving squad members filed in. "He's awake! Ho, Blandius, looked for a while like you wouldn't make it," one of them said.

"Yeah, and because of your silly foot, of all things. If you would have died from that cut, you'd never live that down," another said to erupting loud laughter. His friends knew what he needed most now. Camaraderie and teasing would keep him from feeling too sorry for himself.

***

"Thank you for letting me know," Nico told the medical helper who had just given him the news that Andrippos, the Cretan's first decanus, was still alive against all odds. He walked out of his tent, followed by a couple of other Cretans at a slight distance, and headed straight for Andrippos's squad tent. When he walked in, he wondered for a moment why there was so much empty space. Then it hit him like a brick. There was little need for superfluous cots here. *All this empty space was filled with living, breathing people just two nights ago.*

He glanced at his escort. None of them were allowed to go anywhere by themselves, as was customary for soldiers who had recently lost most of their units. Even with this kind of precaution, the rate of attempted suicides was bound to be high, and now he had the experience to understand why—his own survivor's guilt felt like a boulder pushing down on him. He knew the officers wouldn't stop worrying about him and the survivors until the next battle. He had heard that the one emotion overriding any wish to depart from this senseless life was the need to help the man next to you. *I hope that will be true for me as well when the time comes. I just need to hold on to get there.*

Nico looked at Andrippos, whose eyes were closed in uneasy slumber and whose hot forehead had beads of sweat running down the sides. He found a rag on the table and managed to pick it up with his left hand before moving it slowly over to his right. He was careful not to move his right arm and to keep the weight in the sling. Lifting a pitcher off the table with his left, he poured some water over the rag. He put the water down and switched the piece of cloth back to his left so he could dab Andrippos's forehead. He only glanced up when he heard the medicus come in. The man had a servant in tow to help carry a bowl and two small amphorae.

"Ah, how goes the broken clavicle?" the medicus asked Nico. "Or your hairline cut?" The man was a miracle worker when it came to saving people, though by now he looked so pale and ragged as to fall over any moment. He had treated the wounded nonstop for two days, making house calls after the patients had been moved into their squad tents. The man had no head for names, though he could always remember injuries.

"My clavicle is fine, thank you, and so is my head. The stitches hurt, but it will all heal in time. I am not so sure the same goes for Andrippos here," Nico answered, lowering his head.

The medicus moved in to pull off the blanket, and then the wrappings and bandages. "All in good time. Since he's still with us today, he might yet be with us tomorrow." He touched Andrippos's stomach and pushed hard a couple of times. "I cannot hear any liquids in there, which is a very good sign. Now, it all depends on his fever breaking." The medicus took a sponge from his helper's hands and waited for the man to fill his bowl with red wine vinegar. He dipped the sponge in and proceeded to soak the many wounds. All the big ones were stitched, including the hole in the upper stomach. The vinegar ran down the side of Andrippos' body to stain the blanket and the cot beneath. "So far, so good, but still too early to call." The medicus switched to a rag and let his servant pour a generous amount of olive oil over it. Then he proceeded to wipe the wounds with that.

"As long as it doesn't get red and inflamed, he has a chance. Though if he makes it, he won't be beautiful anymore," he said before laughing at his own joke, pointing at Andrippos's deep cut up the chin that split the lower lip in two—the stitched sides were slightly misaligned. "I know how to save lives, but my stitches just aren't good enough to make pretty scars." Nico joined in the laughter which somehow came easy because it felt right. Looking good was the last thing on anybody's mind right now.

693 AUC (61 BC), summer
High Plateau of the Stella Mountains, lands of the Lancienses Transcudani, Hispania

The Transcudani chiefs held another emergency assembly. This time they sat out in the open, close to the bigger lake of the high plateau. Just days earlier, everybody had been proud and boastful—Retukenos remembered statements like "Let the Romans come, we'll show them!" and "They can't hurt us in our mountains." They had all felt invincible. Until yesterday. The simple attack on a handful of Romans digging trenches had ended in utter disaster. He had lost his older son in the scuffle and come to the realization they stood no chance in another open fight. So, he had sent word to the remainder of his family to come up to join him on the western high plateau. Nights were much colder up here, but they would be safer. After seeing what a small detachment of Romans could do, he had lost faith in the fortifications securing the valley's approaches.

The discussion was muted, and he only listened half-heartedly without engaging. Topics fluctuated between possible defensive actions, food distribution, and blankets for the late arrivals that frequently needed better clothing against the mountain cold. *They still do not understand. None of these things matter anymore.*

Though, all the tough talk of taking the fight to the Roman army was gone. Once everything was said that needed saying, the meeting broke apart and the chieftains dispersed. He watched most of them go north, back to their camps in the valleys below. He still stood there, deep in thought, when he heard a voice behind him. "Retukenos, there you are, I thought you had left already." He turned and saw an old friend walking over to him. Koitina was currently the only woman chieftain on the Transcudani high council. "I need to ask you, because you were down in the thick of things yesterday. Did the Romans fight as hard as I was told? Did they truly beat us back with far inferior numbers, even without having their fort finished?"

"Yes, Koitina. It's true, and it was worse than whatever you heard. I lost my oldest boy down there." He sighed. "I'm now convinced we can't withstand them, not even here, in our mountains. If their main leader is as good as the one who led the few soldiers yesterday, they'll come for us, and they won't stop until we surrender or are all dead." He looked around and saw a few other chieftains lingering close by. "Come, walk with me," he told her. When they were far enough to not be overheard, he stopped. "I have sent word to all family and friends to move up here from the valleys. I suggest you do the same. If you want them to live." After a moment, he turned to keep walking, glancing back over his shoulder to see her shocked face. "You know I'm no coward, but we should not fight with odds so bad."

693 AUC (61 BC), summer
East of the Stella Mountains, lands of the Lancienses Transcudani, Hispania

"Here comes that older Numidian again. I don't know what you two see in these people. They're stupid barbarians and you know it," Opiter Maximus, one of the newest centurions within the second cohort, grumbled at Titus Balventius and Gaius Seppius.

Balventius's face turned sour. "Opiter, just shut up. Those Numidians saved my entire century. They are good people, and we'll gladly have them cover our rear in any battle," he retorted. "Why don't you do yourself a favor and just leave right now, while you can. If you don't, I will need to punch in that ugly nose of yours." Balventius put as much venom into his look as he could, until Maximus wisely decided to walk away. Titus Pullo, Maximus's Optio, opened his arms in apology for the centurion. Balventius sighed, his face relaxing. Seppius shook his head, and they turned to face their visitor.

"Capussia, how goes today's march for your men? Not too many in need of extra breaks?" Balventius called out with a dead-pan face. All seven cohorts and auxilia forces had stopped for a short break while their cavalry was out scouting and foraging, except for a few turmae of mounted Cretans who acted as guards for the column and rode up and down the sides. The Numidians marched with the legionaries, and Capussia kept his turma intentionally right behind Balventius's century. After years of fighting together, the men shared a strong bond of trust.

"Balventius!" Capussia responded with a wide grin. The man had obviously picked up his teasing. "My men can march just as well as yours, and you know it!" The Numidian walked up, and the two men clasped arms. "I wanted to ask you about the three cohorts we left this morning." He looked around, making sure nobody else was close enough to overhear him. "Do you think they are strong enough to hold the pass? Three cohorts and ninety Cretans? Against how many did Sabinius estimate? At minimum, a hundred thousand people in the mountains?" he whispered. "With no idea how many of them are at that southern pass, I fear for the Romans there, and Andrippos."

"I share your worry," Balventius replied, "though Sabinius's number was for all their people, including their old and children. He also said the majority of them are in the valleys. Still, that likely leaves a few thousand warriors to watch that pass. Who knows? I just can't figure out why Vatinius insisted on the legion moving on instead of helping to get the fort built and secured. Well, nothing left now but to hope for the best."

"We must be close to the northern pass into the mountains, right?" Capussia said. "Did you see the ravine a while back? Why didn't we camp close to that? It looked like it could lead all the way up to the plateau. Also, where we are now? I can see what our cavalry commander meant about the wooded lower mountains." He pointed to their left. "You could lead the whole legion up and over in the dark."

"I think we'll make camp soon enough, then let our scouts backtrack. I don't agree with the decision about the southern pass, but I think it makes good sense not to give away our intentions to any of them spying on us from up there."

Capussia nodded. "Ah, I guess that makes sense indeed." He put his hand on Balventius's shoulder. "Thank you, my friend. And let's pray to the gods we see Andrippos again."

Balventius anxiously watched his friend turn and walk back to his men. *I am as worried as you about Andrippos. Curse you, careless Vatinius, you son of a dog.*

***

Long before the afternoon was over, the legion made early camp. A messenger came for Oz, telling him to come to the eastern gate with his turma's tent group and to leave shields and armor in their tent.

They soon arrived at the open space in front of the gate, which happened to be the one located away from the mountains. He told his men to stay alert and stepped towards the other officers. *Ah, Capussia is here as well.*

When his friend and superior winked at him, he groaned, realizing that he had been volunteered once again. Still, he trusted Capussia's judgment and moved forward to listen in on the conversation. The only thing left now was to find out what exactly he was supposed to do.

"Your group will ride north around the northern pass, to see the lay of the land and scout the fortifications the enemy has put in place," their cavalry commander, a man named Quintus Titurius Sabinius, explained to a decurion of the Celtic cavalry. "Capussia's two Numidian squads will lead the other two exploration parties, with one legionary squad each for security. That's meant to increase the odds of at least a few men making it back to report in case things go sideways." He turned to Oz, the other Numidian decurions and the two legionary squad leaders. "Everybody needs to go unarmored to keep quiet, and the camp prefect's men here are to hand out dark woolen cloaks for all to help you remain unseen." Sabinius looked at Capussia, signaling him to continue the instructions.

"Zelal, your mission is to backtrack and investigate the ravine to the south. See if the enemy has finished their wall there and if there is any weakness we can exploit," the Numidian leader instructed before turning to Oz. "Your mission is to scout the tall wooded mountainside just to the south of here." He pointed at Sabinius. "Our praefectus legiones here will personally join you for a look at the other side."

Oz nodded, understanding now why he had been volunteered. The prefect needed to be kept safe at all costs, and Capussia trusted him to do just that. He looked at the sky, and how the sun, far in the west already, caused the first shadows on the mountain side. "Sirs, I suggest we get close to the ridge before nightfall and camp till first daylight. That way the morning's sunlight will give us a clear view of the valley."

Sabinius nodded. "Lead the way."

A couple hours later, Oz, Adhe, Massi, and Gulussa were far up the mountain side, walking ahead and well away from the group of legionaries shepherded by the remaining six men of Oz's squad. Sabinius had so readily agreed to this deployment that Oz wondered about what Capussia had told the man. Likely some inflated story about their ill-fated campaign three years ago.

What was that?

Oz held up his hand. He had heard what sounded like snapping twigs ahead, off to one side. Daylight was waning, but they had made it close to the top of the ridge. His nephew and friends stopped and kneeled. *No movement?*

He touched Gulussa's shoulder to get his attention, then pointed behind them. His friend nodded his understanding, then slunk away, heading back to stop the main group from following. Next, Oz touched Massi's shoulder and pointed to a wide tree trunk his friend could wait behind. Now looking at Adhe, he pointed first sideways, then forward, then made a circular motion. Adhe nodded. The boy would walk around the noise in a big circle to approach from the other side. He watched both leave before creeping towards the noise himself. After thirty feet he could make out the back of someone urinating against a tree. Oz waited patiently for the man to pull up his long pants, secure them around his waist with a loose leather string, and start walking. He followed slowly until a small camp came into view. Another warrior was leaning against a tree trunk under a heavy woolen blanket. *It's already bitter cold, the nights must be freezing up here.*

The returned companion slid down another trunk close by. "Wish we could have a fire," he said in their Celtic dialect. The other man replied with a grunt. Oz had seen enough and turned, backing up with slow metered steps, aware any noise would give him away.

He made it back to Massi and his tree a few minutes before Adhe. He held up two fingers for his nephew. Adhe nodded, holding up two himself and using his other hand to cover the fingers as a question. Oz shook his head, and pointed to their right, away from the two Transcudani scouts. When they had scouted about a half mile without encountering any other enemies, they backtracked five hundred feet and stopped.

The three men crouched down and leaned their heads close to each other to whisper. "We don't want to take their scouts out yet, that would show them we're interested in this ridge. Adhe, go back to the others and lead them straight here. Massi, you stay and wait. Tell them not to move from here. I'll go up and find us a clear spot below the ridge."

Adhe nodded. "I'll get them, no worries."

Massi also nodded. "I'll be here. Just come back soon, Oz, before we run out of light."

Adhe took off in the opposite direction from him, and Oz made the remaining two hundred feet to the ridge with caution. *No more watchers down here? They are not as worried about us as they should be.*

He looked around the wide, flat-topped ridge from the cover of a bush. After a few minutes of slowing his breath he could make out distant voices not far to his right. He crawled backwards, moving down between the trees for a ways, and tracked a couple hundred feet to his left before crawling back up on the ridge. This time, he could see a small fire in the distance where he'd heard the voices. The flames, hidden in a dip from anybody coming from the east, were visible from the side. Several figures huddled around the warmth, and Oz, chilled to the bone despite his climb, looked over in envy.

He took his eyes away and scanned to his left, waiting until he could focus in the waning light. The stars were coming out, but the moon was nowhere to be seen. He chanced it and moved across the ridge flat to the drop on the other side. There he searched and found some brush cover to crawl into.

He determined to note roughly what time the moonrise happened, knowing that it would be an hour later the next night, and so on. When he was reasonably sure there were no enemies stationed close to this spot, he crawled back to move across the ridge. Right below his descent was a stand of trees hidden from above. *Perfect cover right up to the top.*

Satisfied, he went back to get Massi and the two squads.

***

Early the next morning, Oz nodded at Sabinius. The man followed his example and dropped down to crawl forward through the bushes. They were rewarded with the first rays of a bright morning sun illuminating the scenery in front of them. Oz knew he had gotten lucky with this perfect spot; this part of the flat ridge was hidden from both sides by thick lavender bushes emitting a nearly overpowering smell. Their view out front of the thicket though was clear and showed them a village in the valley right below. The settlement had a vast amount of people camping out in the open around the houses, easily quadrupling its footprint. Very few inhabitants stirred at this early hour, and he was excited to see a fenced off area close to the ridge they were on, holding a sizeable number of the enemy's horses. *If we end up coming through here, we can keep these horses from them instead of facing more mounted warriors later.*

To his left, in the south, the valley ended in a steep incline up to the eastern one of two high table mountains. A small river originated up there somewhere to run through the valley along the side of the village. Off to the north, a long wooden wall ran across the width of the valley, with a small town located close to the gates. He could also make out a big opening in the mountains located to the west with a bigger river running out of it and flowing right between the two settlements to the wooden walls and beyond. That opening must lead to more of the valleys Sabinius had mentioned earlier. He scanned the opposite mountainside across the valley below. It looked easy to climb. *But it's also fully exposed, with no trees or bushes on the upper thirds.*

After a few minutes, Sabinius nodded to Oz and crawled backwards. *It will be interesting to hear his take on what we just saw.*

They collected the others and carefully backtracked their way down to camp.

***

The legate, his cohort prefects, the first decurions, and the tribunes were all waiting in front of the commander's tent. Oz and Sabinius walked up and joined the other scout team leaders.

"Good, since we're all here, shall we begin?" the legate asked. "How about we discuss what you found at the ravine first." He looked to his right at the man who had led that mission.

"Ah, of course, sir. We got there before dark. The palisade wall across the path is close to the top of the eastern plateau, and it has been completed. It was also heavily guarded, and they made us leave in a hurry. Their archers were coming down hard and we lost half of our team to their arrows. I estimate there's at least several hundred manning that wall, though we didn't get a close enough look to be sure." The centurion sounded and looked defeated, not making eye contact with anybody throughout the report.

The legate waved the last comment off as if it wasn't of much importance. "Thank you for trying." He's gaze moved on. "How about the northern pass?"

Uxentio, the leader of the Ninth's Celtic cavalry, stood straight. "We rode through the pass itself and noticed a few sentries observing us from the surrounding heights. The pass has a good-sized river running through it. It comes from behind the wall that cuts of the whole valley. The wall reaches the steeper mountain inclines on both sides, so we'd have a hard climb to get around. It's a fifteen-foot-tall wooden palisade with a raised walkway at least ten-foot-tall on the inside."

"Did you see if they shored it up with gravel and dirt and a shorter inside palisade like we've seen in the smaller towns?" Vatinius asked.

"No, sir. We couldn't see that, though I think it might be the case. This wall has two massive gates, one for each side of the river. They're similar in size to those in a decent city wall, and the walkway spans across the water. We tried to get closer until they challenged us and we left. Farther out, we found a ford across the river and went around the northwestern mountains. We could see only a few more hills to the north, and after those the land flattens out." Uxentio looked down as if to collect his thoughts before he continued. "Once around the next mountain, there is another enclosed valley with a small deserted town. From there we found two possible paths into the next valleys. The first looks like a steep climb and the other had another full wall built across. Both had plenty of guards at the top."

"Thank you, as we expected. Now, Sabinius, let's hear what you found at the wooded mountainside," the legate said.

"First, I want to note that we made it up undetected, and also left undetected. There are enemy watchmen guarding the ridge, but not enough to stop us if we go in force. I believe if we time it right, we can get a sizeable detachment across the ridge to catch them with their pants down. We should get in position late evening and wait till first light before taking out the scouts on this side of the ridge, that way we'll surprise them down in the valley. I had a clear view of a village full of refugees right below the ridge. It has a small stream which spills into a much bigger river that flows from other valleys in the west. That river also runs down towards the wall and out through the pass, as Uxentio said. Close to the wall, there's a small town on the east side of the river with a nice bridge across."

Sabinius paused for a brief moment. "I would suggest moving two detachments across the ridge. One to move to the northern wall from the inside to open the gates for our cavalry. Once that's done, the cavalry can lead that detachment west to the other valleys. The other force should engage the village below the ridge, pinning the enemy in place until they give up or flee. Later, that detachment can climb over the mountain behind to surprise anybody in the other valleys."

Oz was impressed by Sabinius's analysis of the land and his sense of tactics. The man was obviously a smart thinker.

Vatinius cleared his throat. "Thank you for your input, Quintus. I will take your plan under advisement. With the enormous numbers of Transcudani in there," he waved over at the peaks, "we won't do anything until we see reinforcements from the Eighth."

693 AUC (61 BC), summer
Stella Mountains, northern pass, lands of the Lancienses
Transcudani, Hispania

Lucius Cornelius Cinna rode behind Quintus Titurius Sabinius, the legion prefect for the Ninth's cavalry. Cinna looked at the tall and likeable man's brown curly hair, which was so similar to his own, its red tinge visible in the moonlight. The hair color, though, was where the similarity ended. Sabinius's hair had started to recede, and though tall, he had a rather stocky build compared to Cinna's lanky features. He glanced back into the darkness, barely making out the first few dozen riders behind them. Their contingent included all Celtic cavalry, a few Roman messengers and scouts, and the seven remaining turmae of Cretan archers.

Since the moon had risen well before they left the fort, he figured they had now maybe one hour left before sunrise. He looked up as some of the full moon's light poked through heavy clouds, and his mind drifted to his recent change in fortunes.

Seventeen years ago, he had made the fateful decision to follow his friend Marcus Perpenna Vento to Hispania to escape Sulla's proscriptions and had been in exile ever since. Soon after they had thrown their lot in with the Marian renegade Sertorius, Vento had assassinated the brilliant general who had welcomed them with open arms in a fit of jealous rage. After all his many victories against Sulla's generals, Sertorius had been brought down by a close ally. Cinna shook his head. *Perpenna was such an idiot. A cup filled to the brim with self-importance, plus the stupidity to think he could do better than Sertorius himself if given the chance.*

When young Gnaeus Pompeius had arrived with his army, Perpenna bungled the battle and promptly surrendered, asking for clemency. Pompeius had him executed after a mock trial. Even though Sertorius was Sulla's enemy, he had still held the rank of a Roman citizen and senator. *Good riddance, Perpenna, filthy sack of slime. You failed us all.*

When he received a letter from his former brother-in-law Gaius Julius Caesar, Cinna had been ecstatic to travel immediately to Corduba. The missive had contained an offer to serve as tribune, followed later by a return to Rome. Even though Cinna hadn't seen Caesar in many years, he had hugged the man on sight in gratefulness. He still teared up at the fact that Caesar, once husband to his beloved sister Cornelia, was the only one of his many friends and acquaintances that had not forgotten him, handing him a chance for redemption out of the blue.

Now Cinna, as tribune of the Eighth legion, had brought long-awaited reinforcements of four understrength legionary cohorts and ten turmae of Celtic cavalry to the Ninth. The lengthy siege against the Lancienses Oppidani had ended in a bloody battle when the city's defenders had finally chosen to fight instead of slowly starving to death. He knew the Ninth's commander had patiently waited here for several weeks, likely to Caesar's displeasure. *For my brother-in-law, the lack of time must be the biggest worry. Well, with the men I brought, Vatinius is finally attacking*.

"What's on your mind, Cinna?" Sabinius asked from his side, fully bringing him back from his musings.

"Just thinking about what's ahead. Did the Ninth have any major clashes with these Transcudani yet?"

"Our small detachment at the southern pass had a close encounter during fort building, but they survived and secured the approach. We built another small fort in front of their wall here in the northern pass, with our own wall parallel to theirs to cut them off from fresh supplies. Though, there are so many little goat trails everywhere, stuff still gets through despite our patrols."

Cinna figured they must have reached the northern pass when the lead riders stopped. The reflection of moonlight from the head of the column's polished armor sparkled, surely bright enough to be visible to the Transcudani watchers on the adjoining ridge.

Sabinius raised his hand, turned his horse around, and shouted. "Keep the men in the woods. No fires or torches, stay invisible to the enemy up there," he commanded the decurions, gesticulating to the ridge to their left. "But keep a couple of men in the pass with a view of our fort and the gate to relay back. When our own wall gate opens, ride for all you're worth." The prefect turned and looked at Cinna. "I will lead this one turma here to the fort. Why don't you come with me? We'll find a good spot on the wall to enjoy the view until the enemy gate opens."

Cinna nodded and kicked his horse to follow Sabinius and the three squads.

693 AUC (61 BC), summer
Stella Mountains, eastern ridge, valleys and high plateau, lands of the Lancienses Transcudani, Hispania

Even well-laid plans can fall apart thanks to the smallest oversights, and Oz admitted it could have easily been avoided this time. He figured it was close to an hour before sunrise as per the moon rising behind the heavy clouds. There was just enough illumination for the two groups of legionaries to gather early below the Transcudani watchmen on the ridge. How he wished they would have waited a little longer! The continuous cluttering had alerted the watchers, and one of them now blew a carnyx to sound alarm.

"Take them out, now!" Capussia shouted.

Oz ran ahead to guide the Numidians to the area between the two defensive groups, his own squad sticking close. He took up Capussia's call, urging the archers onto the ridge. As soon as they had the vantage point, they split into two groups and attacked the two clusters of defenders from behind. This gave them the much-needed advantage of surprise, one that the legionaries attacking from below didn't get. The Transcudani were locked in a tight shield-wall formation against the Romans storming up, leaving them unprepared for the Numidian's charge. The fight was brief, with few casualties on the Roman side. *The real damage, though, was letting them sound the alarm. Nothing left but to hurry.*

Oz saw the legionaries of the Eighth's cohorts form at the valley side of the ridge to get ready for their attack on the village. There was no time to waste. His Numidians would stick with the Ninth's four cohorts and go for the gate. The plan had been for his group to go first, to slip unnoticed by the town on their way to the gate. Now, these twenty-three hundred legionaries and Numidian archers had to rely on speed alone and the level heads of their cohort prefects. He looked to his left to see the Eighth's sixteen hundred legionaries running hard for the valley. When the first few made it to the horse fence, several carnyx in the village picked up the earlier alarm from the ridge. To his right, the town and the wall's gate area still remained quiet. *That will change very, very soon.*

Finally, they were ready, and the cohort prefects ordered their men to go. "Move!" Oz screamed. The Ninth's legionaries started down the hill, many of Oz's own men stumbling in the gloomy illumination. The lead runners pushed to the right until the terrain became flatter and the men fell into an easy trot, the fastest they could sustain in full armor without ending up winded. The distance to the town shrank as the soldiers jogged along. Nobody spoke, the only noises the clanking of gladius sheaths on chainmail and pilum heads hitting shields. The front runners now climbed slightly uphill to keep more distance to the town and the refugees camping outside, though before they were even with the first houses, several of the town's war horns sounded alarm.

Oz urged his men to run faster when several hundred male and female warriors swarmed out from houses and tents. The numbers soon swelled into the thousands, all shouting and screaming to each other while running desperately to cut the Roman force off from their wall and gates.

The legionaries kept jogging until a few hundred of the enemy managed to crowd in front of them. Oz heard the call to form "triple rank," the standard battle line of three ranks deep. The soldiers all slowed and fell into a growing line, now turning to face a rushing enemy who started attacking the moment the Romans came into reach.

The quiet morning turned into a cacophony of epic proportions, the battle noise so loud the only thing Oz could hear above the din was a new bugle call of agmen formate, the change to square formation. By having the standard bearers signal which units were to move, they anchored the square at the northernmost part of the line, allowing the soldiers farthest behind to fold towards the mountain, then fold again towards the north.

As more legionaries came in along the mountainside, they caught up with the men closest to the wall, slowly closing the formation that now resembled a stretched rectangle some six hundred feet long. The Numidian horns had taken up their own command, moving all auxiliaries to share the inside of the square with the officers, standard bearers, and horn blowers.

With the formation completed, the entire rectangle now moved in the direction of the wall. The speed was impeded by the two longer sides, where the men had to move their feet sideways. The legionaries at the bottom of the rectangle moved by continuously switching out their ranks, having to slow down or overrun the sides. Oz knew from many training maneuvers he had watched that the rear had to avoid tripping while walking backwards, which would leave them behind the line and open to a quick death by the pursuing enemy. The maneuver reduced the distance to the wall to about fifty feet, compressing the mass of five hundred Transcudani warriors who'd managed to squeeze into the space. The cohorts' cornua and tubae blew the command to stop, which the standard bearers relayed only to the units of the northern-most facing men, contracting the sides of the rectangle and spreading it wider. After a few minutes of this, the command changed again to momentarily stop everybody, followed by a call to advance to the north.

"Step forward!" the centurions around Oz urged their men. "Inpello! Push through," they called.

"Follow them!" he shouted, changing from blindly shooting into the masses to picking out targets on the wall itself. The legionary ranks in front all stepped together, pushing into the enemy with their shields and throwing some of them back into their fellow warriors. The limited space between their shields discouraged probing Transcudani blades from finding flesh.

After a few repetitions of the standard legionary rhythm of rotate, stab out, lock shields and push forward, the enemy found itself so squeezed against the inside of their wall that they hampered each other's attempts to get back at the Romans.

The next command reverberated. "Rear ranks, pila iacite! Throw pila!" The effect on the warriors trapped between the legionaries and the wall was horrible. Many pila found flesh and killed on impact, while penetrated shields added to the confusion in tight quarters. Another call of "Pila iacite!" told the rear ranks to throw their second pila, many targeting enemy archers spread across the wall. That salvo caused many injured and dead to fall off and land on top of their brethren below. *Yet still they hold out, fighting for their people with a ferocity that needs to be respected,* Oz marveled.

Next, the cornua and tubae called a testudo formation. The second and third ranks moved close to the first to cover all three ranks with their shields against arrows. Oz was caught by surprise when the few centurions not standing in rank ran up to join the backside of the line and the archers on the wall changed their aim to the Numidian archers. "Close with the line, quickly!" Oz called to his men. Their small leather shields provided little protection from direct hits.

The legionaries in front slowed down when enough dead bodies had amassed to create a physical barrier. Another command was given, reaching the century in the middle of the line in front of a set of stairs leading up the wall. This happened to be the part of the Ninth's Second cohort directly in front of Oz and his squad.

"Cuneum formate, form a wedge!" Centurion Opiter Maximus shouted from a few feet away. The center of the line pushed out. Legionaries climbed over the bodies on double step and continued forward. This created a triangular protrusion from the line with its point leading right at the stairs. "Move up!" Oz told his men, who filled the empty space at the back of the wedge as the legionaries continued to push and stab. The wedge hit the wall, allowing the first men to run up the stairs and use their big shields to shove the defenders onto their backs, where they could be easily dispatched from under the legionaries' shields. As he followed, Oz saw several warriors tumble down close by after being pushed off the wall. The legionaries secured the landing at the top and the men moved into lines across the walkway, separately for each side.

As they started to push apart, a second rank formed behind the first, then a third, followed by a fourth and fifth until Oz and his men made it up the wall, aiming below at the easy targets trapped against it. After Oz finished the last of his ten quivers, he looked around the walkway for more arrows, mechanically pulling left-overs with little regard as to their origins, either from dead archer's quivers or directly from dead bodies.

The legionary square below them at last overwhelmed the remaining warriors and closed with the wall, after which the whole square received command to head for the gate. Each step was a push with their shields, and a stab out in turn. Every step closer got harder. The call blew for the ranks to rotate. *The green boys in the first rank must be at their end.*

With the second rank now up front, the push was renewed. The men stepped over downed bodies until they stopped twenty feet past the gate. *This should be enough to cover our guys below.*

Oz caught the tips of the two gate doors peaking from below the walkway as they swung inwards. *Finally. Now we'll get some help.*

The air suddenly became more humid, solidifying a strong stench of death already permeating everything. He wrinkled his nose in disgust just before the gods decided to open heaven's floodgate, starting a heavy downpour to wash away all the offending odors of viscera and bodily fluids.

The legionaries on the wall followed the leading rank below. Oz's squad trailed closely, widening the gap to the other legionary lines, who were now far behind them and still defending the catwalk from surviving warriors on the eastern end of the wall. "They are breaking through!" Adhe shouted, and Oz turned to see those same warriors on the eastern wall cut deep into the lines of the legionaries. As the Transcudani pushed, some soldiers were thrown off the wall, while others were trapped against the parapet on the outside of the walkway. The warriors pushed through the last line of soldiers and ran right at the Numidians.

"They're coming at us from behind!" Oz shouted at the legionaries close to him before bending down to grab a dead Transcudani woman's spear and rushing forward along the inner side of the wall. Adhe, fifty feet ahead, shot a man from up close, then dropped his bow to pull his long knife.

Oz looked at the weapons of the men and women storming at them with a sinking feeling in his gut. Their small Numidian leather shields were no good for this kind of fight. He ran, watching Adhe move towards the parapet with Gulussa by his side and Massi behind. A fourth man got hit and fell off the wall. *Who was that?*

An extraordinarily big woman pushed a heavy iron-rimmed shield at his nephew in an attempt to bowl him over. She was solid and at least a foot taller than Adhe, who casually moved his right foot behind as a brace and managed to keep his own shield up. In response, she swung her large sword at the boy with her right, cutting through the rim and deep into the leather. *Just hold on, please, just hold on.*

Adhe moved fast and decisively, letting the woman fully extend her arm before stepping into her reach and rotating in behind her shield. In one smooth motion, he stabbed her under her sword arm, the knife sinking deep into her armpit through the opening of her chainmail. She dropped hard.

Just as he reached Massi, his friend went down under a sword swing from the side before Oz could run his attacker through. He desperately tried to pull the spear out while the next enemy approached, pointing a long lance's wide-leafed iron tip at his chest. He abandoned the stuck weapon and pulled his knife instead. His years of combat training took over. He moved his shield, feinting an opening that would invite a quick stab to his middle. When the expected attack came, he rotated to his left and used his knife to knock the spearhead off target. Trapped in the forward momentum, the man could not pull his weapon back soon enough. Oz dropped his own shield and grabbed the lance with his left hand, about a foot behind the tip. The warrior stopped to pull back as hard as he could. Oz now reversed, stepped forward and pushed, hard. The man now braced to avoid falling backward, which left his side wide open. Thin leather armor protecting the stomach proved little resistance to Oz's blade. As he pulled his knife back out, he heard a loud shout from behind. Opiter Maximus ran through between him and Gulussa, sprinting hard enough that his outstretched shield flung the next warrior backwards on impact.

As Oz turned forward, a tall warrior's shield came right at him. The impact made him lose his footing and tumble over the wall. Falling through the air, he waved his arms to straighten a fall that ended on a dead warrior. His head hit the dead man's shield, and the world around him turned black.

***

When Lucius Cornelius Cinna and Quintus Titurius Sabinius arrived at the small fort's southern wall, they handed their reins over to a camp servant. They joined the Ninth's Legatus, Publius Vatinius, and the fort's three cohort prefects, all scanning the enemy fortifications. In the soft pre-dawn light, Cinna was surprised to see movement on top of the Transcudani wall. *Of course, something has gone wrong. The plan was for any action to start at or shortly after first light.*

As he looked on, the morning's first sunrays penetrated the heavy clouds to illuminate the peaks of the surrounding mountains, adding clarity to his view. Though the enemy manned the wall in decent numbers, their warriors showed only their backs. He could only assume that meant the ground behind the walls must be swarming with legionaries. Now the first legionaries became visible, pushing out from their point of access. If the gate could be taken, it would happen soon or not at all. He turned his sight to their own camp and the troops standing ready in marching lines pointed at the fort's closed gate. Cinna's gaze went back to the Transcudani wall, and he watched intently as Roman troops pushed closer and closer to the gate.

"Do the troops on the ground mirror the men on the wall?" he said, breaking the silence and receiving only a vague nod from Sabinius in response. *He is as tense as I am, willing the unseen cohorts forward.*

As the fighting on the distant wall made it to within steps of the enemy wall's entrance, legate Vatinius moved into action. "Open our gates!" he shouted down to the soldiers. The Roman wall opened first, followed by the doors in the fort. The legionaries started to cover the thousand feet to the Transcudani fortifications, while most officers still hurried back to their horses. Vatinius and the legion prefects joined the aides and standard bearers at the end of the marching column, while Sabinius and Cinna joined a few Celtic cavalry riders standing ready at the wall.

"Where are they?" he asked impatiently before the thunder of many hundreds of hoofs roared ever louder. Just then, dark clouds decided to empty their heavy load of water over the six hundred hard-riding Celtic cavalry followed by two hundred Cretan archers. He waited until the first hundred had galloped through the gate, then kicked his horse to join the rush. In the dim light, Cinna could see the enemy gate was wide open. They passed the quick-marching legionaries and approached the opening while a corridor formed for them on the other side. They were close to riding through when some of the enemy foolishly moved into their path, eager to get to the gate's doors. Brave though they were, the unfortunate warriors were far too slow, and the first rank of the Celtic horse them like a hammer. *Here we go, time to remove my Spatha from its scabbard.*

Without slowing down, the cavalry with Cinna and Sabinius in their midst moved ever deeper into a sea of enemies. Cinna slashed down again and again, until they were through to the other side. He turned to see the Cretans coming out as well, their own swords hacking. As the last men came out of the throng, Sabinius screamed, "Again, push through one more time!" while rotating his sword over his head to indicate the need to turn horses. Cinna rode ahead, finding himself with the Cretans when hitting the enemy again.

***

Titus Balventius cheered at the Ninth's cavalry thundering when it stormed through the gates behind him, and at the loud thudding noise that sounded like a nearby lightning strike when the riders hit the enemy masses. He was just to the west of the gate, fighting in the front line after having let himself and Seppius rotate into the first rank. It was unwritten law that centurions had to earn the men's respect by getting their hands dirty, or bloody, as in this occasion. Balventius regripped his gladius several times when it became slippery with blood, and silently praised the mental clarity the cool rain brought him.

After his last opponent fell backwards, he had a brief break in the fight, enough to get a glance at the Roman cavalry. Some fought off Transcudani cavalry that had emerged from the opening to the other valleys, but most were already coming back, slashing at the enemy soldiers from behind. *We won this battle already. They just don't know it yet.*

He pushed out with his shield, rotated it slightly, then stabbed. All their men shouted the repeating rhythm together, keeping the line synchronized. The tubae behind him gave a different command, and he picked it up as loud as he could. "Inpello! Push!" he shouted, and the soldiers around him picked it up quickly. They now added a full step forward to each shield push, moving their line into the enemies, inflicting more pressure instead of simply holding their positions. Every step forward saw many of the Transcudani warriors cut down, while others were pushed back into the men and women behind them.

After moving a full hundred steps forward, Balventius came upon a much bigger opening. The enemy's mass was thinning rapidly. Starting at the south-eastern corner, warriors peeled off from their main host to flee. The Eighth's cohorts must have succeeded with the village and turned north to threaten the enemy from behind. He stepped forward to the next opponent, too busy with fighting and staying alive to think about anything else until after he downed another woman warrior. Suddenly, only the backs of running Transcudani were before him. The enemy had broken, all rushing through the pass into the western valleys.

In the distance, a line of the Eighth's four cohorts marched towards him, helping to herd the enemies west. He cheered with the rest of his century and cleaned his gladius before sheathing it, then turned towards their cohort standards in expectation. He was as ready for the call as his men were. The moment the horns sounded the command to fast trot, they gave chase.

***

Legatus Vatinius rode up to Lucius Cinna. "Ride over to your cohorts and tell them to cross the mountain to the west now, and to make haste. Your men need to cut the Transcudani off at the ascent to the tableau. If we trap enough of them in the valleys, this whole thing is done and over with."

"Will do, sir!" Cinna shouted back, touching the fingers of his right hand to the side of his helmet in acknowledgement. He kicked his horse and rode hard for the troops of the Eighth. The cohort prefects already moving their line toward the incline in anticipation.

He reined in. "Have your men start climbing immediately! The legate wants you to cut the enemy off as close to the tableau as possible. Trap as many as you can."

The prefects and some of the present centurions saluted, touching their eyebrows before turning and barking orders. The centuries formed into a long line facing the incline before finally taking off up the mountainside in a mad scramble.

Cinna shivered and turned to look at the clouds. The rain had reduced to a trickle. *I wouldn't mind seeing some of that hidden summer sun. It's entirely too cold in these mountains.*

He encouraged his mare to speed across the muddy ground after the cavalry, on to the next valley and the next Transcudani town.

***

Ozalkis came to and yelped as a slap shook his face. Then another one came. He held up his hand to stop the third blow.

"Ah, he's truly back from the dead," he heard and opened his eyes to find the hitting hand now offering to help him up. He grabbed without hesitation before realizing it belonged to Opiter Maximus, the unfriendly centurion from the second cohort. Oz was confused. The man made no secret of his loathing for the dirty foreigners of the auxilia forces.

"Thank you," he said, mystified.

"Oh, not at all. Thank you and your men. Those warriors would have wiped us out from behind if you hadn't been there. You fought bravely, especially considering the flimsy excuses you people have for shields and swords. I saw you get thrown off the wall earlier, so I figured I should come and find you." He waved behind, where most of Oz's squad walked up, and grinned. "I guess I beat your guys to it."

Oz grinned back at Opiter. He had never thought to share a smile with the man, let alone a civil conversation. Over the centurion's shoulder, he spotted Adhe slowly moving down from the wall while supporting their friend Massi. With a thankful nod to Maximus and his optio Pullo, he turned and walked over to his nephew. Adhe was shaking. Oz squeezed his shoulder in support. He knew from his own experience that fighting up close and personal was the worst. This kind of killing would haunt his nephew, just as it did him. *Every damn day of my life.*

He inspected Massi's long cut in his lower cheek. "You sure took a beating," he wisecracked, happy his friend wasn't worse off.

"Looks like my arm is broken. Well, and I added a new beauty mark," his pale friend joked back, "but thanks again for getting us chainmail. I wouldn't be here without it."

Oz looked his squad over and realized it was light. "Where is Salla?" He saw heads shake. "Muusa? No?" He sighed. They had lost two more of their old team, though it could have been worse. So much worse. Looking around for the medici, he hoped they had already set up shop. His top priority was to leave Massi in capable hands while he and the rest of the squad caught up to the other forces. He spotted some of the battlefield medic's helpers about to collect the wounded and pointed in that direction. His friend waved back at him and walked away.

"Let's go!" The legionaries and Oz's squad started to run.

***

As Oz, Maximus, and their men ran up the valley, they encountered chaos everywhere. What had started as a retreat for the Transcudani warriors had transformed into wild panic. Hundreds of them had been cut off by pursuing cavalry forces, and some simply gave up, their weapons thrown into the mud. Once wrists and ankles were bound, the Roman soldiers moved on, leaving only a small guard force. Other groups of Transcudani, though, kept fighting, clearly intent on dying. After running through the middle of a forcefully emptied town, Oz passed several more legionary centuries caught up in these senseless struggles. The men were boxing the warriors in behind a continuous shield wall, and dispatched them briefly and viciously. Oz shook his head, though on some level he understood the choice these warriors made. *So much senseless death. I'm not sure I can take any more of this.*

As their small force came out of a second town, they came across huge numbers of surrendered enemies, all cut off from escape to the high plateau by the soldiers of the Eighth legion. Most of the gathered groups totaled in the lower thousands, but the biggest assembly, cornered against the three-thousand-foot-tall sheer wall of the high eastern plateau, counted at least ten thousand. At the base of the steep incline, a handful of agile warriors attempted a last-minute escape by climbing. Oz's eyes followed them up and widened at the sight of tens of thousands of Transcudani standing along the edge of the plateau, helplessly staring down at the trapped people in the valley. On the long incline between the two tabletops, a big mass of locals successfully defended the winding path, denying the legionaries any further passage.

Oz and Maximus stopped their men when they reached the soldiers of their second cohort, who formed part of a loose line around a few thousand captives. Devoid of all hope, some Transcudani were pale, sitting on the ground in shock, while others were standing and wailing loudly. Many walked back and forth, often crying violently. Oz let his eyes scan through the sad mass of people.

Horrifying. So many children, guarded only by grandparents. What? He scanned back. *There. Two small children, all alone.*

He held his breath. A small girl hugged a little toddler boy, both crying. The other Transcudani around them didn't seem to care, leaving the space around the two lonely children wide open as if nobody wanted to take responsibility for them. *Their family must be among the many dead.*

As Oz watched the girl get up to stand protectively in front of the little boy, a dam of long pent-up emotions broke inside of him. He started sobbing violently, the losses of all his many loved ones hitting him at once. *No, no, no. This is too much, I can bear this any longer.*

As tears threatened to block his sight, he acted suddenly and without conscious thought. Wiping his eyes, he ran out of the circle of soldiers and into the mass. A path opened for him, fearful faces following his progress. He grabbed both children and turned around. Clutching them tightly in his arms, he sprinted back. The young girl kept hitting him with her little fists as hard as she could, screaming all the way. He made shushing sounds, saying, "It's alright, it's alright" in Numidian, although he knew the words couldn't calm her or himself down. As he approached the soldiers, Adhe, Gulussa, and several others from his squad protectively rushed at him. All shed tears as they surrounded him, hiding the children from prying legionary eyes.

***

Retukenos stood next to his favorite chieftain colleague at the edge of the western high plateau. They looked out at the scene below them, neither speaking a word. From the corner of his eye, he noticed Koitina's worried glances. After a few minutes, she put her hand on his shoulder. "Sit for a moment, old friend." He did, caught too much in his own grief to reply.

The survivors who had made it up the path were now grieving for the many families and friends who hadn't. Retukenos watched on as big groups below stopped fighting and surrendered, while some smaller groups of warriors chose death over slavery. He took a deep breath. "I hope you'll be up for this, my friend. We need to form a group of emissaries to negotiate with the Roman general. They can starve us up here, surrounded as we are. If we offer full surrender, maybe they'll spare some of our people from slavery." He looked at her. She nodded and helped him back up. "Let's see who survived."

They walked off to gather a few elders and a handful of surviving council members. Once they numbered twenty, Retukenos figured it would have to do.

"We can't keep looking for more elders," he said to the small assembly. "We need to go down to the Romans now and end this before they start building more walls to trap us up here. All they need to do is wait, and many of us will die from hunger." He looked at Koitina. "Are we all in agreement?" He examined every face in turn. Some of the men still looked shocked, others clearly grieved about loved ones. Two of the men just looked angry. "Do we have a problem?" he asked them.

"No, we don't. Even though I hate the idea of surrendering to these dishonorable dogs, I know there's nothing more we can do," one of them said.

"We all share that thought," Retukenos replied.

***

Vatinius walked up to Cinna and Sabinius. "Get the slave traders!" he commanded before moving on. Sabinius left Cinna sitting on a boulder to find a cavalry man to bring the legion's three resident slave traders over from the main camp. The slavers had been part of the Ninth legion's entourage from the very beginning of the campaign. Sabinius found his scout, barked orders, and walked back.

"Won't take them very long to show up. They're likely already halfway here," Sabinius quipped after he returned to the boulder.

Only twenty minutes later, Cinna spoke. "You were right, here they are." The slave traders and their men made their way through the different groups of Transcudani, carefully counting and studying along the way. A few legionary centuries continued to bind untied hands and ankles in the bigger groups, while the remainder of the cohorts had moved on to start digging for siege fortifications to cut off the two high tableaus.

Half an hour later the sky cleared, and young Crassus led the slavers by their boulder. "What's next?" Sabinius asked, stopping the tribune.

"They're done with their count, so now they will meet with Vatinius and our camp prefect," Crassus answered.

"I don't want to miss this." Cinna stood up, Sabinius following him a moment later. Everybody involved in the fight against the Transcudani would get a cut from the spoils, Cinna and the cohorts on loan included.

The Ninth's commander sat on a folding stool, animatedly chatting with his camp prefect, when Crassus brought his entourage.

"Ave!" Vatinius addressed the three traders. "Have you come up with your numbers?" Cinna saw all three heads nod.

One of them stepped forward as the spokesperson. "First off, I need to let you know that we will not bid against each other. We don't have enough manpower individually to move all the captives, at least not without involving methods that would inflict heavy losses. So, we need to work together on this. On numbers, we came up with roughly twenty-five thousand men, women and children. I am asking to buy ten thousand head, and my colleagues here want seven and a half thousand each. Our offer is a generic two-hundred-fifty sesterce a piece."

Vatinius looked to his camp prefect, who ran quick numbers in his head and whispered them to the legate. Vatinius shook his head. "That's not enough. I want you to pay four hundred sesterces a head, or I'll dispatch half my legion to bring them back to Scalabis where we can get much better prices."

Cinna saw the slave traders' faces suddenly go blank. A moment later, he realized the men were actually amused, working hard to suppress smiles. He raised his eyebrow to look questioningly at Sabinius. "They know the legatus would never attempt this kind of endeavor himself," Sabinius whispered. "They have the upper hand and can push for wholesale prices. Why else would they follow the legions to the ends of the world?"

The slavers' spokesman made hand gestures back at his fellows, and both of them nodded. "We are willing to pay three hundred per head. That's our final offer."

The legate nodded. "Very well, agreed. Thank you, gentlemen. Please, work with our prefect on the needed paperwork." Vatinius turned and walked away.

"Legate, may I have a word?" Sabinius asked while hurrying after him, Cinna following closely. "About taking the tableaus; do you have a plan yet? Their defensive situation is very good. I worry this could become quite bloody if we try brute force." Cinna nodded in agreement.

Vatinius laughed. "I have to say I don't know, not yet. If we could stay, we would wait for them to starve. But we don't have time to hang around. Caesar needs us to move north. My hope rests on them not knowing our hurry." Just at that moment, they all gazed at the steep path below the tableau above. A delegation of twenty older men and one woman was rushing down the incline. All were well dressed, holding their hands out with palms up in a gesture of peace and supplication. Cinna would have never guessed it would happen this soon, and clearly neither had the legate. Chuckling, the man raised his fists in triumph.

"Speaking of my hope!" Vatinius said. The man seemed outright giddy from today's success. "Whatever they ask, all I'm offering is that none of the ones up on the tableaus get sold into slavery, and for that I want anything of value they have left." He paused. "They will take my offer, mark my words."

The delegates were soon surrounded by legionaries escorting them to the legate. Some of the chieftains were clearly shaken, their faces masks of incredible sadness. Others kept their heads bowed to avoid eye contact with the Romans around them. The bigger part of the group wore angry defiance in their locked jaws and narrowed brows.

"Who speaks for you?" Vatinius asked. A translator started to speak but was waved off by an old man standing rigidly erect.

"I am Retukenos," he said in passable Latin. "What are your terms for surrender?"

While the legate laughed out loud in triumph, the old chieftain seemed to wither. The formerly regal looking patriarch now seemed nothing more than a huddled, elderly grandfather.

Cinna had seen and heard enough, and he knew that, now, the deal would be struck just as predicted. He grinned at Vatinius and showed him a raised thumb before leaving. With fighting over for the day, he wanted to check on the Eighth's troops

"See you in camp!" he said to Sabinius, who was deep in thought. *No doubt pondering the sale of the slaves. Not bad, seven and a half million sesterces. That makes an incredible one million eight hundred and seventy-five thousand denarii; we will all get a nice bonus.*

A nobleman only needed to own twenty-five thousand denarii, in any mix of estate or cash, to be counted as a knight of the high equites class. As far as Cinna knew, Senate eligibility was worth a few hundred thousand denarii. Of course, Caesar would take a big share as was his due as governor and overall general. Although, he wondered if the whole war would be enough for his brother-in-law, considering the rumors of his legendary amount of debt.

As he slowly made his way back to his horse, he speculated what his total cut would be once the campaign was all over. He was glad the Eighth's commander was somebody trustworthy when it came to money, not like the Ninth's Vatinius. Maybe he could talk to Caesar to urge close scrutiny on the man. A somewhat capable commander, he had to admit. *But with Vatinius' reputation for personal greed and extortion, I don't understand why he would be trusted with a single sesterce, and most certainly not why Caesar trusts him with a whole legion's spoils.*

693 AUC (61 BC), early fall
Lands of the Banienses, Hispania

Oz woke up with a start. He scanned the tent until his eyes rested on Adhe, who tossed back and forth on his cot. The boy's forehead was drenched in sweat. Not surprising; nightmares had become nightly companions for all of them. *I wish I knew how to help him with those. I'd like to get rid of my own as well.*

He listened to his tent members sleep; some were snoring. *Is it early morning? Definitely. Well after midnight, based on the bright moon shining through the tent leather's holes.*

His eyes lingered over his friends as they lay sleeping. Massi still looked uncomfortable with his broken arm, but at least he no longer let out involuntary groans like he had for a few weeks right after the battle. Gulussa was clearly uncomfortable as well, but by his own choice. Oz had to grin at the sight. Daleninar had become his friend's woman, and now lay as if draped over him. It was a feat of contortion for two grown people to share a small army cot. Looking at her arm and shapely leg hanging over the side, he felt eternal gratitude. Her offer to care for his two little Transcudani children indebted him to the bright-eyed girl. Despite her protests, he had insisted on a small fee in return. The two siblings were currently sharing the empty cot right next to him, sleeping peacefully despite their rough experience, like only small children could.

Now encamped in the land of the Banienses, the legion had stayed put for a second day in a row. For the first time after countless days of marching and nightly camp building, many of the men had jumped at the opportunity to bring their loved ones into the squad tents. The lack of privacy bothered many raw recruits, but the more experience the legionaries and auxiliaries all shared together, the more they saw each other as brothers in arms, and the less individual privacy seemed to matter. *I don't even think any more about the many slights and derogatory comments the Roman legionaries threw at us barbarians after our arrival in Hispania. Or the even worse condescension we received from the Cretans. We are all equals now, more or less brothers.*

The lines had become more and more blurred, their varied origins or backgrounds didn't seem to matter anymore. Sharing more hardship with each other than they ever could with any blood relatives seemed to do that.

In his own dreams, Oz often relived some of the battles. The unbidden scenes were always the worst and most violent ones, filled with death and destruction. What made his episodes especially vile was the inability to change things. He knew what was coming, yet despite his struggles was never able to save a friend or a fellow soldier from sure death. Having everything replay in his head left him with a feeling of complete helplessness. Adhe's dreams were similar, and the boy was often depressed. Still, in the bigger scheme of things, he knew they were among the lucky ones. A legionary from the sixth cohort had recently woken up disoriented enough to kill three of his tent mates with a cooking knife before snapping out of it. The soldier had been publicly put to death shortly thereafter, head hanging in shame through the whole ordeal of his execution.

Some of his tent mates and friends had started to walk away from any conversations touching on previous battles or deceased pals. He sighed. Different personalities coped differently with their experiences, and the one saving constant binding them all was their camaraderie. He settled back down in the knowledge of the morning call still being hours away. He wouldn't be able to go back to sleep, but he could stay as quiet as possible to allow his tent mates their well-deserved rest.

***

The next morning, Oz sat on his cot and wondered about the homey scene that had unfolded around him. Daleninar had used a hand mill to grind generous amounts of wheat into flour while Adhe formed small loaves for the entire tent's morning bread. The other archers sat outside around the tent's fire, already lit in preparation for the bread oven, while the two small children took advantage of the now open dirt floor between the cots to play. He corrected himself. The dark-haired little girl watched over her two-year-old brother as he explored the tent. No, not just the little girl. She was *his* little girl now, and her name was Stena. She was a five-year-old desperately acting tough to keep her brother from harm. Little Sakaristar ended up at his side, and Oz pulled the boy into a quick hug before dropping him down again. He looked to the tent entry when he heard a throat being cleared and saw Capussia's face peeking in, eyebrows raised in wonder. "I need to talk to you!"

Oz hesitated only a short moment before answering, "Come on in."

"I need you to come out instead. Sorry. Walk with me to my morning meeting at the legate's tent."

"Alright, I'll be right out," Oz replied, hurriedly changing into a fresh tunic, mentally noting not to forget to have his other two washed today. He pushed out through the tent flap and caught up to his waiting friend. "What can I do for you, Capussia?"

"We lost two Numidian decurions during the battle with the Transcudani. The two turmae in question have elected new ones, but we need one more. One of the dead was my overall second decurion. You know the second and third decurions are my official assistants and next in line for command over our Numidian auxiliaries if I die." He looked Ozalkis in the eyes. "I want to propose you for the job, if you're up for it." He chuckled.

"Of course, you may not have any time since you now seem to be babysitting children." Oz knew Capussia expected him to laugh with him. Instead, he put his arm on his superior's shoulder and cleared his throat. "Just to be clear, the children are mine. I should have told you earlier; I took them from the Transcudani captives. When I saw them, I could not let them go into slavery with everybody else." He took a deep breath. "I would appreciate it if you kept quiet about this. Gulussa's woman Daleninar is looking after them for me, so they wouldn't interfere with my new duties."

In answer, Capussia smiled knowingly and clapped him on his shoulder. "Don't worry about me, I applaud you for doing it. I guess we share a soft spot for children. I hope to find the right woman to have a few more myself before my time is up."

Oz breathed easier. He had dreaded for days what Capussia's reaction might be once he found out. Taking Stena and little Saki as his own equaled stealing from the legion's coffers, after all. *I should have known better. Once again, he proves to be a true friend.*

693 AUC (61 BC), early fall
Lands of the Seurbi, Hispania

"The Callaeci delegation is here," Hirtius announced. Caesar had received several messages from local powers over the last few days, urging him to stop hostilities and meet with their highest chieftains. He had decided to grant the audience and had sent word to all his legions to stop marching.

To maximize his negotiating power, he had also decided to treat the envoys as a nuisance, barely worthy of his attention. *I have just the right setting.*

He grinned at Hirtius. "Send them over to where the camp prefect has the latrines extended," he instructed. Noticing

Hirtius' raised eyebrow, he broke into a chuckle. It was a hot fall day, and the area would be unbearable.

He collected some officers on his way and positioned himself right next to the expansion area, making a show of being undisturbed by the stink while glancing toward the road from the corner of his eyes. Hirtius walked the delegation up to his group, and he was satisfied to notice many scrunched noses on shocked faces. *Good. That should maximize the effect I am after.*

"Tell them I'll be with them shortly," Caesar said, turning away from the group to head straight for the digging legionaries. "What have you poor sods done to get this duty?" Caesar shouted at them, smiling. The legionaries looked up, briefly stopping their work. "Nothing I want to tell our mighty leader about, sir, sorry!" One of them replied with a deadpan face. The whole group broke out into laughter.

"See these folks behind me?" Caesar added, after the laughter died down. The soldiers all looked past him at the delegation. "They want to urgently negotiate terms since they are scared of us. Should we let them use our latrines before they need new pants?" The legionaries laughed even harder this time. "Are you ready to be done with this campaign? How do the words winter quarters sound to you?" This time, he was answered with cheers and hoots. *They probably stewed long enough, let's deal with these people.*

He sauntered back to the group of Callaeci, seemingly interested in anything but them. Time to negotiate favorable terms for plunder without sacrificing another single legionary. "Where were we?" He asked Hirtius, briefly winking at his aide before putting on a look of absolute boredom.

693 AUC (61 BC), winter
Scalabis, Roman Headquarter for Lusitania, Hispania

"Again, I am forever in your debt," Cinna said.

"We are forever bound by Cornelia," Caesar replied. "There is no need for you to grovel." His former brother-in-law gestured to the small table and stools on a small patio of the town house that had become the de facto city headquarters. They both sat down. "My plans are to help you back to a career on the Cursus Honorum. You lost too many good years in exile."

"That is beyond my wildest dreams," Cinna responded. "Most of my old friends won't even respond to my letters. I must be persona non-grata in Rome, somebody to be avoided at all costs."

"Not for much longer. While you keep serving as tribune, I will work on the Senate to approve your eligibility for higher office. It's near impossible to get Sulla's law that marked your father a traitor thrown out, so I plan to get you exempted based on personal service to me, and therefore to the Republic."

"Thank you for all you're doing for me." Cinna's gaze went over to beds of blooming flowers in the small garden. "How is my niece Julia these days? I hope I can meet her in person someday."

"She's fifteen now, and strikingly beautiful. I'm happy to say that she takes after her mother, though she reminds me so much of her sometimes that it hurts," Caesar mused.

"Does she get along with your new wife? What was her name, Pompeia?" *How I wish I would have been there for you, Cornelia, my sweet sister.*

"Oh, they got along just fine. Pompeia was a nice enough person, though I divorced her earlier this year," Caesar replied.

Cinna raised his left eyebrow at him. "You divorced her? Sorry, I hadn't heard."

"The marriage was a political arrangement, though I tried to fall in love with her, I really did. But the fact is she's not Cornelia." Caesar paused for a moment before showing Cinna a slight smile. "I should have divorced her much sooner. Once I realized that I will never love her, I felt free to have my fun. I've made a sport out of sleeping with the wives of my staunchest opponents in the Senate." Caesar must have noticed the surprise in his friend's face because he started to laugh. After a brief moment of hesitation, Cinna joined him. "When you come to Rome, I'll walk you across the Forum Romanum before one of the senate meetings, so I can introduce you to the senators I'm working with. I am even on a civil footing with senator Decimus Junius Silanus these days. The man used to loath me, though he's changed his view thanks to his lovely wife Servilia. She has become a close friend since we started seeing each other three years ago."

Cinna shook his head in wonder. *This is not the same Caesar I remember. Surely, he is no longer the principled man I once knew.*

As if reading his thoughts, his brother-in-law him looked back pensively. "Cornelia is gone, and the best of me went with her. I just sometimes forget how much I have changed, while you, dear Cinna, still seem the same idealist as ever." Caesar stood up. "Would you have some wine with me? Yes? Let me go and get some."

As his friend left for the kitchen, Cinna wondered if he would still recognize Rome. There had to be so many changes since the time of Marius, buildings and people alike.

***

"And he said it was the best eatery in all of Scalabis?" Oz asked Massi.

"Yes, he said that and more. Once he got going, he couldn't shut up about the place," his friend answered. They had asked around for a good local place. All of them were tired of legion fare.

Oz, Adhe, and Massi passed the winter camps of the Eighth and Tenth legions on their way to town. The Seventh had long since departed overland, back to its province, with Caesar's three legions all slated to move back to Corduba in the spring.

"The man's point was that the eatery's customers are all local Roman colonists, so all dishes are based on Italian recipes. He swore the food was better than his own mama's cooking on holidays."

"Let's hope that doesn't mean his mother was a horrible cook," Adhe said before his expression changed. "I understand why Gulussa is not leaving Daleninar alone, but why did we leave Stena and Saki in camp?"

"Roman style eateries might be rowdy. They aren't what you would call child friendly," Oz answered. "I figured, better safe than sorry. We'll see when we get there." He had left the children with Gulussa and a heavily pregnant Daleninar.

They passed several other auxiliary soldiers and legionaries on leave, all of them shouting greetings, no matter their legion, with accompanying friendly nods or waves. Oz felt he and his friends belonged to something much bigger than themselves. "Would either of you have believed this when we signed on?" he asked. The others shook their heads.

"No way," Adhe answered. "Remember how the Romans all looked down on the Numidians, us especially?" He held up his dark-skinned arm for emphasis and chuckled. "Actually, not too different from some of our own Numidians. You remember that guy who called us a troop of apes back in Cirta?"

"Didn't he share his water with you on our march back to Scalabis?" Massi asked.

"He did. I was so surprised when he walked up to me and offered that I didn't know what to say."

"That man," Oz said, "was the only survivor of his squad after the battle in the Stella mountains. That could change anyone's perspective on things." They remained silent, and Oz looked over the massive open gates leading them into city proper.

"Just a few more blocks," Massi said, and Oz sped up, hungry as he was. "Look, there's the sign hanging from the wall. Nicely painted." Massi pointed at a wooden board, hung from the side of the building by two short pieces of chain. His friends guffawed.

"Nicely painted? If I wouldn't know that it's supposed to be wild pheasants, I would think they serve oddly shaped turds inside," Oz joked in reply. They all laughed.

Massi led the way through the doorway and into a wide-open space defined by long, rough tables and benches. A central cooking area at the back of the building opened to the outside below an upper story held up by a row of columns, allowing for many smaller tables all the way out into the backyard.

"I don't think I ever thought an eatery could be this big," Adhe said excitedly while looking around the busy place. Most of the tables in the big room were occupied, and the noise level was overwhelming.

Oz had been told by many legionaries that a small L-shaped bar with a very limited food selection was the norm for Italian style eateries. If you wanted variety, you had to pick another eatery—not a challenge since eateries were commonplace in bigger in Roman cities. "This is certainly not your run-of-the-mill thermopolium. Amazing!" Oz agreed, delighted at the sight.

A serving girl walked by with her arms full of food dishes. "You can sit wherever you like. One of us will be with you shortly. Oh, and if you haven't been here before, the food options are painted on the wall over there." She turned away to deliver the plates.

"That smelled great. Let's see that wall." Oz walked over to the food depictions. "Fortunately, painted much better than the sign outside. They are big on meat here." For the legion's people, meat was a luxury item. "These here are all sausages, right? And are these meatballs? Olives and cheese over there and some kind of stew, plus another stew next to it. What's the bowl after that, or the last thing?"

"No idea, we need to ask the serving girl. I want her to explain all the options before we choose. Should we get a table first?" Massi asked, scanning the room. There were maybe fifty legionaries crowding the long tables against the inner walls. The smaller tables at the back and the outside were all filled by locals, mostly free workers and craftsmen, by the look of their simple clothing.

Massi led the group to one end of the only unoccupied massive table, located between the soldiers and the locals. "I don't see any of the wealthier Romans in here, though they walk the streets outside with everybody else. I wonder why not." Adhe suddenly said.

"From what I know, higher-class Romans frown on public eateries. Maybe because the serving staff is supposed to work as prostitutes for extra money," Oz answered. Adhe raised his eyebrows and looked back at the cute serving girl from earlier in disbelief.

"I think they might not come here because a place like this serves lower class people. I'm sure that rented rooms rarely have kitchens in these cities," Adhe countered.

They expectantly waited for a few minutes until the attractive young woman from earlier came over.

"What would you like to eat? Do you have any questions?" she asked.

"Could you run us through the dishes on the wall, please? We need more info about all of them. Also, please let us know what everything costs," Adhe replied.

"Sure thing, sweetie," she said, winking her long lashes with a seductive smile. "We have something here to suit any coin purse. Starting from the left, there's our house specialty, sausages from pork or lamb, Italian style with fennel and pine nuts, fresh every day and served with garum fish sauce. Next are steamed meatballs, or skewered boar and pheasant. Those are all five sesterces." She looked at them, Oz thought, as if she expected some quip about the outrageously steep price of the main dishes. The table stayed silent, however, expecting her to continue. She listed the whole menu from the most to least expensive items and explained the available choices of red, white, and black wines. "Now, what would you like?"

Oz looked at his two friends. "Are we doing this?" He saw Adhe and Massi enthusiastically nod. "Great." He looked at their waitress. "We'll take one of each dish." The waitress's eyebrows rose, expecting Oz to say he was joking. "I'm serious! We'll share everything with our friends back at camp." He grinned. "And we came prepared." They all pulled out pieces of loose cloth in anticipation of wrapping leftovers.

"And a pitcher of the red wine, please. We had way too much cheap black these last three years." They all laughed. Wine bought by the legion's quartermasters tended to err on the side of vinegar, though the soldiers usually didn't mind. Watered wine was known as a cure-all when combined with food loaded with copious amounts of garlic. If the wine was of the black variety, it added extra strength for the drinker, or so the cohort's regular medicus insisted.

As the serving girl walked to the kitchen, they brought out their purses to count out coins. They stopped when they reached the total, and all added an additional sesterce as a generous tip for the girl.

"We couldn't buy the expensive meat dishes every day. Look over at the local tables, they are only eating from the cheap side of the menu," Oz observed. The other two turned to have a look.

"You're right," Massi said, "but the legionaries are sure going for it," he added, making Oz turn to the tables behind him. Meat dishes along with wine were sprinkled generously on the tables, likely the reason why the majority of the noise in the room originated there. They didn't have to wait long before receiving their wine, followed by the food.

"That earthenware is decent, just as good as the legion's," Massi said. The waitress took the pile of coins and flashed them a happy smile. "Please, let me know if I can do anything else for any of you. We have a quiet corner in the yard or a few small rooms upstairs if you prefer some privacy. You can also ask anyone else from our staff for sex, just have a look around."

"Ah, thanks, we'll think about it," Oz answered with a lopsided smile.

"You weren't kidding," Adhe said after the girl had left their table.

Massi laughed at uncle and nephew's apparent discomfort. "You guys never paid for it?"

"Nope," Oz said, while Adhe just shook his head. "We never had to or wanted to. Adhe always had his share of local girl admirers." He looked at his flushing nephew, who was usually too shy to take advantage of the offers. "Maybe we should get to know some of the locals better instead," he added, pointing at a far table that held a group of local women of different ages, apparently all friends.

Adhe slowly whistled through his teeth when he followed Oz's finger. "Very interesting—pretty, and well-dressed. Decent local women."

They enjoyed the various dishes, slowing down well before making a real dent in the huge amount of food. "I can think of a couple of children that will be excited at breakfast tomorrow," Oz said while pointing at the sausages.

Massi leaned back and rested his hands on a full stomach. "These are so filling, I don't think I could have another one,"

"And that red wine is strong stuff," Adhe added, finishing his cup. "Goes to your head quickly."

A legionary stumbled past. "Talk about wine, or too much of it," Oz said. His eyes followed the man straight to the table with the local women. "Oh no, here comes trouble."

The soldier made lewd gestures at one of the pretty young women, seemingly illustrating what he wished to do with her. The whole table around her erupted in loud protests and various shouts for the man to go away. When he made no attempt to leave, several of the adjoining local diners stood up in solidarity with the women.

Three of the legionary's friends walked over to stand with the drunk troublemaker. Two of them were laughing about the incident, clearly quite intoxicated themselves. The third one, though, looked like he was in a trance, restless eyes darting around from an otherwise stony face. *That guy looks like he's still on a battlefield somewhere. Merda, all of them brought their swords.*

"Please, get your friend here to back off," one of the men at the adjoining table told the legionaries. "These women are all upstanding Roman citizens. They are decent ladies from good families and are married or betrothed. If your friend wants sex, there's plenty of that to be had here." He pointed at the eatery's wait staff, who watched the stand-off from the kitchen area.

The aggressive drunkard now walked over to the local man, showing the room a wide grin on the way. When he stood face to face with him, the legionary slowly moved his head backwards. "You really think you can tell me what to do?" He slurred before flinging his head forward into the man's face. Oz cringed at the juicy sound of a nose getting crushed. The local's friends quickly grabbed their stunned and profusely bleeding fellow and retreated. All looked angry, but some also had the smarts to look scared. *As they should be, armed veterans are no joke.*

The table of women, all standing at this point, hurried towards the entry in a huddled group. Three of the four soldiers followed, while the silent one ran to head them off at the doorway.

Oz, Adhe, and Massi stood up at the same time as most of the other legionaries in the room. He recognized the big group closest to the entryway as part of the third cohort of their Ninth legion.

"Let the women go, friends!" one of the soldiers at that table shouted, before turning to his fellows to continue in a quieter voice that Oz could barely hear. "Let's take them down, but quietly and gently, alright?" His friends spread out to encircle the women and the four soldiers, before pulling the locals out through their lines, getting them out of harm's way one by one.

"Looks like they have this well under control," Adhe said. Oz sat back down, still watching intently with everyone else.

The bigger group of soldiers slowly tightened their circle around the four drunken legionaries, and the same man from earlier spoke up again. "I am decanus Albatius. Let's not have any problems here, alright? This is no Lusitanian town where you can do whatever you like." The drunken soldiers looked annoyed. *Well, they will calm down now.* A quick glance back into the room showed Oz patrons trying to laugh off the incident, tensions relaxing. "We are all Legion here. Let us escort you home to your camp, alright? You are all from the Eighth?"

The original troublemaker stood close to the non-com officer. Several emotions played across the man's face until furious anger won out. "Fuck you!" he shouted, exploding into a vicious lunge at the decanus and landing a surprise punch. Though after a quick recovery, the squad leader seemed able to keep the drunkard at bay.

Oz's eyes wandered over the crowd to the entry, just in time to see the shifty-eyed legionary draw his gladius. "Watch out!" he shouted, but the warning came too late. The man violently stabbed the next legionary's stomach before swinging around in one smooth motion to cut through the throat of the man on his other side. As everybody else pulled their own swords, the silent killer slashed at the decanus, who turned his torso and head away at the last moment. The sword tip slashed his right cheek open from the lower jaw to the side of his head, cutting off and launching the lower half of his right ear into the air.

The decanus now followed his men's example and drew his own gladius. "No more chances!" he shouted. The men from the Ninth's third cohort stepped forward as one, stabbing their blades into the men from all sides. When they moved back, four lifeless bodies slumped to the ground. As weapons were cleaned before sheathing them, Oz realized the decanus also bled from a long cut on his left arm. *I wonder, does he even realize how much he's been hurt?*

Albatius looked over at their table. "You are from the Ninth, right? I'd be in your debt if you could go back to camp and ask for centurion Maecius. Tell him that Sextus Albatius, from the third centuria, third cohort, needs his help." He turned away, attempting to get his carefully cleaned sword back into its scabbard. Several of his friends seemed to want to speak, opening their mouths but deciding to stay quiet after all. *Nobody wants to be the one to give him the bad news. His face is not a pretty sight.*

694 AUC (60 BC), summer
Petinesca, Free Gallia, Nation of the Helvetii

"There is a young warrior here. He says he came a long way to speak to you and would not give me his name," one of Divico's farm hands said. "I had him wait at the hay barn."

"Is the man thin and tall, with a slight limp?" Divico asked, receiving a confirming nod. "Thanks, I'll go see him right away." He grabbed a piece of cloth to wipe away his sweat and started from the horse corral to the barn. Despite a layer of dramatic looking clouds, it was a hot day, even at the mountain valley's high elevation.

"You were gone for a long time," he told the visitor before shaking his hand. He looked around to see several of his retainers close by. "Let's take a walk, shall we?" He led the way out of the homestead and onto a small trail, eventually passing through a small stand of trees. Once they came out into open cow pastures at the bottom of a hill, he stopped to look at the vista of the huge valley walled by massive snow-capped peaks on its eastern side and loudly cleared his throat. "So, what did you find out?"

"I followed Orgetorix and his men into the lands of the Sequani. He met with a chieftain council member there. I'm sure they made a deal because he was in a good mood when they left and headed west."

"West?" Divico asked in curiosity as he unconsciously twirled the ends of his enormous white mustache. *How interesting. What exactly is he up to?*

"He went into the lands of the Aedui. I followed him all the way to Bibracte. There, he met with a council member that dislikes the Romans. The man hated that his people asked Rome for help after their catastrophic loss to the Sequani at Magetobriga," the spy reported. "I asked around about him. It wasn't hard to find out about his greed and ambition, though I had no way of finding out what they discussed with him or what they agreed to."

Divico paused to brood about the situation. He considered himself to be among the first and foremost of the Helvetii leaders, but Orgetorix was on his way to the very top. The man was just as driven as himself, and the scion of an ancient noble family to boot. He was sure Orgetorix was already plotting to become a war king himself, the ultimate power among the nation of Helvetii. Somehow, these two foreign councilors played a role in the man's plans, likely in how he meant to keep that power for good. *But, how? How does it all fit together?*

A year ago, Orgetorix had spoken to the council about the nation leaving their homelands in search of richer farmland in the west, as they had fifty years earlier under his father's and

Divico's leadership, but without ending in a shameful retreat from the Romans this time. Divico had immediately smelled the opportunities such a move would bring and had supported the endeavor wholeheartedly. The motion had been carried and a departure date set for two years from now. Swaying the council had proven much easier than expected, thanks to Divico's many battle successes in the past and the incessant complaints the councilors had been exposed to over the years thanks to raids against their people from Germania in the north.

"There is one more interesting part to this. He travelled to Bibracte with two of his daughters. Only one came back with him."

Ah. That means he did find what he looked for, a strong ally. Somebody important enough to cement the deal with his daughter's hand.

"Did any of his men see you?" Divico asked.

"I don't think so," replied the spy.

"Good. In that case I have more work for you." Divico turned back toward the farmstead. "First, let's get you paid for your good deeds so far."

6694 AUC (60 BC), summer
Bailenua, Free Gallia, Eastern part of the Aedui Nation

"I am so sorry about little Boud. I wish I could have come when father's letter reached me," her little brother Morcant said, putting his hand on her arm. "My testing for journeyman was only a few days away, and the tests themselves take weeks."

"I figured as much, don't worry." Aina sadly looked into the distance. "It was so sudden. He had a week of fever, and just when I thought he had pulled through, he closed his eyes and was gone." Her tears rolled down her face, dropping onto her little daughter Nara resting in a sling hanging from her shoulders. She hugged her precious sleeping child. "Having this little one helps take the pain." *Though I miss him terribly.*

After a moment of solitary silence, Morcant asked, "How is Bradan holding up? I hope you two are getting along, I've seen many couples split over much less."

"No complaints there, our marriage is still intact. He's extra gentle and understanding since our loss, and he helps me however he can with the new baby. Most important is he still treats me as his equal, always. I know how lucky I am; I've seen how badly some of my childhood friends get treated by their husbands."

They stood on top of a hill a mile outside of town, overlooking a lush meadow. She adjusted little Nara's sling to position her in front of her stomach and let her eyes scan the forest's edge below. Bradan, her brother Elsed, her father Drestan, her friend Rionach and many other warriors were spread out close to the foot of the hill, all holding drawn bows ready to shoot, except for three men holding long boar spears. These weapons had iron crossbars a foot behind the head, needed to keep a safe distance from dangerous tusks in case the hounds and drivers ended up flushing out a boar or two.

She focused on her attractive husband standing next to her brother, now the husband of Brenna. That at least had ended up as she had hoped for. Her best friend had stayed home today thanks to her fast-approaching due day. They would raise two children close in age. *Please gods, I beg of you, let little Nara survive to become the woman she is meant to be.*

She looked back at Morcant and focused on his new silver brooch pinned to the chest of his white tunic, signifying his status as a journeyman Druid. "It's an oak tree, right?" He nodded. "How long will you be able to stay home this time?"

"I am not sure. I'll help and study with our master Druid here, but I might have to leave again if there's a greater need somewhere else."

"A master Druid's knowledge! I'm curious. I wish you could share something."

Morcant smiled at her. Aina shrugged and smiled back. The druids were the most knowledgeable and also the most secretive people in Celtic society. Most often seen in their function as priests, they were also reputable healers and scientists. The master Druids were the unchallenged leaders of society, with several of the most powerful having seats on the Aedui nation's council.

"I am sorry, sister." He sighed. "I wish I could share my knowledge freely, that would help us all. Yet, I was sworn to secrecy in front of the Aedui Druid master council, and that means never talking about our lore to anybody who is not a Druid. Not even to sweet and prodding older sisters." They both laughed. "And I won't be done with studying anytime soon. It will take me another decade before I get a chance at the master Druid tests. Once I am master, it will be my turn to teach the apprentices and journeymen, to make sure there are always enough holding our knowledge so none of it gets lost."

Aina nodded. She knew what a paranoid bunch the Druids were. Nothing was ever written down, and they used only oral repetition for teaching. She looked down to the forest again. "Did you hear that? Not long now." The barking of the dogs and the bells of the drivers were fast approaching, the prey close. As she scanned the tree line, the first deer jumped out and was quickly cut down by several arrows. This left a small window for following deer and elk, and several made it through unscathed to the side of the hill. Still, about ten animals in total were taken down. "We'll have a grand feast tonight," she stated. As they walked down the hill, she remembered something else she wanted to ask her well-informed brother. "The council has paid tribute to the Sequani for two years now. Do you think they will eventually honor our payments and stop the Suebi from raiding north? Magetobriga cost us all dearly, and when the Suebi come here, there will be no help for us from Bibracte."

Her brother shook his head in reply. "Nothing will change. Ariovist, the Suebi king, is trouble for the Sequani. He settles all his tribesman in Sequani lands, and there are constantly more coming from Germania. I heard the last group were twenty-four thousand Harudi warriors, which means he will evict that many Sequani from their own farms. Our neighbors are cowed enough now to let the Suebi do whatever they want. Believe me, things will get even worse for us."

So much for my hopes. "What about the Romans, are they going to help us?"

"I don't think so. When our father's old friend Divitiaco was Aedui Vergobret the year after Magetobriga, he sent them several requests for aid. After a year without replies, he traveled to Rome. He held a long speech there in front of the senators. They applauded and gave their condolences, but they never helped. Being a friend to Rome doesn't seem worth a whole lot." They kept walking downhill until they reached the hunters.

"Aina, we'll have lots of meat for the feast tonight," Bradan beamed, hugging her sideways as to not disturb the baby. "I can't believe little Nara slept through it all."

Aina warmly smiled at her man. *At least some things don't need much improvement.*

They walked over to her father Drestan for a chat, and from there on to their horses. Time to ride back to town.

***

Aina sat at a table in the town's great hall, in the midst of her family. The festivities to celebrate the passing of fifteen years since the new town's founding had been planned for months. Fifteen meant three times five, an auspicious set of numbers pleasing to the Celtic gods. Aina sat between her father Drestan and her brother Morcant, opposite Elsed. She smiled across the table as her older brother ate his gamey stew by using his wooden spoon to ladle meat and grains onto his piece of bread. Brenna sat next to him, currently suffering through a lecture from Morcant. "Seriously, you shouldn't do all your chores anymore this late in your pregnancy," he told her.

Her friend was annoyed at her brother's know-it-all attitude and ignored him to listen to their friend Rionach instead. Though their childhood friend had only eyes for her lover Orlagh, who sat next to her brother and his children and at the other end of the long table. *I think its high time for a rescue.*

"Brenna, how are you today?" Aina asked, cutting through Morcant's monologue.

Her friend smiled and leaned away from the table before shoving her empty bowl away from the table's edge. "I feel great, considering, and I can still eat for two. But my stomach is squeezed so tight I don't know how it all fits." Brenna's tense features relaxed, and her smile turned into a grin as she folded her hands over her baby bump. Elsed finished his own bowl and also leaned back, reaching with his right arm around Brenna to pull her closer to him.

"I sure hope this will be over soon," he said wistfully, pointing at Brenna's stomach. "I would like to have my wife back." Most of the adults at the table broke out into unabashed laughter.

"Only a new husband would think to say something as stupid as that. You have much to learn!" Rionach's brother shouted from the far end of the table. More laughter followed. Aina smiled at Elsed when she realized how out of sorts he was. *I will tell you later what it means to have a newborn around. New mothers are always tired, you'll be a far second priority for Brenna from here on out.*

Bradan now joined the table with his own fresh bowl of stew, oblivious to the last exchange. "Nara is finally asleep. Took a long time, she slept too much during the day," he told her before looking across the table. "Elsed, once your child is out of there," he said, pointing at Brenna's stomach "your life will change. You have no idea how much."

Aina wiped fresh tears of laughter from her eyes before lifting her drinking horn. "To family!" she shouted.

Everybody lifted their horns and joined in. "To family!" her father repeated from her side. The other tables in the hall followed suit.

She was content. Here, amidst her loved ones, everything was as it should be. She put her arm around Bradan and snuggled close.

694 AUC (60 BC), fall
Aricia, 16 miles south of Rome, Italia

"Ave my friends, would you like to follow me into the garden? There is a nicely shaded table ready for us." Marcus Licinius Crassus showed Caesar and Publius Claudius Pulcher to his home. Crassus had walked out from his villa just in time to meet them in the courtyard. The property was close to Aricia, a small town in the middle of a neighborhood of senatorial properties. A straight shot from Rome, the sixteen miles south could be traveled conveniently on the Via Appia, and the town could be reached within a few hours. Caesar admired the setting on the side of a hill, presenting a perfect view of the many acres belonging to the property. The villa, though, was massive and opulent, as to be expected from the richest man of Rome, who happened to own thousands of slaves specialized in construction.

"The servants will bring us my best wine and cool water. I'm rather proud of the grapes. I spent a fortune years ago to get plant starts from the Falernian estates south of Neapolis," Crassus boasted as he led the way.

Caesar followed, glancing back at their entourage who still remained in the courtyard. His old friends Aulus Hirtius and Lucius Cornelius Cinna stood with young Marcus Antonius, who held an intense conversation with Pulcher's brawlers. Antonius was the son of a distant cousin of Caesar's and had fallen in with Pulcher and his gang. He was already second in command despite his young age of seventeen. *What a weird combination of people I consort with these days. Dear friends mixed with people I barely accept as necessary evil. The lines are blurring, and I am worried I won't be able to keep the two apart for much longer.*

Caesar followed Pulcher and Crassus to a round table in the shade of a gigantic old olive tree bordered by rows of small mastic trees and oleander bushes. He sat and nodded to the three men leaning against the massive trunk of the old tree. "Salve Luctatus, Salve Fraucus!" He raised his eyebrows when he got to the third man. "I don't remember your name, sorry."

"Postumus, sir," came the reply. Caesar knew these men acted as Crassus's trusted bodyguards and sometimes even as servants. Hirtius, Cinna, and Antonius quietly arrived at the tree as well, close enough to hear everything said at the table.

"Tertulla and both Marcus Junior and Publius will be here later to join us for dinner. Did you pass their carriage on the road? I am sure Tertulla insisted on traveling in her carpentum. My sons both hate the monstrosity. It's pulled by six brown horses, so you wouldn't have been able to miss it. No? They likely started out much later than you lot." Crassus chuckled. It was no secret that Caesar was an early riser, no matter the circumstances. "Were you able to arrange for Marcus to become pontifex of Jupiter as we discussed?"

"Yes, it's as good as done. We can talk with him about the details over dinner," Caesar answered.

"Excellent! He will be overjoyed, and we will have yet another set of ears to listen in on the back-row discussions of the Senate." He paused to take a sip of his wine. "You know, he has nothing but good words about you since your campaign in Hispania. About that, how are your finances coming along?" A hint of a smile spread on Crassus's face.

"Hispania much improved things, though you well know how much new debt I incurred to run for next year's consul," Caesar answered, annoyed at Crassus's mocking. His ally had been the one to loan him the huge sum needed to secure the election. Caesar shifted in his seat, uncomfortable with the subject. He did not want constant reminders of his debt. "It's nice out here, much cooler than Rome."

"Where it's scorching hot for a whole week now. I get why so many senators have villas out here," Pulcher said. "I'm thinking of buying one myself; I'm sure my wife would love that."

"Our wives' happiness is certainly a big motivator, right?" Crassus joked with a deadpan face. They all laughed at the irony of the statement. Between the three of them only Crassus didn't have extramarital affairs. Though Caesar's exploits with married women of the Roman upper classes had caused many rumors to spread across the city, Publius Claudius Pulcher's sexual depredations put him into a category all by himself.

The laughter died down, and Caesar spoke up first, looking at Pulcher. "I'd like to discuss something more serious. Specifically, I am worried about our waning street support since the Optimates strengthened their gangs. I heard they're trying to recruit Titus Annius Milo as a leader. He's refused so far, though it's no secret he hates you. He hates you so much; he surely wants you dead. Which makes me believe he will eventually join them just to spite you," he said.

"What did you do to the man? Did you sleep with his mother? Or with him, then leave him behind as a spurned lover?" Crassus asked Pulcher before roaring with more laughter.

Pulcher grinned wide in response. "Close, dear Marcus. It was his younger sister."

"By Jupiter, you must tell us all the sordid details," Crassus replied, "but let's get business out of the way first." He nodded at Caesar to continue before turning back to Pulcher.

"The elections are behind us, but we can't relax. I've heard much slander in the Senate about my motivations for the campaign in Hispania. It seems that several of the tribal councils managed to send letters to Optimates senators, and you know of the two delegations that made it to Rome to accuse me of misconduct. We've successfully rebuffed it all, but some of it always sticks with the public. The moment anybody hears about preparations for legal proceedings against me, you come running to let me know, you hear? I ask that of both of you." Caesar looked over to Crassus. After both nodded in agreement, his focus turned back to Pulcher. "If that were to happen, I can count on you and your men to do what needs to be done?" He received another decisive nod and sighed. "Thank you. Now I want to talk about Marcus Bibulus."

"His vote count came in far second to yours, and as the junior consul he won't have the power the Optimates were hoping for," Pulcher said. "But he will still try to be a pain in your rear."

"I agree, he will veto every single senate proposition coming from any of us or our allies. Since this will be our most important year yet, I propose we set our brawlers on him. If we could make him leave town, we would gain free reign. What do you say?" Caesar asked.

Crassus and Pulcher were both grinning broadly. "I will most certainly enjoy seeing that pompous little twit run for his life," Crassus responded. "Let's just make sure our people don't kill him. We want him gone, not give our dear Optimates a vacancy for consul to be filled by someone more capable."

Caesar agreed, switching his attention back to Pulcher. "I do want to add my thanks to you and your people for how you exposed Cato the Younger. We are all in your debt for that, he will never live this down."

Pulcher looked pleased by the compliment. The old families of the Optimates faction had always held Cato in highest regard, though now the man had finally lost his impeccable reputation of incorruptibility and honesty. Pulcher had arranged for him to be caught red-handed, buying electoral votes for Bibulus. "Righteous Cato had it coming. And I'll also enjoy scaring Bibulus with a righteous beating," he replied. Caesar shared Pulcher's gleeful smile, though when he glanced back at the men under the tree, he noted that Hirtius looked pensive rather than amused, while Cinna was clearly troubled over the discussion. *Maybe I should not bring these two to our meetings anymore.*

After a moment of silence, Crassus gave Caesar a questioning look with a nod towards the third man at the table. Caesar understood and addressed Pulcher.

"Thank you, you know what needs to be done. We'll meet you later."

Understanding he was being dismissed, Pulcher pushed his chair back and looked at Crassus. "By your leave, I will explore your beautiful villa."

Crassus waved at one of the house slaves waiting at the rear entrance to the villa. "Show our guest around."

Caesar turned to the men at the tree. "Could you please check that our men are settled? We'll join you in a moment."

He watched all six men enter the long colonnade at the back of the villa, leaving only the two of them at the table. Crassus spoke up once the last man was out of sight. "I'm worried about Pulcher. He's been a great asset these last couple of years, but he seems so capricious to me, always impulsive, and his violence on the streets knows no bounds. He never seems to know when to stop." His ally groaned. "Can we keep him loyal? I don't want him to turn on us at the wrong time."

"Have no fear on that account, Marcus. If anything, his failed attempts to get at Cicero and the Optimates have made him more determined. Did I tell you about his latest plot yet? He returned from his stint as quaestor for Sicilia with this idea of changing from patrician to plebeian status, just so he can get elected as Tribune of the Plebs next year. For Pulcher, it's all about revenge against Cicero."

"But he won't succeed. Cicero is too careful and too popular," Crassus said.

Caesar chuckled. "You and I know that, but our dear friend doesn't. Becoming a plebeian is a crazy scheme, even for him. He'll legally renounce his name, but only by changing his main nomen from the patrician Claudius to the plebeian Clodius. Yet another way of making fun of the Optimates by butchering ancient traditions."

Crassus burst out into roaring laughter. "I can already hear Cicero ranting about that fact alone. This goes against everything our Optimates hold dear." He continued, mimicking Cicero's high-pitched voice. "We simply must keep our noble elite pure, in thought as in deeds, so we can keep the ideals of our great ancestors firmly in place." Caesar chuckled at Crassus' impersonation, honed to perfection over the years.

"The best part is that our Pulcher found his adopter already, a young plebeian in dire need of funds. The official paperwork will legalize the whole thing, though the real scandal is that his new father will be younger than himself," Caesar said. They shared another laugh.

Crassus beamed at him. "I'm glad your election worked out. We'll be able to push all our planned laws through, and we'll set you up with a lucrative proconsul governorship for after. Having your young Legatus Publius Vatinius as Tribune of the Plebs will be a big help. He is just the man to introduce the law to stretch your term as governor to five years. If Pulcher's crazy scheme works, he can support us as tribune of the plebs after Vatinius is done with his term." Crassus paused and turned pensive, making Caesar wonder what else was on his mind.

"We've worked well together, and I consider you a friend, so I want to share this with you," Crassus continued. "I have only two ambitions left I truly care to achieve in life. First, I want to grow all my business ventures until my wealth is so vast that nobody else will ever come close. For that, I need to keep most of my activities secret. If the Senate ever finds out how much trade

I'm involved in, I'll get shut down, or worse, they might kick me out. So, they can never know more than what's publicly visible."

Every senator was supposed to achieve his wealth from owning land, and nothing more, something Crassus hadn't felt limited to for a long time. *This much I knew about you. What's the second thing you want?*

Crassus's determined face changed, and his eyes seemed to look far into the distance. "My other ambition… since I was a child, I dreamt of Rome conquering Parthia and making it into a province. I'd like to take a few legions and pick up where the Greeks stopped after they beat the Persians at Salamis and Plataea. Xerxes was on his knees, but instead of following through, all they did was celebrate. They should have invaded his homeland in retribution."

Caesar raised his eyebrows. All Roman noblemen grew up with the tales of ancient Greece's struggles, including the heroics of three hundred Spartans holding back the might of Persia at Thermopylae four hundred years ago, giving all of Graecia time to gather its armies in defense. Another well-known tale about the vast eastern lands now belonging to the Parthian Empire were Alexander the Great's exploits two hundred years later.

"Only Alexander ever conquered Persia, though he never tamed it. Everything was left in place when he died, so just think about the treasures to be found there. Even now, the Parthians keep buying hundreds of thousands of slaves from Greek markets every year." Crassus sighed. "But more important than the riches is the glory." Caesar raised his eyebrows, causing Crassus to laugh out loud and hold up his hand in acknowledgement of his friend's surprise. "I know how that sounds coming from me, but by now you must know my vanity. The idea of being known as the conqueror of Parthia throughout eternity quite appeals to me."

Nothing ever seems to be enough. The richer he becomes, the more he still needs. And since richer than anybody else won't do, he needs to add glory. It's like a sickness.

Caesar cleared his throat. "I would like to discuss another matter with you, and I urge you to keep an open mind. You know I've been working in the courts every bit of free time I have, ever since I came back from Hispania."

"Of course," Crassus replied. "Your eloquent rhetoric there is adding to your already stellar reputation as a statesman," Marcus cut in. "Plus, you're winning bonus points with the populace by going after the worst of the former offenders. Some just don't know when to keep their mouths shut about what they did in their province. They don't deserve better than what they get from you. It's expected for any governor to bleed his province, but there's still a fine line not to be crossed. Opportunities for future revenues need to stay intact, and that's why uprisings need to be avoided at all cost."

I should have figured that this is how he views my work. It's always about money.

"Thank you for your support. But did you know that my younger sister's husband Marcus Atius Balbus is the cousin of Gnaeus Pompeius Magnus? Balbus helped me negotiate mutual support with him for several court cases, and I wondered about possible long-term prospects. You've never gotten along with our great Pompeius, especially not since Sulla's death, but could you imagine the possibilities if we were to ally with him?"

Caesar held his breath. To his relief, Crassus appeared to be pondering the idea instead of outright dismissing it. "He would only indirectly support the Populares while officially keeping both feet in the Optimates camp," Caesar continued. "We can switch him to our side if we help him with rich lands in the east for his veterans. He'd jump at the opportunity to deliver on that old promise. His so-called friends have shut his senate proposal down twice. If we help him push that law through, he'll join a long-term alliance, and I'll give him my Julia's hand to cement it. She turned seventeen not long ago, and I'll break her current engagement if you agree."

He watched Crassus' face go from pensive to amused in a split second. "Pompeius is forty-seven now, right? Julia is young and beautiful. He will jump at the opportunity to marry her." Caesar must have shown his pain at the thought of the lecherous old man since Crassus paused to laugh in his face. "I just hope she will forgive you for this. Don't look so unhappy! You have to admit, the thought of him marrying your daughter is quite ironic. After all, he divorced his third wife because of the persistent rumors of her affair with you. Which I remember were quite true."

Caesar smiled in response and looked out over the beauty of the Latium countryside so many wall painters tried to capture. *I hope you will forgive me, dear daughter. In my mind, I am still the vulnerable young man running from Sulla in search of allies to keep me safe and untouchable.*

Crassus cut into his silence. "If we can form that alliance with Pompeius, the three of us would be the most powerful political entity Rome has ever known. Think about it: you, the nobleman from your impeccable family, loved by the masses. Me, the adored hero of the slave uprising. Add the great Pompeius, the most successful general of our time, the man who rid the Mediterranean of Piracy six years ago. In only three months and with only two hundred seventy Roman galleys to boot. With us together, nobody could stand in our way. Whatever we want to happen…"

"…will happen," Caesar finished his sentence. They both grinned at each other. *I knew you would bite. With this alliance I will never have to worry again. Finally.*

Crassus stood up. "Let's see what the others are up to, shall we? High time to keep Pulcher and young Antonius away from my prettier servants."

Caesar chuckled as he followed his ally to the villa.

695 AUC (59 BC), summer
Clusium, Etruria, Italia

"Lethie, I don't know what do," Velia Churinas complained. They sat on a settee in her best friend's new room a couple of floors up from what was now Velia's bakery. She was shaking from grief and impotent rage. "You know things have gone from bad to worse since my father died." *Already a week ago, but it feels like yesterday that I couldn't pay for his funeral. I had to let them burn his body on the garbage pile outside the city walls like so much refuse.*

She took a deep breath. "I tried to deliver the weekly loan payment today, but Minatus refused to take it. He said it needed to come from my father, or in his absence from his son."

"That mangy dog! May the gods curse all dishonest usurers," Lethie replied in disgust. "Did you send your letter to Numerius?" she asked.

Velia nodded. "I sent it off to Hispania yesterday with a trader, but it cost most of my remaining money. Which means I can't buy enough grain now to keep the bakery going without taking from the loan payment." Despite her attempts to talk him out of it, her brother had followed his friend Vibius to the legionary recruiters late last year, and the two had shipped out to Hispania after their four months of basic training. *Another one of my failures.*

Though Numerius had promised to stay in contact and send money home, she hadn't received any news since his departure.

"I told him about our father's death and the situation with Minatus. I just don't know what he can do from Hispania besides send money. Which would be too late to help with whatever is going to happen."

Lethie moved in close to hug her friend. "I wish I could do something myself. My father hasn't been able to work for weeks since he fell ill. I am supporting him and my mother with every spare sesterce."

"And it's not like you have much to start with," Velia replied. Her friend worked as a cook for a small eatery, dreaming of eventually running her own or becoming a personal chef for a wealthy family. Velia knew from her visits at the eatery how Lethie struggled with the unwanted advances of overly eager male customers unable to distinguish her from the servers offering their sexual services on the side. She finally let go of her friend and stood up. "I should go. You need to get ready for your dinner shift."

Lethie nodded in thanks. "Good night, Velia."

"See you tomorrow." She left Lethie's apartment and climbed the stairs to the bakery's side door at ground level. Once inside, she closed the door, hoping to keep this bad day from following her inside.

***

Two weeks later, Minatus's men bullied their way into the bakery to confiscate all utensils. "Your father's loan has been filed as forfeit with the local magistrate, on account of non-payment," one of them told her, handing her receipts for a handful of sesterces to count against the full debt. The remainder totaled eight hundred sesterces. Though the usurer hadn't taken her money, the law held her liable as the closest available relative to the original debtor. She had asked everyone she knew for help, but though willing, nobody had enough money to make a difference. *If I could afford legal help, I might have a chance. I feel helpless.*

As of this morning, she had acquired a shadow, somebody following her everywhere she went. The man had even introduced himself and apologized. Minatus had ordered him to ensure she wouldn't run away or, gods forbid, take her own life. She currently walked back home from yet another attempt to secure a loan from a different loan shark in the city. If successful, she could still pay off her debt at the magistrate's office and continue running the bakery, but the man shadowing her was well known as Minatus's man. None of the lenders was willing to cross him.

Her shadow followed her to Lethie's door. Her knock wasn't answered, so she went back downstairs to the side door of the bakery. When she tried to close the door behind her, the man shoved his foot in the opening. "I need to come inside with you," he said before stepping through. "I also urge you to collect your most important things. Tomorrow morning, you will leave with me, and you won't be coming back."

She had figured they would evict her from the bakery sooner or later. *How can I let Lethie know now?*

She walked to the back of the room and opened a small leather bag to pull out her parentes statues, carefully arranging them on the sideboard of her sleeping corner. She knelt and felt tears well up in her eyes. *What will happen to me now?*

A cough behind her made her turn her head. The man slid down a wall to sit on the floor while curiously staring at her. She closed her eyes, wishing the unwelcome intruder far away. "Vesta, goddess of the hearth, watch over this family," she whispered. "Keep our spirits connected, so we can support each other." She held her breath. *I am losing everything. My father is dead, Numerius is gone, and so is the bakery. And tomorrow, it will be me, and then there is nothing left.*

A tightness moved into her chest, making it harder to breath. Something else rose inside of her; a desperate fear which took hold, bringing tears to her eyes. A deep and calming breath helped, and she shoved the thought aside, at least for the moment. She opened her eyes and drew two of her family figurines forward; roughly carved depictions of a male and a female figure representing the spirits of her mother and father. She cleared her throat and spoke loudly. "Father, Mother I hope you are watching. Please, please, help me figure out what I can do." When she tried to continue, her voice faltered, and she reverted to whispering. "If Minatus were an honest man, I would now run the bakery. Instead, I'm now convinced he'll sell me as a slave tomorrow." She raised her hands up and hissed "Father, Mother, please help me!"

The man behind her chortled. Her feeling of helplessness fell away, replaced by anger. Tears still streaming down her cheeks, she turned to stare at the figure sitting on her floor. The shameless man was amused! But she kept her eyes fixed at him until he finally stopped grinning and raised his hands in silent surrender. She turned back to the sideboard and moved the two statues back to pull a third forward.

"Numerius, hear me. I have never needed you as much as I do now." She screamed loudly into the ether that connected everything. "Don't forget your little sister."

She rolled her statues into her shawl and lay down, clutching the bundle tightly. *Maybe they are listening, yet I have never felt this alone in my life.*

Wherever she would end up, she hoped she would be allowed to keep her parentes figures. Her family's spirits were now her only comfort.

695 AUC (59 BC), summer
Aquileia, Roman Province of Gallia Cisalpina

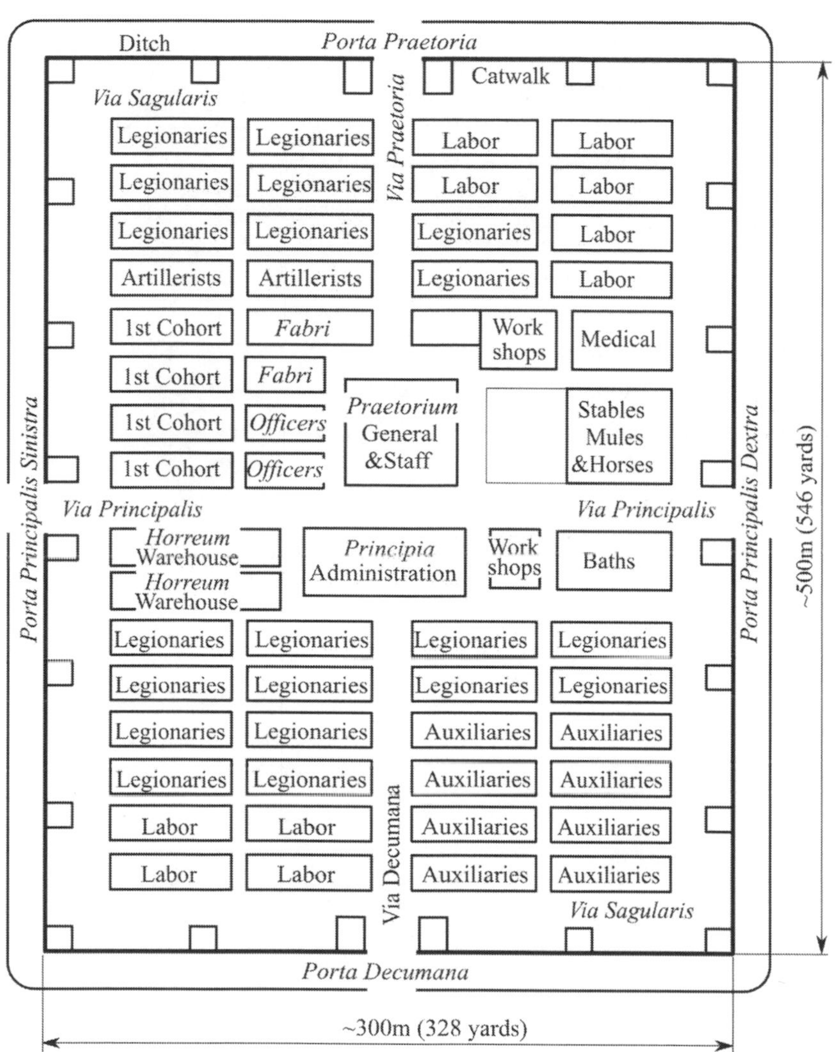

Illustration: Typical permanent Roman legion fort

"Are we agreed?" Oz asked the camp prefect's man.

"We are." They clasped their arms in the Roman fashion to seal the deal. "You will get thirty custom cavalry shields for your turma, pricing as just discussed."

"Thank you. Now we'll be better prepared for wherever Caesar leads us this time." Oz smiled at the man. The rumors of who their new commander-in-chief was going to be had been recently confirmed, and since the relocation of the Seventh, Eighth, and Ninth legions to Aquileia in Northern Italia a few months ago, the Numidian archers had all received horses. Besides the issues of many of them having to learn to shoot from horseback, the question of trading in light-weight shields for something better had come to the forefront again. The Roman style cavalry shield seemed like a good compromise—small enough not to interfere with their bows, it had an iron-reinforced rim keeping it safe from splitting apart on a first or second sword hit. The fighting in Hispania had shown that any of them could be pulled into hand-to-hand combat, and he was glad that Capussia had followed his example by making chainmail a mandatory upgrade for all his auxiliaries. The only grumbling about it came from recently arrived new recruits, who disliked the extra weight. The veterans knew the value of metal shirts.

Oz raised his hand in goodbye before leaving the massive warehouse tent and stepped out to the Via Principalis, one of two main streets crisscrossing the camp's center. From there, he ambled back to their barracks building to show the men the armory sample he had received. He wanted them to decide if they wanted to use a common color. If so, he would buy paint and ask the craftsman of the first cohort's fabri century for help with appealing designs. He was walking around the backside of the administrative building when Adhe rushed towards him from the bathhouse latrines.

"So that's the one!" Adhe exclaimed. Oz handed the shield over. "Nice, I think this will be the perfect type of shield for us, once it has the additional leather straps like the Cretans have on theirs," Adhe said.

"I won't like this on my arm when shooting, I think it's too heavy. But we'll figure out a way for quick attachment to our saddles. Should it hang on the same side as our hasta?" Oz mused. As another result of the Lusitanian campaign, all Numidians now regularly trained with the Roman hasta, a long lance with a wide double-edged head. The legion's officers had encouraged cross-training of the auxilia forces to gain more deployment options in the field.

The two walked up to massive wooden barracks, a huge improvement from their old camp in Hispania, and pure luxury compared to the tents used on campaigns. Each of the buildings housed one-hundred-twenty people with ample space left over for horses and community areas. "After I drop this off with the men, I'll go see the children. Do you want to come along?" Oz asked.

"Sure thing, I'm always happy to see my little cousins," Adhe replied and fell in beside Oz, whistling a merry tune.

***

Oz watched his nephew hurry after the children. At twenty-three, Adhe was handsome and somewhat exotic-looking to many of the camp followers and the Celtic inhabitants of northern Italia.

With a smile, Oz hurried to catch up to Adhe, seven-year old Stena, and four-year old Saki, now all far ahead. "Wait up!" he called after them.

"Good luck with that," Adhe shouted back. They were following the excited children through the camp's satellite settlement to an area behind used as a children's playground. The suburb around them had sprung up on both sides of the road to Aquileia, just far enough away from the Porta Praetoria, the camp's main gate, not to interfere with defensive needs. It resembled an average small town with blacksmiths, traders, eateries, bars, bordellos, and of course the ever-present slave traders prominently situated along the main road. What made the development feel like a real town, though, were all the soldiers' families, housed in communal buildings very similar to the legionary barracks located right behind the many shops and offices. It might have been against the rules for legionaries to marry, the right strictly reserved for officers at centurion level or higher, but the majority of soldiers couldn't care less and started unofficial civil unions with local women whenever they fell in love. Most camp wives were from Hispania, though there was a recent influx of locals from Gallia Cisalpina, like the group of attractive young women Oz and Adhe now encountered bringing back freshly washed legionary tunics from the river. Several of them were without iron or bronze wedding rings on their left ring fingers and smiled openly at Adhe as they hurried past.

"What's the matter with you? At least take a look," Oz muttered after they had passed without Adhe even looking up. He knew the young man was interested in women but still struggled. Well, Oz had his own issues in that regard, emotionally damaged and so far unwilling to make strong connections. Their shared grief saw to that, though the brutal fighting in Hispania had added another layer of complexity. "Don't answer that," he said when he caught up with Adhe and put his hand on his shoulder. "Let the kids go, we know where they're headed." He turned around to glance back at the retreating women. His own outlook had transformed recently. He dreamed of having a steady woman in his life again. *Maybe caring for two children is what changed me. Little Saki and Stena have opened my heart again. I didn't think anything would ever be able to.*

Though, these particular women were all too young for him. At thirty-four, he couldn't imagine life with a teenage girl. Instead, he hoped to find somebody closer to his own age, preferably with life experience and acceptance for his emotional baggage. Though, most importantly, they needed to be fine with his children.

Stena ran back to them. "Papa! The red-haired girl from yesterday and her little brother are back. The four of us will play hide-and-seek in the trees down there, if you agree."

"No problem. We'll check on you in a little bit," he answered, waving her on. It was hard to remember how full of mistrust little Stena had been. *Was it really just two years ago that we met on that fateful day?*

He had never wavered in his loving treatment of the children, and he'd slowly won her over. At this point, he couldn't imagine his life without them.

"So, you really think we'll be moving out again soon?" Adhe asked.

"Yes, I do, and sooner rather than later. Think about it, we just received close to fifteen hundred fresh recruits, and I heard there's a few more on the way. The cavalry got more Celtic warriors, and the Cretans and us have been brought up to full strength. Plus, we now have four hundred slingers from the Balearic Islands."

They turned around to look back at the massive camp in the background, easily visible behind the suburb and an imposing sight to behold with its high walls. "I don't know the exact numbers, but the Ninth alone must be close to sixty-five hundred fighting men. The legion wouldn't pay for all these reinforcements if there were no plans for needing them, and soon."

695 AUC (59 BC), summer
Close to Bailenua, Free Gallia, Eastern part of the Aedui Nation

Elsed watched Drestan ride up and rein in his tall black mare. "They took the bait and are coming this way," his father said. "It's a mix of Harudi and Suebi, about two hundred and fifty riders, each on their own horse. It seems they gave up on their old habits of sharing ponies."

"Why wouldn't they, after becoming rich in Celtic lands," Elsed replied. "My group is ready. Please, father, don't wait too long before you hit them in the rear."

His eyes followed Drestan ride across the open field to another small patch of old growth forest, similar to the one in which his two hundred fifty riders waited. Close to town, the landscape consisted of fields, some worked, some fallow, and patches of forest sprinkled between. He turned back for a quick glance at his wife Brenna standing next to his sister Aina a few feet behind him. *Mother, please watch over us.*

He raised his hand to signal everybody to mount. With his father leading a similarly sized band, the town only had another three hundred warriors in reserve as a guard force. Their clan's fighting force had steadily eroded over the last years thanks to continuous raids from the south by the Suebi.

Aina guided her horse forward to the edge of the woods. "Let's hope your plan works," she said.

"It should," he replied. "See?" Their scouts were coming back at full gallop with the raiders in hot pursuit. He turned around in his saddle. "It's time!" He hurried his horse toward the field where the Harudi and Suebi were expected to arrive, while staying carefully hidden from sight by the copse's trees. The distant noise of approaching riders turned into a rumble when they entered the field. "Follow me!" he screamed and kicked his horse, his people riding out before arranging themselves into a line facing their own approaching riders. The first horses came within a hundred feet of the defenders, and the town's people moved apart to let them through. The raiders behind them slowed down before reining to a full stop. *Good, they look surprised. The plan worked.*

The Aedui around him broke out into a war cry. "Baile nua abu! Baile nua abu! Baile nua abu!" Elsed grinned, proud of his people. The name of Bailenua, simply "new town" in Celtic, had become the clan's new identity, to which they'd added abu as a call for victory. The few of their people that had brought a carnyx now blew their instruments with all the breath they could muster.

The Aedui line exploded into movement, the warriors kicking their mounts into frenzy in their attempts to reach the enemy. The front line smoothly flowed around the scout party, which reined in to turn and follow. The enemies responded by spurring their own panting horses back into a canter and adding their own battle cries.

When the two parties crashed into each other, the resulting deep booms and clangs of horse running into horse, of blade hitting blade or shield, and the mix of voices of men or women shouting in defiance or in pain were deafening. Elsed added his own noise, screaming out his anger at the hated intruders. A horse opposite him neighed and reared to avoid a collision with his own, moving sideways into the next horse, hoofs hitting the rider and eliciting an ear-piercing shriek of pain. Fighters all around him stabbed with their spears or hewed around with long swords, the stench of emptying bowels from people dying adding to the metallic smell of blood already permeating the field. Focused on the enemy in front of him, he barely noticed a spear dart his way from the corner of his eye. His horse bucked and launched him out of his saddle. The impact took his breath away. *Crap, that hurts, but I can still move. Lucky, I guess. These damn Suebi are no pushovers.*

Quickly rolling into a crouch on loam steaming from warm blood and other bodily fluids, he picked up his sword and ran to support one of his beleaguered townspeople. Moving in front of the attacking warrior with his shield raised high, he followed through with a sideways cut into the man's right side. That fighter dispatched, he looked to his left just in time to meet a massive Harudi charging his horse at him. Elsed threw himself to the side while holding up his shield. *By the gods, this guy is a giant.*

The impact of the enemy's heavy spear tip was too much for the shield's upper rim, and two of its sections opened up. As he used it to block another stab, it broke apart, leaving only a third of the wood sandwiched between shield boss and handle. Elsed threw the now worthless remains at the rider and danced to stay out of his reach. The sheer force behind the attack had rattled him. Somehow, he had to make this quick. *This bastard is too good, I can't get my sword close enough.*

A few feet away, he glimpsed a long lance embedded in a dead warrior's chest and jumped for it, dropping his sword to the ground in order to pull the shaft out of dead hands. With the sharp head swinging, he turned, expecting to face the massive warrior. The man had moved away to fight somebody else. *Did he think I meant to run away from him?*

Gripping the lance tighter, he advanced. "Hey, dead man! Yes, I mean you, ugly bag carrier, comb of a castrated cockerel!" he screamed. When the taunt finally made the warrior glance back, he sprinted at him, jumping and driving the long weapon deep into his chest. The steel head easily penetrated fine Celtic chainmail and pushed him off his horse. The Harudi's falling body ripped the shaft out of Elsed's hands, leaving him weaponless. While he frantically searched for his sword on the ground, several Suebi converged on him. He quickly grabbed the closest shield off the ground, just in the nick of time to deflect the first spear swing. Carefully retreating, he attempted to get a riderless horse between himself and the new attackers. As he moved towards the horse, it spooked and reared up, pushing him back into two of the Suebi. They all went down hard, and Elsed lost his grip on the shield.

He rose back up and heard Celtic trumpets that signaled his father's attack on the rear of the enemy. With empty hands, he ran as fast as he could, scanning the ground for weapons and briefly glancing at the enemy warriors in close pursuit. Just as he tripped over a dead body, he heard somebody shout, "Elsed!"

From down in the dirt he saw his brother in-law Bradan leading a group of several still horsed Aedui right into the pursuing warriors. *That was a close call. Thank you, old friend.*

He had a moment to choose a dead Harudi woman's shield and a decent sword lying close to the body of an Aedui warrior. *Sorry, I will bring it back for your family.*

Elsed rushed after Bradan's group to help kill the last of his original attackers. They moved on together, cutting down many more of the enemy before meeting the warriors from Drestan's team.

The battle now clearly won, a few of the remaining Harudi and Suebi clustered around their women and children, intent on fighting to the death. The Aedui made quick work of them. Thankfully, most survivors threw away their weapons and dropped to the ground. *These people will work our fields until we can use them to barter with a Roman trader, for wine and other luxury goods.*

He moved through the battlefield to look for his former personal opponents and proceeded to cut off the heads of several Harudi and Suebi he had killed, including the big man he had unhorsed.

"Have you heard that the Romans think this barbarous?" Bradan said from behind, as he, too, searched the battlefield for heads to collect. "They hang people from wooden crosses for slow and painful deaths, but they think we are the barbarians for collecting heads from people already dead."

"The head may be the center of a person's soul, but that soul surely departs at the moment of death. The Romans must think too differently to understand our customs," Elsed mused. Showing off heads of enemies killed in battle was a status symbol for any Celtic warrior. With his sword out, he couldn't carry more than the two heads he had, so he chose a riderless horse and tied his trophies to the saddle before searching for more. Once he had his sixth, he was satisfied and stuck with Bradan, who kept collecting until he had a well-deserved eight.

He scanned the battlefield as they led their horses across. Only fifty of their enemies were still alive, though at least a hundred of their Aedui warriors lay dead on the ground as well. Brenna came into view on the field's far side. She had one of her arms loosely dressed and looked with Rionach and Orlagh for her own heads to sever. He waited for her to look up and waved until she waved back. As he scanned the other side of the battlefield, he saw his father slowly moving towards him, supported by Aina. He looked pale, and his legs were drenched with blood. Elsed's heart dropped, Somehow, his father had always seemed invincible. *Oh no, oh no. That looks bad.*

Elsed ran over to help. When he took Drestan's left side, it became clear that his father was about to fall over. "I am sorry, my son, this was my last battle. Got this deep cut in my leg right at the initial charge. I've been bleeding out since." He motioned with his head to the far side of the field. "Please help me over to the trees. I would like to sit against a yew if you can find one, or at least a strong and tall oak." They made their way to the trees. Through wet eyes, Elsed spotted an old yew, just a few feet inside the edge of the small copse.

He and Aina gently lowered their father against the tree trunk. Drestan raised his head until he could see the tree's massive foliage overhead and sighed contentedly. "Thank you," he said. Yews were the most sacred trees, being the longest living things anywhere, offering an occasional branch for an excellent bow, or their foliage as poison to ease somebody's suffering. "I feel close to the whole world here, to nature and the gods,"

Drestan said in his usual strong and sure voice. "Here, I have a chance to go straight to the Otherworld instead of having my soul linger." He settled down and held his hands out for Elsed and Aina. "I hope to see your siblings soon, my children, your brothers and sisters who passed to the other side while they were still little." Drestan closed his eyes and Elsed couldn't hold his tears back any longer. The reality of the situation finally hit him like a battering ram, and his chest convulsed in deep sobs. *I know it's too late, but please, gods, I don't want him to go, not yet.*

He looked at his sister's face and saw she wept just as hard. Then his father spoke again, softly, yet amazingly clear and unmistakably happy. "I am coming, dear. We will celebrate and hold each other again," Drestan let go of Elsed's and Aina's hands to raise his own in greeting. He opened his eyes. "And here you are! Ganna, my love, take my hand, help me up." With a smile of endless joy, he slipped away.

695 AUC (59 BC), summer
Free Gallia, Lands of the Helvetii Nation

Behind the wall of mountains in the west, a descending sun colored the low hanging bank of clouds in fascinating shades of pink and orange. Divico heard the riders' approach and let go of the beautiful display the gods had provided.

"There you are." He appraised the men as they walked to him, as he stood on the top steps leading into the Great Hall of the Helvetii council, as was fitting for this official transaction. Well, mostly official.

He smiled at the two young retainers. "I have two courier bags for you. Both of you need to be on your way at first light tomorrow morning."

He chose the burly man with the long mustache for the lesser of the two jobs. "You need to hand this to the Sequani Council. It contains proof of the treachery of one of their members. Providing this proof will produce some goodwill for when we need it," he said. "Be on your way, and please report back the moment you return.

He waited while the man walked back to his horse, pulled himself up onto his saddle, and rode away, before turning to the second man, a tall, lanky and even younger warrior than the first. He handed him the remaining bag. "You have the most important mission. Go to Bibracte and find a chieftain on their nation's council. His name is in the bag, with a letter addressed to him and coins for you to give him. This part is important, so listen closely. Do not address him in public; instead, shadow him until there is a chance to catch him alone. I don't care how long it takes, it's very important he is not seen with you. I need you to swear to that."

The young man's eyebrows rose in wonder. "I swear it. May the gods punish me if I don't hold to it."

"Once you have him alone, hand him the letter and the coin purse and wait for a written response before you come back." Divico lifted his right hand, showing the man his index finger. "When you do have his response, you will come straight back. You do not make stops or talk to anybody else until you have delivered that man's word to me, understood?"

The courier nodded.

"Very good. Now go!" Divico twirled the ends of his white mustache as he watched the young warrior rush to his mount and ride away. He chuckled to himself as he walked the last few steps to the Great Hall.

***

Three weeks later, Divico made his move by betraying Orgetorix's motives to the Helvetii council. When they heard how his rival had planned to become war king, by force if necessary, and how he had conspired with a Sequani councilor named Castico to help him stay in power after, the council at once sent all their retainers to find and arrest him. *Though you will not have the opportunity to tell them about your ally among the Aedui. I have my own plans for that man.*

A day after the arrest came the harder part—convincing the council to stick to the laid plans for the nation's migration. Their first impulse had been to cancel the whole endeavor, though he succeeded and won the councilors over. With the official affairs settled, he visited the guard house of the Helvetii Great Hall where Orgetorix and a few of his retainers were held. *He must think he is to be executed. That's usually the only reason why anybody is held in this building.*

"Let me in," he told the guard at the door. "I am here to fetch Orgetorix."

He patiently waited for the door to be unlocked and walked through. He stopped in disgust at the stink of unwashed men and overflowing chamber pots and tried to find his young rival in the twilight. There he was, a rather short man with blue tattoos up the side of his neck and cheeks. Divico smiled. His own were carefully limited to his chest and arms. He had always thought the tastes of his nation's young men too flashy.

"Orgetorix, you're free to go, with compliments of the council," he stated loudly. Every man in the room rose in surprise. He held up his hand. "Nobody else, only him."

The man looked at him with suspicion and obvious mistrust. *As you should.*

Divico turned and walked back out, only stopping once he reached the wide stairs leading up. The captive walked out of the guard house, took one last look at him and the Council chambers, and walked down the main road to the gates. *You are making this far too easy for me.*

Divico continued up the stairs and into the Great Hall, careful to be seen by the guards. He walked through the whole building and out the back door, where the single guard was in his pocket. From there, he walked a few houses over before doubling back towards the gate. His retainers waited for him, out of sight of the road. "He went out only five minutes ago. Plenty of time to catch up," one of them said.

"Lead on," Divico said. "And don't worry about me, I can keep up, white hair or not."

The entire group started to run and quickly caught up to Orgetorix. "Wait up, friend!" he called.

Though clearly uncomfortable, the man chose to stop and wait. "What do you want now?"

"I want to clarify that I hold no hard feelings, and neither does the council. In fact, I am to deliver a gift. Please, follow me." He led the fellow councilor a quarter mile off the road to a small altar stone in a clearing.

"What is the meaning of this?" Orgetorix finally asked. Just as he turned to Divico, one of the men gripped him from behind, while two others pulled his arms forward. "This gift is a blessing from me to your family," he said, pulling out an ornate knife and inflicting two deep cuts into his wrists. "This way, your children will not be tainted by your actions. In fact, I have plans for your oldest son to help me make the council see things my way."

"Gently," he directed his men, who lowered a wailing and heavily bleeding Orgetorix to the ground, leaning his back and head against the altar. He watched on as the lifeblood drained out. "Farewell," Divico whispered as he laid the knife down in the grass, close to his victim's left hand. He stepped back and nodded in satisfaction at the scene. *Honorable suicide is by far the best choice.*

TERTIUS

Nova Familia (A New Family)

"All Gallia is divided into three parts, one of which the Belgae inhabit, the Aquitani another, those who in their own language are called Celts, in our Galli, the third. All these differ from each other in language, customs and laws. The river Garumna separates the Galli from the Aquitani; the Matrona and the Sequana separate them from the Belgae. Of all these, the Belgae are the bravest, because they are furthest from the civilization and refinement of [our] Province, and merchants least frequently resort to them, and import those things which tend to effeminate the mind; and they are the nearest to the Germans, who dwell beyond the Rhenus, with whom they are continually waging war; for which reason the Helvetii also surpass the rest of the Galli in valor, as they contend with the Germans in almost daily battles, when they either repel them from their own territories, or themselves wage war on their frontiers."

Julius Caesar, De Bello Gallico, Book 1 / Chapter 1

695 AUC (59 BC), summer
Rome, Italia, Capital of the Roman Republic

"You're late," Marcus Licinius Crassus said once he recognized the person walking out of the early morning dark into the light of the few oil lamps and torches held by people behind him. Suddenly, more light came around the street corner behind the approaching man, highlighting the outline of the newly minted commoner Publius Claudius Pulcher, who had led his gang of Populares brawlers down into this small street full of stinking garbage. Of course, Pulcher would have to pick a spot like this as their rallying point.

"What does it matter? We did what we set out to do," came the defiant reply.

"And where is Marcus Antonius with the veterans?" Crassus stepped out from between his men to shake Pulcher's hand in congratulations, his man Luctatus and his brother Fraucus sticking to his side, while their friend Postumus remained behind him, all keeping their cudgels ready.

"They ran after the survivors. We caught a group of two hundred Optimates brawlers between us and left at least a hundred of them dead or dying. The rest ran like dogs with their tails between their legs," a bloody Pulcher replied. The torch in his hand highlighted the spatters covering his face and tunic, his wide eyes above his vicious grin shifting quickly. The clamor became louder as more men pushed into the street behind him. "And here he comes! Salve Antonius, did you catch more of them?"

Caesar's relative approached from the other end of the alley with a few of his younger followers. The torchlight made Antonius seem like a monster from the underworld. He was broadly grinning despite the open gash in his forehead, blood running down from dark-blond hair across his left forehead and over a swollen eye.

"Of course, we did! They never stood a chance against real veterans." He nodded behind him at the hundred battle-hardened soldiers in civilian clothes now filing into the street. *Caesar was right. We are invincible now that we hold the streets of Rome itself.*

"Well done, men, and I mean all of you!" Crassus shouted across the street. "But no celebrations yet, we are only halfway there. We need to make a showing for the Senate this morning, I need all of you at the west end of the forum at first light. After the senate meeting starts, you can drink and party through the day on my coin, that's the least I can do."

Let's see what our Optimates senators do today once they see these men. Most of them are weak-minded and care only for their luxuries. They're properly afraid to go against us. Today, the few of the Optimates senators that were made from sterner stuff were either out of town or not influential enough to make a difference. *Caesar timed this perfectly.*

***

Later that morning, Gaius Julius Caesar walked through the ancient Forum Romanum at the head of his twelve lictors to join a senate emergency meeting called by Gnaeus Pompeius Magnus. Crassus joined him at the edge of the open plaza in front of the Curia Hostilia. "Good morning, I trust everything is in order?" Caesar asked.

"You could say that," Crassus replied, pointing to the southside of the plaza.

Caesar's gaze followed Crassus finger to the Populares gang at the western end of the forum. He noticed with satisfaction how the other senators kept as far away as possible. The brawlers were crowded too closely to count, though he knew they were several hundred strong. "They didn't even clean up," he commented when he noticed the blood-stained clothing.

"Nice touch, don't you think? I figured it would strengthen the message," Crassus replied with a chuckle.

Loud exclamations from behind alerted him to a group of Optimates senators enter the plaza, Pompeius in the lead.

When he looked back at the brawlers, many of the ones in the back raised their hands in greeting. Those were Pompeius' veterans, acknowledging their old commander. Though the old general didn't wave back, the slight smile displayed was enough for Caesar. *He is pleased with our arrangement. This is truly happening.*

The group of senators walked on, oblivious to what was about to happen. *Today is the birth of the strongest alliance Rome has ever seen, and I will be an equal partner in it.*

Once the meeting started, the Senate proved sufficiently cowed to allow Pompeius's renewed proposal to move forward. The Populares would all vote for it, and enough of the Optimates would follow Pompeius's example to ensure a majority, giving their new ally the eastern lands he had wanted for his discharged veterans. *And Crassus and I have his goodwill and cooperation in return.*

***

"You really think your time as bachelor might be over?" Lucius Cornelius Cinna asked in disbelief. Caesar nodded. They marched down the city sidewalk, surrounded by his lictors and twenty of his clients for security.

"It's not like I planned this; I had meant to stay single for the time being. A couple of months ago, Lucius Calpurnius Piso Caesoninus asked me to come to his house for a strategy dinner to help me succeed this year. As one of last year's two consuls, I didn't suspect his motives in the least." Caesar chuckled. "When I got to his house, the only other dinner guest was his daughter Calpurnia. She's seventeen. He used every possible excuse throughout the evening to leave me alone with her. And his ploy worked. I'm quite smitten with the girl."

It was a nice evening, and Caesar enjoyed the stroll. The group aimed for the house of Quintus Tullius Cicero. Caesar's clients kept up a steady stream of happy banter and chit-chat that drowned out other street noises.

"Are you serious?" Cinna asked incredulously. "She's only seventeen."

"I know, I shouldn't even consider it. She's younger than Julia. At first glance, she seems shy and humble, but I was hooked. There's a deep fire burning behind that lovely face," Caesar said. "You can let me know what you think after tonight. She's on the guest list."

Cinna shook his head. Caesar didn't know if in wonder or disgust, though he hoped it was the first. His beloved Cornelia was gone for over ten years now, and the end to his loveless marriage to Pompeia had come three years ago. The biggest obstacles to a new marriage were his own feelings about his five-year-long affair with Servilia, senator Silanus's wife, or rather the deep love he had developed for the attractive and intelligent woman. He sighed. Servilia had recently told him that her one-year-old Junia Tertia was his daughter. *But she will never divorce Silanus, and I will never be able to publicly acknowledge that child.*

A few minutes later, they arrived at the city block containing the younger Cicero brother's house. It would be good to see his old friend who had been out of town for three years, serving as propraetor governor of Asia province.

"When did Quintus Cicero come back?" Cinna asked.

"Only a week ago. He has yet to step foot into the Senate," Caesar answered. "I think he doesn't want to face his brother Marcus quite yet, they are in another one of their stubborn quarrels. It seems Marcus figured out that Pulcher works closely with Crassus and me, and he urges Quintus to disassociate from me over the matter." The whole ordeal was very painful for Caesar, who had a long bond with both brothers. A stoic at heart, the older Cicero had publicly praised Caesar's efforts as lawyer for the provinces many times, at least until recently. *I hope he comes around again. All I can do for now is to mitigate some of Pulcher's actions before any real and irreparable harm comes to my old friend.*

One of Caesar's lictors knocked on the front door, and as soon as it opened, most of the party filed through into the residence's atrium. The bodyguards laid down their rods and got comfortable around the pool area, while his entourage of clients had to wander down the street in search of a public eatery.

Cleisthenes, his Athenian manservant, handed him and Cinna indoor sandals, and Caesar sat down on a bench to take off his closed leather shoes. "Thank you. You are excused to leave for the kitchen."

"Thank you, master, I will take my leave," the old slave said before heading to a hallway leading off the atrium's side.

Caesar stood up and approached the residence's majordomo. "Lead the way, please." The servant brought them into the triclinium, the townhouse's beautiful smaller and more intimate dining room. All traditional dining rooms had three deep and open couches set up to create a big U, but these specimens looked to be brand-new with several fluffy-looking cushions for each occupant. The lounges were quite wide, and their surfaces sloped away from the center of the room in the traditional ancient Greek style, allowing for three diners per couch resting on their left sides. *I need to give our hostess a compliment for her good taste.*

The men remained in the entryway to wait for their hosts and the other guest. "Did you see the open scroll on the table in the hallway?" Cinna asked.

"Yes, I did," he replied. "Looks like Marcus Cicero's latest work, doesn't it?" All the man's court speeches had been combined into a book and thousands of copies made and distributed across Rome's refined households. "Please, don't comment on that," Caesar continued. "He'd be unhappy to hear we noticed. Quintus isn't fond of the glory Marcus reaps, especially for his latest book. People all over the city are lauding his brother as a master of Latin prose and the greatest orator of all time."

"Thanks for the warning," Cinna replied, looking at the several small tables in the center of the room within reach of the couches. They would hold plates of food during dinner. "Any idea what will be served tonight?"

"Probably something Greek. Quintus wrote me that he picked up new household staff in Pergamum," Caesar replied with a shrug. "The food is really of no concern to me." *I am here for the conversation. I'd be just as happy eating field rations.*

Their hosts soon approached, their loud voices echoing down the hallway. "You really had to do that? You know I don't like it, not at all," Quintus was shouting at his wife Pomponia.

"Yes, I did," she shouted back as the couple walked towards the triclinium. "And why should I always worry about what you like when you never care about what I like anyway?" Those two had been married for eleven years, yet had never seen eye to eye on anything as long as Caesar could remember. It was clear nobody had told the hosts that guests had arrived. An uncomfortable-looking majordomo rushed out to lead his masters into the room.

Quintus Cicero made straight for Caesar for a tight arm clasp that quickly turned into a hug. "Thank you for coming, old friend."

"How could I not?" Caesar smiled and turned to the hostess. "Salve Pomponia, it is so good to see you again. Thank you for letting me visit your home, it turned out beautiful. I love the tasteful style," he said with a wide grin, indicating the couches behind him.

Pomponia beamed back at him, clearly pleased by the compliment. It was obvious she had invested much effort and money into the house in her husband's absence. "Thank you. I hope you will like both the food and company tonight." She gave him a saucy wink. "I last met Calpurnia at a dinner party five years ago when she was just a pretty little thing. She was shy and didn't say more than please and thank you." She looked over to her husband. "I didn't get many dinner invitations while my husband was in Asia. I'm so happy to have him back home. You know, I took our son and visited him in Asia province for a few months, but that wasn't nearly long enough. Quintus junior is seven, and he needs a full-time father as a role model."

Caesar blushed. Pomponia's comments prickled his conscience. He could have easily invited her and her son over for a dinner event. Furthermore, he had meant to ask his old friend tonight to sign on as legate, taking him away from his family again in a short few months. When Caesar's year of consulship was at an end, he would leave for the provinces. Well, he had already secured several loyal commanders. He smiled back at Pomponia. *Maybe I will wait with asking Quintus to join me for a year or two.*

As if reading his thoughts, Cicero turned to him. "I heard the Senate confirmed you for both Gallia Cisalpina and Illyricum provinces for your proconsul term. How in the world did you manage that?"

With support from both sides of the aisle. He wasn't ready to share that yet. "By placating enough senators to see it my way. Did you hear that Quintus Caecilius Metellus Celer died a few days ago?" Caesar asked.

Cicero shook his head. "I didn't, and you know I haven't been back at the Senate yet. I figured to make tomorrow's meeting my first one."

"You're in for a surprise, then. Yesterday, Vatinius proposed to add old Celer's province of Gallia Transalpina to my other two, and the Senate voted and confirmed it." He grinned when he saw the raised eyebrows. He and Crassus had planned for his future governorship the moment his election as consul was confirmed. Part of that plan had included the relocation of three of his old legions from Hispania to Aquileia in northern Italia. The last administration had slated his old and loyal Tenth to move to

Narbo Martius in Gallia Transalpina for Celer's post. *And now even that is mine, a gift from the gods.*

"I imagine I'll spend most of my time in Aquileia since that's the most centrally located of the three provincial capitals." *At least at the beginning. It's the perfect starting point to conquer the free Dalmatian tribes and the rich kingdom of Dacia.*

"And you will be going with him?" Cicero asked Cinna.

"Of course," Cinna answered with a grin, "and some other mutual friends like Aulus Hirtius and Lucius Cornelius Balbus will join us as well."

Hirtius will be handy to raise more legions before sending them all east for more loot. Caesar was tired of his financial difficulties, which had started so long ago it felt like he'd been in debt his whole life.

Pomponia cut through all his thoughts. "Here are our other guests." She walked out of the room and opened her arms. "Our star of the evening! Welcome to our home, dear Calpurnia. You look lovely." After a quick hug and broad smiles for everybody else, she brought her guests into the triclinium.

Caesar stepped back from the doorway, eyes fixed on the young woman who'd just entered. Calpurnia was tall and slender and looked mature for her seventeen years. She wore a large brown palla, the traditional Roman women's five-foot by eleven-foot shawl, wrapped around her as a cloak to completely cover her figure and gorgeous auburn hair. *Just as society demands from a decent woman in public.*

Though when she removed the palla and handed it to one of the attendants, it revealed a bright and form-fitting orange Greek-style peplos. She locked eyes with him, a slight smile playing on her lips. "Salve, my dear. I was very happy when I received the invitation for this dinner." *Oh, my. That smile, like a sunrise. Those eyes, like deep pools. I might already be done for.*

Caesar suddenly realized that the other guests were all waiting for him. He turned to greet his old friend and fellow senator Gaius Oppius and his wife Petreia. Next was Lucius

Cornelius Balbus from Gades in Hispania Ulterior, a reputable engineer that had served as praefectus fabrum in the Tenth legion during Caesar's time as governor of southern Hispania. Close friend to both Caesar and Pompeius, Balbus had been the necessary connection to make the current alliance a reality.

They went through the seating process, which resulted in Caesar and Calpurnia lying on the same couch right next to each other. He was transfixed by her company and her witty conversation throughout dinner. He hardly tasted the different fruits brought out as the first course, nor all the different meats, vegetables, and seafood of the second, or the fine sweets and desserts toward the end. The remainder of the evening proceeded like a blur, and afterward he remembered only two things with perfect clarity.

The first was his shock when he learned about a side of Quintus Tullius Cicero that he hadn't previously been aware of. The conversations had veered towards recent and memorable experiences, and his old friend shared about having to tour the province during his time as governor of Asia to dole out justice. "The man was accused of patricide. Can you believe that, patricide, the most heinous crime imaginable? I couldn't allow the defense to finish and told them to shut up or be shut up. I was so angry, I sentenced him to our traditional Roman punishment. A beating to within an inch of his life before being sewn into a leather bag with a dog, a snake, a rooster, and a monkey, all to be thrown into the sea together. The only issue was that we were too far from the ocean, so we had to make do with throwing the sack into a river." He laughed heartily. "I thought he was long dead when we got there. He could have succumbed to the beating, or suffocated in the sack, or maybe that local snake was poisonous after all. But as the sack was thrown from the cliff, he started screaming and kept screaming all the way down."

He didn't like the happy smile on his friend's face. *I will need a good man at his side to counter this intense streak of cruelty.*

The other part Caesar remembered clearly was Calpurnia's plea to him toward the end of the dinner, when she turned over on their couch to face him. She took his hand and started to whisper. "I hope it's clear to you by now how I adore you. I'm sure this is mutual, so please go and see my father. I urge you to make arrangements as soon as you can."

695 AUC (59 BC), summer to late summer Corduba, Capital of Roman Province Hispania Ulterior to Aquileia, Capital of Roman Province of Gallia Cisalpina

"I don't know how much more of this I can take," one of the other young legionaries behind him said. He was loud enough to be heard over the din of their long marching column.

Numerius Churinas nodded in agreement, too tired to talk. He looked up to see his old friend Vibius Clarus two rows ahead, just as exhausted as all their fellow soldiers. Ten centuries of fresh recruits had shipped out in early summer to join the Ninth legion in southern Hispania. Upon arrival, the local administration had told them the legion had relocated to northern Italia based on urgent orders from the Senate. The senior centurion, may the gods curse his soul, had the glorious idea of marching instead of chartering ships.

At just two weeks in, he had vivid daydreams about marching forever. *Surely a punishment from the gods, though I don't know what crime I have committed to be chastised so.*

"It will be good for your stamina, and it's going to be your first adventure as true legionaries," his neighbor mumbled. Numerius smiled. These were the exact words the centurion had used in his speech in Corduba. That adventure turned out to be a string of many days filled by ten-hour marches, followed by dreamless nights fueled by exhaustion.

The single buccina among the horn blowers blew for their midmorning break. The men hurried to the side of the road to get a break from the sun relentlessly reflecting off the light-colored stone pavement, the glare much too bright for tired eyes. The hills here were barren and the heat outright cruel. Numerius touched Vibius' shoulder. "How are your feet?"

"Not as bad as yours," Vibius replied. "Mine seem to have recovered. I'm getting pretty thick calluses where my blisters were, and the caligae feel comfortable now."

Numerius lowered his body to the ground and sighed in relief. The bulky chainmail alone weighed close to fifteen pounds, and the hardest lesson over the first few days had been that you couldn't wear your belt too loosely around the mail, or all the weight pulled on your shoulders. Full battle gear added another ten to fifteen pounds for each man, consisting of helmet, shield, gladius and pila. All that was bad enough by itself, though they had to carry another forty pounds of personal packs, tied to a T- or Y-shaped rod and carried over their left shoulder.

Numerius opened the oiled skin around his pack and started rummaging in the wicker basket. Moving his field spade, his glazed bowl and cup, spoon and knife, his hand finally found his bag of field rations. He pulled out the last piece of this morning's bread and began chewing, washing down the dry mouthfuls with swigs of water from his metal canteen. His gaze wandered over to their tent squad's mule. It was just as heavily loaded as they were. *At long last I understand why Marius' veterans of old called themselves his mules, but why were they proud of it?*

***

Three and a half months and fifteen hundred miles later, Numerius found himself happily marching through northern Italia. The men often sung to keep in step, and the mood was euphoric this close to their destination. He looked left to his friend Vibius walking next to him. *Amazing how thick his calves are. I didn't know legs could grow like this.*

"Summer is going to be over soon, and we spent all of it marching," Numerius muttered.

"So? What else would you do anyway?" Vibius retorted before they both started laughing. "I'll be sad when it's over."

It had taken a while, but once the legionaries had grown accustomed to their daily exertion, light banter while marching had become easy, everyone's mood had improved, and the trip had turned into adventure as promised.

"I'll be glad to stay in one place for a while," Numerius said, "but I agree, we certainly got to see a lot. And we had some interesting exploits along the way."

"You could say that! Do you remember the old ragged fellow in Saguntum that sold the *very best balm for weary feet?*" Vibius said, mimicking the dirty man's husky voice. They both burst out into laughter loud enough to garner a glance back from their decurion marching two rows ahead.

"That stuff… I never want to see or smell that again, ever," Numerius answered. The ointment stunk to the heavens, and the tent mates had kicked them out for a few days until it was properly washed off. "How about the weird fermented paste we bought in Tarraco? We never figured out what that was."

"No, we didn't, only that it's to be avoided like the plague." They had quite liked the flavor, though not the result of having to remain close to the latrines for several nights.

"Vibius!" Numerius suddenly called out. "Look ahead, could that be it…?"

"Yes, that must be it. Our new legion's camp. We made it!" he shouted. His excited comerades gave several hoots and hoorays. "Let's see if they give us a few days off. I'd like some rest."

"That would be the decent thing to do, but I have the feeling we'll be up early tomorrow for more training, mark my words."

696 AUC (58 BC), late spring
South of Bailenua, Free Gallia, Eastern part of the Aedui Nation

"How many able-bodied warriors do we have left, aside from our party?" Brenna asked.

"About as many as are riding with us, another three hundred," Elsed answered.

Brenna held her breath in shock. "I did not realize how bad things are. We can't keep going like this."

"I agree, but what are our options? You know Bibracte will not help us, not since Magetobriga."

They were leading the town's warriors in pursuit of yet another enemy raiding party. Word of two hundred Harudi raiders had reached them only yesterday morning, and they had been in hot pursuit ever since. The raiders had given them a merry chase, always staying slightly ahead of them. *As if they know we follow them, carefully staying ahead without trying to get away.*

As he scanned the group riding through a forest clearing, he took in the exhaustion of everybody and slowed his horse. He worried his wife Brenna might fall out of the saddle at any moment and Morcant and Bradan were in only marginally better shape. *Time to call it quits.*

"Ho!" he called out, reining in with his left and raising his right hand before dismounting.

"Are we finally giving up on this wild goose chase?" Rionach asked, following suit.

Elsed smiled at the woman, best friend to both his sister and his wife. "I think we must." Orlagh, usually keen on showing her fierce and hardened warrior face, reined up next to Rionach with a weary, yet warm smile, meant for her love. Their longstanding relationship had caused much turmoil lately, with Rionach resisting all attempts by her family to become a bride for one of a long line of male suitors. He watched their happy banter as he stretched his weary muscles from too much saddle time. *Our usually tolerant culture frowns on lack of procreation. The real issue is they aren't trying to have children.*

As the clan's new chieftain, he had listened to all kinds of complaints about the two women. He sighed. Rionach's brother had died fighting another raiding party just a few months ago, leaving the women as substitute parents to the man's son and daughter, which had quieted the loudest voices. "We should head back home. I'd like to eat a proper meal and sleep in my bed tonight," he said loudly.

"You mean share a bed with me?" Brenna called as she walked up, causing many chuckles and smiles. *How did I get so lucky? Marrying that woman is the best thing that ever happened to me.*

He looked forward to being back home.

***

"Come on you two, let little Faela sleep," Aina scolded her daughter Nara, now three years old, and two-year-old nephew Coraidan, Faela's older brother. "Come away." Her hope for a break was suddenly disturbed by a long and piercing noise from outside.

"What was that, Mamm?" her daughter asked.

"That was from our people on the wall, it's the carnyx blowing alarm. We need to find out what's going on. Get your things, I'll be back with Iudica." She ran over to the neighbor's house. "Iudica? Are you there?"

"I am here, Aina, what's going on?" the young teenage girl said on her way out the door. She was home alone, with her father out with Elsed to catch the latest raiders and her mother long dead.

"I'm not sure, but I mean to find out. Will you help with the children, please?" After Iudica gave a decisive nod, they rushed back to her house, where she fastened a long rectangular cloth around Iudica's shoulders as a sling for little Faela. Satisfied with her work, she bent down to Nara and Coraidan. "It's very important you listen to me now." The children's big eyes meant they understood the seriousness. "You have to either hold my hand or Iudica's, no walking alone. We will go to the wall and see what's going on, and I don't want to leave you here. Do you understand?" She looked them in the eyes until they both nodded. "Alright, let's go."

She held Nara's hand and led, soon arriving at the town's wall close to the gate. "Stay with Iudica for a moment. I will be right back," she said to Nara. Joining several warriors frantically running up the stairs, she made it up and searched for who was in charge. Fedelmida, her mother's best friend, was in command.

"Aina!" Fedelmida called. "Have a look, this is truly bad." She pointed south. Aina followed the direction with her eyes and held her breath in shock. Far away in the distance, thousands of riders poured into the fields between two patches of forest. *Even with Elsed and his force here we could not defend our wall against this many. I hope at least he is still out there and wasn't ambushed by these masses.* "Suebi?" She asked, and Fedelmida nodded. "What should we do?"

"Pray, child," her mother's old friend said quietly before giving herself a visible jolt. "We need to get some of our people over the wall on our north side, with the children. It's risky, but we need to try. Who knows how long it will take these people to get around to the backside of our walls? We might have enough time." The old woman scanned the buildings until she stopped at a fenced patch with a couple of grazing horses. "We have maybe sixty horses left in town. How about we mount warriors, each with a child, and send them out through the gate before the Suebi close in?"

"That would help get at least some of the little ones out. Any that get away won't grow up as slaves."

"That's settled. We'll send out our young and able warriors, and as many small children as we can. I want you to lead them, Aina," Fedelmida said. "No discussion!"

Aina sighed. "Alright, though I can't say I like leaving you here. Also, I'll need help collecting the horses. Everybody is to meet at the inside of the gate." She threw one last glance out over the fields at the steadily approaching enemy, close enough now to leave no doubt they were Suebi and Germanic allies, and hurried back to the stairs. Behind her, Fedelmida issued orders to some of the other younger warriors to leave the wall and fetch horses.

"Go!" After the loud send-off, everybody rushed down the stairs after her.

"Iudica! The Suebi are here, and there are too many to try to defend the town. We need to save as many of the children as we can. Let's fetch horses. Come with me to our stall, you can ride one of ours."

The young woman turned and ran for the stable, little Faela bouncing in her sling. Aina grabbed Nara and Coraidan by the hands and rushed after.

***

She sat in her saddle at the fringes of the crowded open space in front of the gate, now filled with sixty horses and their riders. Nara was right behind her, tied to the two rear horns of the saddle with a piece of cloth. Iudica's horse was close by with little Coraidan sitting the same way, clasping the horns for all he was worth. Faela was wailing from Iudica's sling.

"Everybody ready?" she shouted. Pale faces looked at her for guidance, and her stomach plummeted from worry about them all. Some of the little children wailed and many of the young warriors wiped tears from their eyes, though most of the others nodded back at her in quiet resolve.

Fedelmida called down from the wall. "Go, they're closing in too fast, don't wait. Head west the moment you are through the gate. We'll buy you some time."

She looked up at the many youngsters and old folks manning the wall, gripping their swords and spears with white knuckles and sporting grim faces. *None of you deserve what's coming. Thank you and may the gods bless you.*

Two grizzled warriors opened the portal doors and Aina shouted "Ride! Move!" She waited impatiently for all the riders to get through the gate until, finally, Iudica made it out and she could follow. The moment she was through, she knew it had taken too long. A group of riders bore down on them at full gallop, attempting to cut them off. She kicked her horse again and again, until the mare ran as fast as she possibly could, little Nara screaming in fear and discomfort behind her.

***

Elsed rode close behind Bradan, anxious to get home.

"By the gods!" his best friend called out.

"What is it?" Elsed asked but received no reply. He rode up and reined in. "By all that's holy, no!"

The rest of the group came out from the trees and stopped. "What should we do, Elsed?" Brenna asked with panic in her voice. "There are too many for us to fight, but we can't leave our children!"

"I know, let me think a moment. Maybe we should ride to the northern part of the wall. Perhaps the Suebi aren't there yet. If we could get some of our people to climb over the wall…" His hands shook with fear for his people and his own little ones.

"We'll try for that. Let us head north and stay out of sight," Bradan replied, already turning his horse.

About twenty minutes later, Elsed moved out from behind another patch of forest. He could look down the length of the wall from this spot, all the way to the gate where a slew of riders had just left the town. Likely their own people, though they were a little too far away for certainty. He reined in and turned in his saddle. "Lead everybody else to the north wall, Brenna. I'll stay with a few warriors and get closer. If they are Suebi, we'll try to slow them down. If they're ours, we'll try to help."

"Just come back to me! Meet us on the main road heading west," Brenna shouted at him before riding on.

Several of their close friends had stopped, intent on following him. He drove his tired horse into a canter towards the gate. As the distance shrunk, he recognized the riders as their young warriors and children. A troop of enemy in pursuit was gaining. He drew his sword as he approached, determined to defend his family. When he passed the first of the fleeing Aedui, the enemy riders converge with the end of the group. Trying to fight the Suebi off, the last of the townspeople were now slowly falling behind. His heart skipped a beat when he got a clear view of their last rider. *Aina!*

He kept riding until he crashed into the first Suebi. Bradan passed him at full gallop, narrowly avoiding another warrior, intent on the end of the line. Elsed barely countered a ferocious attack, able to dispatch the enemy with a stab of his sword only once Rionach distracted the man from the other side. He looked ahead to see Bradan within twenty feet of Aina, who was trying to keep an attacker off her left side. Another Suebi slowly came up from her right and caught her with his spear. Her loud scream echoed in his ears when she fell out of her saddle. Only now did he realize his little niece was on his sister's horse, clinging to the rear horns of the saddle. *Gods, show mercy.*

He kicked his horse hard, barely recognizing Iudica riding by with his own children. Bradan, still far ahead of him, crashed into the Suebi who'd killed his sister. Both horses went down in a big tumble, his brother-in-law getting flung and landing hard. After rising to his knees, his best friend picked up the German rider's spear and stood up. Raising the weapon and gripping it in both hands, he swayed. *He's hurt! Hold on, hold on, I am coming.*

But Bradan didn't waiting for him, he ran for the man holding Aina's horse and daughter instead. The warrior let go of the reins to raise his shield in preparation for his attack, though another Suebi warrior now approached his friend from behind.

"Watch out!" Elsed called, though it was no use. Just before Bradan reached his target, the other rider punched a spearhead right through his back, lifting him clear off his feet. The remainder of the Suebi riders now made it onto the scene and pushed between, taking away any chance for Elsed to reach Bradan or his niece. He mentally prepared for a suicidal attack, only changing his mind when he remembered his wife and children behind him. *They still need me.*

With tears of loss and frustration, he turned his horse to follow the fleeing Aedui.

***

Brenna tightly held on to the young boy after helping him down from the northern wall. *It's too many to carry for our few horses, looks like everybody is here except for the warriors holding the wall.*

"Grab only the smaller children, the others have to run for the forest and hide," she shouted at the other riders, guiding her horse away from the wall. A few elders stood on the fringes of the growing group. "Please, lead them into hiding, keep moving as far away from the town as you can. We'll come back with food and water, and more horses if we can find some."

"Thank you, Brenna, we will get them to safety," one of the older women yelled back, already walking off to gather people. Brenna nodded and turned back to the wall. Most of the town had made it over, and only a few stragglers were left. Scanning the growing group, she started to panic. *Where are my children?*

Rionach came over, her nephew holding on tightly to her saddle. "Somebody just told me Aina and Iudica took the young warriors and all the remaining horses out the gate with some of the children, yours too."

She took a deep breath and let her eyes wander over the mounted warriors. Everybody had children with them in front of their saddles, behind, or both. *Please, gods, let mine be well.*

"We need to go, and we need to lure the Suebi away if we find them heading here. If they follow us for a while, our people will have"—she pointed with her head to all the town's inhabitants now running for the nearest patch of forest—"a much better chance."

She rode off without looking back at the town, their home for so many years. When they turned around the bend in the wall to ride straight west, she noticed in satisfaction a group of Suebi choosing to follow them rather than finish their ride around the wall.

695 AUC (59 BC), late summer
Twenty-five miles southwest of Vesontio, Free Gallia, heartland of the Sequani Nation

"Where should we focus next?" Ariovist, king of the Suebi and Sequani, asked, from his oversized chair on the back of the dais. He sat with his council of chieftains at a long table in the new great hall he used as his seat of power . The issue at hand was the arrival of another five thousand warriors just last week from across the Rhenus.

"I want to suggest the area just east of where the Dubis bends south, halfway between Vesontio and the Vosago mountains. It is very rich land, and many of the farmers there raise horses," one of his men replied. Several members of the council talked to each other in greedy excitement until Ariovist raised his hand.

"I agree, the prospect of liberating more horses during the resettlement of the Sequani farmers is exhilarating. I agree with your suggestion, Celtic horses are a treasure." He grinned. *This soft land already made me richer than my father ever was.*

"My King!" one of his retainers shouted from the entry way of the great hall. "There is a Roman trader outside who wishes to speak with you. He is asking that you grant him hospitum based on the good news he brings you."

"Hospitum?" Ariovist asked. He had heard that this word was very important to the Romans. It didn't just mean hospitality, it also invoked divine guest rights, including the status of friendship and mandatory exchanges of gifts. "Tell him he will receive it only if the news he brings are worthy of such. Show him in," Ariovist commanded, rising from the table to walk over to his throne. His retainer returned shortly with a tall and grossly overweight Roman dressed in a pristinely clean and white toga. Ariovist frowned in disgust at the man. *Why does he wear something so impractical? Maybe to distract from his physical weakness.*

"Salve, king Ariovistus!" the trader greeted him jovially before bowing slightly. "My name is Marcus Mettius, purveyor of fine goods. Our Roman Senate entrusted me with a letter for you." He opened a bag hanging from his shoulder and removed a wrapped scroll. "It seems you have powerful friends. Congratulations, you are now the latest friend and ally of the Senate and People of Rome."

Ariovist jumped up in excitement. He couldn't stop himself from offering the detestable man his hand in friendship. *I can't believe my ploy worked. My gold must have reached the right people. Now that we have the same status, the Roman people will never help the Aedui against me.*

695 AUC (59 BC), late winter
Rome, Italia, Capital of the Roman Republic

Caesar waited, fidgeting like a boy. His mother Aurelia came up from behind and squeezed his shoulder. "Not long now, I'd imagine. They must be nearly here," she said in a soothing tone.

They stood in his townhouse's atrium, waiting for Calpurnia's arrival. His extended family crowded all around him, including both his sisters with their families and his daughter Julia with her new husband Gnaeus Pompeius Magnus. A few friends like Aulus Hirtius, Gaius Oppius, and Marcus Licinius Crassus stood against the back wall. *This is my third one, why am I still nervous?*

Since Caesar himself was now Pontifex Maximus, the highest priest in Rome, the lower Flamen Dialis had to officiate the wedding by himself, presiding over ten witnesses collected from the guests to attest that the marriage had taken place.

He walked close to the open doorway, just in time to see his bride and her family approach. Calpurnia wore a sparklingly white wedding gown, the sight of which made him smile in joy. She had insisted on following tradition to the letter, even though it had taken her many weeks to weave the woolen cloth herself. *The gown turned out amazing. She looks spectacular.*

A belt around her waist was fastened by the traditional "knot of Hercules," a symbolic safety measure to ensure only the husband would open it. On her head, she wore a floral wreath covered by a slightly translucent yellow veil to symbolize chastity and purity. A young cousin of hers walked in front holding a lit torch, whose flame had been transferred from her parent's hearth this morning and carried all the way to the Subura. *I'm sure she offered the traditional copper coin to the local neighborhood spirit on her way here. She joins the local community, making everything is as auspicious as possible.*

"I give you water and fire," one of Caesar's nephews announced, stopping the bridal group before handing over a cup of water and another torch lit by the fire of his own hearth.

Once the old torch was extinguished, her family carried Calpurnia over the threshold. As she was let down to stand by herself, she greeted Caesar. "Where you are Gaius, I am Gaia," she spoke the ancient words of the Earth goddess. Caesar's same first name was pure coincidence.

"Where you are Gaia, I am Gaius," Caesar answered and walked up to clasp her hands. The Flamen Dialis now brought a small cake made from spelt flower as part of the patrician wedding tradition. Caesar and Calpurnia held it in one hand each and tore it apart between them, eating the resulting pieces.

"On to the sacrifice," Caesar said to her. They moved over to a makeshift altar holding a bound and sedated sow. Cleisthenes handed him a ceremonial knife which he put into Calpurnia's hand before wrapping his own hand around hers. She looked away as they stepped towards the animal. "Mother Earth, receive this sacrifice and bless this union," they both said in unison.

The deed done, they retreated a few steps, now officially married. The room broke out into cheers, and the guests formed a line to congratulate the new couple. When his daughter Julia reached him, she hugged him tightly and put her face close to his ear. "Hello father. I wanted you to know that I forgive you. I hated you for trading me to Gnaeus Pompeius without asking for my consent, but I realize now that I could have done much worse. It certainly helps that he treats me like a goddess," she whispered. Though he knew Julia had meant to make him feel better, his conscience gave him a twinge for what he'd done to her. He sighed and kissed her cheek. "Thank you, my dear, I appreciate you telling me."

Next, a beaming Gnaeus Pompeius stepped in to shake Caesar's hand. "Congratulations, and may you be as happy as we are." He moved in close. "I will forever be in your debt about Julia."

"I am glad and grateful for your support. We can talk more at the wedding dinner tomorrow," he answered.

"Murcia and both my boys will be there as well," Crassus, who was next in line, said. Though the wedding dinner was traditionally reserved for family alone, Caesar had invited some of his closest friends and allies to the ceremony. The feast that would take place the next day was a different matter as it was supposed to be an open affair, including many hundreds of people.

The last stragglers filed out of the house, and his mother closed the front door. Cleisthenes busily directed the household servant's efforts to clean a big puddle of blood on the atrium floor. Previously unnoticed by the celebrating couple, the move of the sacrificed animal to the kitchen had made a big mess.

"I'll deal with that later, don't you worry," Aurelia said, stepping in for a tight hug with her son. Calpurnia leaned in and put her arm over her mother-in-law's shoulder. Though he knew his mother still thought the age difference scandalous, he was glad she didn't hold it against his new wife. "Let's go," Aurelia said before leading them to the back of the house. "I have your bedroom ready." As was proper for a wedding night, the bedroom contained no lamps, forcing the couple to undress in the hallway. Aurelia stood in front of the doorway, her lit oil lamp the only illumination, and winked at her son. "You better be quick about getting your clothes off."

"Thank you, mother." Caesar smiled. As he turned to his new wife, he saw her hold the belt's knot up to him. He had to laugh at her eagerness, and after a moment of uncertainty, Calpurnia freely joined his laughter. *That's a good start.*

696 AUC (58 BC), late spring
Clusium, Etruria, Italia

How could I be so stupid to think Minatus would sell me legally? Velia stopped in the dark hallway outside of her chamber, thinking back at that fateful moment, now some nine months ago. She would have fetched a good price at public auction, maybe three to four thousand sesterces. That would have paid off her debt of eight hundred sesterces and awarded her the difference, making for a good head start to buy her freedom back. But, instead, the despicable man had made a backroom deal with the manager of a lupanar, a common brothel, for the exact amount of the debt. Her new owner Fastie was a brute of a man who hadn't looked at her once throughout the whole sale process.

"Everything alright, honey?" Titia asked in the hallway. The older woman had befriended her right from the start. A gentle soul, she was the age exception among the other, much younger sex workers.

"Yeah, I'm fine. Just thinking about the unfairness of it all. You know, nothing new," she replied, giving her new friend a bitter smile. "Maybe it would help me to let this go, but I can't stop hating Minatus for what he did. I daydream of what I'll do to him if I ever get the chance." The man had not just made a shady backroom deal. As it turned out, the scam was much bigger. Minatus was the secret owner of the brothel, and dealing with Velia's debt this way would earn him ten times the amount she owed for every single year she worked here.

"Nothing wrong with a little daydreaming, especially if it keeps you going," Titia replied. "Come on, let's get to the atrium."

"Ah, here comes the favorite," Fastie said when they rounded the corner into the open space. Velia ignored the man, hoping he would let her pass without his usual mocking. Every morning, the women mingled here for the mandatory cup of tea and breakfast; the only chance for socializing since the other two meals of the day were brought into their rooms.

Before leaving their rooms, they had to sponge bathe and then make their way to the front of the atrium to receive a cup of silphium tea. She had long since figured out that it kept her bleeding regular. *Having any of us pregnant would cost Minatus money.*

Titia had already finished her cup and looked over. "Are you all right, honey?" She asked, as if it wasn't obvious. How could anything be all right again, ever? She had days in which she wanted to die, just so she could be done with this horrid place. A dark corner in Hades would be such an improvement over these men every day, their rough and unwanted hands touching her. She shuddered. *They are not what brought me here. That was all Minatus.*

"I'm fine," she finally said. "Just thinking of what I'd like to do to that scum bucket Minatus if I ever get my hands on him."

Velia saw it vividly in her mind's eye. How she would torture him, and gore him, but slowly. *More than anything, I want him to feel what I feel every day when all these men violate me. Him and that pig Faustie both.*

With some effort she put her hatred aside. It wouldn't help her to survive. Instead, she needed to be strong, endure the unwashed bodies on her every day. All she could now was to survive and wait for a chance to change things.

She glanced at her friend. Titia's constant support had helped bring up something from within, a strength she didn't know she had. *Eventually, I will find a way out of this horror. Though paying for my freedom won't be what gets me out of here, ever.*

Fastie charged the men between four and six sesterces for her, depending on what she was supposed to do, but she only received a single per visit, a small coin equal to a quarter sesterce. Most of those small coins were collected to pay the rent for her small room, the scant clothing pieces she had to wear, and the small portions of food she was allowed every day.

"Where is Velthurus?" Velia asked in alarm. She had just realized the boy was missing from the common area.

The young towheaded water bearer served the main corridor that connected both their rooms, his job bringing wash water to the women between customers. At only six years old, he had already been branded by Fastie as a repeat runaway. The tattoo on his forehead spelled FUG, the abbreviation for fugitivus. Velia had long since opened her heart to the boy without reservation. "Let's find him, or he'll go hungry," Titia responded.

The two women walked down both main hallways, calling for the boy, until they reached the small walled garden at the back of the domus. There, he sat with his hands in front of his face, and Velia knelt for a closer look. His eyes were red from crying, and the left side of his face black and blue from a recent beating. He fought her as she tried to pull him into a hug, but then changed his mind, hugging her back so tightly it hurt.

"There, my dear. Do you want to talk about it?" Velia whispered into his blond hair. In reaction, he cried even harder and increased his grip until she thought her ribs would crack.

She abhorred and detested what she had to do every day, knowing that her body would never feel clean again for the rest of her life. But the abuse of the helpless boy at the hands of Fastie was something else entirely. It made her soul scream in anguish. She locked eyes with her friend Titia, though her friend had no answers either. *Will this ever end?*

Waiting here much longer would invite Faustie's wrath; he was always suspicious about the women wanting to shirk their duties. "Come, let's go, so you can still get some food," she said, dragging the boy up to his feet. They made their way back to the atrium, just in time before the breakfast dishes were put away. *Oh brother, how I wish you wouldn't have signed up, though I fear going back in time might be impossible even for the gods.*

696 AUC (58 BC), late spring
Mediolanum, Roman Province of Gallia Cisalpina and border area between Roman Province of Gallia Transalpina and Free Gallia, lands of the Helvetii.

"How is Labienus these days?" Aulus Hirtius asked. "I admit I was surprised when you tapped him as the Tenth's next Legatus. He's known to be Pompeius' man through and through."

"From what I can tell, he's done a fine job in getting the Tenth into fighting shape. They were ready when I left Narbo Martius and will be here in another three weeks at most," Caesar replied. "As to him being a Pompeius man, I'm very much aware of that. The entire Labienus family of Picenum Asculum has been clients of the Pompeii since time immemorial. Don't forget though, our great Pompeius is now also my son-in-law. I've also worked with Labienus in the courts for years and know him to be dependable. I have no reason to doubt his faithful service."

The early morning fog hanging over the field's fresh growth added an eerie mood to an otherwise beautiful landscape surrounding this new Roman road south of the city of Mediolanum. The thoroughfare had been built to connect several major routes from the South, the East, and the West with the city itself, and Caesar had set a gentle pace for the few cavalry men and his ever-present lictors. The only traffic they had encountered so far were the occasional early produce carts of local farmers heading to market. "What exactly are the numbers for our two new legions up to?" Caesar asked.

"We're past three quarters. The word is spreading, young men are coming from fifty miles around. Nearly all of the ones we've signed are still in basic training, though we are running them hard in case you need us to shortcut the four months. That said, I wouldn't go anywhere with them until we do at least three. You'll see when we get there."

They were on their way to visit the first of several training grounds west of the city, and there were still many miles to travel. Hirtius suddenly pointed back. One of Caesar's lictors rode up. "There's a courier here, wishing to speak with you, sir. He says it's urgent."

Caesar reined in. "Bring him to me."

The man waved back until a colleague rode up with a lone rider in tow. The stranger wore the official sigil of the senatorial courier service around his neck, and his horse's mouth and sides were caked with foam. The animal had been pushed hard.

"Ave, sirs, I've came from Narbo Martius with an urgent letter from the Provincial headquarters for governor Gaius Julius Caesar," the man said.

"You found him. Please hand me the scroll and let me sign for it. And wait until I know if I need to send a response to whatever this is," Caesar answered before dismounting. His lictors followed suit. He signed the man's receipt, broke the seal on the scroll and started reading.

"What's the urgent news?" Hirtius asked.

"Trouble for Gallia Transalpina. The nation of the Helvetii has petitioned me to allow the use of our provincial road westward from their lands in the mountains. They want to travel through our lands to the free Gallic tribes beyond." Everybody knew free Celtic tribes used raids on their neighbors to hone their skills of war. There was no chance a whole nation would wander peacefully through a Roman province.

Caesar turned to the courier. "Come with me, I need to write two letters for you to take back. The first for Titus Labienus, commander of the Tenth legion, currently on the move. You might have passed them on the road here." The man nodded. "The other needs to go back to Narbo Martius and be delivered to the deputy governor of Gallia Transalpina. He needs to officially send word to the Helvetii that I am thinking about their request, and that they'll have an answer soon."

He mounted again. "Geneva is the closest provincial city to their lands. Any idea how long it will take to travel there from here?" he asked Hirtius.

His friend shook his head. "No, but I'm sure we are about to find out."

***

Only a few weeks had passed since his encounter with the courier. "Bring the men to the bridge," Caesar told the centurion. "I'll meet you there."

He sauntered along the water's edge ahead of his lictors to where the water of the lake flowed out into the Rhodanus river. The wall of the city of Geneva was close behind him, and a few farms and settlements were visible along the lake shore across the water. He stopped to study the bridge crossing the mighty river a few hundred feet from the lake. *If we remove these cross braces... that might be the easiest way to take down one of the segments in a way that can be restored at a later time.*

The oversized century of soldiers approached him from behind. "What do you need us to do, sir?" he asked.

Caesar looked at the young men, the first of the new Eleventh legion to have passed basic training.

"I need you to take the bridge apart. We need to deny the Helvetii out there"—he pointed across the river—"any easy way of crossing. Let me show you what I think will be easiest." Caesar took the lead down the bank to the river and pointed at the braces he had in mind.

A week later, an elderly Helvetius showed up in Caesar's small camp. "Salve, mighty proconsul. I am a retainer of Divico, foremost chieftain of our nation and elected war king. We had word that you are here in person, so I was sent to ask if you have decided to allow our nation access to your road along the

Rhodanus. We will make it worth your while with many lavish gifts."

"I am sorry, I have not made up my mind yet. I'm inclined to give you a favorable decision, though this will have to wait until a later time. Tell Divico to send a delegation in two weeks. It needs to be ready for some negotiations. Please give your king my best regards." *I want these people thinking that I can be bought, at least until the Tenth is here in a few days.*

***

The legion had arrived late yesterday, building its customary camp close to the dismantled bridge. The morning was miserable, cold, and full of promise for heavy rain. Yet Caesar couldn't wait for better weather. Time was short.

He marched straight up to the legion's command tent. "Are you here, old friend?"

"I'm back here. Good morning," Labienus replied. His voice exuded tiredness, and he was rubbing his hands for warmth at one of the braziers.

"I know you and the men just arrived, but I need to put them to work immediately. Please, have them assemble so I can address them."

"Better you than me," Labienus said. "Can we at least wait until after they've had some breakfast? That should make them more receptive to whatever you have to tell them."

Caesar nodded. "Thank you, that will help. Please bring them out to the field in front of the Porta Praetoria after. I'll wait there for the call to assemble." He headed back out in search of a wagon to stand on during his speech. He needed to be seen by as many as possible.

An hour later, the men formed up into centuries and cohorts in the middle of a heavy downpour. Caesar closed his bright-red military cape to help with the chilly morning and smiled to himself. His new sagum, as the big piece of wool was called, had been a gift from his young wife, handed to him when he'd said good-bye to leave for the provinces. *"You told me that you needed to be clearly seen and recognized by your men during battle. Well, my dear, now you will be," she had said with a glint in her eyes. "Everybody who sees you will want one for themselves." He had been puzzled until he opened the wrapped package and saw the bright color.*

The legionaries continued to assemble, all wearing their own cloaks ranging from light browns to deep greens. As long as the wool got regular treatment of lanolin from fresh sheep's skin, it would stave off the wet on cold days such as this. The officers now moved up to stand in front of the cohorts, their sagums in traditional deep purple, and his smile turned into a grin. *I have to remember that thinking of my dear Calpurnia helps with the jitters before giving speeches.*

He mounted the wagon's platform. All the men could see him now, and he projected his voice over the rain to be heard as far beyond the front ranks as possible. "Welcome, loyal legionaries of the Tenth Legion. All of you have sworn your oath of loyalty to me twice. First in Hispania as raw recruits, and again two months ago in Narbo Martius."

He turned to address the auxilia. The archers, slingers, and cavalry men had lined up beyond the big square formation.

"I want to thank every single one of you for hurrying here. Let me tell you why you were asked to come to this place. The whole nation of the Helvetii wants to travel through our province of Gallia Transalpina. We cannot let them do this. They must be stopped here at the border, or they will burn and pillage our lands in the process."

Good, the men are hanging on my every word. He added a dramatic pause before continuing. "I am sorry to have to ask you to keep up your haste. I need your shovels, your baskets, and your axes. If we want to keep out the Helvetii, which are a numerous nation, we must build a long wall from this lake to the nearest mountain." He pointed west. "I know wet dirt is hard to move, but we can't wait for better weather because we would be too late." He scanned the crowd up and down again, nodding to many of the men he recognized. "I was proud to march with the Tenth through Hispania. You men are the finest legionaries any commander could hope for. Therefore, I know you will not let me down, but will make me proud again!"

A few of the men started a cheer before he stepped off the wagon. The cry was quickly picked up by others and gained momentum across the troops. *Better than I expected. They will do as I ask.*

On his way to the legate a few hundred feet away, he came across his old friend Lucius Cornelius Balbus, prefect of the legion's engineers. "Come with me!" he called and marched on until he reached Labienus. "I'll ride out with Balbus and his engineers to figure out the construction details. I need you to be ready to break camp. We need to spread the men along the south side of the river in several smaller forts, otherwise we can't garrison such a long stretch effectively. The best wall is one we can build quickly, so our standard ten-foot-high palisade along the river's southern side will do. It should be located above the banks and behind the ditch, with regular towers to allow signals as calls for reinforcements." The wall would stretch for a full nineteen miles, all the way from the southern tip of the lake to the first cliffs of the Jura mountains. He turned to Balbus. "Are you ready? Please, gather your men."

***

Only a few days later, Caesar supervised the final parts of the huge building project, his men closing off the last stretch to the lake. "Did we deploy the heavy bolt throwers yet?" he asked.

"Yes, we have them on each watchtower now, and one stands ready for this one," Balbus answered.

Good, nearly done. And that gods-forsaken rain finally stopped as well.

He walked up to a tired looking legionary and took the man's shovel. "Sit down, you deserve a rest." Time to do some labor himself. *And show the men that I'm not above sharing their hard work.*

He sunk knee deep into the mud in his attempt to dig the bottom of the trench. An hour later, he was thankful for Publius Licinius Crassus interrupting him.

"Sir, there is a Helvetii embassy here that wants to speak to you." Though still very young, at twenty-three, his ally's second son was looking more and more like a good catch. Though his age meant he couldn't be advanced past his status of tribune for the time being, the man was both sharp and already a proven leader. *I'll keep an open mind about him.*

"Bring them here," Caesar answered, climbing out of the ditch and wiping his hands on the hem of his tunic. He didn't have to wait long and was duly impressed by the sight. The delegation contained only two men, though exemplary specimen of their nation, wearing the finest available to them. Long pants covered the upper rims of soft leather boots, and long, colorful cloaks wrapped their bodies against the cold. They looked splendid, clearly leaders among their own, with small blue tattoos peeking out at the wrists and necks to show their status. Broad leather belts did double duty by keeping their cloaks closed and providing a place to hold beautifully decorated sword sheaths. The cloaks, the sheaths, and even the belts were all ornately trimmed in gold. Their hair was cut short, and they were both clean-shaven except for impressively thick mustaches. Caesar took in all of it until his eyes rested on the massive Celtic gold torcs they wore around their necks, sticking out from their cloaks. Made of three cords formed from multiple strands of gold wire all braided together, they formed a heavy representation of power. *Pure gold, the ultimate status symbol for these men.*

When young Crassus pointed at him, the two men stood silent and stared in disbelief. Caesar laughed. Was it the thought of the Roman general dirty top to bottom, or was it the other surprise, the massive wall that had sprung up all along the riverbank behind him as far as the eye could see?

The smaller one of the two men addressed him in perfect Latin. "Salve Caesar. I am council member Bricio, son of Orgetorix. The Helvetii nation wants you to know that we cannot wait any longer for your response. King Divico demands your answer now—will you, or will you not allow us to pass through the lands of the Allobroges along the northern border of your Roman province?"

The other man spoke up. "Let it be, Bricio. We already have our answer. That wall was built to keep us out."

Caesar nodded as he looked them up and down. At this pivotal moment, covered in dirt and cold sweat, he decided to put his plans for conquest of Dacia on hold. *Why go anywhere else? The riches I need can be had right here, in Gallia.*

"You are correct, this wall is your answer. I cannot, will not let you pass. I know what would happen to our province if your warriors were to wander through." He gestured at the wall. "Try to force the issue if you must. We're ready for you."

He addressed tribune Crassus. "Please escort these men back to their boat. There is nothing more to discuss."

***

Two weeks later, Caesar ran along the wall at the head of a small relief force. The signal towers had indicated yet another attack, this time between the seventh and eighth towers as counted from the lake. The run made him sweat hard despite the cool morning hour. The Helvetii had been crossing the river in small groups for several days now, probing for weaknesses in the Roman defense. *So far, we've repelled every one of their sorties. The watchtowers have proven their worth over and over, and so have our auxiliaries.*

The Tenth's archers and slingers had stayed spread out along the wall sections, raining arrows, rocks, and lead shot on the enemy at every opportunity.

Caesar reached a section packed tightly with legionaries. "Who is in charge here?" he asked the first centurion he encountered.

"That would be tribune Crassus," the man replied. "Just keep going toward the next tower, you can't miss him."

Caesar nodded and ran on. He didn't have to go far before he came upon a cluster of officers, standard bearers, and horn blowers. As soon as he saw him, Crassus walked toward him. "Salve proconsul! We beat them back, at least for now. How many did you bring?"

"Two full centuries," Caesar replied. "Will they try here one more time?"

"Possibly, or a few hundred feet over. I'd appreciate you staying close for the next hour or two." The young tribune looked tired and dirty. Nobody had gotten much sleep thanks to frequent alarms up and down the wall. "I just hope they won't ever do more than test us."

"I agree. They could overrun us with ease if they ever gathered more than just a few hundred fighters in one place. The Helvetii have many tens of thousands of warriors," Caesar said. "I'll tell the men I brought to get comfortable for now, we'll stay nearby."

He walked back and told the two centuries to stretch out on a lesser populated wall section. They waited for three uneventful hours before he led them back to the closest camp.

A few more hours passed without attacks or as much as a sighting of the enemy, and Caesar sent a courier with instructions for the Tenth's cavalry prefect to bring Celtic scouts across to the other side of the river. *What are they up to now?*

***

Two days later, the flap of Caesar's tent swung inward and his servant Cleisthenes's head popped in. "The first of the scouts has returned."

"Bring him, bring him in!" Caesar said in excitement.

The Celtic cavalry man walked in and gave him a Roman-style salute. Caesar smiled in response. "What can you tell me of the Helvetii forces? Why have they stopped attacking?

"They are all gone. Every family, every man, woman, child, and dog in the area. I couldn't believe it at first, so I searched in ever wider circles until I found their trail. They took all their wagons and moved toward a narrow pass through the Jura mountains. As far as I know, it leads directly to the southern border of the lands of the Sequani."

And here it is. If they are still planning to go west as before, they will not enter the Sequani nation, instead they'll move through the lands of the Aedui—friends and allies of Rome. The Helvetii had just given him the perfect excuse to go after them.

"Thank you, good work." He shook the man's hand and dismissed him. "Cleisthenes, send someone to bring Titus Labienus to me. I need to see him at once." Sitting down at his folding table, he pulled out a stack of map scrolls, unrolling them one after the other. After an hour of brooding, he briefly heard the heavy thudding of a man running in armor, followed by Labienus's flushed face appearing through the tent flap.

"Come in my friend, have a seat. I talked to the first of the returning scouts, and he told me that the Helvetii are all gone. Stay here for another three weeks, and if nothing else happens, take down the camps and move west. Let me show you where I want you to go." He moved the scrolls around until he found the best depiction of southern Gallia. "Right here." He grinned when he saw Labienus' raised eyebrows. "The Helvetii are about to enter the lands of the Aedui. In a few weeks' time, I will meet you where the Arar flows into the Rhodanus. First, I need to go back to Mediolanum."

696 AUC (58 BC), late spring
Aquileia, Roman Province of Gallia Cisalpina

"Always feels good to watch somebody else doing the drilling, doesn't it?" Oz said.

"You could say that," Gulussa answered with a laugh. Oz's turma had wall duty, and he had stopped at Gulussa's post as he did his round to check in with everybody. He looked out over a wide field filled by yet another cohort of legionaries performing maneuver drills.

The ranks included many raw recruits who had signed up a year or less ago, brought in to bring the Ninth back to full strength. One of these young men kept missing turns, clearly not remembering left from right.

After several wrong turns, the commanding centurion had enough. "Column, *haaalt*!"

The noncom walked to the legionary and stood in front of him for a couple of minutes. Without further warning, he lifted his right leg and stomped down hard, hitting his victim's left foot with a hobnailed caliga. The unfortunate young man fell over screaming.

"From here on you *will* remember where left is. It's the side that hurts!" the centurion shouted. "Now, go and see the medicus."

Oz flinched as boy hobbled off the field. *Hopefully it's not too bad and the medicus can help. They will make him drill and march again soon, and then he better be ready.*

"There you are!" Capussia approached him from behind—the direction of the camp. "I just left a meeting in the command tent. Good times are over, we're deploying," he told them. "The camp prefect's staff has already started to pack their supplies, and the legion as a whole is to break camp tomorrow morning. Lucius Cotta, our new legate, received an urgent courier this morning from Gaius Julius Caesar himself."

"Any idea where to?" Gulussa asked.

He looked to his right where the slowly hobbling legionary had made it through the camp gate amid some loud moans of pain. *Sorry, poor boy, rotten timing for you.*

"West, to wherever the Tenth is. That's all Cotta told us," Capussia replied.

Oz nodded. The where didn't really matter. Wherever the governor told them to go, they would, and they'd get the job done.

696 AUC (58 BC), early summer
Eastern part of Roman Province of Gallia Cisalpina

"I thought we were moving fast when we were three legions marching together from Aquileia," Numerius said. "Now we're five, and we haven't slowed down at all." He looked at his friend marching next to him. *I am so glad that you made it, Vibius. I wouldn't want to be here without you.*

"Don't know if you noticed, but it's too fast for the families to keep up," his friend replied. "Most must be several days behind now. We're moving, what, an average of twenty miles a day?"

Three weeks ago, they had marched north into the low plains at the southern edge of the Alps and turned west onto the Via Postumia, a well-built public road leading west to Mediolanum, where their governor Caesar had waited for them with two new legions numbered Eleventh and Twelfth.

"But now we're marching straight for some steep-looking mountains. If we don't slow down soon, the families and servants will be on their own, with only the supply train for company," Numerius observed. "Many of the older veterans are worried."

The call to make camp came just as they entered the foothills of the mountain range in front of them. "It's still early in the day, maybe the front ranks ran into an enemy. Not likely, without us hearing a call to arms. So, could be we're camping to wait for the supply train. If so, I guess the veterans won't have to worry anymore."

Half an hour later, they were both digging. "Are you glad that your foot is holding up well enough for full duty?" their decanus asked Vibius with a smile on his lips.

"My answer depends on when in the day you ask me," Vibius replied. The whole squad laughed and kept on digging. The sooner they were done, the sooner they could expect to pitch their tents, leaving time for clean-up and some leisure to cook dinner.

A couple hours later, Numerius watched his friend remove his left caliga. They had another hour of rest before lights out, and most of the men sat outside around the cooking fire, leaving the tent relatively empty. Numerius sat on the cot next to Vibius's, holding a couple of oil lamps to help his friend see better. "Your foot looks so much better. Even the bruises are mostly gone."

"I will never forget where left is," Vibius said, and they both laughed.

"And you have a friend for life now. That centurion was so impressed by you marching on as if nothing happened despite your black and blue bruising."

"Yeah, but his timing could have been better," Vibius answered regretfully.

"Is Numerius Churinas here? I have a letter for him," they heard someone ask their tent mates outside.

"I'm here," he called loudly as he got up. "I'm coming out."

The voice belonged to a servant of the camp prefect, who handed him a scroll. "Looks like this was on the road for a while." With a nod, the man turned and walked away.

"Is it mail from home?" one of his comrades asked.

"Maybe, it's hard to tell with all the marks and notes on the outside," he said as he used his small knife to cut through the wax seal of the paper wrapping. He unrolled the papyrus and began to read. "Yes, it's from my sister back home."

He shook his head at the rowdy inquiries about her availability and level of attractiveness and walked back into the tent. He sat down on the cot and continued to read the letter. His stomach dropped, and tears started falling as he had to reread to make sure he hadn't glanced over anything.

Finally, he laid the document down. Vibius finished rubbing salve on his foot and glanced over, straightening with a worried expression. "What happened? Tell me."

Numerius was unable to speak. He wiped his eyes and handed the letter to his friend. "By the gods, your father," Vibius said after reading silently for a while. "I'm so sorry."

"Read on," Numerius whispered.

"She says that your father's moneylender swindled her, and she thinks she'll be sold as a slave. By the gods!" Vibius came over to give him a hug. After a brief moment, his friend spoke up again, now deep in thought. "Do you know how old that letter is?"

Numerius handed the paper wrapper to Vibius, who studied all the notes added to the original. "It went all the way to Hispania and from there to Aquileia. It's a miracle that it got delivered at all, most letters end up in a fire if they can't be handed over at the first place. If it's been all the way to Hispania first…"

"It could be nearly a year old." Numerius took a deep breath. "That also means that none of my letters or the money I sent made it to her." He touched his friend's hand. "Would you help me? I need to go to Clusium and look for her."

If anything, Vibius looked even more shocked. "No, I can't. You've seen what happens to deserters when they get caught.

"Well, yes, I've seen it a couple of times now." *Ordered beaten to death by your closest comrades is not a good way to go.*

"There might be other ways to help her," Vibius said. "How much do you have saved?"

"I have about four hundred sesterces. Only half of what's owed," Numerius said. A feeling of helplessness washed over him.

"That's no problem then. I will gladly add four hundred more. The question is how to get the money to her. We're stuck here in the legion, and we're on campaign, so sending letters back and forth will take time and won't be reliable." They both stayed silent for a moment, until Vibius continued. "I wonder if the legion could help. Let's ask, it can't hurt. Is the decanus back yet? First, we talk to him, then maybe he can take us to see the centurion."

Thank you, my friend! Without you I'd likely be on the run tomorrow, to end up with a bashed-in head once I got caught.

696 AUC (58 BC), early summer
Twenty-five miles southwest of Vesontio, Free Gallia, heartland of the Sequani Nation

Ariovist opened the door to find the woman's little girl blocking his way. In her own world, the child quietly played stretched out on the floor of the small room. He shrugged and kicked her out of his way. The girl screamed in pain, and the hissing response by the woman on the cot made him smile. "I pity you," he said in his broken Celtic. "I own you now, chieftain's daughter of the Aedui. Your husband is dead, and you lost your other child." He nodded at her stomach. "But you will have more, you are healing and are young still. Maybe you want a son or two, from me?" He laughed at her expression of revolt and disgust. "Don't be so quick to judge. It would be an honor for you to become my third wife."

Even pale and weak from her recent tragedy, there was no mistaking how pretty she was, and how strong-willed. She had value as a hostage, though marrying her would be even better. She would accelerate his plans, her blood ties giving him a claim to Aedui lands.

He sat down on the single stool in the room's corner and held her angry stare. The girl had settled back down to play as far away from him as the room allowed, oblivious to her mother's plight. *She is strong, but her little girl is all the leverage I'll ever need.*

He had come so far. As the third son of Adalbern, the greatest Suebi king his nation had ever seen, he had grown up underneath an oversized shadow, amidst serious rivalry from older brothers. When the envoys from the Arverni and Sequani had come to seek help against the Aedui, Ariovist had jumped at the chance, seeing a way to prove himself and escape the yoke of his family. Everybody he had brought along, now all part of his nation, were prospering beyond their wildest dreams.

"I still don't know your name, woman. I only know your father was a chieftain, brother to councilors and vergobrets," he told her while coldly studying the child.

"My name is Aina, daughter of Drestan," she said, sitting up straight. "I'll warn you only once. If you hurt my daughter again, I'll kill you." He quite liked the way she turned menacing despite her dirty appearance and her filthy clothes.

Ariovist laughed. *Just as I thought, as pliable as wax in my hands.*

"I like your spirit. I think it's time I let my wives and their servants take care of you. They'll get you washed up and dress you in clean clothes. It must be weeks since you last saw some of your Celtic soap." He touched her tunic on her shoulder with a single finger. "I will make them burn this filthy thing."

His sour mood was gone, replaced by elation. Marrying this young woman held much appeal. He watched her unconsciously lift her hand to fidget with the ends of a torc no longer around her neck. "I can get you a new one, once our arrangements are official, made like whatever your old one was. Solid gold, I'd imagine?" He laughed again at how uncomfortable she was with him. A good challenge, though it would have to wait a while. He would enjoy breaking her until she finally understood that she belonged to him.

He turned his gaze back at the girl moving little sticks around the floor. When she looked up at him, he smiled at her. "I'll see you again soon," he said to them both and stood up. He whistled loudly by the time he reached the door. He walked out, carefully locking the door behind him.

696 AUC (58 BC), early summer
Clusium, Etruria, Italia

Velia followed a customer out into the hallway and asked Velthurus for fresh water. As it happened, Titia was following her own customer out as well. *It will need to be soon. It has to be.*

"Can we talk for a moment?" she asked Titia. Her friend nodded and followed into her room.

"I want to run away, I just can't take it anymore," she whispered. "Are you coming with me?"

Titia's eyes grew wide. "I can't tell you how much I want to, though I'm afraid about what happens when they catch us. Look at poor Velthurus. If he were to ever run away again, it would cost him his life." Her friend sighed and gave her a hug. "I'm sorry, I won't go with you, I can't risk it. But if you must go, I'll help you anyway I can."

So, I will have to go alone and leave Titia and Velthurus behind. She closed her eyes to keep from crying. "Please, go, and send the boy in."

Velthurus saw her damp eyes and raised an eyebrow in silent question. She just shook her head and pointed at the water bowl.

He poured fresh water before putting down the bucket and laying his hand on her arm. Now she couldn't hold back her tears any longer. Velthurus squeezed her tight. *I can't stay here, and having to leave you behind is killing me. But Titia is right. I can't chance you getting killed.*

The next morning, she woke her friend early so they could be first in line for their daily tea and breakfast. That way, they had a few spare minutes before getting ready for business hours. A bowl of porridge in hand, she nudged Titia towards the rear garden. One of the Lupanar's guards stood watch there, like always during daytime hours. Velia turned to whisper away from the man's ears. "Do you know if anybody has fled over the garden wall before?"

"Yes, one young girl tried one night, just a few weeks before you got here. The domus on the other side is a store for fine import goods, and it's guarded by a trained fighting dog. Every night after they leave for the day, the dog has access to the garden. It got her, and she didn't survive." Titia shivered. "I still remember her screams."

"Alright, not over the garden wall." She looked around, deep in thought. *I'll figure something else out. I just have to.*

At the call that breakfast time was over, they walked back inside. Time to get ready to be on display in the atrium.

***

She went to bed at lights out, patiently waiting for the guard in the atrium to fall asleep. Earlier in the day, the man had traded for extra wine rations—she wouldn't get another chance like this again. When he finally fell asleep in the early morning hours, she snuck out of her room and to the back of the house, careful to stay quiet. Every little clink and scrape sounded loud as thunder in her ears. Surely, somebody must have heard her by now! Slowly unlatching the back door, she paused before opening it. Her heart pounded so hard she had to hold on to the door jamb while she listened. Nothing. If anybody woke up, she would miss this chance, and there were no guarantees she would ever have another one.

Outside, the moon provided decent lighting. After getting her bearings, she quietly heaved the small wooden table to the corner and added a chair on top for extra reach. Next, she lifted herself up on the table and slowly stepped onto the chair. Now the first row of clay tiles cemented to each other were in reach. With enough grip to get one leg up, she slowly pulled her torso up until her other leg could follow. Crouching, she carefully crawled over to the adjacent building. *No alarms. So far, so good, but too early to get excited. I am not out of the woods yet.*

At the end of the city block, she scanned the sidewalk below for the best way to get down. There, through the twilight, a couple of old crates leaned against the wall just a few feet away. She slipped off the roof and came down hard enough on the crate that one of her feet slipped off. Swearing silently at the pain of a sprained ankle, she hopped down the sidewalk. A wave of elation came over her. *I can't believe it. I am free.*

First things first. She needed to see her best friend and let her know what had happened. If Numerius had already come back for her, or if he was still coming, Lethie was the person for him to see. *And I need a change of clothes, these few things leave me half-naked and easily recognized for what I am now. A cheap prostitute.*

Fastie would waste no time having notices posted all over the city; she was just another runaway slave from his Lupanar. No other choice, she needed to leave town. Moving as fast as possible, she knocked on Lethie's door half an hour later. No answer. Another attempt, louder this time. Still nothing. Lethie was not home. *Now what?*

She weighed leaving town during the night against waiting for her friend to come home, however long it might take. *I don't have a choice. I need new clothes to stand a chance, and I need to let Lethie know about what happened to me.*

Leaning against the door, she sat and soon fell asleep despite her excitement. A hand on her leg woke her up. "Velia? Is that really you?" Eyes open, she saw her friend crouching close by. "Where have you been? Come on in." Lethie used a heavy key to open the door and walked inside to a short counter to light a lamp.

"Sit down, please. On the bed, or the chair, wherever is fine. I have some olives if you're hungry." She put a bowl full of green olives next to the lamp and turned back, the lamp illuminating Velia's cheap makeup and skimpy clothes.

"Oh, Velia. What in the world happened to you?"

"It was that criminal Minatus. He didn't legally sell me as a slave." She sighed. "I'll tell you everything, and you need to tell Numerius if he ever comes back." Her friend leaned forward to listen, and after Velia finished, Lethie slowly unfolded her white fingers from tightly clenched fists. She slowly closed her jaw, tears running into her mouth from wide open eyes. "I hate to ask this of you, but would you have a few clothes you could spare? I ran away and won't get far in these," Velia said while pointing at her revealing underwear.

Lethie moved in and hugged her. "Of course, let me see what I can give you." She let go and walked to her clothes basket. "Here's a tunic, though I'm sorry to say it's nearly worn out."

"Thank you, you can't imagine what a treasure this is." She pulled it over her head. Lethie now also held a stola out for her. "I can't take that, that shawl looks brand-new."

"Please take it, I only wish I could give you more. The stola can cover your head and conceal a good bit of your face." Lethie put the cloth loosely around Velia's neck. "What are you going to do now? You need to leave town, right? What direction are you thinking off?"

"I figured I'll go north, all the way to Arretium. Maybe I'll stay there for a while."

"I can give you a few coins to get you started, but I just can't leave my parents alone, sorry. I am so glad to see you; I was worried when you vanished last year. I feared the worst."

"Thank you. I should go, the sooner the better," Velia said. Lethie packed her some food, they had a final hug, and then she ran down the stairs and through the front door of the building. She looked around, realizing it was already much closer to daylight than she had hoped. *Merda, I wanted to be long gone from Clusium by now.*

She turned north to walk toward the city gate. A young man sitting on the sidewalk not far from the apartment building's entry door followed her with his eyes. She started to worry. *Was he already there when I arrived?*

Half an hour later, she was outside the city and breathed easier. *Is Arretium far enough not to be caught? I will have to figure out how to be invisible there.*

The first rays of morning light fought through the clouds, illuminating a trail leading away from the road. She was about two miles out of the city. Taking the path would help her stay out of sight. As she stepped off the road, though, the sound of horses made her look behind her. *Slave catchers! Already? Please, gods, not yet.*

Growing despair turned her mood dark, and she rushed through the trees despite the pain in her ankle. *I need to go through some of the underbrush, deeper where they can't follow me.*

Some of the men ran into the woods after her, shouting for her to stop. She couldn't keep up this speed for long; her pain was severe and she was badly out of shape. *Merda, I am no match for them.*

As they gained ground on her, she frantically looked for a better direction, when her foot encountered a big tree root. She hit the ground hard. *No, no, no. It can't be over, please, no!*

"Leave me alone, I beg you! Just let me go..." She broke into convulsions when strong hands grabbed her, lashing out with her hands and feet as long as possible, crying uncontrollably while her hands where bound. Knowing she had failed was unbearable.

696 AUC (58 BC), early summer
Border area, Roman Province of Gallia Transalpina and Free Gallia, lands of the Ambarri

Caesar and his five legions had successfully made their way across high mountain passes and through several skirmishes with isolated local tribes not acknowledging Roman rule. Now they were closing in on the meeting place with the Tenth.

"Is this the Arar river flowing into the Rhodanus over there? It must be," Caesar told his old friend and personal aide, tribune Aulus Hirtius. It was the morning of the third day since reaching the Rhodanus in their march north. "That means the bridge where the Tenth is waiting must be nearby."

He met the Tenth's scouts soon after, and an hour later they came to the old stone bridge and the full legion waiting next to it, prepared and ready for travel. *A full-strength legion, yet it looks small compared to the huge army already behind me.*

"Tell them to cross now, we'll sort out the marching order on the other side," he yelled at one of the ever-present couriers.

Later that same day, dirty from digging the trench of their nightly camp, Caesar put down his spade to watch the legionaries erect a segment of the wall. He estimated they had made it twenty miles north on the ancient Gallic road following the banks of the Arar before they found this defensible position. He waved at Lucius Cornelius Balbus, who insisted on personally supervising camp erection every evening, and stretched before climbing out of the ditch. He nodded to the men around him. *Enough for today, they've seen me get dirty enough.*

His twelve lictors fanned out with their axes ready, always on the lookout for potential threats. The legionaries rammed in pole after pole, bracing and tying them in place. As Caesar admired their work, someone walked up to him. "We have envoys at the camp's edge, both from the Aedui nation and from the Ambarri, the Aedui's local relations. They want to talk to you at your earliest convenience. Most urgently, of course," Hirtius said, smiling.

"Walk with me, Aulus. Let's see if my tent is ready," Caesar said in answer.

They strolled towards the middle of the enormous camp, now big enough to hold over thirty-five thousand fighting men and close to half that number in non-combatants. Caesar's servants had already pitched his tent, set up the furniture, and even fired up a little foculi at the tent center, a portable coal brazier effective against the cool of the early evening.

Grateful for the comfort, Caesar reached for an already filled cup of water. "The Aedui are our friends, we're officially here to help them against invaders, so I guess I better change." Hirtius laughed. Caesar knew the story of how he had received the Helvetii delegation had quickly spread from the Tenth to the other legions. "Before you have them brought to me, please ask all our Legates to attend."

He walked over to the curtain leading to his private chamber. "Oh, and let the envoys wait a little. Maybe have them detour through the camp to give me a few minutes to catch up with everyone." Hirtius nodded with a smile and gave Caesar a brief salute, putting his right hand up to his helmet before leaving. "Thank you," Caesar shouted after his friend and entered his private chamber. "Cleisthenes, thank you for getting the tent ready so quickly. Your help is still needed, please fetch more chairs or stools for the main room."

A few minutes later, a clean Caesar sat at his writing table in the main room when the first of his legion commanders arrived. Titus Labienus, the wiry legate of the Tenth, was ahead of tall and gangly nephew Quintus Pedius, son of the older of his two sisters. Even though he liked Pedius, a young man seemingly afflicted with a rare combination of high energy and high integrity, he was still unproven as a field commander. Caesar had given him the Seventh legion despite his reservations, though he would review as things progressed. He stood up and walked over to the two men, first clasping arms with Labienus. "It's good to have you and the Tenth with me again." Next, he moved over to Pedius, also clasping arms. "And my dear Quintus," he said, "we haven't talked much since you joined your new legion a few days ago. Is your task as legatus going well? And how is my sister these days?"

"Fortunately, excellent staff helps and I'm coming up to speed. I wanted to let you know, I was so excited to receive your letter I left Rome the very next day," Pedius replied. "I am grateful for the opportunity." *He seems very enthusiastic, good.*

The young man now continued with a broad grin. "As to my mother, she's fine. As you know, she had a hard time last year after my father's death, but I think she's past the worst. Now that she's out of mourning, there seems no shortage of suitors. She might yet marry again." Caesar smiled back, happy at the thought.

The rustle of the tent flap announced the arrival of the remaining legates. Publius Vatinius was in front. After complaints about misappropriation of some of the Ninth's spoils in Hispania, Caesar had thought it wise to move him to the Eighth. Behind him was Lucius Aurunculeius Cotta, a young man with curly light brown hair. Another family member, Cotta, was an ambitious distant cousin from his mother's side. Being from plebeian stock, he had loyally served him as a cohort prefect for the Tenth in Hispania. *Your promotion to legate for the Ninth is well deserved.*

Behind Cotta walked Servius Sulpicius Galba, legate of the new Twelfth legion. Galba was short and stocky, mostly bald with a rim of dark brown hair, and an old friend and supporter of Caesar. *And so eager to make a name for himself. I'll give you your chance.*

Next came Gnaeus Domitius Calvinus, the freshly confirmed commander of the new Eleventh. The bullish looking man was another long-time friend and had served as tribune of the Plebs last year with Vatinius, tipping the scale by supporting every single one of his bills and laws. *And he plans to stand for next year's aedile elections. I will arrange for him to stand in absentia, but that still means I need to reshuffle my legates soon.*

The last man to walk in was young Publius Licinius Crassus. Though technically just a tribune, Caesar had given him full command of all cavalry detachments. *You showed strength and leadership on the wall against the Helvetii. Who better than you to lead the needed combined cavalry force?*

Caesar walked among his executive leadership, clasping arms and shaking hands before moving back to his desk. "Gentlemen, now to the reason for this meeting. Aulus Hirtius is bringing a delegation of Aedui and Ambarri envoys to the tent. The latter are the local outlier of the Aedui nation and currently have the Helvetii ravaging through their lands. They should have a good idea of their forces' setup and baggage train. I have already sent for seats."

As if on cue, Cleisthenes and a crowd of appropriated servants appeared at the tent entry with stools and folding chairs, and Caesar gave them instructions on how to arrange seats. Soon after, Aulus arrived with six Aedui and three Ambarri in tow.

With the last stool in place, Caesar waved the servants out and turned his full attention to the newcomers. He immediately recognized the Aedui leader, a tall man with piercing blue eyes known to the Romans as Divitiacus. Famous for being both master druid and renowned warrior king, the man had visited Rome to plead the Aedui's case against the Suebi and the Sequani after the loss of the nation's great army at Magetobriga. Caesar extended his hand in friendship. "Welcome to our camp, Divitiacus." He opened his arms to include all the Celts in his welcome. "Welcome all of you, friends of Rome!" He ushered them all to the seats, arranged in two arcs with the writing table in the center of the smaller one. "Let me introduce my officers to you." He started from left to right, introducing every legate by name, and adding tribune Crassus. Once finished, he nodded at Divitiacus to do the same.

"Proconsul, honored officers, let me introduce our envoys. Next to me is my younger brother Dumnorix, member of the Aedui high council." The man looked like a younger version of his brother, though he made no eye contact with Caesar during the introduction and, in stark contrast to the speaker's friendliness, seemed rather sullen. Caesar raised an eyebrow, though ended up dismissing the rude behavior. *They might look alike, but that does not mean they are.*

"This man here is Liscus, old friend, fellow council member, and current Vergobretus of all Aedui. This is Elsed, son of Liscus's brother Drestan. Elsed is a newly elected chieftain of an eastern clan. This is Elsed's wife Brenna and his brother Morcant, a fellow druid." He continued with the contingent of Ambarri. "These two are Arthfael and Cynbael, both among the foremost Ambarri chieftains, and this fair lady here is Lughna, personal friend of mine and fellow master druid."

Caesar took the opportunity to have his servant offer cups of wine and water all around. The Romans had all settled around Caesar, facing the nine Celts. "Please, continue, Divitiacus."

"Proconsul, honored Romans, you must know why we're here. The Helvetii are traveling through Ambarri lands, stealing food, burning fields, pillaging farmsteads, and enslaving our families. Their trajectory leads straight to the heart of the Aedui nation. As long-term friends and allies of Rome we ask for your help. Our Ambarri envoys have seen their host with their own eyes and can give you many details, including estimates of their overall numbers."

Caesar nodded. "I will speak for all of us and the Senate and People of Rome. We are here now to stand with our brothers and sisters of the Aedui against the invasion of the Helvetii nation." He looked at his officers, most nodding enthusiastically in support. "I understand that you are still hard pressed for warriors thanks to that fateful battle at Magetobriga, and, as I understand, continuous raids by the Suebi. We will take the brunt of the fighting, as long as we can establish our food supply in your lands. I think you might appreciate selling to us for fair compensation." *Especially when the alternative is pillaging of your lands by the enemy.*

It was Divitiacus' turn to nod. "Food will be no problem. We can supply you great amounts of wheat, and we'll add legumes and other fresh vegetables straight from our fields." He looked at his fellow Aedui. "I have much hope that the big force you brought will prevail against the Helvetii"—he cleared his throat before continuing—" but I am also charged by our council with a second plea. We still need your support against the Suebi king. Ariovistus is ruling all the Sequani lands now and constantly brings more of his Suebi and allied tribes across the Rhenus river. Even though pay tribute, his warriors keep raiding and devastating our eastern lands. The Arverni have already distanced themselves from it all. Easy for them since they are sheltered from the Suebi by Aedui lands, although they plotted with the Sequani to bring the Suebi across the Rhenus in the first place. The Sequani bitterly rue the day they called to Germania for help." He held up his hand to stop Caesar from replying. "Before you answer, please let me add that Elsed and his people are here with an offer. His tribe is reduced to a thousand warriors and their families, all displaced from their homes. He has personally lost his father, sister, and best friend to the Suebi. His people are desperate for vengeance and are willing to ride with you now as cavalry against the Helvetii, if only you declare your support against Ariovistus."

Caesar had no reason to hesitate. *This gives me another rich target once we are done with the Helvetii. I couldn't have asked for more.*

He knew the majority of his legates would agree, either because they felt swayed by the plight of the allied Gallic nation, or because they hoped for more plunder to share. He stood up and circled the desk to approach Divitiacus. The Aedui leader also got off his stool, searching his face for any hints, until Caesar broke into a big smile and offered his hand. In response, a sigh of relief emanated from most of the Aedui. After shaking hands with Divitiacus, Caesar continued on to Elsed. "I giv word that I will assist you against Ariovistus. We shall not rest until the man and his Suebi are gone from Gallic lands." *And until I have enough spoils to pay off all my debt several times over.*

Caesar moved back to his desk and looked to the Ambarri. "Now, please give us details about the Helvetii host. Are their four cantons traveling separately?"

"Yes, the four main tribes travel apart. Three keep close to each other, but the Tigurini tribe is far behind, likely because they are worse when it comes to raiding," Cynbael answered.

The Tigurini canton was infamous for having annihilated a Roman army half a century earlier, consisting of three legions led by Lucius Cassius, consul and friend of Caesar's uncle Marius, and a certain Lucius Piso, grandfather of his new wife Calpurnia. Turning in his seat to the officers behind him, he glimpsed the recognition and fire in their eyes. *Good. Righting that old stain on Rome's honor will go a long way to appease both the populace and the Senate back home.*

696 AUC (58 BC), summer
River Arar, Free Gallia, Border between Ambarri and Segusiavi

Caesar scanned the horizon. The afternoon sun had lowered to soften the landscape of peaceful farmland intermixed with a few fortified Ambarri settlements. *I hope the camp prefect's men get lucky and find some provisions for us.*

"Proconsul, you have to hear this!" shouted Crassus as he rode over with a scout in tow.

"What have you got for me?" Caesar called back.

Crassus reined in and beckoned the scout forward. "This is Publius Ventidius Bassus, decurion of the Ninth." Crassus nodded to the man to take over. "He has found them."

"Salve, proconsul. The Helvetii are crossing a wide section of the Arar about ten miles north of here, with many small boats and rafts. It looks like a slow crossing, considering all their belongings, livestock, and wagons. They bring the latter across in parts to reassemble on the other side. By my estimate, the first two cantons are across, with the third mostly done. The fourth, however..." Bassus added a dramatic pause. "They are still arriving." He smiled. "I would consider that a perfect target."

Caesar grinned back at the scout. "Good news indeed. I promise you we will make good use of your information." After turning his horse to ride on, he changed his mind and pulled on the reins. "I have to ask, Crassus introduced you as a Ventidius. Are you the eques from Picenum I've heard about? The muleteer that turned his fellows into cavalry to save two of the Ninth's cohorts in Hispania?"

"Ah… yes, sir, that would be me," Bassus replied, visibly uncomfortable with his fame.

"Good man! You showed initiative when it really counted." Caesar turned his horse back to shake the man's hand. "Please keep an eye on the situation and let us know if anything changes. I want us to attack at first light."

Bassus saluted with a brief tip of his fingers to the side of his forehead and rode away.

"Keep a close eye on that man, Crassus. He's wasted as a scout leader."

***

Oz sat on his horse in the midst of his men in the middle of fifteen hundred cavalry—three-quarters of the legions' available mounted forces.

Ahead, the group's first riders were just reaching emerging out of the old forest they were passing through and into wide open country. When he left the tree cover himself, he entered an open space rimmed by more forest in the distance. *This will be our first real battle on horseback. Won't take long now. Ah, there are all their wagons, close to the river.*

"Do you know why there are only three?" Adhe asked him from his left.

Oz turned around for a glance at the three legions marching behind him. The Seventh, Eighth, and Tenth had set out at first light to follow the cavalry. The camp had been broken down, and the other three legions had left as well with five hundred cavalrymen, but in the direction of the Arar.

"I'm not sure. All I can do is speculate. I figure we will know soon enough." *I just hope this force is enough for what we are about to do.*

He spotted proconsul Caesar not far behind, riding at the head of the Tenth in the middle of his lictors, next to Titus Labienus. *Knowing he's with us helps.*

The legions now left the forest and fanned out to march in three separate lines, approaching the Tigurini camp. They were only half a mile from the enemy. The Tigurini had obviously given no thought to defense. Panic took hold among them when their carnyx blew alarm, with some people on the outskirts trying to hook up oxen to drive the wagons off. Many others frantically began to unload the blocked wagons instead to carry goods away. He shook his head. *After seeing us, they are worried about their possessions? Really?*

Tribune Crassus raised his hand. The cavalry's horn blowers took the man's cue, their litui sounding the attack. *Here we go.*

Oz kicked his horse into a full-out gallop. The cavalry moved towards the space between the enemy wagons and the forest on the north side, encircling the Helvetii with their small numbers as far as possible. Oz saw an enemy force of several hundred warriors riding out to engage them.

"They're coming for us, be ready!" he shouted.

***

Numerius stood next to his friend Vibius in a continuous basket line when he glanced up at the approaching rumble. "Here comes our work for when we're done playing with this muck," he said.

Vibius handed the next basket of dirt to him and looked up, breaking out into shrill laughter at the sight of the arriving mules. "I clearly remember the words of our recruiter." His friend changed his voice, sounding like a market seller. "In peacetime, your legion will drill maneuvers and train to hone your fighting skills. You will learn how roads and aqueducts are built. When your legion is on campaign, though, you will be so busy as to never get bored." Numerius and several of the other men in the line joined in hooting laughter.

The Ninth's cohorts were creating a gently declining ramp down to the riverside, cutting through the high bank a mile west from last night's encampment. The river here was narrower than they'd seen before and flowed a bit faster. Based on the comments of the engineer directing their Second cohort, they understood this new tongue of dirt would form the basis for a road surface leading up to a new bridge. The legion's mules and some of their wagons were delivering the first loads of rough-hewn logs from the nearby woods. Numerius wiped the sweat off his forehead with the back of his left arm. "But nobody ever said anything about having to dig for a new camp every day we march, or about building a little bridge in our spare time," another legionary called.

Out of the corner of his eye, Numerius followed the progress of the six centuriae of fabri, the several hundred craftsmen of the legions' First cohorts, stacking dry palisade logs into several crisscrossing layers to create floating rafts. Another of their teams had strung a strong rope across the river. *Will the floats be tied to the rope?*

He had heard from the veteran legionaries about endless building projects between campaigns, but he was still surprised at the efficiency and the little amount of complaining. *And those few complaints are spoken in jest. Amazing.*

***

Titus Balventius stood on one corner of the raft as part of a four-man team, pushing away from the riverbank with a long pole. The job was tricky as the faster flowing water towards the middle tried to rotate them. The men with him had all volunteered for the job after a call for decent swimmers made it through the ranks. Lucius Cornelius Balbus, the Ninth's Praefectus Fabrum, stood on the stack of timbers in the middle of the raft and gave his orders. "Hold steady now, come on, we're nearly there." The man grabbed the rope spanning from the last completed bridge segment to several pilings driven into the ground on the other side of the river, pulling it between one of two pairs of the float's uprights. "Quickly now," Balbus said. Balventius laid down his pole and rushed a small crossbar to the prefect, who lashed it to the uprights before moving to the second pair of vertical beams, fully securing the raft to the rope and making it the newest official part of the rapidly forming bridge. The men at the last adjoining section now brought two long logs forward, and Balventius and the other three pole handlers moved into position to receive the ends. The first one came in fine for the two men on the other side of the rope and was fastened securely. Balventius' log, though, came at too much of an angle, and as he worked with his partner to push the piece into position, he lost his footing and slipped off the raft, hitting his side on the rough-cut timber on the way down. *Merda, that hurts!*

As he swam back to the raft, he was glad the cool river water numbed his side. Balbus waited for him and heaved him onto the raft, where he sat for a moment to catch his breath. In the meantime, the other team had moved to help secure the second log.

"Thank you," he told the prefect leader of the engineers as he used his fingers to feel his side.

"Are you alright?" Balbus asked him.

"Actually, not too bad. Maybe I cracked a rib, but it doesn't seem to be broken through."

"Pain alone won't slow you down, right?" Balbus added with a grin.

"Join the legions for some adventure!" he replied, and they both laughed in response.

The prefect nodded in acknowledgement and moved on to where the center planking had been laid. The horde of legionaries that came next dumped and tamped loads of dirt as base for two lines of planking that would serve as roadway for cart and wagon wheels. Behind him, the next raft was already moving into place. Balventius carefully stood and climbed up to the nearly finished roadway. Even though a veteran of many years, the speed of three legions building something still impressed him. *Such efficiency needs to be seen to be believed.*

***

"Time for quick step, don't you think?" Gaius Julius Caesar said to Titus Labienus, who rode next to him. Now out of the forest, they were clearly visible to the Helvetii. The Tenth's legate nodded and shouted at the signalers walking right behind Caesar's fierce-looking ax-bearing lictors. The legion, still marching in a wide line three ranks deep, switched to a trot of ten steps jogging, ten steps marching, with all the legionaries loudly counting out together. He noticed with satisfaction that the Seventh and Eighth immediately followed suit. This would get them swiftly to the enemy without losing formation, or so the theory went since the lines pulled apart anyway. They reached the last hundred feet in front of the enemy baggage train, and Caesar nodded in thanks at Labienus who already shouted to the legion's signalers to call for falling back to standard march. The cornua and tubae once again blew loudly, the line reforming properly just in time for the engagement. Caesar sighed a breath of relief. *Now we'll see if a speedy river crossing was worth leaving me with only half our force.*

He had couriers standing ready to bring other legions for support if needed, though he could only fully rely on the Ninth. Fresh legions were a liability in their first serious fight, known to break rather than follow a call for an orderly retreat. *Too late for second guessing. Let's see what the Tigurini are going to do.*

From the vantage of his horse, he saw many families running away from his oncoming legions, though at least some of the Helvetii warriors rallied to rush out between the abandoned wagons in a continuous wave. The vehicles were many, and there would be a lot of spoils to divide as long as they prevailed. *And hopefully fresh food for our empty stores.*

The enemy approached the first legionary rank and raised their weapons. The mounted Roman officers around him moved apart to give less of a centralized target, though a Helvetii close to his position focused on him, throwing his spear with incredible power. Caesar raised his shield and turned sideways in his saddle to allow the weapon's point to glance off. Unfortunately, it had enough force to hit a lictor marching behind him. Caesar winced at the loud scream. Even after all these years, the guilt for the death of his men hadn't gone away. The legionary shield wall engaged the enemy warriors, and once it moved forward, the soldiers of the second rank stabbed down to put the wounded out of their misery.

The front line soon flowed around the abandoned wagons, and he maneuvered his horse enough into the Helvetii camp to observe a good number of horses and wagons racing away to the woods in the north. The Roman cavalry was heavily engaged while trying to stem the flood of fleeing enemies. *This is no fight, it's a rout. They were utterly unprepared and couldn't fathom that we might have the guts to attack them.*

The Helvetii in camp now all fled from the legionaries to avoid slaughter or capture. "Keep two cohorts behind to secure the baggage train and guard against boats crossing back over," he told Labienus. "Any preference?"

"I'd rather keep the first if you don't mind," Labienus responded without hesitation. The oversized first cohort matched two normal cohorts in size, and its troops were considered the elite of the legion.

"Very well," Caesar answered. "I'll lead the remainder after the fleeing Celts to catch as many as we can." He called over to the signalers. "Call quick step for all except first cohort."

***

"Just keep on shooting until you're out, but at least try to aim at warriors, you hear?" Oz shouted. The Legions' combined Celtic cavalry had engaged the Helvetii riders, and Crassus had sent the Numidian and Cretan auxilia farther to target the fleeing masses. *I know he needed to slow the exodus, but I will forever hate him for making us do this.*

The initial rush of fleeing families slowed to a trickle, discouraged from attempting the gauntlet by the steady rain of arrows. *It worked, but the gods will judge us for shooting at old people and children.*

The Helvetii cavalry disengaged the Roman cavalry, riding for the auxiliary archers instead. Oz noticed them galloping over and shouted, "turn to your left! Put your bows away and grab your hastae. Don't forget your shields, and be quick about it!" He already untied his own spear. Soon, a long line of steel tips was pointed at the enemy warriors. "Let's show them what Numidians can do!" he screamed and kicked his horse forward. The two hosts collided, and chaotic one-on-one fighting ensued. Oz stabbed and twisted with his long weapon, the spear finally feeling natural to him after he intensely trained with it for over a year. His instincts took over and the first warrior in front of him went down, then the second. The third was a small woman with striking orange-red hair, and he briefly hesitated. *By the gods, I'd think of her as quite attractive under different circumstances.*

Ducking under the slash of her sword, he waited for her to move in close in an attempt to gain the advantage over his longer reach. Once she did, he twisted towards her, swinging his new, heavy roman cavalry buckler right at her face with as much force as his left arm could muster. She raised her own shield into the way, but the heft of his thrust crashed its rim into her face with a loud crunch. She groaned and fell sideways off her horse, away from him. Oz scanned around and saw that Gulussa was in trouble. He turned his horse towards his friend, but another Helvetii intercepted him within a few feet. *Merda!*

Screaming out in anger and helplessness, he slashed out with his hasta.

***

"The Romans, the Romans!" a warrior shouted while running into the tent set up for the high council. War king Divico and the chieftains all rose at once.

"To arms! What direction are they coming from?" Divico demanded.

"From the south, on the other side of the river," the man answered, short of breath from the hard run. "They are attacking the Tigurini."

My people. And I am over here in this tent instead of leading them against the Romans. He drew his sword and broke into a run. Out of the tent, through the camp, and to the riverbank, he shouted non-stop, "to arms, to arms!" along the way. After he reached the river ahead of a force of thousands, he stopped to reorient himself. His sword pointed north at the shallow stretch of riverbank where the boats and floats had been pulled up. "To the boats! We have to help them!" he screamed.

"Stop, Divico, stop!" Bricio shouted from his side. The son of Orgetorix, now his most treasured and trusted aide, had kept up with him during his run and now laid a calming hand on his shoulder. "Look, just look!" he said, pointing across the river.

He stopped to take in the scene, and his heart dropped. The camp was already overrun, and the families were rushing to the forest in the north with Roman legionaries in pursuit. After taking a deep breath, he forced himself to think. "We should still set over to distract the Romans."

"No. All we could do is get maybe five hundred warriors ferried over at the same time, and the Roman soldiers are waiting for us," Bricio said and pointed at the Tigurini wagons. "I can't let you throw away your life."

Divico squinted and scanned the shoreline again. His shoulders slumped in defeat when he spotted the Roman foot soldiers lying in wait behind the first few rows of wagons closest to the river. *All is lost. My heart bleeds for you, my people. I failed you.*

"We can't change the outcome. I'm sorry. It's too late."

Divico put his hands over his face to hide his tears. He fell to his knees, freely crying for his tribe, for the first time feeling his age of more than seven decades. After a while, he calmed down enough to risk another look across the water. The Romans were still pillaging through his people's possessions and collecting food. At the sight of long lines of Tigurini tied and hobbled being led off the field by the legionaries, he cried again. The helplessness he felt was like nothing he had ever known. Bricio was right, all that was left now was revenge. *Should I have let you lead us after all, Orgetorix? The Romans, these stinking dogs. They will pay for this, by Taranis.*

He stayed there on his knees, unable to leave the bank until close to sundown when Bricio urged him to return to the council tent. Scouts had arrived there with more bad news.

***

Nico shot his bow next to his commander and close friend Andrippos, long since recovered from his injuries in Hispania. The most visible remnant was the man's lopsided smile, an already legendary identifier for the older Cretan. The Numidian litui blew, and Nico looked over to see their fellow auxiliaries turn to engage the enemy cavalry riding against them.

"Follow their lead!" Andrippos shouted.

They feverishly lashed their bows to their saddles, shoved their shields in place, and urged their horses to follow the Numidians.

Nico reached them just as the dark-skinned man in front of him went down. A tall Helvetii warrior had delivered a brutal cut into the man's neck before surprising another Numidian who was already fighting off a different warrior. Nico pushed his horse between to disrupt the enemy's swing, stabbing his kopis into the exposed armpit of the man's sword arm. The warrior slid off his horse, dead before hitting the ground.

He sighed in relief when he saw their own Celtic cavalry had caught up from behind the enemy. Nico took out a second man by deeply chopping into his exposed thigh, creating a spray of blood from the leg's artery. He searched for the next opponent, but there were none left to fight. The remainder of the Helvetii cavalry had disengaged to join the wild flight for the forest. He slid off his horse and walked to the downed Numidian. After sheathing his sword and moving his buckler back up onto his arm, he turned the man onto his back. *Sorry, friend, it's too late for you.*

The cut had gone cleanly through the clavicle and deep into his torso. Somebody approached Nico from behind, and he turned, moving his hand back to the handle of his kopis. It was a tall and dark-skinned young archer, with several more of the Numidian auxilia dismounting behind him.

"Thank you for saving me," the man said and held out his hand. "My name is Adherbal, or Adhe for short."

"I am Nicolaos," he answered. "Nico for short." He shook the offered hand.

The Numidian stepped around him to kneel at the body on the ground. "And this was Gulussa, a good friend." He closed the dead man's eyes and turned to the left where more Numidians came walking over. "Sorry, Massi, it's Gulussa," he shouted. A man rushed over, followed closely by a Numidian decurion. "No, my brother. Why you, why you," he wailed as he dropped on his knees to hug the now lifeless body. Unfocused eyes wet with tears, the man turned to the decurion. "Oz, please let me be the one to tell Daleninar," he pleaded.

The officer patted the man's shoulder. "Of course, Massi, whatever you want. I'm so sorry."

Nico moved away to leave these people to their grief. *Too much of that going around. It never stops.*

***

The two scouts were waiting in the council tent.

"Here's our war king," Bricio announced. "Divico, listen to what these two observed today."

The warriors stepped forward, one looking at the other to start. With a jolt, the left one opened his mouth. "We were south by about three miles. We rode up a small hill hoping to get a good view of the surroundings. What we found was a Roman bridge over the Arar."

Divico held up his hand. "How could that be possible? We had scouts ride up and down the river for many miles looking for bridges or a ford for our own crossing, and they found nothing."

"We couldn't believe it either. The Romans built the damn thing in a single day. When we found them in the early afternoon the bridge was halfway across the river. When we rode back to camp a few hours later, they had reached the other side."

"I've never seen anything like it," the other scout agreed. "They are well organized, and by the looks of it, the men building the bridge were all soldiers. From the numbers, I'd guess another two or three legions."

"How can they do something like that?" one of the other councilors asked, clearly unnerved.

"They might be superior in building things, but that doesn't mean they can't be beaten in battle. They were lucky today because they caught us apart and by surprise. Don't ever forget that I led the Tigurini to victory before against three full Roman legions. That was one of our tribes against half of what Caesar has today." He scanned the faces of his councilors. "We still have three full tribes all around us. We will beat the Romans again," Divico told them with an iron conviction. "Get ready to break camp in the morning."

***

Early the next day, the call to arms echoed across the large Roman camp two short miles south of the Helvetii. Caesar threw his armor on and ran out of the tent while tightening the leather straps. "Where are they coming from?" he asked the next centurion he saw.

"Must be the western wall, sir, that's where I'm headed. Just follow me!"

He raced after the centurion. Once on the earthen catwalk, he took account of the situation. The enemy had come in force, the Helvetii warriors amassing just outside of the Balearic slingers' reach, though he figured the centuries' scorpios could easily get to them if needed. Cavalry litui made a call. To the south, several wagons loaded with wood were trying to make the camp's gate. *That must be lumber from the bridge.*

After the deals with the slave traders for around thirty thousand captives had been finalized, he'd had them, their teams, and the slaves escorted south for a few miles before partially dismantling the bridge to deny their opponents a way of crossing back.

The southern gate opened to let the Roman cavalry force ride out and position itself between the wagons and the Helvetii. The Numidians and Cretans had their bows drawn, ready to fight it out. *I am glad I followed Pompeius's example with the auxiliaries. They have proven worth their weight in gold, over and over.*

He looked back at the enemy. They held at a distance. A small group of envoys was approaching the camp. The riders held their shields above their heads as a signal for parley.

"Let them in!" he called down. "But stay ready for anything." Several cohorts formed a square around the gate before the doors opened to receive their guests.

***

Divico saw the strong fortifications of the Romans and knew that attacking it would be costly, if not futile. Still, he figured he might find out exactly what they were up against. Though risky, the best way for that was to visit the camp for a parley, so he rode toward the closest Roman gates in the middle of a small group of his chieftains. The doors opened, and they rode through into a mass of Roman soldiers standing ready. Looking over their heads, he took in the massive space on the inside of the camp. *Incredible. The sheer size of it, filled with row after row of precisely arranged tents.*

Caesar had at least five, maybe six or more legions. It didn't make a difference. He would draw them to open battle and annihilate them.

A Roman officer with a big plume on his helmet stepped out. "Ave, the Proconsul will speak to you. Please, follow me." They were led to a magnificent tent, though once inside he was surprised by the sparse furnishings. *And there he is, the man who murdered so many of my people and sold more into slavery. Hate is too small a word for what I feel.*

Divico stroked his long white beard in an effort to keep calm and appear civil. The Roman opened his mouth first. "I am Gaius Julius Caesar, proconsul governor of Roman Gallia and friend and ally to the Aedui, on whose land you currently reside. Why did you come to our camp?"

He took a deep breath, finally calm enough to speak. "I am Divico, war king of the great nation of the Helvetii. I have come to ask you for the future of my people: Name a location we can go to and where you will leave us in peace." *Would you ever leave us alone now? Not likely.*

"How about you go back to your mountains?" Caesar replied. "I cannot guarantee peace in any other location." The man looked at Divico's group, his eyes coming to rest on Bricio. "First, we need to exchange hostages. I suggest we start with some of the people you brought."

Divico laughed. "We are a powerful nation, used to receiving hostages, but never giving any in return. Leaving our people with you is not a practice I can condone under any circumstances." *Enough, time to leave.*

He turned to move out of the tent but stopped on the way, looking back at Caesar. "We will fight, and I want you to think about the Roman army that perished at the hands of the Tigurini. I was the one who led my people to victory then. Now I lead three tribes, enough to kill all your people twice over. Don't say I didn't warn you."

***

The next morning, the Roman army followed the Helvetii trail to their abandoned camp. The enemy had moved up the old road leading to Bibracte and the Aedui heartlands, and the legions followed in pursuit. Lucius Cornelius Cinna rode behind his friend Quintus Titurius Sabinius and the five other cavalry prefects, all following the young cavalry commander Publius Licinius Crassus. Caesar had sent them ahead to harass the Helvetii's rear. "What do you think of Divitiacus and his friend Liscus?" a brooding Cinna asked Sabinius while watching the two Aedui riding in the midst of their people.

"I have to admit I like them a lot more than Dumnorix. That man gives me the shivers."

Cinna nodded. "I am glad I'm not the only one. I don't think Crassus should have let him ride ahead with his hundreds of warriors. Divitiacus explained that his brother got rich through trade. Considering that the older one himself has only twenty retainers, I can't help but wonder."

"I guess you're right. Divitiacus was Vergobretus of the Aedui at least a couple of times, and he's a master druid. You'd think he'd have more warriors than his younger brother," Sabinius replied. "The way he looks at us, it's as if he dislikes us more than he does the Helvetii. Someone should keep a close eye on that one."

Cinna smiled at Sabinius. *Looks like we're in agreement.*

His eyes wandered over the groups around him. In addition to the Aedui noblemen, the cavalry officers consisted of the higher ranked decurions of the mounted auxilia archers and the latest arrival, a Celtic cavalry commander named Lucius Aemilius. The latter was a chieftain of the Volcae nation in the southwest of Gallia Transalpina, full of pride over his Roman name and in charge of a thousand fresh recruits brought from the south this very morning.

A rider emerged from a small wood at the top of a nearby hill and galloped straight for their group. Some swords were drawn, but, "It's one of our scouts!" Cinna said loudly. As the rider came close enough to be recognized, he added: "Not just any scout, it's Ventidius Bassus from the Ninth." The swords went back into their sheaths.

"Ave!" Bassus shouted, reining in at the last minute. "There is a big group of Celts approaching. It could be enemy forces, though I think it unlikely."

Crassus raised his hand. "Signal halt!" he told the liticen. The signal blew and the group of officers rode out close to the edge of their host to get a good view. Soon, a thousand riders appeared on the hill crest, with many more people walking behind, including many children.

"These are our kin!" Divitiacus shouted. "It's Elsed, leading his people to join the fight as he promised." The master druid and his friend Liscus rode forward. Crassus followed after a brief moment of hesitation, and Cinna and Sabinius joined as well.

"Welcome, and well met!" Crassus shouted, reaching out his hand to the young Aedui chieftain. "I am glad you made it."

"Where do you want us?" Elsed asked while shaking Crassus' hand, his wife and brother reining in next to him.

"Why don't you join us towards the middle. Just have your warriors fall in," Crassus answered. "We should have plenty of warning if the enemy shows. Divitiacus' brother Dumnorix and his men are our spearhead."

Cinna and Sabinius shared an uncomfortable glance. Sabinius shrugged. *He's right, not much we can do right now, and with these warriors, our cavalry just swelled to over four thousand. A far cry from the tens of thousands Helvetii, but nonetheless, double from just two days ago.*

696 AUC (58 BC), summer
Eighteen miles southwest to ten miles south of Bibracte, Free Gallia, Nation of the Aedui

"I can't believe this, I just can't. How could I be so blind? And worse, none of you said anything to me about your suspicions!" Caesar screamed. Three weeks of a game of cat and mouse had been played between the Roman forces and the Helvetii on the road to Bibracte, all to no avail. Caesar was livid, and he didn't particularly care that his friend Hirtius was tiptoeing around him. "First, we lose a perfect opportunity to ambush them at night."

Old veteran Publius Considius had told the officers the enemy held the hill Labienus and his Tenth had been waiting on. The perfect ambush had been called off, and Considius sent home in disgrace once Labienus had come back to contradict his story.

"Now, Liscus tells us in confidence he found out it was one of Dumnorix' men lying to Considius about who held the hill. And much worse, Dumnorix is sabotaging his brother's efforts to get us food." He took a deep breath. "I call that betrayal of the highest order." *The night ambush would have been perfect, and this would be over.*

The food issue had reared its ugly head again and again, and the stores had finally shrunk to only a few days' worth of rations. Liscus had received word from another council member that Divitiacus' brother was bribing other councilors to delay the food collections and had come to inform Caesar. *I don't understand why that man would do this. What does he gain by helping their enemies? Or is this about sabotaging us?*

"Go and tell Divitiacus and Dumnorix to come see me," he told Hirtius. He turned to his lictors. "And I need you to be ready to arrest either of them if necessary." The men fanned out through the tent, prepared for anything. Half stayed close; the rest moved to the tent walls on both sides of the entry.

Ten minutes later, Hirtius walked back in with Divitiacus in tow. "One of Dumnorix's warriors told me he isn't available to meet. I was alone, so I decided not to push the issue."

Divitiacus's eyes grew big at Hirtius's comment. Caesar waved for the man to sit down. "Old friend, I am very disappointed. Let me come straight to it. We know there's no food coming and that your brother has sabotaged all your efforts." Caesar barely kept himself from shouting in his rage. "I will have your brother arrested and punished harshly for his betrayal, but I am more disappointed in you for not telling me about the problems and your brother's actions the moment you knew."

Divitiacus's shoulders slumped, and he dropped his head into his hands. When he finally looked back, he had tears in his eyes.

"I am sorry I've failed you, and I'm ashamed for my brother and my inability to overcome his treachery. He has undermined and weakened my position in the council for some time. Only a few days ago, I found out he married a daughter of the Helvetii chieftain Orgetorix. It was years ago after having made some deal or alliance for money. I still can't believe my brother kept her and their children hidden from me all this time. Knowing that, it's clear why he's been working against me, or should I say, helping the Helvetii all along." The once so proud Vergobret and chieftain dropped to the floor to prostrate himself. "Please, show mercy. Dumnorix is my only remaining family. Punish me if you must, for my inability and for not telling you of my own account, but I beg you, don't hurt him."

They remained in silence. Caesar's anger at Divitiacus simmered down until it vanished. He shook his head in wonder, remembering how he would have given anything to have more time with his precious Cornelia or his father. If the situation were reversed, he would have fought with everything he had for a close loved one to be spared. *What else in life is as important as family? In all my anger, I can't bring myself to inflict more pain.*

"I can see that you're suffering from your brother's actions, and I give you my word that I will not harm him by my own account. Though I will need to confront him over his actions and employ spies to follow him. Trust in Dumnorix is a commodity I can no longer rely on." Caesar walked up to Divitiacus and helped him up.

"Thank you, you are a better friend then I deserve. You'll have my eternal gratitude for your mercy," Divitiacus said, still unable to hold eye contact.

Caesar put his hand on the man's shoulder. "I can't help but feel sorry for you. Please, leave me now, I need to think."

With the visitor gone, Caesar turned to tribune Hirtius. "Take a heavy escort with you and bring me Dumnorix. Make it at least five centuries so he knows he has no choice—that man has given me his last excuse. Though, first, please have somebody find tribune Crassus for me."

A few minutes later, the young tribune's head popped in through the flap. "Proconsul?"

"Come in, I have an urgent request for you. We need to head to Bibracte, and I need details about the lay of the land between here and there. We must leave the Helvetii behind for the time being and march to get food. We're down to a few days of rations."

***

The council members around him were in an uproar over what they'd just heard. *I can't believe this myself.*

"Let me restate what you just said," Divico told the young scout. "The Roman army, after harassing and toying with us for three weeks all the way from the Arar, retreating to their camp when we fight back, packed up this morning and is now marching away from us?"

"Yes, exactly. They took the road to Bibracte."

Several councilors let out gleeful laughter, and many chieftains tried to speak at the same time, all wanting to voice their happiness to be out from under the Roman threat. The rowdy tent had suddenly become too crowded and too small for Divico. He stood up and raised his hands. "Quiet! Please!" he shouted. Once the table calmed down, he added: "I'd like to tell you what I think our options are." He looked into the round.

"Let's hear it, Divico," Bricio shouted. He had acted as a mentor for the young council member, and his protégé had shown him nothing but gratitude in return.

"Thank you, my friend. Yes, without the Romans chasing us, we could simply keep moving west, leave the Aedui lands, and conquer the weaker nations at the coast as we had planned. However, in my opinion, the Roman province will never be far enough away from us. If not Caesar, then some other future Roman general will come after us." He added a dramatic pause. "I believe that we must give this army of theirs a sound thrashing. Yes, I want to punish them for what they did to the Tigurini, to my people, but more importantly, we need to make the Romans fear us if we want them to stay away. We will never have a better opportunity for that than with this army already on the run from us. What say my fellow councilors?"

One after another the other chieftains rose in support. "Let's go after them!" Bricio shouted.

"It's decided," Divico said. "Bring wine, we'll drink to their impending defeat." A few minutes later he made a silent toast into the direction of Bibracte, raising his horn. *Soon you and your dogs will be dead, and your head will be on my spike.*

696 AUC (58 BC), summer
Twenty-five miles southwest of Vesontio, Free Gallia, heartland of the Sequani Nation

"Come here, girl, bring your child. Sit down, sit down!" Osburga, Ariovist's first wife, commanded her. Aina sat down and pulled Nara on her lap, scanning the big main room of the great hall rather than looking at the hated woman at the opposite side of the table. The king's men took Nara away from her at night, but she was allowed to spend the days with her. Aina was able to keep herself clean and properly dressed, if only by Suebi customs. The woolen skirt was nice enough, though it would become annoying if she was ever allowed to ride again, and she would have preferred to wear a little more cloth on her upper body.

"I will never understand what my husband sees in you," Osburga said, "or why in the gods' names he would need to marry you. He has no need for a third wife, his first and second are already more than he can handle." The woman made a lewd sexual gesture with her hands, visible from the corner of Aina's left eye, and laughed heartily at her own joke.

Ignoring the voice as best she could, she looked straight to where Ariovist lounged on the throne-like chair, receiving his retainers and supplicants. *At least he's waiting with the marriage until fall. Whatever his reason, I am thankful for every extra day.*

A glance to the side showed her the ever-present shadows guarding her, even in the middle of Ariovist's great hall. *Where my future husband reigns. The thought alone makes me sick.*

Suddenly some of the voices turned angry. Four wealthy looking Sequani farmstead owners stood in front of the throne, loudly complaining about the brutality with which the Suebi warriors had forcefully relocated fellow Celts from ancient lands. "Theft, rape of wives and daughters, and outright murder of servants and slaves. This cannot continue!" one of them shouted.

So, at least some of you have some courage left, though too little, too late.

At first pensive and thoughtful, Ariovist's face suddenly brightened. "You think it is your right to ask for consequences or recompense," he said, loud enough that the entire hall could hear him. The men nodded eagerly. "I tell you that you do not have that right, as you and yours don't have the same value to the gods as my own people. Though I will be merciful in my punishment for your overreach." With a wide grin, he waved at his men to either side of his chair. "I will keep one of you alive. Keep them from leaving!"

She heard the murmur of protest from the other people mingling around the great hall, Suebi and Sequani alike. Ariovist stood up. "You four, give these brave men your spears." His men handed over their weapons to the bewildered Sequani. "Take them," he commanded.

"There is no need for this," one of the Sequani meekly protested. The Suebi warriors stepped back from the dais and formed a loose circle.

Ariovist drew his sword. "Oh, but there is. You wanted consequences; here they are. I am giving you a chance to punish me for what my men did." Aina saw the four older men arrange themselves defensively around the king before he exploded into motion. *I've seen the man spar; not many stand a chance against his speed.*

Aina turned Nara around and hugged her tight, keeping her from seeing the scene that was about to unfold. *Only a few more months before I am to be this despicable man's wife…*

"Please, Esus, Toutatis and Taranis, haven't our people sacrificed enough of their blood for you yet? Can you start to intervene?" she whispered. "I do not ask for myself. Just give me a chance to get Nara away from here."

696 AUC (58 BC), summer
Ten miles south of Bibracte, Free Gallia, Nation of the Aedui.

"Here is what we need to do," Caesar shouted at his officers to ensure he would be heard over the noise. They rode through wide open terrain and had no time to stop. "We send all our cavalry to engage the pursuing Helvetii host. If we can slow them down, it will allow the legions, the baggage train, and the families to go up and dig in on a hill I scouted yesterday." He saw some approval, but also many worried faces. "The four veteran legions will block the approach, the two new legions will fortify, while the auxiliaries protect the laborers, women, and children."

"How much time do we need to buy you?" Crassus asked from his side. Cinna and Sabinius rode next to him, both anxiously nodding. Caesar felt pained over the question. *I'm sorry, boys, attacking the massive enemy army with our few thousand seems like suicide. I hope the engagement won't be long enough for their numbers to count.*

"You won't need to buy us a lot. The key outcome I need is for Divico and his chieftains to see you stand ready for them. He will stop their host to analyze the situation. When they start moving again, you will attack and fight for a few minutes. You need someone at a good lookout point. I want you to disengage the moment our last wagons get to the hill." He pointed forward where the flat changed into several hills, growing taller in the distance. "Do you see the medium height one with the forested top?" he asked. "That's the one. It has only steep approaches except for the one from the front. I'll have our legions cover that side. The hilltop is wide and flat, perfect for the baggage train and fortifications. Crassus's scouts are waiting there to give directions."

He looked around at all the men. "Any other questions?" A few faces looked back with eyes widened from fear, though most appeared determined. *Good, they have some hope that this will work. That will help make it so.*

"Go to your troops and get ready. Dismissed!"

He loosened his helmet strap to take it off, needing a moment to dab away sweat from his forehead. It was still late morning, but clear skies and hot.

Aeolus, I pray to you. Let loose Venti Favonius so that he may bring us a western breeze to keep my men cool in their armor. Today, we need every advantage we can get.

***

Oz held his horse steady. The combined Roman cavalry force had reined in, facing down the approaching front lines of the Helvetii. The massive host stopped half a mile away. *Looks like they are done discussing and moving again.*

Capussia gave the signal for the liticen to blow their horns. "Get ready," Oz shouted as his turma. "Are you alright, Adhe?" he asked his nephew in a lower voice.

"I'm fine. Just thinking that it seems insane for us to try to stop this"—he nodded at the ocean of Helvetii consisting of who knew how many tens of thousands of warriors, plus wagons and families coming their way—"flood with our little band."

Oz grinned at his nephew with more confidence than he felt. "Capussia will send us back before we're done with the first quiver. You heard him, we and the Cretans are needed to man the fortifications, so these poor people," he nodded behind them at the Roman Celtic cavalry, "will take the brunt of it. Hopefully not for long."

"Here they come!" Capussia yelled. The Numidians and Cretans were stretched out in a long line three horses deep, with wide paths left open between them. *Those paths are what will keep us alive.*

They held their bows ready, arrows nocked. The first Helvetii riders came within a hundred yards. "Steady!" Oz shouted. At fifty yards, the Litui blew the note for release. He let go of his arrow and pulled and shot the next one and the next, until he heard the cavalry signal for attack. Moments later, the Roman riders burst through the archer's line straight at the enemy. For a moment, he watched the ferocity of the counterattack, until the Numidian and Cretan signals for retreat sounded over the din. He nodded and raised his hand. As one, his mounted archers turned and galloped for the hill looming on the horizon.

***

Elsed rode out of the group and turned his horse. He scanned his beloved people's faces. So many were gone, but the remainder had followed him to this place where giant forces were at play. He smiled at Rionach and Orlagh and many other familiar faces in greeting. Nodding to every face, he decided to forgo a speech. *There is really nothing I can add, they are all here with me despite having to face down hundreds of thousands of people.*

Of course, they were here to help the Romans keep these enemies from ravaging Aedui lands, so that the Romans would help them against the hated Suebi in return, though all thought faded away when confronted by the incredible size of the nation in front of them. *I'm glad for not seeing Brenna's face here. I know she is unhappy leaving me alone, but this way there's some hope our children won't grow up as orphans.*

Morcant had stayed with Brenna and the children, anticipating the need for his healing skills once the wounded arrived at camp. Elsed turned to face the battlefield, where the archers were letting their first arrows fly. Then came a second salvo, followed by a third. The cavalry litui blew for attack, and he drew his sword. "This means us!" he shouted and rode out, leading his clan through the lines of archers and into the fray. He screamed at the first Helvetii warrior in his path, hacking down at the man's shield with all his might. It split on the second swing and left the warrior wide open for his follow through. His Aedui fanned out around him, and soon they were all embroiled in a vicious melee. No matter how many enemies they downed, still more pushed in to replace them. "Stay together!" he shouted. If they were stretched too thin, disengaging would cost even more of their lives. *Please, gods, lead my people out of this before we all die.*

***

A mile of hard riding and Nico reached the hill. There, he followed the Cretan and Numidian archers through the openings between the four legion's columns. After riding through the open gate area of a hill fort under construction, he lead his animal to the rear and tied it to a stake already prepared by camp staff. "Follow me to the wall!" Andrippos shouted. Nico marched after him to the hill's west side wall, overlooking the approach and the action below. Their men moved around the Balearic slingers, who had taken the center position, with the Numidians filling the right flank and the Cretans the left.

Nico came to a stop next to Alketas, close friend and one of a handful of fellow survivors of the southern pass battle against the Transcudani, who whistled appreciatively. "The legionaries have been very busy in a very short amount of time." Nico looked down at soldiers of the Eleventh and Twelfth legions, hurriedly digging additional defensive moats in front of the wall and filling ready sections with sharpened stakes. He lowered his bow from his shoulder and opened a fresh quiver to have the arrows ready. That's all there was to do for now besides watching the fight in the plain below.

"Ah, our cavalry is finally disengaging. Our troops are ready for the Helvetii," Alketas said.

They silently watched as their riders rushed back, closely chased by the enormous mass of enemy riders. Once the last of them made it through the openings provided by the legionaries, the soldiers closed their line, holding Pila at the ready. The mounted enemy troops turned sideways to keep their distance rather than engaging. *So far, so good.*

Nico looked over at the legion's Celts riding through the fort's gate. Two women warriors at the end of the line shared a single horse. They had to be part of the recently joined Aedui clan since the Roman's did not recruit women into their auxilia forces. The one up front bled profusely and leaned into the horse's mane, close to falling off.

"These Aedui have some fierce women warriors. I hope she makes it," Alketas said.

Nico nodded. *I couldn't agree more. The Aedui and the raw recruits from the south haven't been with us more than a few days, yet they just attacked an overwhelming force without complaint to buy us all the time we needed.*

***

"Yes, this is the best view. We'll stay here and see how it develops," Caesar told Labienus and Hirtius. The two had followed him to the top of a big boulder a few hundred feet below the fortifications, the vantage point unobstructed by patches of forest. The gentle breeze the Roman wind deity had sent startled him. "Thank you, Favonius," he whispered in gratefulness.

He'd left the other high-ranking officers with their legions, valuing Labienus's experienced perspective for strategy above all others. The enemy host below had gathered two-thirds of a mile from the hill, arranging their wagons into a circle to create a defensible position. All their horses and draw animals were brought into the center. *Interesting, why no more cavalry?*

An astoundingly big mass of foot soldiers now left the wagon fort on the east side and set out toward the Romans. As they came within a few hundred feet, the front line of the oncoming warriors started to form a protrusion. "Look at that. They are creating a phalanx to try to push through our line," Labienus observed.

"Let's see what our Pila will do to that formation," Caesar said. "I'm not too worried about us holding the hill. Our defensive position is strong enough, though I wonder how we can achieve a crushing victory."

They stood in silence for a moment, until Labienus cleared his throat. "We can't win by staying in our fortification, and we can't win with a frontal attack. Their numbers are just too great, they'd wear us down."

"I generally agree with both, although I think adding the baggage train with their families into the equation might be the needed lynchpin," Caesar mused. "If we can somehow drive a wedge between that and their army, they might lose their heads." He scanned the surroundings and focused on an even higher hilltop a mile away. An idea began to form. "How about we do this…"

***

"Coraidan! Get back here!" Brenna screamed at the top of her lungs while running after her son, holding tight to little Faela bouncing in a sling bound around her shoulders. She couldn't believe the speed her two-year-old demonstrated at the most inopportune time—the tyke headed straight for the legion's artillery teams, who were assembling heavy weapons meant for the platforms on the fortification walls. The closest of them were trying to turn over the heavy wooden frame of a catapult. "Stop, Coraidan, stop!" she yelled in growing desperation. Suddenly, a young girl ran in from the side and grabbed the boy before he reached the big timber frame. A moment later, the artillerymen succeeded in tipping the frame over, landing it with a solid thump on the wild grass Coraidan had headed towards just a moment earlier. *Oh, my gods!*

Brenna caught up with the girl still holding Coraidan's arm in a tight grip. "Thank you!" she told the girl in Latin before spontaneously hugging her. "Thank you so, so much, you saved my son! Without you..."

"No problem," the girl answered. "I have a younger brother who always gets into trouble. Why don't you bring your son over to our group?" She pointed to several families with children to the west side of the open space. "He can play with Saki while I keep an eye on both. Looks like you could use the help, you already have your hands full." She waved at Brenna's group, which consisted of a handful of adults vastly outnumbered by a horde of children. The girl stepped back and held out her hand. "I'm Stena. My papa is with the Numidian auxiliary."

She took the girl's hand. "Thank you, Stena. My name is Brenna and I'm grateful for your offer. If we all get through this, I'll pay you back any way I can," she replied.

Stena shook her head. "No need, I'm happy to help." She turned to Brenna's son. "So, what was your name—Coraidan? Am I saying it correctly?" He nodded with a smile.

Brenna watched Stena take her son by the hand and slowly lead him away. *Thank you, gods. There is hope for this world.*

***

"Elsed!" Brenna shouted as she ran at her husband, throwing herself into his embrace. "I am glad you're back. How bad was it?"

"Bad enough, we lost more people," he said. "Though I suppose it could have been much worse." He let go to look at her closely. "I'll take over with the children. I think you might want to stay with your friend." He moved his head sideways, indicating Orlagh and Morcant behind supporting somebody shuffling along.

"Rionach!" she called, rushing forward. "What happened?"

"That woman!" Orlagh answered. She figured I needed saving, that's what happened. I had lost my horse, and all she could think of was how to get to me instead of worrying about the Helvetii around her."

Rionach's niece Epona and nephew Caom, now ten and eight respectively, ran up. Their big eyes and tears running down ashen faces showed just how worried they were for their aunt. The group made it as far as the wagons when a legion medicus spotted them. "Bring her over to the Valetudinaria!" he called. When he saw their blank faces, he added "Our medical tent. We don't have many legionaries in there yet, so I can take a look."

Morcant frowned. After a brief inner battle, her brother-in-law answered, "All right, lead the way." *He can always intervene if he doesn't like what he sees.*

They made it to a big tent full of empty cots and gently laid Rionach down. The medicus efficiently assessed and cleaned the injuries under their watchful eyes, though once he started closing the wounds, Morcant spoke up.

"I'll take over now if you don't mind. Looks like you're needed elsewhere," he said, pointing at the busy tent entry where wounded legionaries started showing in big numbers. "Thank you for your good work. I could not have done better myself."

The man mock-bowed with an amused smile. "Please, put the needle and thread over on that table when you're done," he said before hurrying to his new patients.

She could tell Morcant had something to say, but her brother waited until the Roman medicus was well out of earshot. "He's skilled, except for the crude stitching. Let me fix what he already did so we can get out of here. There are more of our people in need of my help," he said, carefully guiding the needle. "She needs some rest, but she'll be fine," he told the girl and boy standing behind her cot. Then he turned to Orlagh, "and I'll keep her pretty for you, don't you worry." Brenna laughed in relief, joined by a calming Orlagh a moment later.

***

"Get your pila ready!" his centurion yelled from right next to him after rotating into first rank. Numerius obediently sheathed his gladius and picked up the first of his two pila from his left hand's shield grip, leaving the second for later. When he risked a glance over to Vibius, standing two men away in the same position, his friend looked back at him. *Let's hope we survive this, maybe we won't be first rank again next time.*

His heart beating hard in anticipation, he moved his eyes back to the Helvetii phalanx climbing up the slight incline, heading straight for them. He regripped the pilum, his sweaty hands making things worse. "Hold it! Steady, men!" the centurion roared. Numerius had enough trust in his superior that just hearing the man reassured him immensely. *Here they come, the first enemy warriors only twenty feet away. They are so close, when are we finally throwing?*

"And release! Pila iacite!"

He hurled his pilum as hard as he could. It went straight towards the face of the second man in the tip of the phalanx, who raised his shield at the last moment to catch it, though another missile hit his now exposed thigh and downed him, just like other pila did so many others. The still standing Helvetii slowed down, most trying to remove the Pila from their shields. Finding the soft iron tips solidly embedded, they ended up dropping the shields to the ground. Suddenly, the weakened phalanx broke apart, warriors rushing the Roman line in a frenzy.

"Ready your second Pilum!" the centurion bellowed. Numerius moved his remaining pilum out from his shield hand.

"Pila iacite! Pila iacite!"

More of the Helvetii went down, and once again a great number of the enemy line had to drop their shields during their run at the Roman front line.

"Here comes your warmup, boys!" The centurion shouted. The legion's shield wall closed in anticipation, everybody pulling their swords and bracing for impact. Numerius peaked out over his shield rim and saw a tall Helvetii rushing in with a long sword swinging down. At least two heads shorter than the charging warrior, Numerius raised his shield higher. Realizing it might not be enough, he raised his gladius above his head. The Celt's sword cut deep into his own edge. His move had worked, stopping the blade right above his head. Numerius now pushed the man back with his shield, slowing him down enough for his line neighbor to get a stab in. "Thanks, centurion!" he shouted. The centurion's answering chuckle was nearly lost in the noise of battle. The frontline rhythm started: push shields forward, rotate the shields slightly left to create a small opening on your right. Dart out your gladius for exposed skin or weak parts of armor. The Helvetii front lines kept going down in huge numbers. *As long as all their warriors push against us, their men in front have no room to evade our stabs. We might survive this onslaught.*

He lost all track of time while following the rhythm. The same movements over and over, calming in a way. Some undetermined time later, the Helvetii warriors briefly thinned, creating a buffer space that gave the enemy time to regroup. *Are they finally weary of the slaughter?*

He stabbed out with his gladius and couldn't find any targets close by. A new command sounded over the din, introducing a major change to his rhythm right after the shield closing. Instead of just pushing the shield forward to keep the enemy off balance, the whole line stepped as one with a shoving motion, first closing the distance to the enemy, then pushing hard into the warriors before opening shields for the next stab. The pressure was immense, and the entire Roman line wavered briefly as the enemy masses pushed back. But the move successfully blocked the front line of Helvetii warriors, leaving them no room to move and or evade Roman blades. The tubae changed their call back from push to hold, and the slaughter continued. Another two rounds of stationary action, then another call to move forward.

We're using their big numbers against them in a most disturbing fashion.

A movement to his right caught Numerius's attention, and he saw a legionary from the second rank hastily step over their centurion's wide helmet plume, which lay on the ground. His heart dropped. He had always liked and admired the man. *Merda, don't think about him now, stay focused.*

He concentrated on keeping his movements steady and put the fate of his superior out of his mind. *Left foot in front, shove and brace with my right. Open shield. Stab. Close. And again.*

His entire line kept moving forward. Slow and steady.

***

Caesar had thought the Ninth's call to advance a risky move but silently commended Cotta for his initiative when he saw how successful the counter push turned out. *Now it's time to send Hirtius to Cotta with new orders, and for me to inform the Seventh with theirs.*

"Are you absolutely clear on what I want done?" he asked Hirtius and Labienus.

"Yes," they both answered in unison.

"Very well, let's go and make this happen." He jumped off the boulder and ran to his lictors holding their horses. Hirtius overtook him, sprinting by in excitement. As Caesar mounted his horse, Labienus peeled off for the Tenth, positioned next to the Ninth's southern end and currently joining the fray, the men closest to the Helvetii masses throwing their pila.

A staccato of loud bangs came from behind him, followed by whooshing noises created by nearly four hundred oversized scorpio arrows flying overhead. *Finally, the artillery is getting in on the action.*

Caesar reached the Seventh and reined in close to his nephew Quintus Pedius. "We need to follow the Tenth. When they move, attach the Seventh to their end to extend the line between the Helvetii and their wagons." He looked over the Roman legionaries at the Helvetii masses. Where the massive scorpio bolts hit, the impact was enough to down several warriors at once.

Now it was up to Labienus. The entire length of the Tenth rotated, using the connection with the Ninth as their hinge point. The Tenth succeeded with pushing the Helvetii back where the line was already engaged. *Good men, just as I asked.*

The legionaries of the Seventh trailed and caught up when the Tenth came to a stop facing the enemy. The new line now cut right between the Helvetii and their baggage train behind the legions. *Let's hope the rest goes as smoothly.*

***

The chaos around him was complete. Divico saw the oversized Roman bolts, shot from somewhere close to the top of the hill, hit his warriors with incredible force,. *How did they set these up so quickly? I knew their cavalry attack was meant to buy time, but they didn't gain much.*

Grim faces were all around him, many of his men losing their determination. "Divico, Divico!" came from his right. He turned to see Bricio pushing through the Helvetii warriors. "They are trying to cut us off!" his protégé screamed over the cacophony of noise. "We need to secure the baggage train!" Divico looked back to their wagon fort just as Roman line finished its rotation into the formerly open space. *How are they doing this? Fifty years ago, the Romans I faced seemed…so much less capable.*

"Take as many as you can and go, keep the wagons secure!" Divico shouted back, waving him on to take off. One of the incoming scorpio missiles crashed right into a group of warriors close to Bricio, and the people hit bowled over several bystanders, the young councilor included. A moment later, those of the men and women who'd remained unhurt scrambled back up, and Bricio dusted himself off before running and screaming at chiefs and warriors to follow him as he passed them by. A good number rallied and took off to flank the end of the Roman line. *Pray they can hold out until we are done with these curs in front of us.*

"Keep pushing! Focus on one point and punch through their line!" he screamed at his people and their chieftains in growing frustration.

***

Caesar rode with Quintus Pedius and the Seventh, now marching to attach their line to the open end of the Tenth. The soldiers started to extend the line just after a party of maybe ten thousand warriors rushed out from behind the Tenth, running for the baggage train. *Let them, that's not nearly enough to change the outcome there.*

The Seventh's legionaries effectively blocked the retreat for any more of the Helvetii. Caesar was close to the center of the legion and had a good view of the enemy when the Roman artillery commanders opened fire with heavy ballista bolts and catapult rocks. *That means that most of our one hundred eighty artillery pieces are in place; the artillerymen usually compete with each other over who'll set up the fastest.*

The height advantage made the first shots go wide, but the specialists homed in on the enemy host with their second and third barrages. Where the big rocks hit the tightly packed masses, the path of destruction was devastating. *This has to be wreaking havoc on their morale. Yes, there, the first warriors are already moving away from our hill.*

The rush of survivors from around the impacts pushed the other Helvetii into complete panic, and soon the entire force started to disengage. When the artillery shot their tenth barrage, the Helvetii were in complete retreat. *It's working. They can't see a clear path to their wagons anymore, the majority is heading for the hill behind them instead. And now the rest follows as well.*

Caesar raised his fist in satisfaction and watched until the first of the Helvetii reached the hillside in the distance. "Have the Seventh turn around. We're going for the baggage train," he told Pedius. "I need messengers!" he yelled next, waiting for several men to come running. "You two, bring word to the legates of the Ninth and Tenth to join the Seventh against the wagons, and you there, tell the Eighth to follow the main enemy forces to their hill.

"You, go to the legates of the Eleventh and Twelfth and tell them I want them supporting the Eighth in pinning down the Helvetii host against the far hill, and you, go tell tribune Crassus to take the Celtic cavalry and support the Eighth, and tell the Archers and Slingers to join us against the wagons. Now, run!"

***

There was little daylight left. "Our food problems are finally solved, at least for a while," Seppius told Balventius while walking around the enemy camp, taken only a short time ago. Many of the captured wagons were full of fresh grains and produce.

"I wonder about all those beautiful Gallic horses," Balventius said. "Have you ever seen such a sight?" The amount of hobbled horses looked to be at least thirty thousand, maybe more. They walked on past another cluster of wagons and finally came upon a big group of officers. "Ah, here they are."

Titus Labienus, Quintus Pedius, and Lucius Cotta stood in the middle of their cohort prefects and centurions, engaged in animated discussion. "Have your men walk the captives up the hill. The nobles we caught, including councilor Bricio, should ride in the first wagons," Labienus told Cotta. "Pedius and I will follow the proconsul to the hill the Helvetii hold, and we'll be quick about it. He already took the Cretans and the slingers, should the Numidians go as well?"

"I'd like them to ride escort for the wagons and the captives. Their drawn bows will do more to deter them from escaping than our tired legionaries," Cotta replied.

"Very well, it's decided then. Your Ninth took the brunt of the original attack, so they're in charge of moving all of this up to our hill fortification," Labienus said. "And the Seventh and Tenth will march quick step to support Caesar." The Tenth's commander paused to examine the faces around him, all nodding in agreement. "Dismissed!"

Balventius turned to Opiter Maximus, who stood nearby. "Hey, Opiter, nice to be a wagon driver for a change, aye?"

The fellow centurion responded with a laugh. "If you're game, we can make it into a race. I have an eye for which team of oxen is going to be faster."

Balventius joined in the laughter and turned to an amused Capussia and a chuckling Oz, who stood between Maximus and Pullo. *I need to give Maximus credit for changing his attitude about our Auxilia soldiers. I would have never thought that possible.*

He was surprised to find that he'd come to like the crude man.

***

What is he doing? The cornua and tubae of the Eighth had just sounded the command to attack. The Eighth should pursue the Helvetii down the hill. It was early morning, and after a whole night of relentless fighting, the enemy had broken, their warriors rushing down the backside of the hill in small bands and groups.

Caesar sprinted after Vatinius. "Let them go! Let them go!" he shouted, finally close enough to be heard.

The legate turned to Caesar with a haughty and annoyed look, though upon recognizing the man who'd shouted, Vatinius forced his face into a blank expression. "Proconsul! Why should we stop now? If we go after them, we can kill thousands more," he replied.

"I know, and I see the temptation, but Rome needs them alive and back in their mountains to keep the Germanic tribes at a distance from us," Caesar explained between breaths. "Think about it." The proconsul's chest was still heaving from his fast run.

Vatinius raised an eyebrow in response before slowly turning to issue the command for retreat. The chase stopped, and the legionaries of the Eighth turned back.

"For now, they will try to leave the lands of the Aedui as fast as they can. If they keep their current direction, they will run northeast to the Lingones. I'll have messengers sent to them asking to deny the Helvetii assistance." Caesar smiled. "These warriors lost everything today. Their families, their possessions, their supplies, and their pride. All we need to get the kind of official surrender I want is to follow them." *Which will get me a signed document as unalterable proof of success to keep my enemies in the Senate at bay.*

696 AUC (58 BC), late summer
Clusium, Etruria, Italia

Velia studied the mosaics on the walls of the atrium. She'd seen them hundreds of times and had usually looked away in disgust, though now she had lost all emotion toward them. She marveled at the incredible craftsmanship that had gone into putting together the small stones and pieces of tile to depict all possible—and some surely impossible—sexual positions, achieved with grossly oversized genitalia as if to elevate the detail. Since her failed attempt at escape a few weeks ago, she had been cold and uncaring to the world around her. Even Titia's attempts at conversation bothered her, she would only engage for a sentence or two in the hope of being left alone. However, explaining to Titia that she was didn't feel or care about anything made things worse. Her friend seemed alarmed and didn't back off. *Can't she just leave me alone? Even my hate for Fastie and Minatus is meaningless now. I am dead inside, stuck in this place. All I want is to die; maybe I can make one of my customers mad enough to do it. The underworld will be a happier place.*

Fastie's punishment after her failed escape had been brutal, meant to inflict maximum pain without leaving scars. He was always careful about the latter; she was a moneymaking investment after all. She had patiently suffered through it all until he added what he called a valuable lesson, making her watch as he beat and mistreated Velthurus. *That was the worst thing he ever did to me, telling me the pain he inflicts on the boy is my fault. Somehow, I believe him.*

Velia had expected to receive a tattoo similar to the boy's. Instead, Fastie fastened a bronze band around her neck, engraved on front and back in Latin with, "I have run away. Bring me back to my master Fastius at the Lupanar for a reward."

And then, one morning Fastie had released her from his room and sent her back to work. As a lasting reminder, knowing how precious the boy had become to her, he moved Velthurus to the hallway on the other side of the building. The only time she saw him now were the mornings.

Velia walked along the atrium wall's mosaics and absently fingered her neckband when she heard breathing close behind her. Somebody had walked up without her noticing. She sighed.

"Are you Velia?"

She turned around to look at the customer. He was muscular and would have been quite handsome if not for the air of toughness and danger about him. On the skin visible outside the standard off-white toga, the sign of a freeborn Roman citizen, deep scars marred the man's face, neck and arms. She involuntarily stepped back, her eyes now focusing on his milky white right eye. Realizing she was staring, she looked down in embarrassment. That's when she noticed that the front portion of his right military-style, calf-high sandal was empty, half his foot missing. She swallowed hard before answering. "Yes, I am Velia. Would you like my services?"

The man looked to the front door, then back at her.

"I'm a friend, and I'd like to talk to you, but not out here. Which of your services will keep us in your room the longest?"

Velia took a step back. It wasn't just his hard looks. She felt in her gut how dangerous this man was, unexpected fear growing and cutting through her lethargy. *Leave me alone. I am miserable enough.*

He stepped forward to close the distance but stopped short with a quizzical look. "You don't have to be afraid of me, I only want to talk, I promise," he said in a low voice. "Just tell me what I need to pay so we can go to your room."

Velia hesitated, searching the man's face for a sign. When he showed her an oddly endearing lopsided smile, she felt it to be honest. She nodded to the front of the room. "Tell the manager you want the full treatment for eight sesterces. That'll give us some time."

Her eyes followed the man back to Fastie's counter near the entry. The stranger ambled over as if he didn't have a care in the world, but she could tell it was for show. Under that exterior was a man wound tight and ready to spring to action. She saw him put coins on the wooden surface, point back at her and return. She took a deep breath. "Follow me," she said before taking him by the hand through the hallway and into her room. She gestured to the bed before closing the curtain behind her.

"Why don't you sit down first. Please," the man said, remaining on his feet. He waited until she plopped down on her bed before he sat down next to her. She suddenly felt uneasy with him in the room. *Did I make a mistake with this one? Should I scream for help? Or, maybe I should hope he'll kill me…*

He started to whisper. "Your friend Lethie told me where to find you. Nice woman, with great concern for you." He cleared his throat. "My name is Gaius Blandius. I'm with the Ninth Legion and here to help. Now tell me everything that happened since you sent your letter to your brother." Velia's fear suddenly dropped, and her spirits lifted. *This scary man is here to help me! What a difference a few words can make.*

***

"Hello, I'm here because I need a loan," Blandius told the bouncer at the door. "This is the lender Minatus's office, right?" The man stepped back and nodded for him to enter. Blandius shuffled in, dragging his bad right foot all the way until he stood waiting, hunched over, in the middle of the room.

"Why do you need money?" a clerk asked him from behind a counter to his left.

"To open a business." He looked around as if worried about who was listening. "Maybe not the kind of business I should talk about in public, but it's lucrative." He laughed. "Very lucrative."

"Very well, you might be in the right place. Let me check if Minatus will see you now, or if you need to come back later," the clerk said and got out from behind the counter. "Be right back." Blandius took the opportunity to smile at the bouncer. The man gave him a bored look, and then ignored him. *So far, this works better than I expected. Just another harmless sap, easily taken advantage of.*

The clerk came back into the main room. "He'll see you, just go right in."

"Thank you." He shuffled through the door into Minatus' office, who looked up from the papers on his desk. The man smoothed some of his orange-blond hair, while trying to read what type of customer Blandius was. "Sit down, please," he said with a warm smile, gesturing to the chairs in front of his desk. "My clerk tells me you need a loan. I can certainly help with that, though depending on your kind of business, I might be able to do more than just give you money. I have the best contacts."

Blandius eagerly leaned forward, pulling a long knife from beneath his toga in the process. He toppled a chair over in his rush to get behind the desk and point the tip at Minatus's throat.

"Well, I lied. I don't need a loan. I'm here to pay one off instead. Hold still and hear me out, or I'll slit your throat and ask your clerk for help instead. Your choice," Blandius said coldly.

Minatus's eyes widened in shock. *Looks like I played the polite cripple well enough. Surprise.*

The bouncer had heard the commotion and came to the office's door. "Everything fine, boss?"

Blandius was careful to stay between the door and Minatus to keep the knife out of the line of sight. The lender hesitated, and he leaned forward to whisper. "I know what you did with Velia Churinas. Better tell him everything is fine," he hissed, moving the knife closer and closer to the man's throat until a small drop of blood ran down into Minatus' tunic.

The money lender swallowed hard. Sweat started to bead on his forehead, some of it running into his eyes, causing several involuntary and rapid blinks. *Good, I need him terrified for this to work.* "Everything is fine. Go back and guard the front door," Minatus told his man.

Blandius waited until the bouncer had left. "That just saved your life. As I said, I know what you did with Velia. Too bad for you that she has a brother in the Ninth Legion." Minatus sat back, trying to get away from the knife. "Yes, I see you realize what that means. I am a veteran, and I'm sure you've heard some of the stories. The ones like me who survive a few battles love to kill just so we can count bodies afterward. Better if you don't mess with me."

"I'll tell you everything you want to know. Yes, I sold her, and perhaps I shouldn't have, but it was a fair price; I swear she got the difference herself. If you have any issues, you need to take it up with the person I sold her to," Minatus offered.

Blandius smiled again. *It would be so easy to end this slimy piece of scum.* It took him some effort, but he finally overcame his revulsion at the man and pulled the knife back. He took a deep breath. "Spare your lies for somebody else. You have exactly two choices. We can do this the easy way, which is by far better than you deserve. I'll pay you four-hundred, half of what her father owned you." Minatus gave him a look so full of hatred that he had to chuckle. "It's not like I'm trying to steal from you. I know she earned you the difference in her very first month." Minatus opened his mouth to speak, but Blandius moved his knife forward again. "I don't want to hear a word from you. This is not a discussion. I know you own the brothel, and I know your sale was not legal, you never filed the proper paperwork at the magistrate. So, I know you are the right person to sign a letter of emancipation. You will write that the money for her freedom was paid." Blandius added a dramatic pause. "I'll tell you what, I'll still give you the full eight-hundred, but for that, you also include a little boy by the name of Velthurus and a woman named Titia. Same deal for both, write out full papers."

"What if I refuse?" Minatus whispered. Blandius smiled and moved the knife forward to right above the man's jugular. Another big drop of blood ran a second line all the way down into Minatus's clean tunic.

"You really want me to spell that out? I'm disappointed, I figured you'd be smarter than that. Let me be very clear. I'll leave three dead bodies in your office and go see Fastie next, who I am sure will be more accommodating. If you're gone, he might see himself as the real owner of your place. I bet he'd love that." Blandius said with a chuckle.

"Alright, stop, please!" When the knife retreated, Minatus slumped forward in resignation, his hand rubbing his throat. "I can write the letters up right now. You have the money?"

"Of course. Two hundred denarii. I don't trust you to keep your word, so you'll get it when I have the women and the boy. I think it's best I leave the cash with Fastie as we walk out of your brothel." He waved the tip of his knife and smiled again. "I hope we agree?"

Minatus nodded instantly. "Of course, considering the circumstances." The man pulled out a stack of fine Papyrus and started to write.

A few minutes later, Blandius rushed out the front door with three tied scrolls. He waved across to where his friend stood watch before turning left to run down the street. The man jumped from the curb onto the road surface and caught up with him. "Albatius," Blandius called as they met. "We don't have much time. That bag of slime will send his thugs after us, you can bet on that. We need to get the women and the boy out of the brothel while we can."

He smiled at his friend, who easily kept up with his own wobble of a jog. He was enjoying himself, happy to be of use and able to help a legion comrade out by coming here. Having his best friend Albatius by his side was a bonus. They had a lot in common, including the Ninth as their home since the legion's very first days back in Hispania. Both crippled three years earlier, Blandius had lost most of his right foot in the first battle against the Transcudani, while Albatius had lost his ear in a brawl between legionaries in winter quarters in Scalabis. His left arm had followed the ear into the underworld soon after thanks to an infected cut. Blandius still thought of both of them as very lucky, remembering many fellow soldiers who'd died from harmless looking scrapes and cuts. After the injuries, they had expected to receive an honorable discharge, but the camp prefect's team had surprised them with offers to join the army's supply team, dependent on their ability to write and count. They had separately passed that muster and had finally met in their training as wagon drivers. After a few months as apprentices, they had become friends and were elevated together to full members of the camp prefect's staff.

"Are you glad we took this job?" Albatius asked him with a smile.

"You bet I am. I was getting bored with our boys doing all the fighting and us just driving wagons back and forth. Frankly, I can't think of anything better to do than messing with somebody as slimy as that dung bucket Minatus." Blandius replied with a wide grin.

Many months ago, Albatius had been approached about this search and rescue mission by an old tent mate, risen to decanus of his own tent squad. A fresh recruit had serious worries about his sister back in Clusium. They had both been eager to help, wanting to pay forward the mercy the legion had shown them.

Fortunately, a perfect reason to travel had soon presented itself in the form of urgently needed gladii, pila, shields, and other replacement pieces. The supplies had been ordered long ago for the Ninth' armory and needed to be picked up in Rome. So, they had driven their supply wagons south as part of a big convoy, loaded the weapons and armor, and started the trek back north on the Via Cassia before stopping in Clusium to search for young Numerius' sister. There, they had hired a couple of locals for a few days to help the rest of the team with their wagons and bought three horses as a means to catch up later.

Only a few minutes after leaving Minatus's office, they entered the road leading to the brothel. *Good, I don't think I could have run much further.*

"Merda, my foot hurts like the missing piece is undergoing torture in the underworld," he joked.

They slowed down for the last block and walked up to the door. "You need to go in alone," Albatius said. "Minatus and his men don't know me, so I'll keep watch at the door. If they show up, I'll follow them in."

Blandius nodded and held out his right hand for Albatius to hand him the bag of coins. Two hundred denarii were significantly less bulky than eight-hundred sesterces but still made for a heavy load. Money bag in hand, Blandius stepped to the door as his friend moved a few feet to the side and leaned against the wall.

He walked in and gave a nod to Fastie behind his counter before heading to Velia.

"I can't tell you how glad I am to see you out in the atrium right now. Take these scrolls and follow me." He walked back to the counter.

"I need your help with some business," he told Fastie, receiving only a raised eyebrow and a sneer in response. "Very well, let me rephrase this. I just came from your boss Minatus, and we made a deal that includes your help. Do you have an office where we can talk?"

"This better be good." Fastie came out from behind the counter and motioned for one of his brawlers to follow. He led Blandius into a small office on the side of the atrium.

"I've given the girl three papers of emancipation. For her, Titia, and a boy named Velthurus. They were written personally by Minatus, have his signature, and show that the money was paid. For that last part to become true, I will pay you when we all walk out of here." He held up the bag. "I suggest that your man gets Titia and the boy, then I'll hand you the money, and we're done."

Fastie just stared at him. Blandius sighed. *That phallus is going to make trouble. Why couldn't this go easy*?

Suddenly, the brothel manager made his decision. "Baricus, hold the girl!" he shouted at the bouncer before pulling out a long cudgel hidden behind the desk.

Blandius ducking under the manager's swing and then punched him squarely in the jaw with the bag of denarii. Fastie dropped to the ground like a sack of wheat.

He turned to the brawler behind him, who held a knife to Velia's throat. "Stop or I'll hurt her," the man grunted.

Blandius pulled his own long knife out from under his toga and grinned again. "If you don't let her go now, I will kill you." He took a step forward. "That's a promise."

The man swallowed hard before shoving Velia into the room, retreating as fast as he could. "Come here! *Now!*" the brawler called across the atrium to another one of Fastie's men, who happened to be in the rom. "This guy just took Fastie out. Let's get him together." The other man, tall and built from solid muscle, pulled his knife and advanced on the office door. Customers were already leaving in haste behind the two bouncers, avoiding what was clearly not their business. The working women hurried away to the other side of the atrium, leaving the space in front of the office wide open.

"You alright?" Blandius asked Velia, who rubbed her neck but nodded. "When I'm done with these two guys, can you find your friend and the boy? We need to get out of here, quick like."

Velia nodded again. "I can get them. It won't take more than a couple of minutes."

"Good." He moved closer to the doorway. There, the two men had to come at him one at a time. As expected, the one from earlier let the bigger man rush through first. Blandius jumped back from a wild side to side swing before stepping back into the man's reach. His blade stabbed into a wide-open stomach. Once on the ground, the brute started to sob in misery and crawled away. The first man now backed away from the office, beads of sweat on his forehead betraying his fear. "Merda, merda, merda! Are you legion?" he asked as he continued to move backward. Blandius gave him a curt nod. "I'm putting my blade down, see? I'll stay out of your way, I promise." The bouncer dropped his knife to the floor and shoved it towards the office.

"Velia, now. Go!" Blandius shouted.

***

She ran and picked the knife off the floor before hurrying through the rear hallways to fetch Velthurus and her friend. She decided to take the left first to go for the boy. "Velthurus? You are coming with me. We are leaving this place forever. Do you want to get anything from your closet?"

"All I have is an old blanket. Fastie never lets me keep anything." Velthurus replied with saucer-like eyes.

"That means you're ready. We'll pick up Titia and go." They hurried down to the other corridor. When she reached her friend's chamber, she pulled the curtain. A middle-aged man stood close to the doorway, alarmed by the screaming voices from the atrium and undecided what to do. Titia stood in front of her bed.

"You just stay out of the way, you hear me?" Velia shouted, pointing the long knife she held at the client.

He lifted both hands and stepped away until he reached the wall. "I don't want any trouble."

"Good. Titia, we need to go. I have papers for both of us and Velthurus. We're free, you hear me? But we need to go now. If you have anything of value, grab it."

"What? What kind of cruel joke are you playing?" Titia stepped back, unbelieving.

"It's legal, I promise, though we must go *now*. Come on!"

She walked to her friend, grabbed her arm and pulled. Finally, with a jerk, Titia started to move. She grabbed an old stola on her way out, her sole possession important enough to take. "Wait, I need to fetch my family statuettes," Velia suddenly remembered before rushing into her own room.

***

Eight rough looking fellows entered the brothel. *Must be Minatus' men already. Didn't take long.*

They held a variety of weapons, mostly knives and cudgels, though one gripped a rusty old spatha. "A lot of good that long sword will do in close quarters," Blandius muttered to himself with a chuckle. The men were all brutes, though he doubted any of them had proper training. *Or they wouldn't work for a sleazy lender like Minatus.*

He smiled when the door closed behind them, a loud clang indicating the inside crossbar falling into place. *Thank you, Albatius.*

Grinning wide at the armed men, Blandius stepped forward, long knife in hand.

"Sorry, people, I should apologize. This fight hardly seems fair," he shouted to the brawlers.

"Too late for apologies, you fool. Minatus wants you dead. Not our fault if the fight ain't fair," the bearer of the rusty cavalry sword yelled before spitting on the floor.

Blandius laughed. "You misunderstand me. It's your fault, really; you should have brought a lot more men." He could hear Albatius laughing heartily at his joke from the far side of the room before the first of the brawlers back there screamed. Apparently, his friend had started without him. Blandius jumped at the closest man, dodging a swing of a wooden cudgel on the way, and pushed aside his target's knife-wielding arm before stabbing into his side.

He stayed close to the wall, ignoring for now the loudmouth with the sword—likely the least dangerous among them. Easily avoiding another wide sword swing, he turned to the next cudgel holder instead. The spatha impacted the wall behind him and was jerked out of the brawler's hands, clanging into the mosaic floor. *Ha, I can still call who's the greatest fool. I haven't lost my knack yet.*

Genuine fear was written on the face of the man facing him, a nervous tick playing over his opponent's left eyelid. *I am sorry for you; I can't stop now.*

Though when the time came for him to stab into the man's armpit, he chose to push the knife lower and forward to slash deeply across several ribs instead. Painful, yes, but he'd live. He turned around to a face full of anger. The sword wielder had picked up his weapon again. *You, on the other hand, I don't feel any pity for…*

***

Velia held tight to Velthurus' hand as they arrived back at the hallway leading to the atrium. Loud shouting and screams stopped her short of bursting into the open space. Several men stood between the front door and Fastie's office, and more were on the floor, some moaning, others lying still. Blandius fought those closer to her, but there were also screams from the front door.

She realized it was less of a fight then she had thought, with Blandius quickly dispatching three men in front and another man cutting down two more at the entryway. The man left standing between them threw down his cudgel and raised his hands. "Please, I give up, see? Don't hurt me!" Blandius motioned for him to join Fastie's remaining brawler and the women at the far side of the atrium. He turned to Velia.

"Are you ready? We better go before any more of these idiots show up."

Velia held on to Velthurus as she crossed the open doorway to the office when Fastie reached out to snatch the boy out of her hand. The furious man, despite a bleeding gash on his head from his earlier impact with the floor, held the boy rigidly by the arm while waving his cudgel. She raised her knife to attack. But Titia pushed her out of the way, running past her with balled fists. The cudgel, already swinging for Velia, impacted Titia's head with a loud crunching sound. Fastie screamed as Velthurus bit hard into his arm, and Velia thrust her knife at the hated man's chest. Fastie bent down at the last moment, and her knife tip came close to his face. Without hesitation, she pushed the weapon toward his right eye. As he screamed and jerked back, she let go of the handle. He stepped back, screamed profanities at her, gripping the handle to pull the knife back out. *No, you don't. I've had enough of you.*

Velia's numbness, all her desperation and her fear slipped away from her, replaced by a bottomless rage. She stepped forward and punched the end of the handle with an open palm, driving the knife in until the hilt hit Fastie's face. The hated man finally dropped, his body convulsing briefly before lying still. Velia turned back to Titia, and her anger evaporated, leaving her empty and drained. She lifted her friend by her arms. "Wake up, Titia, please, wake up."

"I am so sorry, Velia," Blandius told her. "She's gone. Her skull... it's over for her." He gently pried her hands from her friend's body and pulled her up. "We need to go, and we can't take her."

"Wait." Velia opened the scrolls to find Titia's. She held it up for the people across the atrium pool. "Do you see this papyrus? It's her legal declaration of freedom. We all three have one, but Fastie didn't want to let us go. He was the criminal here, remember that!" She gently laid the scroll on her friend's still chest.

"I'm ready," she said and followed the two men and the boy to the door.

Blandius carefully looked outside. "No other men, good. Follow me." He ran across the road and into a side street, only slowing down once they were hidden from the Lupanar's entrance. "By the way, there's somebody anxious to see you," Blandius said.

Velia saw her friend waiting for her as they came around the next corner. "Lethie!"

"I'm so glad you are out of there," Lethie said, bursting into tears. Velia hugged her back tightly.

"Sorry to break you up, but we can't remain here," Albatius told them. "We need to move."

Velia released her friend and turned to face the two men. "Fine, but where to? What's next?"

"We thought you should come north with us to the legion," he suggested. "Your brother is there, and he'd be happy to have you close. And there's always plenty of work around the camp, lots of paying jobs available."

"Either way, you can't stay here. If you do, Minatus will contest your freedom," Albatius added.

She stood straighter. "I have no choice, then." She took Velthurus's hand and kneeled in front of him, looking into the boy's eyes. "I know we haven't known each other for more than a year, but you have become very dear to me. Is there anybody else you can go to, or would you consider coming with me?" Velthurus burst into tears and hugged her tight. "I guess that means we'll both go with you," Velia told Blandius. Then she looked at Lethie. "Would you join me as well? With Numerius and Vibius, the four of us together, it would be like old times."

"I'm tempted, but I can't, not now. My father just passed away and I can't leave my mother alone," Lethie replied.

"This is goodbye, then, at least for now. Take care," Velia said. "I'll write once I can afford to."

They continued to a stable near the city gate, retrieving their horses and riding north from Clusium as soon as the saddles were fastened.

"Can we make this our first stop?" Velia asked, pointing at her neck.

"Absolutely, we'll find someone at the next village," Blandius replied.

After two days of uneventful riding on the Via Cassia, they caught up with the wagon train. *I feel like this isn't real. It simply can't be. I must be dreaming, though I pray that I will never wake.*

696 AUC (58 BC), late summer South of Andematunnum, Free Gallia, Southern lands of the Lingones Nation

Why did the Roman commander leave me alive? As part of the peace treaty, he made me promise to lead my people back to our mountains, and I will abide by my word, though there is no honor left for me.

Divico was a broken man. He knew his short fits of restless sleep made him look gaunt and older than his seventy-five years, and for the first time in his life he was no longer ready for anything. He wanted to avoid any sparring, conversing, or anything else that might hold meaning for a future he did not want to be part of anymore. All that was left was to ride, and occasionally eat part of the rations the Romans had handed them.

"I would like to share some of my ale with you." Bricio had ridden up to grace him with his company. Having the young man worried about him made things even worse. *His father would have been the better leader after all.*

He knew there was no use in dwelling in the past. It was history now, there was no way of changing it. Behind him, saw a long trail of families and warriors trudged on. Some looked beaten down, but not all. After everything, many looked forward to their old homes and resuming the lives they knew, comfortable like a pair of worn leather shoes. He couldn't fault them for wanting to be done with the adventure that had come close to killing them all.

How could anyone understand Caesar, the man who let them go, even giving them supplies so they had a chance of surviving the coming winter? Unexpectedly, that hated person had shown mercy to the Helvetii people, the chieftains, and most of all, him, the man responsible for annihilating three Roman legions fifty years ago. *Apparently, killing and enslaving my people at the Arar was enough to satisfy his need for vengeance.*

He had hoped for an honorable death in battle, or, if that was not possible, to be executed by the Romans. He would have left this world in defiance.

"I'm grateful, thank you," he answered Bricio, who handed him a skin full of ale. Drinking greedily despite the fluid's warmth, or perhaps because of it, he considered the cold day.

"You should leave me alone. You don't want to be seen with the man who led his nation to ruin. Don't you understand? I will not, no, cannot be on the council any longer." *Once we're home, I'll spend the rest of my days on my farm in solitude and quiet.*

He handed the skin back to Bricio. That young man was now the best hope for their nation's future. Divico turned away, shivering in the cold drizzle, tightened his coat, and rode on.

***

"My wife wants to visit me in Mediolanum in Gallia Cisalpina next winter when I hold the assizes there for the province. She writes that she plans to leave Rome in mid-October and asked my mother to join her. She wants to make the trip into an adventure, which should be easy, considering she never traveled far from Rome before." The letter had transformed Caesar's previously solemn mood, and he smiled across the desk at Hirtius. *I can't wait to see sweet Calpurnia again.*

His aide laughed at his reaction. "And that's after you've already received a letter from Crassus wanting to visit you and his son. You'll have a busy few months there," he replied.

Caesar nodded. "I should write to him about the Helvetii spoils. It's more than enough to pay back all I owe him. In fact, it should be sufficient to pay back every single outstanding loan. Which is unbelievable, I wasn't sure I'd ever see the day. I'd like to celebrate that later with a small round of friends. Would you care to join me?"

"What else am I going to do? Of course," Hirtius beamed at him. "I'm very happy it finally worked out. I know how much that has weighed on you over the years."

Caesar stood up. "The Legates will be here shortly. We should prepare. Cleisthenes, would you help, please?"

The Athenian servant rushed out of the private chamber section of the tent. "I'm here, what do you need me to do?"

"Please have the big table set up, and we will need a few more chairs. Five should cover it."

A few minutes later the required table and chairs were arranged, and Caesar moved a collection of papyrus scrolls and baskets containing various pieces of vellum over from his desk,. He spread the containers out and waited until his legates walked into the tent.

"Gentlemen, please have a seat. I asked you here to help me sift through all of this," he said while indicating the documents on the table. "The Helvetii left us their council's official correspondence. Please, search for anything useful to us and the Senate. That could be anything relating to their possessions, their motivations, or agreements between their cantons and other tribes and clans." As Caesar started with the vellum in the basket in front of him, his thoughts drifted to the last few days. After the decisive battle, he had given the legions three days to convalesce and bury the dead before hurrying after the fleeing enemy. Even with the wait, they had easily caught up with the majority of the Helvetii, who had no stomach left for fighting. Instead, Divico and his surviving chieftains had sued for peace. *Like I figured they would.*

The council members had willingly signed his agreement, eager to return to their homelands, and promised to never bother the Romans or the Aedui again. As a gesture of goodwill, he had given them wheat brought from Roman Gallia. He needed the survivors to live through the next winter.

"Look at these numbers, Gaius," Pedius said, leaning forward in his chair. "Unbelievable! This should look excellent in your report to the Senate." He handed the piece of vellum to Vatinius, who passed it on to Caesar.

"In Greek letters, and nice handwriting to boot. Let's see. It lists the Helvetii and their sister tribes at three-hundred-seventy-thousand people." Caesar whistled through his teeth. "That number seems too high to believe."

"Maybe they didn't all leave the mountains. Though I think you have to mention these numbers in your next missive," Vatinius added with a wide grin. "You do have that document as proof, and it will make us look even more successful."

Caesar ruefully shook his head. "I don't like to boast, but I think I might have to. We need the help of public opinion." He turned pensive. "I am personally more interested in how many of them survived to go back home."

"You mean in total, including the first battle?" young Crassus asked.

"Those of the Tingurini that managed to flee, not the ones we sold," Caesar answered.

Labienus jumped in. "We counted only one-hundred-ten-thousand in their camp when we caught up to them a few days ago."

"Yes, but that doesn't account for any of the Tigurini who fled earlier, or any of the ones traveling separately," Caesar said. "I guess we'll never know for sure. Do we have the tallies for our own fallen yet?"

"Yes, I have them here," Hirtius chimed in, pulling a folded papyrus from his legionary satchel. "Let's see. In total, we lost close to nine thousand legionaries. That's nearly a third of our troops. We also lost three thousand men from the combined auxilia forces."

Caesar cringed. "We need to start looking for fresh reinforcements." He pondered the situation while everybody kept pulling documents to read. *I had meant to go after Ariovistus soon. Every day I wait, more of my political enemies in the Senate will support the Suebi king in the hope of interfering with my own plans. Crassus wrote that some senators are already calling for me to leave Gallia altogether. But I couldn't; there's so much more to gain here.*

***

"You better make your peace with leaving the council voluntarily, or they will kick you out. If that happens, you can be sure they'll make a show of it. Nobody wants to work with you anymore, not after you collaborated with the Helvetii against your own people and Caesar," Divitiaco lectured his brother Dumnorix.

He glanced over his shoulder at Liscus and all their retainers trailing behind, plodding through open countryside on their way back to Bibracte. The others were far enough away for him not to be overheard.

"Now that Caesar has gotten the Helvetii out of our lands,"—his brother sneered at the mention of the legatus's name—"the council feels nothing but gratefulness for his help. All Aedui are in his debt, and you know about the preparations for our grand assembly. We've invited many nations' Vergobreti, kings, and elder chieftains from all over Gallia. They want to add as many pleas as possible to our own for when we officially petition Caesar to intervene with Ariovist and his Suebi. There's no place for you in any of this, not anymore."

Though Dumnorix stayed sullen and silent, Divitiacus was content. The threat of the Helvetii was no more, his nation's relationship with Rome was better than ever thanks to Julius Caesar, and his brother had been chastised without getting hurt, at least physically. The wounded pride would heal, and who knew, maybe stubborn Dumnorix would eventually forgive his older brother for interfering.

"One more thing. I want to meet that Helvetian wife of yours and your children. They are my family too—can you do that for me?" Dumnorix looked at him with a veiled expression.

"Please?" he added before his brother nodded. He thought he saw the corner of his brother's lips curl slightly. *Maybe that was a smile. Well, it can only get better from here.*

The effort the Aedui council had put into the grand assembly might bring Gallia's nations closer, though he figured there was no need to push Caesar. He had personally heard the man's promise and seen him shake hands with Elsed. *Caesar is obsessed with keeping his word. I have no doubt he will help.*

EPILOGUS

Spero (Hope)

"Accept the things to which fate binds you, and love the people with whom fate brings you together, and do so with all your heart"

Marcus Aurelius

696 AUC (58 BC), late summer
Via Cassia, south of Faesolae, Etruria, Italia

Velthurus told me there is a temple to Feronia in these woods. An old local woman told him yesterday at the trading post from," Velia told Blandius, who sat next to her on the wagon bench. "I know it will slow us down, but we can catch up with the others later."

Their wagons had reached a mansio, one of many official rest stops along the Via Cassia. Blandius drove past it to a wide grassy patch big enough to allow their entire wagon train to camp for the night. He had explained to her that this ancient highway between Rome and several of the former Etruscan cities turned west to merge with the Via Aurelia, which ran along the western Italian coast. In response, she had told him she'd dreamed of seeing the ocean since she was a little girl, though now she didn't seem able to manage much enthusiasm in the prospect. *I need to remember she is not the same person she used to be. What happened to her would change anyone.*

"Let me talk to Albatius," he answered as he climbed off the wagon. "If he's up for it, we can go."

Glancing at the big building reserved for official dignitaries and government messengers, he walked back across the grass to where his friend was finishing parking his wagon. Off to one side were the ubiquitous local farm stands that sold overpriced foodstuff like bread, cheeses, fruit, fresh water, and feed for travelers' animals. He nodded to his colleagues as they walked by on their way to the forest edge to relieve themselves after another afternoon spent on hard wagon benches. He walked on until he reached Albatius and Velthurus.

"Why don't you follow the others, I'll catch up," he told the boy, who gladly took off.

Blandius grinned after him. "I assume you heard about the temple?" he asked his friend.

Albatius laughed. "The boy won't shut up about it." They both glanced back at Velia, now also heading for the forest. "Can't say I know what they've gone through, but they have their hearts set on it. We can make an extra day or two work."

"It's settled, then. Let's tell the others."

***

"I thought we'd never get here. This is far enough into the forest that we'll have to spend the night," Blandius announced. "We wouldn't make it back to the Via Cassia before dark."

The broad clearing around the temple, was filled with an assortment of tied or hobbled horses, mules, and many kinds of wagons, including a few rented raeda big enough for ten people or more, and even a small and luxurious two-wheeled carruca, indicating at least one wealthy visitor. One side of the temple grounds housed an open market with booths and stands.

They'd have difficulty finding a spot to leave their wagon. Velia's companion whistled through his teeth. "All of this far into a big forest?"

"As befits the temple of the goddess protector of all wildlife, fertility, freedom and abundance," she answered. "How about over there?" He followed her advice and parked the wagon, and she jumped off to stretch.

"I'll unhitch the oxen, you go right ahead to the temple," Blandius said.

Velia frowned. "I hate to bother you, but could you please loan us some money?"

"I'm sorry, of course. Don't worry about paying back, please. Here are..." He opened his purse bag and counted out the coins as he took them out. "One, two, three, four denarii. That's sixteen sesterces. Will that be enough for now?"

"I think so, thank you." She turned around to Velthurus. "Let's go." Velia led the boy up the stairs, through the first columns of the temple's colonnade, and onto the temple's front under the shadow of its massive roof. It was as if the goddess suddenly shut off the noise of the market, and she felt some of the emotion of the last days drop off her shoulders. She was relaxed for the first time in a year or more. *The hate for Fastie kept me sane. Now that he is dead and I am forever out of Minatus's reach, why am I still full of fear?*

"Look, Velia. They sell clay tablets. Is that how we are supposed to ask the goddess for a favor?"

"I bet that's what they're for. Wax tablets are easily erased, but clay tablets dry and keep your wish written forever." She turned to the temple servant behind the counter. "One please." She handed a denarius over and received two sesterces back. "Thank you." She handed the tablet to the boy.

"Don't you want one as well?" he asked her.

"I don't need one, my wish has already come true. I'm here to thank the goddess for what she did for us."

She stepped through the main doorway and walked into the inner sanctum, the main part of the temple holding a large and vividly painted marble statue of Feronia. They got in line, slowly moving to the goddess' pedestal. The temple might be out of the way, but nonetheless was a busy place. "Velthurus, write your most heartfelt wish and put it in the bin next to the goddess. She may grant it to you if she feels you are worthy."

He took the tablet and held it awkwardly for a moment before pushing it back at her. "I never learned how to write. Could you please do this for me?" He looked expectantly at her.

"Sure, of course, but how about I start teaching you how to read and write?" Velia asked. "What do you want the tablet to say?"

"I want you to write: Please, remove the mark of shame from my forehead."

Velia burst into tears, her heart overflowing for the child. She hugged him tight before scratching the sentence into the moist layer of clay. The line to the platform advanced slowly, yet she didn't mind in the least. *I am content just to be in this holy place and not to worry for a little while.*

She was gazing at the gentle face of the goddess when Velthurus suddenly pulled on her arm. "It's our turn," he said. She was surprised they had already made it to the front. Velthurus carefully added his tablet to a basket holding a growing collection, while Velia kneeled down to lay Fastie's bronze neckband on the altar as a donation. Next, she opened the bag containing her parents' figurines and pulled them out, arranging them carefully one by one on the edge of Feronia's stone platform, with her parents positioned slightly behind Numerius. "Thank you, Feronia, for watching over me and my family's spirits," she whispered. "Thanks to you and my parents for guiding my brother, and to you, my dear brother, for sending the help we needed. I hope to see you soon."

***

Albatius volunteered to stay and keep watch over the wagons and their load, so Blandius decided to explore the market. He perused stall after stall, stopping at a booth to buy a flaky meat pie, freshly baked and smelling too delicious to pass up. Hot food in hand, he moved to the edge of the market to sit down on a boulder and enjoy his meal. He was done too soon and licking the last bits off his fingers when he noticed a servant exit the back side of the enormous temple with a heavy basket. Intrigued, Blandius followed him into the forest. The path wound through ancient trees for a good third of a mile before ending in a small clearing filled with raised mounds of dirt and one big hole gaping in the ground. The servant of the goddess proceeded straight to the hole and gently lowered the basket to the ground before tipping it forward to spill its contents—many clay tablets that now slid into the hole.

Blandius stepped on a twig, and the man looked up at the sound. "I'm sorry to disturb you. I saw you and followed you out of curiosity. I meant no offense to Feronia or her temple," he apologized.

"None taken. This is part of my daily duties. I have to ask you to keep this clearing to yourself, please. These," he pointed down the hole, "are the worshippers' questions and requests for favors, and we wouldn't want the tablets to ever be stolen or destroyed. They need to stay close to the temple, so our goddess can peruse the wishes on her own time, and grant them if she finds the wishers worthy," the temple servant said.

"Oh, I see. I will keep your secret, I promise. I'm leaving tomorrow anyway. With so many wishes in one place, I am curious what most people want from Feronia. Would you mind telling me?"

"Oh, that's no secret." He waved his arm, indicating the entire clearing. "With very few exceptions, Feronia gets asked to remove the brands or tattoos on former slaves' foreheads. It's usually F or FUG for runaways, or FUR for the ones accused of stealing."

Like most other citizens, Blandius had seen these marks of disgrace on slaves in the streets, but he had grown up in a household too poor to own slaves and had never thought much about them. Until he met Velia and little Velthurus. Now the realization washed over him. *I never gave a thought to how widespread these marks are, or how devastating they would be for a freedman or freedwoman.*

He followed the temple servant back through the forest in silence until another thought struck him. "Do they ever?" he asked.

"I'm sorry?"

"Do the wishers ever get their wishes granted?"

"Yes, at least some of them do. The brands can only be covered or masked, but the ink tattoos can sometimes be removed, depending on what kind of ink has been used," the servant replied.

"Would you mind telling me, do you know how the removal is done?"

"I've heard of two methods, and the more effective one is very painful. You must reopen the skin with a needle and daub on a concoction of lime, gypsum, and salt. Sometimes it works well the first time, but it often takes two or three treatments."

"And the other method? Does it work at all?"

"It does occasionally, and it's quite simple, though you have to use it for a longer time. You need to collect pigeon feces and apply it as a poultice over the tattoo. You should refresh the poultice every two or three days, and it will take many weeks before the tattoo fades. If it works at all." Blandius must have involuntary shown his disgust since the temple worker snickered. "Yeah, I agree, repulsive, right? But surely not so bad if it takes the letters off a forehead, no?"

"You are right about that, my friend. I thank you and your goddess for sharing these remedies with me. I'm traveling with a little boy who might be excited to try them."

696 AUC (58 BC), late summer
South of Andematunnum, Free Gallia, Southern lands of the Lingones Nation

Brenna was still not used to living in the legion's leather tents. Since the Aedui were now employed members of the auxilia, they had received new gear from the camp prefect's warehouses. The one thing she did appreciate were the clever little earthen bread ovens called clibanus, accompanying each package of hides and wooden staves.

She walked up to the fire pit in front of Rionach and Orlagh's tent, which they shared with the children and two other couples. "Hello, Orlagh. How is Rionach?" she asked the warrior who had a clay pot in her hands. A stone hand mill and one of the ovens sat by her side.

"She is doing well, better than hoped for." Orlagh pulled most of the raised sourdough from the clay pot and formed it into a flat loaf in her wet hands before placing it on the bottom plate of the earthen oven. The warmth from the fire would let it rise again before it was time to bake.

Next, she worked on replacing the used dough by grinding wheat into rough flour, adding a little bit of water from her canteen and a dash of salt before mixing it with the small bit of remaining sourdough. "And tomorrow's loaf is done." She put the lid on the pot and moved it aside. "Rionach's still asleep. If you can wait with me, I'll wake her once the bread is ready."

"Certainly, I'm happy to sit with you." Brenna took a seat beside her and handed her a towel for cleanup. "Where are the kids?"

"Gone to the latrines. They'll be back soon," Orlagh wiped her hands on the towel and pulled her knife to cut crisscrossing lines into the loaf, which had now slightly risen. The fire had burned down enough, allowing her to drop the oven plate onto hot coals. She lifted the main lid piece onto the plate, sealing the loaf. She looked up and focused behind Brenna. "And here they come."

Brenna turned around and saw Epona and Caom running through the tent aisles. "Hello, you two! How are you doing?" she called out.

"Good," the boy said, while Epona just shrugged. They both plopped down in the dirt next to Orlagh. "Thank you for making bread." Caom gave her a hug.

Brenna smiled. *I'm glad the children like her.*

A while later, she used an iron hook to lift the hot lid, allowing Orlagh to grab the fresh loaf with a linen used as bread bag. She stood up and followed her into the tent. The delicious smell of bread helped mask the persistent odors of old sweat. *Some airing out would do wonders. The early cold rains don't help, everybody keeps their tents closed.*

"Good morning!" Orlagh greeted Rionach with a quick kiss and sat down on the cot next to her. The children moved in with hugs and kisses as well.

"Ouch," Rionach said with a smile on her lips.

Brenna, who had followed them inside, moved up to give her friend a hug as well, careful to keep it gentle. "I am so glad to see you are better."

"Yes, I'm much better," Rionach sleepily replied. "I can't wait to move around."

"Here, start with some bread, and I'll help you up," Orlagh said tenderly. Brenna moved to give them some space and sat down next to Caom and Epona.

Everybody had gone through so much, shared the loss of home and loved ones. Rionach's brother had died, and so had Brenna's sister in law. And all of their clan, every single one of them, had lost so many, many friends. And after all of that, they had ended up here with the Romans.

The homey scene in front of her made Brenna's heart burst with joy. Part of it was Rionach's obvious recovery, quashing the worry and fear for her life. A bigger portion though might be the abundant love among the people here, all around her. Their love would build their new home, wherever that ended up.

***

"Want to go to Andematunnum later?" Vibius asked. Numerius stood next to him in full battle gear. on a field outside the immense combined multi-legion camp's Porta Decumana. Part of a long parade line of the Ninths' Second cohort, they endured a steadily falling cool drizzle.

"Depends. I'll go with you if we survive this inspection," Numerius replied. From the corner of his eyes, he got a glimpse of the centurions strolling up and down the lines, frequently stopping, sometimes barking in anger.

When they finally came his way, they stopped in front of a man a few feet away to inspect every aspect of his gear. Their century's new leader Gaius Seppius, formerly longest serving optio of the Ninth, shook his head. "The shield is in good shape, the gladius as well, but look at his canteen and his armor." He addressed the legionary directly. "When was the last time you treated your chainmail? Your iron rings are rusty! The camp prefect's men hand out new patches of wool every month. The idea is that you actually use them!" Seppius marked the man on his list. "Latrine cleaning for two weeks." The legionary groaned. "Alright, three weeks it is," Seppius said, "thank you kindly for volunteering."

The group of noncommissioned officers moved on and stopped at Vibius, who was by now sweating profusely. "Ah, I remember talking to this young man about his shield a few days ago. He badly needs a new one." Seppius marked Vibius on his list too. His shield had been nearly hacked in two during the last battle and now was held together by rope. Though they tried, the centurions and optios could find no other issues with Vibius' gear.

As the group moved on to Numerius, Optio Titus Pullo joined, having just walked over from the camp. "It's official, we're out of replacement shields. Even the Helvetii shields we had repainted were all handed out," he told the other officers.

Seppius turned back to Vibius. "Sorry, son, that means you will have to wait a while longer."

"Can we ask the fabri to make new ones?" Centurion Opiter Maximus asked.

"Let's go see our cohort prefect after we're done here," Titus Balventius suggested. "We might already have deliveries on the way." He turned to Titus Pullo. "And I hear congratulations are in order."

Pullo looked surprised. "You mean you've heard something? The prefects haven't told me anything yet."

"Sorry, I just heard before coming out here, I assumed you already knew," Balventius said. Numerius, looking straight ahead, saw the puzzled looks on the noncom officers' faces. Balventius continued. "Let me all introduce you to the newest centurion of the Eleventh legion. They took quite a beating at Bibracte and have several positions open. Though our friend Pullo here didn't just get any centurion position, he was chosen as a centurion of their First Cohort."

The other officers broke out into hoots and congratulations. The troops of the First cohort were considered the elite, and their centurions as well. After the handshakes were done, the officers turned to Numerius, who squirmed under the scrutiny. *Don't let them see my sword. It still cuts, that's all I need it for.*

After seeing that his gear was in decent shape, most of the men moved on, except for centurion Balventius. *Damn.*

"Let me see your gladius!" the man suddenly said. *Oh no, latrine duty, here I come.*

"Here, sir." Numerius handed the weapon over hilt-first. Balventius whistled when he saw the deep cut into its edge below the hilt, deforming the blade enough for the wooden scabbard opening to stop it from going in all the way.

"I tried to grind it out a bit but was worried any more would weaken the blade further, so I stopped." Numerius was now unable to hide his nervousness.

Surprisingly, Balventius grinned at him. "Son, I applaud you for trying to fix it, but you couldn't possibly do that. That piece of steel was merda to begin with." The man stuck the blade into the ground as far as he could, hammering the pommel with his fist for good measure. He turned to the other officers. "Want to bet?"

"I'll only put up twenty sesterces this time. That one does look questionable," Opiter answered.

Seppius shook his head. "Titus, I hold with you on that one. No bet from me." Nobody else commented.

Balventius shrugged and moved sideways into position before kicking the pommel of the sword with the sole of his right caliga, easily snapping the blade in two. He turned back to Numerius. "At least I know we have plenty new swords in store, with much better steel than this," he said. "Go see Seppius later for the requisition paper." He turned back to the officers and grinned. "And thanks for the easy money, Opiter!"

Most of the men laughed and the group moved to the next man in line.

Numerius took a deep breath. *No punishment duties for either of us.*

"You're on for tonight," he whispered to his friend, who beamed. They finally had leave again and would see what the capital of the Lingones nation had to offer.

***

"At last, a bright and sunny day. This dull drizzle was getting to me," Andrippos said to Alketas as they walked in front of Nico, who shook his head in silent disapproval. *I liked the rain, and I am glad there's a mild breeze or we'd be right back to stifling heat.*

Nico followed his friends out of the big camp towards a nearby hill that had become a popular hangout for the camp's families in the two weeks since catching up with the Helvetii. As the view opened to include the hillside and the trees at its bottom, he saw many of the smaller children playing catch, while some of the taller ones climbed trees at the edge of the forest. "It's easy to forget how many children there are," he said.

His little group made it halfway across the hilltop before he identified Capussia, Andrippos close friend, sitting among many other Numidians and their families. As they approached, he made out Adhe and his Numidian decurion, who both stood up. "Welcome, it's good to see you again," Adhe said in perfect Latin before shaking his hand. "This is my uncle Oz. Please sit with us."

As Nico plopped down on one of many laid-out blankets, he waved at another man, who sat close by. "Salve, I'm Nico," he called over.

"I'm Massi," the Numidian replied with a smile. "Good to know your name. This is Daleninar, my brother's widow." He pointed at an attractive woman sitting next to him. Tall, with brown hair and green eyes above a prominent nose, she held a newborn in her lap while feeding olives to a three-year-old boy. Nico smiled and nodded at her, receiving a beautiful smile in return. When he looked back at Massi, he noticed the loving glance the man gave his sister-in-law. *I hope for his sake that she likes him as much as he does her.*

A young girl shouted "Papa," and ran up to Oz to give him a quick hug. "Is it all right if I invite some people over? They have a boy that's Saki's age," she said. "And they love to play together." *Interesting, the girl doesn't look like him at all, and there's no mother around that I can see.*

"Sure, Stena. We have lots of space," Oz said with a wave at the blankets on the ground. The girl ran over to a group of Aedui just arriving from camp. There was so much love and tenderness in the man's look. *I can't help but like these men and their friends. They all seem like good people.*

***

Along the tents of the legion followers and servants, Brenna walked ahead of Elsed and Morcant and a growing group of orphans and adults, all joining them for their outing. "Children!" she called at a group of five young ones playing between the tents. "We're going to the hill outside the camp. Many of the legionary children go there to mingle and play. Come and join us!" It would be good for Aedui children and adults alike to socialize with other camp people, Romans or otherwise. For better or worse, they were now tied to this army, at least until Ariovist was dealt with. Why not make the best of it?

They came to the women's tent housing Rionach and Orlagh. To her surprise, the two stood outside, hand in hand, watching Epona and Caom put out the tent fire.

"We heard you are taking the children out. We'd like to join you," Orlagh said eagerly. "Rionach insists she's up for it."

"Fine with me. The more the merrier," Brenna replied with a warm smile before turning to Rionach. "I am just glad you're up and walking again."

"Me too. We can help you herd the children," her friend said. "Or at least Orlagh will."

Brenna laughed at the smirk on her friend's partner's face in response to being volunteered. "Thank you, I appreciate all the help we can get," she said, smiling at the thirty to forty dirty children of all ages behind them.

***

The big group of Aedui led by little Stena came closer. Nico was surprised how many of the faces he recognized. There were the two warrior women walking with a boy and girl between them, and the young man following them, dressed in white from head to toe. *That clothing would make him stick out anywhere.*

The group included a mass of children, all settling in an open spot about twenty feet away. Most of them soon ran off, eagerly joining the many groups playing on the side of the hill.

Nico overheard Alketas and Andrippos talking about the two women warriors. "The shorter, dark-haired one with the bandages is quite attractive, right?" Alketas said.

"I like the taller blond one, she seems... exotic," the tall and lanky Andrippos replied, showing his lopsided smile. "I wonder if we should go over to introduce ourselves?"

Nico broke out into laughter. "Good luck, you'll need it!" he told them. "You both need to work on your skills of observation. Except for those two children, the women only have eyes for each other. Sorry, I don't think you'd stand a chance with either."

Andrippos's gave Nico his lopsided grin and shrugged. "Oh well, never mind." His expression turned contemplative. "I've seen the Aedui fighting in the final battle against the Helvetii. They were ferocious and have more than earned their equal place here. They can do whatever they want in their free time."

That's why I love you, my friend. You are tolerant and non-judgmental, rare traits indeed.

***

"Here they are!" Stena walked up to Oz with a familiar looking Aedui couple in tow. The woman led a young boy by the hand, and the man held a baby. "This is my Papa," Stena proudly told the woman, pointing at Oz.

"Ave," the woman replied, nodding to the group of Numidians. Oz stood up and the woman held out her hand. "I'm Brenna, and this is my husband Elsed." Next, she pulled a small boy forward from behind her legs. "And this here is Coraidan. He loves to play with your son."

She seems genuinely nice, loves her children, and clearly cares for Stena. Warmth blossomed inside Oz, and he smiled at the couple. "Please, why don't you sit down with us so we can chat? Oh, and we've brought more than enough food to share," he said, ushering them to his blanket.

He gestured towards Adhe. "This is my nephew. Adhe, would you please tell Saki his friend is here?" A moment later, his excited son ran to greet Coraidan. Seeing the boy's happiness, he was overcome with joy, and tears rose to his eyes. At long last, this had become much more than simply group of soldiers. *The legion has become a home, a community.*

No, he thought as he handed a plate of bread slices and olives to Elsed and Brenna. He looked back at the two boys playing together. *Community is not a strong enough word. It's much more than that.*

He took in his Numidian friends around him, and the Cretans. *I know we have bad individuals in the legions as well. But these, here, they are all decent people.*

Glancing toward the camp, he saw Balventius and Seppius approach, likely to visit Capussia and Andrippos. He turned to look out at the hillside. All the playing children, Stena among them, were shouting in excitement. *No, this is so much more.*

Oz relaxed. Unexpectedly, on this small hill, life was wonderful. *Why did it take me this long to realize? We all share so much more than other people do. Our bond makes us brothers and sisters.*

This. This is. Family.

POST SCRIPTUM

Inabsoluto Negotio (Unfinished Business)

"The brave and bold persist even against fortune; the timid and cowardly rush to despair through fear alone"

Cornelius Tacitus

696 AUC (58 BC), early fall
Outside of Oaxos, Crete, Roman Province of Crete et Cyrene

"Husband, there is a man at the house. He's asking for your brother," Eupraxia said. Penthylos added a closely measured amount of vinegar into a huge pot of boiling sheep's milk and stirred. Then he handed the ladle to one of his many nephews. "Keep stirring until you see solids, then pour it through the cloth as I showed you yesterday."

He wiped his hands and followed his wife out of the barn and to the house. "He's looking for Nico? Did he say what it's about?"

"No, only that it's very important to him. He said he came a long way to find him." She hesitated, then added, "and he might be someone important. He wears expensive clothes, and he has an Aethiopean with him."

Penthylos raised his eyebrow. "Oh. Clearly not a local." He was quite anxious by the time he made it to the farmhouse, though once he opened the back door, he found two grown men joking and playing with the children on the floor. One of them looked Greek with his dark hair. Physically very strong, he might have been in his mid to late twenties. *Yes, definitely well-off. Look at those clothes and the ornate sword sheath with its gold decorations.*

The black-skinned man's arms were even more muscled, and he was also well-dressed, though without the many little bits of gold his companion was adorned with.

"Welcome!" he said to the two men. "I hope the children didn't bother you too much. What can I do for you?"

"They were no bother," the Greek man said as they stood up. "We're looking for Nicolaos, who I understand is your brother. I hoped to find him here."

"He left Crete over six years ago. May I ask who you are and why you are looking for him?" Penthylos replied.

"Certainly, my apologies. Your brother showed me much kindness when nobody else would, and my fond memories of him got me through some rough times. I needed to come back to Crete to see him again," the man replied. He reached out his hand. "Let me introduce myself. My name is Timon."

696 AUC (58 BC), early fall
Twenty-five miles southwest of Vesontio, Free Gallia, heartland of the Sequani Nation

"I may know why he's moved your wedding out," Seisilla, the king's second wife, told Aina in confidence. "I overheard him talking to Osburga yesterday. The big Roman army that beat the Helvetii is nearby, and its leader is demanding that Ariovist leave the Aedui alone. Though he thinks his Suebi should win if it comes to a battle, he wants to negotiate first. They have sent many letters back and forth already." A fellow Celtic chieftain's daughter and sister to king Vocion of Noricum on the far side of the Alps, Seisilla had been another involuntary bride, given against her will by her family to cement an alliance. Once Osburga started to leave them alone together, they had fast become friends.

"I would have thought he'd do the opposite and marry me right away to cement his claim. Did he move the wedding out because it might offend the Roman leading the army? Either way, the fact that he changed his plans means he's worried. Maybe not without reason—after all, the Romans beat the entire Helvetii nation," Aina said.

Seisilla nodded in agreement. They were in her bedroom, darning socks and re-stitching some of the king's worn clothes. Nara sat at Aina's feet, playing with Freawaru, Seisilla and Ariovist's daughter, who at two years older showed remarkable patience with the young girl.

"Who knows, they might come to blows. Though we have more Germans here than ever, I think the Sequani would turn on my husband in a heartbeat. That could become dangerous for all of us. If the Romans win, I doubt they'll politely ask if we volunteered to be part of Ariovist's household. They might show you mercy if they find out who you are, but not me."

Aina nodded in agreement. "If that day comes, I'll vouch for you. I hope my word as daughter and sister to Aedui chieftains will count for something." Nara started to cry about a broken toy, and she bent down to give her daughter a hug.

Maybe Esus, Toutatis, and Taranis heard me after all. Is it their doing the Romans are close? Please, gods, all I need is a chance.

696 AUC (58 BC), early fall
South of Andematunnum, Free Gallia, Southern lands of the Lingones Nation

"Salve! What did you think about the many presents the envoys gave me?" a happy Caesar asked his aide Aulus Hirtius on the way back from the officer's latrine.

"How about calling it incredible? That was a lot of chests," Hirtius answered with a shrug.

"Would you mind walking back to the tent with me?"

"That would be a good excuse for procrastinating my paperwork," Hirtius answered in amusement while falling into step. "I thought the many presents were too much. Frankly, it made them look desperate, but from our point of view, it's lots of free gold—you can't disapprove of that."

Liscus, Divitiacus, and many noble envoys had come back from Bibracte to notify Caesar about the end of a meeting of Gallic Nations. A near unanimous conclusion had been reached to implore the proconsul to go after the German invader. Handing over a sealed missive including the signatures of chieftains and kings from all over Gallia, they proceeded to bring forth present after present, some from the Aedui, some from the Arverni, and even a few from Sequani eager to get out from under their Suebi overlord.

"So, what exactly was in their letter if you don't mind sharing?" Hirtius poked.

"That's no secret. The Aedui and many of their allies are begging me to move against Ariovistus, to evict him and his Germans from Gallic lands. If you don't mind, you can help me with the letter I intend to send back with them. I'll agree, of course. I knew I'd go after Ariovistus the moment I shook hands with the young Aedui chieftain's back at the Arar river."

"I remember, though I wonder; you've done a lot of conversing via letters with the Suebi king over the last few weeks. Why bother if we are going to fight him anyway?"

"That, my friend, is called statecraft. Last year, Ariovistus was declared friend and ally of the Senate and People of Rome. The senators behind this bear me ill will, and by writing letters I can publish later, I have proof for the Senate that I tried to negotiate. Of course, I can't agree to anything Ariovistus wants, since the major point is that he leaves Gallia to go back to Germania. He will not do that voluntarily."

The two men entered the command tent. Caesar greeted the guards and a couple of young scribes sitting in the outer room with affection before continuing through to his inner office. He sat down at his desk and picked up three documents, two written on rolled papyrus and one on a sheet of vellum. "I have three letters here," Caesar said, shoving one of the papyrus scrolls across the desk to Hirtius. "This first one is odd. It's from a magistrate in Clusium, asking for recompense and justice. He says that the Ninth Legion is responsible for theft of property, slaves I believe, and several murders."

"Where, here in free Gallia? Or back in Aquileia in Gallia Cisalpina?"

"No, back in Clusium, and just a couple of months ago." Caesar grinned. "Would you please write the man back on my behalf and inform him that the Ninth Legion had been deployed outside of Roman territory several months ago and that he has no legal grounds for any demands."

Hirtius cackled in amusement and nodded while opening his satchel to stash the letter from the Clusium magistrate. "Thank you, that letter will be fun. What else do you have?"

"A letter from Marcus Crassus. Here." Caesar handed the other rolled papyrus to Hirtius. "He informs me that the Optimates senators are already in full swing against me. First, they accuse me of stripping three provinces of all defensive forces without having reasonable cause, and second, for threatening an official ally of Rome by holding my legions in the vicinity of Ariovistus. Of course, the true offense is that I did either without asking the Senate for guidance first."

"As if each of them wouldn't do the same, given half the chance," Hirtius said.

"Exactly. So, short of facing them on the Senate floor, I need an alternative, something that helps to shut up my accusers. Let me run this by you. How about we take the missives I sent to the Senate, work them over in winter quarters, tweak them a bit to make things sound better, and send them to Rome to have them published as a collection? For the title, I thought maybe *The Gallic War*? That kind of book might get the public's opinion behind me," Caesar suggested.

Hirtius nodded his head. "That sounds like a good idea. Though you should call it *Commentaries on the Gallic War* and write every sentence in third person. That way it will read as more objective." They both laughed at the idea.

"I like it," Caesar stated and put Crassus' letter away. He laid down the remaining vellum letter, adding weights to the corners to keep it from rolling back up. "This is the most urgent. It was sent by the Council of the Treviri, whose lands are close to the Rhenus river. In quite passable Latin, no less, they report many Germanic tribes amassing on the far side of the river. They believe it's in preparation to join Ariovistus."

"Ah, merda. We're out of time already," Hirtius answered soberly.

"At least we're freshly stocked with food. The Aedui are more than forthcoming now." He sighed. *No rest, on to the next challenge.*

"Please, arrange a full staff meeting. Include all the tribunes and cohort prefects. We will break camp in the morning and head south for Vesontio and the Suebi."

***

The story continues in INTO DAWN.

COMMENTARIUM

After re-reading all the ancient accounts of Caesar's wars in 2005—for the first time since my years of school Latin in the 80s—I was left with two unique new considerations on the subject matter. The first was an insight into how long many of his soldiers, some of which would become his close friends, fought with him. Anybody joining his oldest legions during the levies in Spain would have served 19 years through tumultuous times of war before receiving land grants as reward once Caesar disbanded them. The second was an even more important insight, at least to me. A huge part of his fighting force and camp followers consisted of people from all walks of life and all over the Mediterranean, with legionary and auxiliary families traveling with the army. That thought stuck with me and ultimately compelled me to tell this story.

A more recent insight developed while I was deep into research twelve years later. I found many parallels between recent, modern time US politics and the Roman system at the end of the Republic. Understandably, the specific details are different, but one of the clear underlying enablers for corruption and circumvention of the checks and balances of ancient and modern systems seems to be private and industrial interests forcing their voice directly into government through financing elections, pushing purely self-serving personalities into office ahead of contenders that might have looked out for the greater good.

Another research facet was the often surprising differences I found between Rome of the late Republic and other societies around them. The educated echelons of Rome had devolved from a culture of more equality, illustrated by early republican women having two full names like their male counterparts, to a male dominated state in which women with only one name were intentionally kept out of positions of power. High-born females were completely excluded from all professions except religious activities. In stark contrast, there is indication that ancient Celtic women were much stronger and more independent than commonly known. The references I found point to women druids and women chieftains. Though perhaps not universal, they still hint at equality in parts of ancient Celtic society and led me to include many Celtic women warriors.

As regards the embedded historical details, it's much easier to state what I didn't find ancient references for than the other way around. I attempted to keep historical accuracy for the biographical parts and at least plausibility for the fictional parts. For readers interested in digging deeper, a brief list of pertinent historical works is included in the Addendum.

- No ancient accounts of Caesar's Lusitania campaign in Hispania survive. It's known that he was accused by senate peers of attacking for plunder, his financial insolvency is well documented, as is his leaving Rome inappropriately early for his post in Spain to avoid his creditors.
- The direct communication Crassus had with Spartacus is speculation. Attested are Crassus trading in slaves and Spartacus being home-free in the north of Italy on his way to Gallia before inexplicably turning south again with his host of 120,000 men, women and children. At the same time, Crassus petitioned the Senate to award him the Roman high command, giving an offer they could not decline, namely the raising of six legions from his own purse. Once active, his forces pushed the slaves farther south. After Crassus trapped them with a wall across the tip of the Italian toe, only a small part got away for a final battle. At the conclusion, the Senate was informed that only 6,000 slaves survived, which is the number Crassus crucified along the Via Appia. The small number of survivors always smelled fishy to me, considering the tempting monetary value of the slaves.

I hope you enjoyed reading about the characters as much as I enjoyed creating them.

C.K. Ruppelt - October, 2018

GRATIA

The most heartfelt THANK YOU goes to my wife, who supported me throughout the painful process of becoming a writer. She told me to give it my all, and to stop worrying about anything else for the duration of the first manuscript.

Thank you to all early readers, some for glowingly supportive comments that kept me going, others for enough critical feedback to nudge me to the conclusion that my writing was in desperate need of professional help. Thank you, Jamie Aikman, Toby Funk, Seth Isenberg, Scott Ketterer, Chris May, Starla McCauley, Bill Mears and Costel Vasiliu.

Special thanks to Jamie's mother Marlene Hanten, who was the only early reader besides my wife to make it through the entire pre-edit version of the manuscript—despite the many issues and generally horrific writing.

Thanks also to Mary Ann Jock, my first editor, for patiently nudging me to absorb some basics of modern writing amidst a handicap of English as my second language, and to my second editor, Ioanna Arka, for sharpening and honing my craft.

C.K. Ruppelt – August, 2020

ADDENDUM

For detailed color versions of the maps, more historical background and artwork visit the author's website at:

www.ruppelt-pdx.com

***

DE SCRIPTOR (Brief Author Bio)

C.K. Ruppelt lives in Oregon with his wife and two children. After spending most of his work life as a Mechanical Design Engineer, he dabbled for a few years in Program Management before moving on to Product Reliability. His penchant for historical fiction is based on growing up in Europe surrounded by ancient sites, coupled with several years of high-school Latin. He considers himself very lucky for discovering his passion for storytelling and wants to keep writing for the rest of his life.

Please check out his author website at www.ruppelt-pdx.com where much support material for his work can be found.

Excerpt of Ancient Sources

Directly related

Comentarii de Bello Gallico (Commentaries on the Gallic War) by Julius Caesar
Commentarii de Bello Civili (Commentaries on the Civil War) by Julius Caesar
De Bello Alexandrino (On the Alexandrine War) by Julius Caesar
De Bello Africo (On the African War) by Julius Caesar
De Bello Hispaniensi (On the Spanish War) by Julius Caesar
De Vita Caesarum (The Twelve Caesars) by Suetonius
Vitae Parallelae (The Parallel Lives) by Plutarch
Historiae Romanae (The Roman History) by Velleius Paterculus
Historia Romana (Rome) by Cassius Dio
Historia Romana (Roman History) by Appian
Bibliotheca historica (Historical Library) by Diodorus Siculus
Letters to brother Quintus and to friends (incl. Julius Caesar) by Cicero

Cultural background

Ab Urbe Condita Libri (Books from the Foundation of the City) by Livy
Bellum Jugurthinum (The Jugurthine War) by Sallust
Germania by Tacitus
De Agri Cultura (On Farming) by Cato the Elder
Origines (Origins) by Cato the Elder
Bellum Catilinae (The War of Catiline) by Sallust
Ta eis heauton (Meditations) by Marcus Aurelius

Cursus Honorum

The *Cursus Honorum* ("Path of Honor") illustration below shows the sequence of public offices for politicians of the late Roman Republic, after the reforms by Sulla.

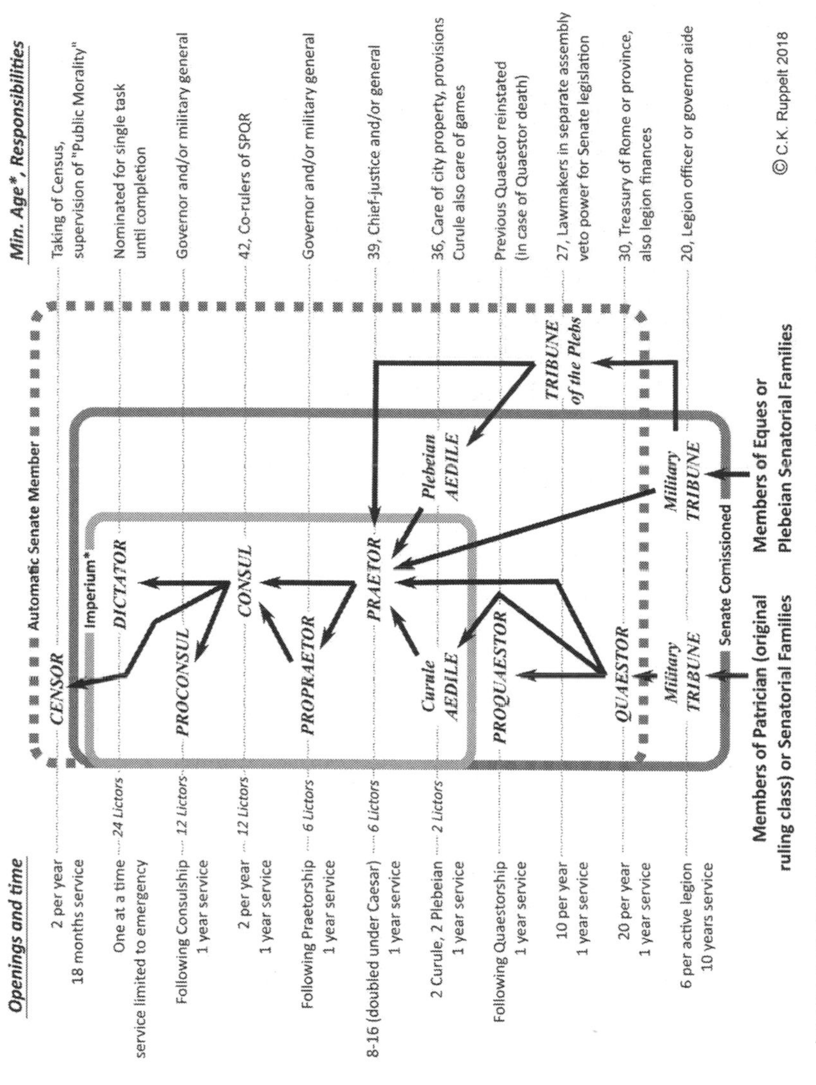

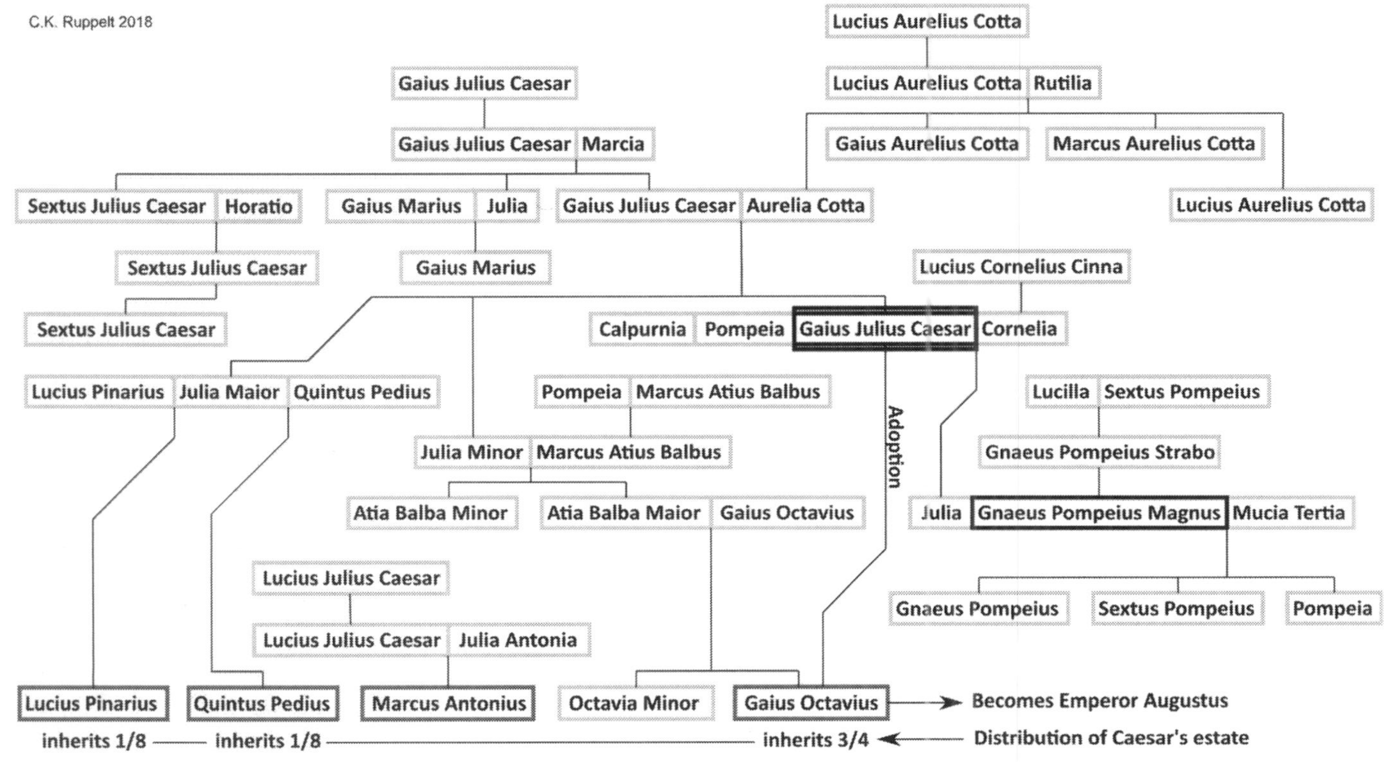
C.K. Ruppelt 2018
Gaius Julius Caesar
Gaius Julius Caesar
Marcia
Lucius Aurelius Cotta
Lucius Aurelius Cotta
Rutilia
Gaius Aurelius Cotta
Marcus Aurelius Cotta
Sextus Julius Caesar
Horatio
Gaius Marius
Julia
Gaius Julius Caesar
Aurelia Cotta
Lucius Aurelius Cotta
Sextus Julius Caesar
Gaius Marius
Lucius Cornelius Cinna
Sextus Julius Caesar
Calpurnia
Pompeia
Gaius Julius Caesar
Cornelia
Lucius Pinarius
Julia Maior
Quintus Pedius
Pompeia
Marcus Atius Balbus
Lucilla
Sextus Pompeius
Adoption
Julia Minor
Marcus Atius Balbus
Gnaeus Pompeius Strabo
Atia Balba Minor
Atia Balba Maior
Gaius Octavius
Julia
Gnaeus Pompeius Magnus
Mucia Tertia
Lucius Julius Caesar
Gnaeus Pompeius
Sextus Pompeius
Pompeia
Lucius Julius Caesar
Julia Antonia
Lucius Pinarius
Quintus Pedius
Marcus Antonius
Octavia Minor
Gaius Octavius
Becomes Emperor Augustus
inherits 1/8
inherits 1/8
inherits 3/4
Distribution of Caesar's estate

Organization of a typical Roman Legion during the Late Republic

Males of patrician, very wealthy and/or senatorial plebeian families typically started their Cursus Honorum career as a military tribune, and often returned to military service later as legatus. File and rank positions were filled by the plebeian poor, all praefectus positions were reserved for plebeian nobility, also called the eques.

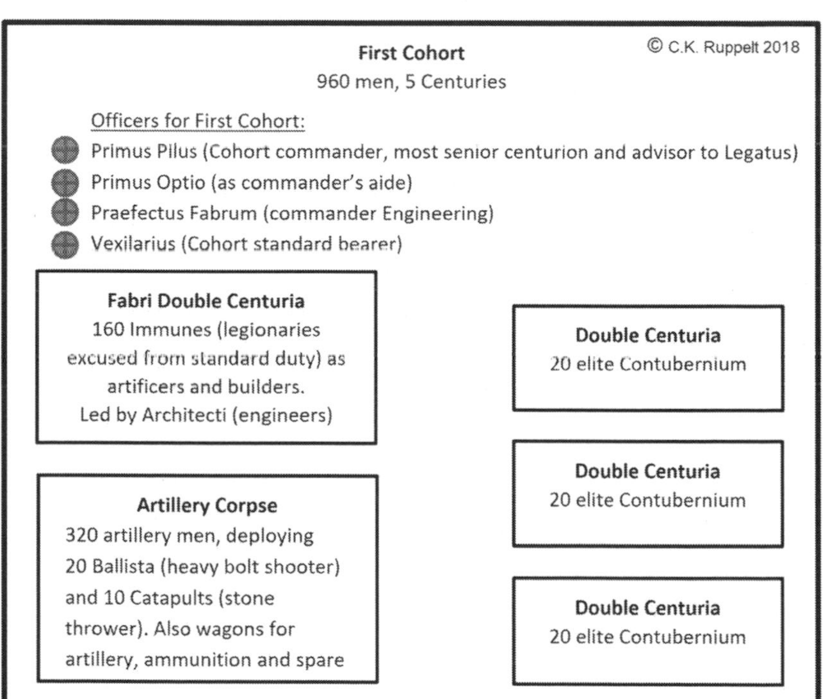

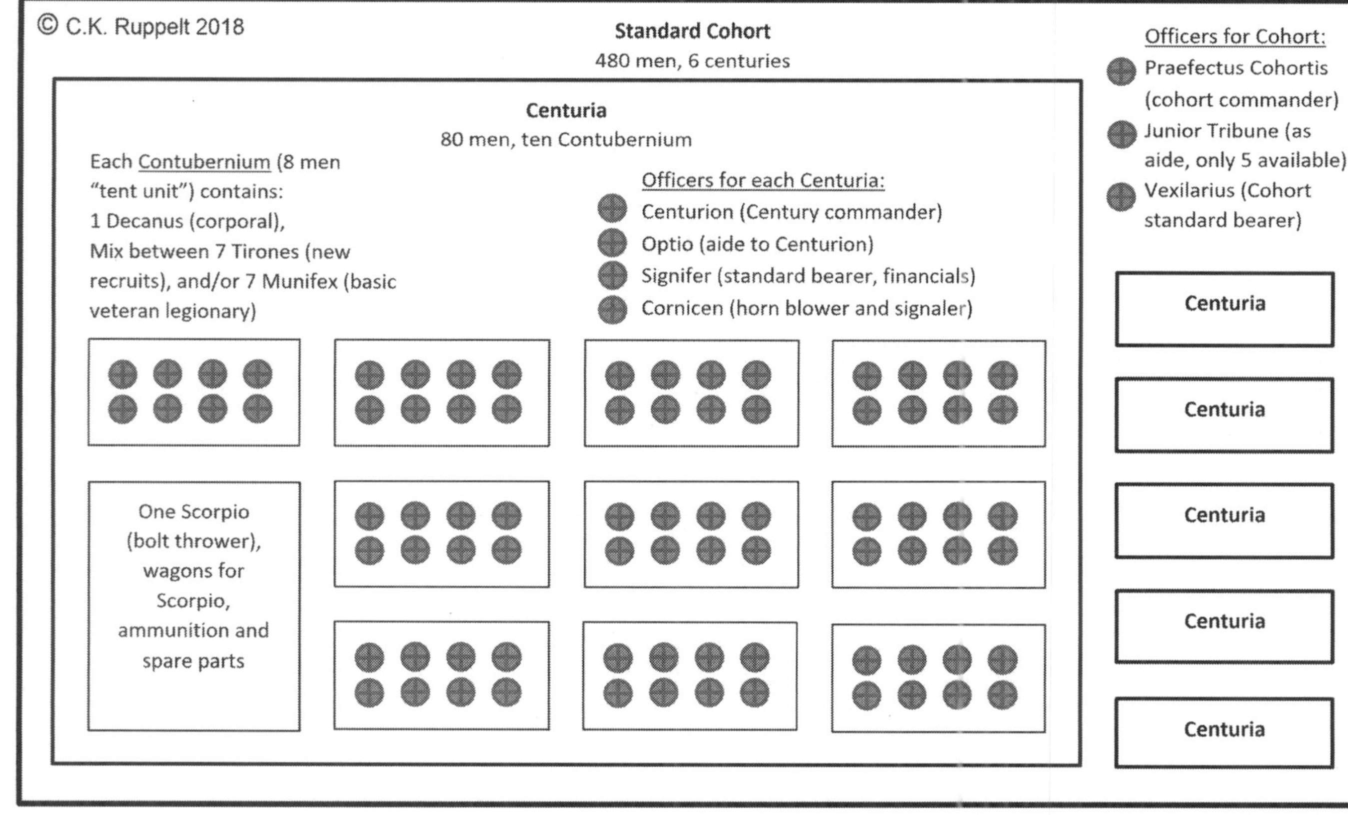
© C.K. Ruppelt 2018
Standard Cohort
480 men, 6 centuries
Centuria
80 men, ten Contubernium
Each Contubernium (8 men "tent unit") contains:
1 Decanus (corporal),
Mix between 7 Tirones (new recruits), and/or 7 Munifex (basic veteran legionary)
Officers for each Centuria:
Centurion (Century commander)
Optio (aide to Centurion)
Signifer (standard bearer, financials)
Cornicen (horn blower and signaler)
One Scorpio (bolt thrower), wagons for Scorpio, ammunition and spare parts
Officers for Cohort:
Praefectus Cohortis (cohort commander)
Junior Tribune (as aide, only 5 available)
Vexilarius (Cohort standard bearer)
Centuria
Centuria
Centuria
Centuria
Centuria

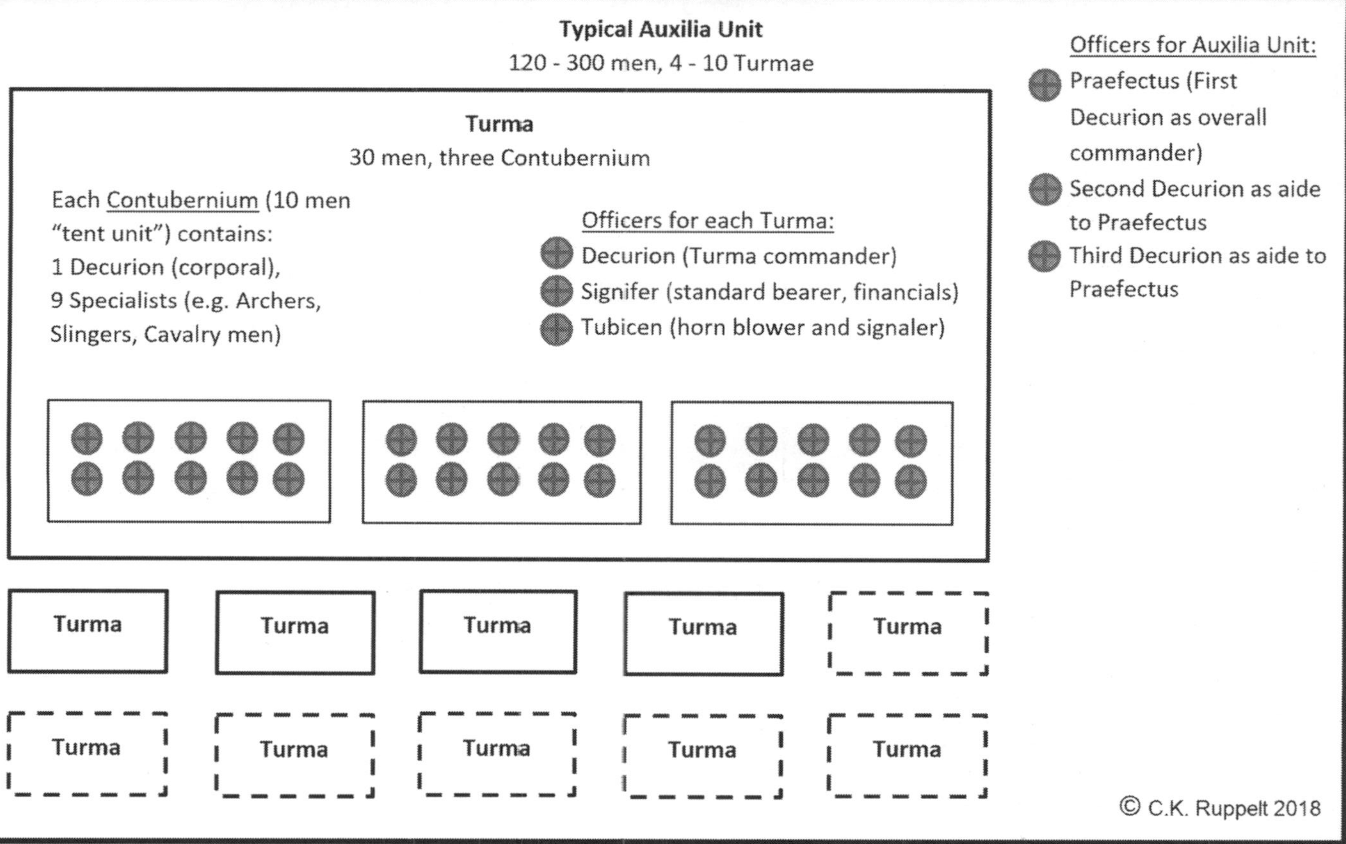
Typical Auxilia Unit
120 - 300 men, 4 - 10 Turmae
Turma
30 men, three Contubernium
Each Contubernium (10 men "tent unit") contains:
1 Decurion (corporal),
9 Specialists (e.g. Archers, Slingers, Cavalry men)
Officers for each Turma:
Decurion (Turma commander)
Signifer (standard bearer, financials)
Tubicen (horn blower and signaler)
Turma
Turma
Turma
Turma
Turma
Turma
Turma
Turma
Turma
Turma
Officers for Auxilia Unit:
Praefectus (First Decurion as overall commander)
Second Decurion as aide to Praefectus
Third Decurion as aide to Praefectus
© C.K. Ruppelt 2018

Typical Roman legion at full strength (around 60BC)
10 cohorts, Equites and Auxiliaries
© C.K. Ruppelt 2018

Officers at legion level:

- Legatus Legiones (legion commander, usually rank of senator)
- Senior Tribune (as commander's aide)
- Aquilifer (bearer of the Legion's Eagle standard)
- Praefectus Castrorum (camp commander)
- Praefectus Legiones (top commander of all cavalry forces)

Standard Cohort
480 men, 6 centuries

First Cohort
960 men, 5 centuries

Standard Cohort
480 men, 6 centuries

Standard Cohort
480 men, 6 centuries

Standard Cohort
480 men, 6 centuries

Standard Cohort
480 men, 6 centuries

Standard Cohort
480 men, 6 centuries

Standard Cohort
480 men, 6 centuries

Standard Cohort
480 men, 6 centuries

Standard Cohort
480 men, 6 centuries

Equites
10-12 Roman light cavalry as scouts and messengers.
Led by Praefectus Equitatus (Cavalry Commander)

Baggage train and camp labor
1500 -2000 non-combatants (men and women) to tend wagons, mules (one mule per Contubernium), and to forage, gather water, wash, clean, etc. Includes personal servants and slaves.

Auxilia
optional special forces

Funditores (Slingers)
Contingent of allied slingers, usually recruited from the Balearic Isles.
Native officers, incl. top commander

Sagittarii (Archers)
Contingent of allied archers, mounted or infantry.
Usually recruited from Numidia or Crete.
Mostly native officers, incl. top commander

Equites Auxilla
Contingent of allied horsemen. In the Roman west, common use of heavy Gallic cavalry. Usually native officers, incl. top commander (Praefectus Equitatus), reporting directly to Praefectus Legiones.

Made in the USA
Middletown, DE
10 May 2022

65573971R00255